SECOND TIME'S THE CHARM

BRENDA JACKSON

HER SECRET BILLIONAIRE

YAHRAH ST. JOHN

MILLS & BOON

First Published in Great Britain 2023
by Mills & Boon, an imprint of HarperCollins*Publishers* Ltd
1 London Bridge Street, London, SE1 9GF

www.harpercollins.co.uk

HarperCollins*Publishers*
Macken House, 39/40 Mayor Street Upper,
Dublin 1, D01 C9W8, Ireland

Second Time's the Charm © 2023 Brenda Streater Jackson
Her Secret Billionaire © 2023 Yahrah Yisrael

ISBN: 978-0-263-31761-9

0623

This book is produced from independently certified FSC™ paper
to ensure responsible forest management.

For more information visit: www.harpercollins.co.uk/green

Printed and Bound in the UK using 100% Renewable Electricity at
CPI Group (UK) Ltd, Croydon, CR0 4YY

SECOND TIME'S
THE CHARM

BRENDA JACKSON

To the man who will always and forever be the love of my life, Gerald Jackson Sr. My first, my last, my everything.

Be devoted to one another in love. Honor one another above yourselves. —Romans 12:10

One

"Charm Outlaw has arrived! Now the real party can begin."
Charm circled the room as she greeted everyone at the bachelorette party. Women she'd known since college or other female acquaintances she'd met through the bride-to-be, Lacey Kilgore. All of them were here at the luxurious five-star Crystalline Resort in Cancún for Lacey's destination wedding.

It didn't take Charm long to work the room, giving hugs to everyone she knew and meeting those she didn't. She wasn't bothered in the least that some thought she was a party girl, although their perception was far from the truth. Granted she liked to have fun, but she knew when, where and how to draw the line. She didn't do drugs, didn't frequent nightclubs, nor did she have sex with men just for the hell of it. Most would gasp in shock to know that at twenty-eight, she'd slept with only one man.

She grabbed a drink off the tray of a passing waiter while being introduced to female relatives of Lacey's fiancé, Vernon Lamont, then headed to the buffet table.

"I can't wait for the wedding tomorrow," Ola Cunningham said, joining Charm.

Ola, Lacey, Charm and Piper Akron had been housemates all four years of college while attending the University of Alaska in Anchorage. Charm smiled at Ola, feeling excited as well. When they'd first become housemates, Charm hadn't been sure how to handle Ola, a forever cheerful, pleasant and agreeable human. She later discovered Ola's positive attitude was contagious. There was no way anyone could be around her for long and not see the bright side to almost everything.

"Neither can I. I just got a text from Garth. He and Regan will arrive in the morning." Charm had five older brothers. Garth was her oldest and Regan was his wife.

"Are any of your other brothers coming?" Piper asked, coming up to join them.

Charm couldn't help but grin as she took a sip of her drink. She'd heard the hopeful sound in Piper's voice. While they were housemates, Lacey, Piper and Ola had always looked forward to Charm's brothers' visits. At the time all five of them had been single. Now they were all happily married. Garth was forty, Jess was thirty-eight, Cash was thirty-six, Sloan was thirty-four and Maverick was thirty-two. And Charm would admit they were brothers she adored.

Maverick, who'd been a junior attending the same university in Anchorage, was supposed to have been one of their housemates as well. At least that had been her father's, Bart Outlaw's, plan when he'd purchased the three-story, five-bedroom house for his daughter's accelerated admission to college. He hadn't wanted his sixteen-year-old to live on campus. What better way of safeguarding Charm than to have one of her brothers live under the same roof? However, little did Bart know, after the first month, Maverick found other beds he preferred sleeping in.

Some people found it amazing that the six Outlaw siblings were so close, considering each of them had a different mother. Charm's mother, Claudia Dermotte, was the only woman Bart had ever loved, and the only one Bart hadn't married…but not for lack of trying. Charm smiled at the thought that twenty-nine years later her father was still trying.

During Charm's turbulent teen years, she'd begun cutting school and getting into all kinds of mischief, including talking back to her mother. That's when Claudia, who had reached her wits' end, contacted the father who hadn't known Charm existed. At fourteen, she'd stood beside her mother at the door of a monstrosity of a house in Fairbanks and come face to face with her father, Bart Outlaw. Her mother's words to him had been… "This is your daughter Charm. I can't handle her sassy mouth anymore. Now you deal with her."

Charm smiled remembering how Bart had dealt with her. He'd spoiled her rotten, which only made matters worse. It had taken her five brothers to give her an attitude adjustment.

"Charm?"

It was then she realized her thoughts had drifted to the past and she hadn't answered Piper's question. "Garth is the only one attending the wedding. The others couldn't make it. Now that they're all married, their wives are keeping them busy. Or should I say, they are keeping their wives busy. Cash's wife, Brianna, is pregnant again, and Sloan became a father earlier this month. True to his word, he and Leslie gave Dad his first granddaughter, and I'm just crazy about my beautiful niece."

"What's her name?"

"Cassidy. Leslie gave their daughter her maiden name."

"Oh, how nice. What about Maverick? His wife is pregnant, too, right?"

"Yes. Maverick and Phire are having a boy next month."

Moments later Brittany, one of Vernon's younger sisters, her face showing her excitement, came up to Charm and asked, "Is it true you know Dylan Emanuel?"

Charm hadn't been expecting that question about the guy

who had broken her heart at eighteen. After drawing in a deep breath, she took a sip of her wine before pasting a smile on her face. "Yes, I know Dylan. We met a long time ago when he attended the University of Alaska's Fairbanks Summer Music Academy."

"Wow! That is so cool," Brittany said in awe. It was easy to see the young woman was one of Dylan's adoring fans. There was no way Charm would burst Brittany's bubble by letting her know Charm wasn't one of them.

Before Brittany could ask her anything else about Dylan, Piper interceded by grabbing hold of Brittany's hand and saying, "I need help setting up tonight's first game."

"Sure."

When Charm and Ola were alone again, Ola leaned in to say, "I should have warned you that might happen. Last night at the bar, when one of Dylan's songs began playing, Lacey mentioned to everyone at the table that the two of you knew each other."

Charm took another sip of her drink. "No harm done. Like I told Brittany, that was a long time ago. I'd almost forgotten about it."

"Liar."

Yes, she was lying. She hated to admit that whenever she heard one of Dylan's songs, she remembered the summer they'd met and the long-distance romance that had lasted two years. For her, it had been love the moment her gaze had met that of the long-haired and super-cute Dylan Emanuel. That day, at sixteen, she'd been convinced he was her soulmate.

"Are you okay, Charm?"

She forced a smile to her lips as she looked into Ola's concerned eyes. "Yes, Ola, I'm fine. Memories are just hard to fight sometimes. The only thing I appreciate about being with Dylan is that we outsmarted Bart that summer."

Her father liked to be in control. She had learned from her brothers very early to never let Bart have the upper hand.

Only to let him think that he did. It didn't take Bart long to find out about her interest in Dylan. When he'd asked her about him, she'd seen no reason to lie and had told him that yes, she was in love with Dylan.

Bart had surprised her when he suggested she invite Dylan to dinner so he could meet her family. Her brothers Cash, Sloan and Maverick had been there. Garth had been away in the military and Jess had been out of town on a business trip.

She should have known her father was up to no good, but for once she'd hoped he would behave like a decent human being. Over dinner, however, Bart told Dylan in no uncertain terms that Charm was too young to have a boyfriend. As her father, he was officially putting an end to any budding romance between them. He'd called it utter teenage nonsense, and further stated that his future plans were for Charm to marry well and not become involved with some two-bit guitar player who would never amount to anything.

Then to make sure she didn't see Dylan anymore, Bart ended her piano lessons, which had brought them together. She and Dylan managed to see each other anyway. The one thing they agreed not to do was let Bart dictate anything about their "budding romance." They were in love and were committed to staying together, no matter what. It wouldn't be easy with Dylan attending school in New York and her in Anchorage, over four thousand miles apart, but they'd come up with a plan to keep their romance a secret and had successfully done so for two years.

"Charm?"

She glanced over at Ola. "Yes?"

"Are you still staying here a week after the wedding?"

"That's the plan."

Ola chuckled. "Must be nice to have a job with your family's company where you can take off whenever you want, make your own hours and write your own job description."

"Whatever."

"Come on. I think they're ready to start the games now," Ola said.

Charm hooked her arm in Ola's and answered, "Yes, it's time for the fun to begin."

Dylan Emanuel smiled as he listened to what the drummer in his band was saying. He and Graham Ives had been best friends ever since the Ives family had moved into his Memphis neighborhood when they'd been in their early teens. After discovering they both had a passion for music, they'd bonded.

Graham and the rest of the band members were enjoying their break from touring by spending the summer in Dublin, Ireland. At any other time, Dylan would have been with them, but he'd been using this time to write several songs that would be included on their next album. Lodged in a villa in Cancún for two weeks, he'd finally finished the project last night.

"We're having a grand time, Dyl. Groupies, you gotta love them. Now that you've finished working, you might as well hop on a plane and join us."

A part of Dylan wished he could, but he knew that wouldn't be happening. "When I leave here, I'm headed for Idaho. You know the promise I made to my grandparents, and Ren has called already to make sure I'm coming."

Renshaw Burgess was the foreman of his family's cattle ranch in Davenport, Idaho and had been for as long as Dylan could remember. The one-hundred-and-fifty-acre ranch had been willed to him by his grandparents. Although it hadn't been stipulated in writing, they had wanted him to make the Red Flame Ranch his primary home when he wasn't touring.

"You're flying out to Idaho today?" Graham asked.

"No. Since I'm booked at this resort for another week, I plan to stay and enjoy myself. Unwind, rest and relax."

The only time he'd left the villa was to run on the beach every morning and again in the evenings. All his meals had been delivered by room service. Now, with nothing to keep him locked inside, he was ready to get out and enjoy himself with plans to keep his identity hidden as much as possible. He loved his fans but they could be intrusive when it came to his privacy.

Hearing music, Dylan wanted to investigate where it was coming from and told Graham he would talk to him later. After sliding open the glass door, he stepped out onto the balcony. He was three stories up and from the looks of things below, a wedding was taking place on the beach.

Dylan would admit the sunset and ocean backdrop made for a beautiful wedding...if you were inclined to get married. He wasn't. His first experience with falling in love had been his last. Music was his only true love and always would be. It would never let him down. Not like a certain woman had done.

Dylan was about to turn to go back inside when he went still at the sight of one of the bridesmaids walking down an aisle of grassy turf lined with a bevy of yellow roses. Although it had been ten years since he'd seen her, he recognized her immediately.

Charm Outlaw.

He was certain it was her. Naturally she was older, but she was as beautiful now as she'd been back then. What were the odds? Just seconds ago he'd thought about the one time he'd fallen in love and the woman who'd let him down. Now she was here of all places, taking part in a wedding.

His gaze locked on the woman who'd caused him so much pain when he had been too young to know better. His father and grandfather had warned him that an Emanuel man would recognize the woman destined to share his life the moment he saw her. His parents, grandparents and great-grandparents had all been high school sweethearts. Even with all their challenges—his parents had even gone to separate colleges—their love for each other had survived because they'd been determined to make things work. Long marriages ran in his family.

Dylan had seen no reason why a long-distance romance wouldn't work for him and Charm as well. The moment he'd seen her, she had staked a claim to his heart. He was convinced he had met the one and only girl for him. The one he would marry. Who would have his children. Share his life. Grow old with him. Love him until the day he died.

Memories of that summer in Alaska came back with vivid clarity. He'd been a couple of weeks shy of his eighteenth birthday and music had been his only love. Until he'd seen Charm. It had been love at first sight for him.

He'd been warned by some of the other music students that she was the spoiled and pampered daughter of one of the most ruthless businessmen in Alaska and if he was smart, he wouldn't get mixed up with her. He had ignored their warnings. Now he wished he hadn't. He doubted he was capable of loving another woman the way he had loved her.

Two years into their romance, she had ended things, saying she didn't want a long-distance relationship any longer. He hadn't seen it coming.

Dylan released a sigh. Feeling disgusted and angry at reliving memories that were still painful, even after ten years. Suddenly, as if Charm knew he was there, she glanced up and met his gaze.

It was Dylan!

Charm Outlaw drew in a ragged breath and tightened her hand around her bouquet. She broke eye contact with him to look toward the front where Ola and Piper were already standing. Although she maintained the smile on her face, she could tell by her two friends' expressions that they knew something was wrong. What had given her away? Had they seen her glance up toward the building? Had the happy expression on her face changed for a second?

When she reached her designated place beside them, she leveled a "you won't believe it" gaze at them in response to their questioning looks. There was no way she'd been mistaken. The man she'd seen had been Dylan. She was certain of it. His eyes had given him away. They were dark, alluring, and had always been the most beautiful pair of eyes she'd ever seen. He'd told her his Native American ancestors had been part of the Shoshone tribe.

He looked older, more mature, and he was gorgeous. Over the years she had seen him on television, photos of him on magazine covers and just this week, when they'd arrived in Cancún, she'd seen a sexy image of him on a huge billboard modeling men's underwear. He had certainly made a name for himself. Definitely not the two-bit guitarist who would never amount to anything that her father had assumed. Dylan was a huge success as a renowned jazz guitarist and singer with numerous awards under his belt. He was a household name with a legion of fans.

She tried to force Dylan from her mind as she watched the rest of the wedding, but couldn't help remembering the summer when she and Dylan had met.

Two

Fairbanks, Alaska, twelve years ago

"Honestly, Regan, why are you in such a hurry to get to class? It's going to be the same boring piano lessons," Charm said, as they alighted from the limo her father Bart had hired to transport them to class every Wednesday and Friday.

No matter how much she complained about having to take piano lessons twice a week, her whining fell on deaf ears. She could get her way with Bart about some things, but for some reason he was hell-bent on having her take these lessons. She suspected it was her brothers' idea. They probably saw it as a way of getting rid of their sixteen-year-old pest of a sister for at least four hours out of the week. Otherwise, she would drive them crazy. That couldn't be helped, though, since she had missed them. Especially when Maverick and Sloan had been away at college. Now they were home for the summer, and she liked giving them her attention. Jess and Cash worked for the family business, Outlaw Freight Lines, and usually traveled most of the time. Her oldest brother, Garth, was away in the military.

"I love my piano lessons, Charm. You would, too, if you gave them a try."

She rolled her eyes at Regan's comments. "You can talk since you're the gifted one." And she meant it. Music seemed to come naturally for her friend. Besides, Regan had been taking lessons a lot longer than Charm. Regan was in the advanced class while Charm was still in the beginners. So what if a lot of the students who'd begun with her were now in the intermediate class. Big deal. Who cared?

When they made it inside the University of Alaska Fairbanks music building she knew this was where she and Regan would part ways for two hours. She liked Regan and even with the three-year difference in their ages, she was the closest thing to a best friend she had. Regan's father was the Outlaws' corporate pilot and had been for years.

"I'll see you in a couple of hours," Regan said, rushing down the hall. That's when Charm noticed the building was a little more crowded than normal. What was up? This was the beginning of summer.

That's when she remembered that each year the University of Alaska Fairbanks held a summer music academy. It awarded over fifty scholarships to students gifted in music from around the country to come to Fairbanks for the summer to study under renowned music instructors. She knew her music teacher, Professor Jovanovich, was one of them.

When she reached her music suite, she glanced at her watch. She didn't understand why Regan had been so eager to get here when they had a good thirty minutes to spare. Charm figured she could hang out in the college break room and wait, but she'd rather not. More than once some of the older guys had mistaken her for a young freshman and thought she was easy pickings. That's where they made their mistake. Her five brothers had taught her how to handle guys like them. More than one had left her alone after walking away with a bruised ego.

She quietly entered the music suite and saw the student ahead of her had finished and was putting his guitar back in the case. Obviously, she hadn't been as soundless as she'd thought, because the student and Mr. Jovanovich turned her way.

Her gaze moved past the professor to land on the student beside him. Immediately her heart went patter-pat. Who on earth was this tall, good-looking guy with almond-brown skin, striking features and a mass of straight black hair that flowed to his shoulders? He was as tall as her brothers and wore a pair of jeans and a button-up shirt that looked good on him. She figured he was a student here at the university.

"Miss Outlaw?"

She blinked when she realized Professor Jovanovich had said her name with force. Did that mean he'd said it twice to get her attention? If that was the case, he still hadn't gotten it. At least not fully because her gaze was still on that guy.

"Yes, Professor Jovanovich?" she asked, still not breaking eye contact with the student. She couldn't understand why she couldn't take her eyes off him. But it seemed he couldn't take his eyes off her either.

"Maybe introductions should be made," Professor Jovanovich said, looking from her to the guy, then back at her. "If you will step over here, Miss Outlaw, I will introduce the two of you."

Charm felt her feet move. It was really strange to be captivated this way. She saw good-looking guys all the time. Her five brothers were handsome and so were the guys they hung out with. Guys who would make most girls drool. She hadn't drooled over them. She wasn't even drooling now. However, something more substantial was taking place. It was something she couldn't explain or define because she had no idea what it was.

When she came to a stop in front of them, Professor Jovanovich said, "Charm Outlaw, I would like you to meet Dylan

Emanuel. Dylan is one of our summer scholarship recipients. He's a guitarist and vocalist." Then without missing a beat, the professor said, "Dylan, this is Charm Outlaw, one of my piano students."

Dylan smiled and extended his hand. "Hello, Charm. Nice meeting you."

She accepted his hand. It felt warm, gentle yet firm. And those dimples in his cheeks when he smiled nearly made her weak in the knees. "Hello, Dylan. Nice meeting you, too."

She tried to place his accent, but couldn't. She'd only visited the lower forty-eight a couple of times. It really didn't matter since she liked the sound of his voice regardless.

It was only when Professor Jovanovich loudly cleared his throat that Dylan released her hand. That's when Charm finally broke eye contact with Dylan to draw in a deep breath. She needed to pull herself together.

Swallowing deeply, she asked, "Are you ready for me now, Professor Jovanovich?"

"No. In fact, there's an emergency board meeting I need to attend that shouldn't last more than thirty minutes. I need to step out. I assume you've practiced your piece for today."

It was a statement and not a question. There was no way she would tell him that he'd assumed wrong. Besides, after Dylan had touched her hand, she wasn't sure if she wanted to touch any piano keys. She wasn't sure she wanted anything to touch her hand again.

"Does your silence mean my assumption was wrong?"

There was no need to lie since he would know the truth when she sat down at the piano. "Yes, your assumption is wrong."

Professor Jovanovich shook his head in the usual way he did when he was disgusted with her, probably wondering why her father paid so much for private lessons she obviously wasn't interested in taking.

He then glanced over at Dylan. "Would you mind practicing Charm's piece with her while I attend my meeting?"

Dylan smiled again, and this one made his dimples even more profound. "I will be glad to, Professor Jovanovich."

"I thought you played the guitar," she said, trying not to melt where she stood when he looked at her.

"I play several instruments including the piano, keyboard, violin, drums, harp and saxophone."

"Wow." She was impressed because she couldn't even master beginning piano.

"Well, if the two of you will excuse me, I'll be back in half an hour. That should give you enough time to practice your piece, Miss Outlaw."

Then without saying anything else, Professor Jovanovich grabbed a packet off his desk and walked out.

As soon as the door closed behind him, Charm glanced back at Dylan. "I'm sorry you got stuck helping me do something I really should have done at home."

"Then why didn't you?"

She was about to say something not so nice, when she saw his lips tilt in a smile that made her breath catch. Charm couldn't help but return his smile.

"I really shouldn't say this to someone who has the ability to play so many instruments, but, as far as I'm concerned, music sucks."

He threw his head back and laughed. Actually laughed. The sound was so rich, hearty and warm. It was the warmth she heard and felt more than anything. "Then I'm going to make sure that by the time I leave Alaska you think just the opposite. You're going to like it, Charm Outlaw."

She wasn't so sure of that and refused to make him any promises. Instead, she took her music notebook out of her backpack and moved toward one of the pianos in the room. "I really don't have any excuse for not practicing. My dad bought me a real nice piano a couple of Christmases ago."

"But the desire to play has to be in here," Dylan said, patting his chest right over his heart. "I take it that learning to play the piano wasn't your idea."

"Heck no. It was my brothers'. All five of them. Even my oldest who's away in the military."

"You have five brothers?"

"Yes, and they are all older. I think I get into their hair sometimes, and they put this idea in my father's head that I should take music. He agreed since Regan was taking it and he'd heard her play a few times."

"Who is Regan?"

"She's my friend who's three years older."

He nodded. "And how old are you?"

"Sixteen."

"So you're not a student here at the university?"

"No."

"You're still in high school then?"

"No."

He lifted a brow. "No?"

"No. I graduated from high school last month."

"At sixteen?"

"Yes. I had home schooling for years and when I entered regular school, I took a placement test and skipped a couple of grades."

"Are you going to college?"

"Yes, but not this one. It's too close to home. I'll be going to the University of Alaska Anchorage. Dad isn't crazy about it since he prefers I stay in town, but luckily, my brothers are supporting me. My brother Maverick will be a junior on campus in Anchorage, so with him there, I'll be fine."

She sat down at the piano and since he'd asked her questions, she felt it was her turn to ask him a few. "So where are you from, Dylan Emanuel?"

"Memphis."

She smiled. "No wonder you like music."

"Yes, I grew up surrounded by it."

"Your parents are musicians?"

"No, Dad is an entertainment attorney who deals mostly with music contracts. My mom is a financial adviser."

"Are your parents together?"

"Yes. Aren't yours?"

"No."

She wouldn't say more than that. There was no need for him to know her parents never married. Not wanting him to ask any questions about it, she said, "You must have gotten your musical gift from someone. What about your grand-parents?"

He chuckled. "My dad's parents are ranchers in Idaho, so were my mom's parents."

She tilted her head and looked at him. "You must have gotten it from somewhere."

He shrugged. "Like I said, my father is an entertainment attorney. Musicians hung around our house a lot, so I guess I picked up my interest in music from them."

She didn't say anything for a minute and then asked, "How old are you, Dylan?"

"Seventeen. However, I turn eighteen two weeks from today."

She wasn't sure why but she immediately filed that infor-mation in her head. She intended to make that birthday spe-cial for him, especially since he was so far from home. "Do you have plans to attend college?"

"Yes. I'll be attending Juilliard in New York."

Even she knew that Juilliard was one of the top perform-ing arts schools in the nation. It had a very impressive alumni and it wasn't easy to get in. "That's wonderful, Dylan. Con-gratulations."

"Thanks." He glanced at his watch. "Professor Jovanovich will be back in less than twenty minutes, so I suggest you began practicing."

"Okay."

Charm hated that he would hear her play. Those times when she did practice at home, her brothers made sure they weren't there. Her father always stayed, and even claimed she did well. For the longest time, she had believed him until one day she'd caught him taking out his earplugs.

After her first piece she glanced over at him. "Well?"

"I suggest you practice more regularly. You know what they say about practice making perfect."

Yes, she'd heard that on more than one occasion, but it didn't work for her. Now he might be the reason for her to try. "How long will you be in Alaska, Dylan?"

"All summer. I'll leave here just in time to return home to Memphis, pack and report to Juilliard after Labor Day. Usually, I spend every summer on my grandparents' ranch in Idaho but not this year."

Knowing he would be in Alaska all summer brightened her day. "And how often will you be here taking lessons?"

"Every day except Fridays and weekends. The university has a special dorm for all the scholarship recipients and that's where I'll stay."

"I hope you've been hard at work practicing while I was away, Miss Outlaw."

They both turned. The only thing Charm had been hard at work doing was getting to know Dylan Emanuel better. When her and Dylan's gazes connected and she saw the warm smile that touched his lips, she was convinced that as unlikely as it might sound, she had fallen in love with Dylan the moment she'd looked into his beautiful dark eyes.

Three

Back to the present...

Piper's mouth dropped open. Then she closed it and asked, "Are you sure the man you saw was Dylan Emanuel, Charm? The sun was bright. Against the glare, you might have seen someone who favored him."

The wedding reception was over and everyone stood waiting for the bride and groom to make an appearance before heading for the airport. Their honeymoon destination was Tahiti where they would be staying in an over-the-water bungalow for two weeks.

Charm took a sip of her champagne. "It was him, Piper. Even with an unshaven look, I recognized him."

"Are you absolutely sure?" Ola chimed in. "Maybe Dylan was still on your mind since his name came up in conversation last night."

Charm frowned. "Still on my mind? Honestly, Ola, I am so over Dylan Emanuel and have been for years. The only time he crosses my mind is when I hear his music."

Piper tilted her head and looked at Charm curiously. "Are you saying you haven't bought not even one of his albums? Downloaded his songs? Streamed any?"

"No, no and no. And I have no desire to do so."

"So, you're not the woman he was singing about in his first big hit song, "Never Again"? If you listen to the lyrics, it tells the story of a man falling in love with a woman, getting hurt and swearing never to fall in love again."

Charm rolled her eyes. Of course she'd heard the song. Who hadn't? "No, that song wasn't about me. Must have been some other woman. A man doesn't love a woman he later dumps."

Ola leaned in to make sure their conversation was not being overheard. "He didn't really dump you, Charm. He got the opportunity of a lifetime to perform in England that summer. Would you have wanted him to pass it up?"

Leave it to Ola to put her positive spin on it. "No, but the decent thing to do was meet with me for lunch as planned and tell me in person. Not send me a text as he was rushing for the airport."

She cringed every time she remembered what the text message said... Rushing to airport. Got a call. Was hired to play at a pub in the UK for the entire summer. Too good an opportunity to pass up. Last night was great, by the way. Will reach out to you when I'm settled.

"You showed us the text, and I admit it was a shitty thing for him to do," Piper said. "Especially since the only reason the four of us had traveled to New York was for you to see him."

Charm nodded. Her three housemates had been her cover when she'd told her father and brothers it was a girls' trip for Lacey's birthday. "And although he claimed he would reach out to me when he got settled, I never heard from him again," she said, recalling the hurt and anger she'd felt then.

"I don't understand how those two years we were together, and struggling to make our long-distance romance work, meant nothing to him. He tossed it all away for what he saw as an opportunity too good to pass up."

When weeks went by and she hadn't heard from him, she figured something awful must have happened. That's when she'd discovered he had blocked her number. After checking his social media page, she saw he was having a great time in England without her.

What hurt her more than anything was that they'd only recently slept together for the first time. She'd given him her virginity and hadn't expected to be treated so shabbily.

"If the guy you saw was Dylan, that means he's here at this resort. Will you hang around here for another week knowing you might run into him?" Piper asked.

Charm had wondered about that very thing. She hadn't been the one to end their relationship. Dylan had. There was no reason to allow him to mess up her plans. "I have no reason to leave, Piper."

"Maybe the two of you meeting up and talking about the past would be good. It could have been all a huge misunderstanding," Ola said, trying to sound positive.

Charm rolled her eyes again. "It wasn't a misunderstanding. Even if our paths cross, Dylan would be the last person I'd let know how much he hurt me. He might not even remember me since I was so many women ago for him. I was barely eighteen and he'd just turned twenty. Ten years is ten years."

At that moment, the cheering and clapping began. They glanced around and saw Vernon and Lacey returning in traveling attire to tell everyone goodbye. Charm was so happy for her friends and admired the loving relationship they shared. The same kind she'd thought she would one day have with Dylan.

Drawing in a deep breath, she reassured herself. Just like

she'd told Piper and Ola, there was no reason not to stay the additional week, like she had planned. This place was huge and if her and Dylan's paths crossed, so be it. He meant nothing to her anymore. Nothing.

Bright and early the next morning, Dylan went running on the beach. He hadn't gotten much sleep and blamed Charm. Seeing her again had shaken him to the core, regardless of the fact that it had been ten years. Yesterday, his gaze had taken in practically every single thing about her.

Naturally she was older, but she was as beautiful now as she'd been back then. The bridesmaid dress had been short, above the knee, and had showed off a pair of gorgeous legs. She'd always had an hourglass figure, but it was rocking even more curves.

When she'd seen him, their gazes had held like they had the first time they'd met. He had thought the entire world revolved around her. He'd thought that summer in Alaska had been the turning point in his life. It was that summer when he'd found something more important to him than music. He had found Charm.

He remembered his second trip to Alaska the following summer. He had used all the money he'd received for his birthday to make the trip back. Knowing he would see her was what had kept him going that first year at Juilliard.

The timing of his trip back to Alaska had been perfect since her father and brothers had been out of the country on a business trip. Both he and Charm were older. She was seventeen and he was nineteen. They had experienced their first year in college and the challenges of a long-distance romance. Although the latter had been hard, they'd made it through and couldn't wait to spend time together. From her text messages and phone calls, she was as eager for his visit as he was.

Although he'd been tempted to sleep with her that summer, he had refused to take things beyond hot and steamy kisses. An unplanned pregnancy was something neither of them needed.

Now, Dylan returned to the villa and showered. While standing under the spray he recalled how his second year of college had been harder than the first. With his studies and frequent band practices, Dylan realized he and Charm weren't talking as much as they used to. When they did, their conversations and text messages were short and hurried. He had wanted to see her, and looked forward to the summer when he would visit her in Alaska again.

Then he'd had to break the news that his band would be playing at a coffee shop all of June, and if the customers liked them, then they would stay on for July and August. However, even with that hiccup, he had been determined to get away at some point during the summer even if for just a few days.

He would never forget that July night when she had walked into the coffee shop where he and his band were playing. He had been both surprised and elated to see her. The moment he'd finished performing, he had walked off stage, pulled her into his arms and kissed her. He then introduced her to Graham and the other members of the band.

When the coffee shop closed, he and Charm had walked around Times Square where he'd shown her the sights. As far as he was concerned, there was nothing more beautiful than seeing New York City at night. She hadn't known he'd been stalling, giving Graham time to rush to the apartment they'd shared, make it presentable and then vanish for the night.

The minute he had her in the privacy of his apartment, one kiss led to another, then another. Unable to hold back the intensity of the need they'd felt after being apart for so long, they'd made love for the first time. Dylan was glad he'd known where Graham had kept his stash of condoms.

That night had been the most beautiful experience of his life. For him it had been all about making love and not merely having sex.

That morning he had put her in a cab to the hotel where she and her girlfriends, who'd made the trip with her, were staying. He and Charm made plans to meet for lunch at a restaurant overlooking the Hudson River.

While getting dressed to meet her for their lunch, he had received a text from her canceling their date. Last night was a mistake, Dylan. I only came to New York to break up with you and didn't mean for things to get out of hand. It would be best if we don't contact each other again. I'm no longer interested in engaging in a long-distance romance.

After reading that text, he'd gotten royally pissed. When he'd tried calling her, he'd discovered she'd blocked his number. Refusing to let her break up with him in a damn text, he had left his apartment for her hotel only to find two goons.

waiting for him at the entrance as if they'd known he would show up.

They had threatened him. Claimed they were Charm's personal bodyguards and reiterated what the text had said, Charm didn't want anything to do with him any longer. They warned him that if he tried contacting her again, they would come after him and break his fingers so he would never play a musical instrument again. Their threat on her behalf devastated him. He'd been a fool to believe he and Charm would have their own teenage love story that would end with a happily-ever-after.

The only good thing that happened amidst all his heartbreak was the call a couple of days later from a promoter who'd heard their music, liked it and wanted to book them for the summer at a club in England. Any penalties for breaking their contract at the coffee shop would be paid, the band's fares to the UK would be covered, and the money they would be paid to perform was three times more than they were getting at the coffee shop. On top of that, they paid for housing. The offer had been too good to be true and in less than a week he and his band were on their way across the pond.

Not wanting to think about that time in his life anymore, he got out of the shower, dried off and put on clothes. Then he ordered breakfast. While eating, he looked at the resort's activities for that day. None interested him. He decided to order his rental car be brought around so he could take the scenic two-hour drive to the Chichén Itzá ruins.

After ordering the car, he was about to go into the bedroom to change clothes when his phone rang. Recognizing the ringtone, he picked it up and said, "If you're calling me again today to gloat about how much fun you're having, Graham, I wish you wouldn't."

Graham chuckled. "No, that's not it. I'm calling to warn you about something."

"What?"

"Elise showed up here last night. I guess that court injunction for her to stay away from you has ended. Those two years came around pretty damn fast."

"How did she know you guys were in Ireland?"

"Probably from the media. We've been partying a lot since we've been here. Anyway, she assumed you were with us. She thinks you'll take her back."

Dylan's jaw tightened. "After she tried destroying my car the way she did? Fat chance."

He had met Elise a few years after his breakup with Charm, and had made the mistake of giving her more attention than he should have. Although he'd told her countless times he wasn't interested in a serious relationship, just safe, responsible sex, she'd refused to take him at his word. When he finally told her he didn't want to see her again, she'd retaliated by slashing his tires, smashing his car windows with a hammer and spraying the exterior with black paint.

"What do you want to warn me about, Graham?"

"Elise got to Jimmi B when he was in one of his delicate moods and he told her where you were."

Dylan released a loud expletive. Jimmi B's "delicate mood" meant he'd been drunk. The band's keyboardist would give you the combination to his safe if you asked for it while he was intoxicated. "I'll alert the front desk. I don't know if I can keep her off this resort but I can make sure she's not allowed anywhere near my villa. I can't deal with Elise right now, especially after seeing Charm."

"Charm? You saw Charm?"

Four

Dylan hadn't intended to mention anything to his best friend about seeing Charm. Graham had met her that summer in New York when she'd surprised Dylan at the coffee shop. She had put on a good act and Graham, who was usually a good judge of character, had liked her.

"Yes, I saw her, but only for a minute and at a distance, from my balcony. There was a wedding yesterday on the beach and she was a bridesmaid."

"You're sure it was her?"

"It was her." No need to tell Graham how she'd gotten even more beautiful. The curves displayed in that dress were those of a woman and not the teenager she used to be.

"Did she see you?"

Dylan released a deep sigh. "Yes, she saw me. I believe she was just as surprised to see me as I was to see her."

"I bet. Well, I'm glad you finished that project you were working on before seeing her."

Dylan knew why Graham had said that. After Charm had dumped him, although he'd performed in England just fine, he hadn't been able to compose any new songs. It was as if his heartbreak had affected his ability to write. When he'd finally recovered from his song-writing slump, that's when he'd composed his hit single "Never Again." It had been his way to bring closure to the pain Charm had caused him.

"Do you think she's still in Cancún? At the resort?" Graham asked.

"If she was here for the wedding then she's probably left." He recalled seeing the resort workers removing all the chairs and wedding props.

"What if she hasn't? I told you what I thought about the entire thing."

Yes, he had. Because Graham had been taken in by Charm's persuasive charm upon meeting her, he thought there was more to the breakup than what Charm had written in her text message. Graham suspected she'd sent that text under duress from her father.

"Bart Outlaw had nothing to do with it, Graham. Charm and I were careful, and there's no way her father could have found out we continued our relationship."

"Are you absolutely certain of that, Dylan?"

Dylan rubbed his hand down his face, annoyed that Graham was going there with him. "I told you I went to her hotel after getting that text. I also told you about those goons. They knew about the text Charm had sent and reiterated what she'd said in it. They threatened me and there was no doubt in my mind they meant business."

What he hadn't told anyone, not even Graham, was that when Dylan returned to the States after their summer in England, instead of flying to visit his grandparents in Idaho, like he'd told everyone he planned to do, he had caught a flight to Alaska, determined to see Charm regardless of the threats those men had made.

He had flown into Anchorage and gone directly to the house she'd shared with three other women near campus. It was a Saturday morning and no one was home. One of her neighbors was kind enough to tell him that Charm and her friends were probably at the coffee shop a block away.

Dylan had found her there, sitting with her girlfriends. When he walked in, they were oohing and aahing over a ring on her finger and she was all smiles, holding it up for them to see. He'd stopped cold in his tracks when one of the women complimented Charm on what a beautiful promise ring it was.

A promise ring... Had she met someone and was promised to him already? The thought had felt like the worst kind of betrayal. Instead of interrupting her and her friends' little gathering and demanding the truth, he had walked out of the coffee shop without Charm even knowing he had been there.

"Well, I hope for your sake Charm has left the resort like you assume."

"Why?"

"Because she hurt you, and regardless of what you've said about moving on, Dyl, I'm not sure you have."

A scowl covered Dylan's face. "What makes you think that?"

"You loved her too much. She was your first girlfriend, and you loved her more than your music. That first week at Juilliard, she's all you talked about. You even talked about her in your sleep."

Dylan would not have been surprised if he had, since he'd been deliriously in love.

"And then there's that other thing."

Dylan raised a brow. "What other thing?"

"The fact that you haven't been involved in a serious re-lationship since Charm Outlaw. That's a long time to hang on to your first love."

Dylan stared out the window at the beach. He had news for Graham. Charm should have been more than his first love. She should have become his wife. At least that's what his foolish mind had convinced him. But that was a long time ago. "Whoa, wait a minute. I've had my share of women over the years."

"Yes, but you've never taken one home to meet your folks."

Of course he hadn't. None of the women he'd been involved with were any he'd want to take home. The only exception had been Charm. He had looked forward to the day he could introduce her to his parents and grandparents.

"At some point you're going to have to move on and open up your heart to love again. I'm sure there's a special woman out there for you."

Dylan rolled his eyes. "Look who's talking. I don't see you taking any woman home for your parents to meet either."

"Of course not. But then I never wanted to be anything other than what I am."

When Dylan heard a knock on the door, he said, "That's probably the hotel staff with my rental car. I plan to take a tour of the ruins."

"Have fun, and as far as Charm goes, if she's still there and you run into her, it might behoove you to remember something."

"What?"

"Second time's the charm."

Dylan then heard the click in his ear.

After several outdoor activities that included a day spent in town shopping at the mall, Charm returned to the resort and changed into her swimsuit to take a dip in the secluded indoor pool. The resort had five pools but this one was on the fifth floor of the building where the spa was located. She liked it for the privacy and the fact it was indoors.

There was a fireworks display happening on the other side of the resort to kick off Mexico's Feast of Corpus Christi. While most of the inhabitants of the resort were there, she would be here, enjoying private time. The only interruption was when a bar staffer came to see if she wanted a refill of her drink.

That morning she'd given Ola and Piper fierce hugs before they'd left for the airport. Then she'd joined Garth and Regan for brunch before they'd left as well. Other than Lacey's and Vernon's parents, and a few other family members, everyone who'd come to Cancún for the wedding had left.

Charm had taken several laps around the pool and was now reclining in a lounger while enjoying a margarita and reading a novel written by her cousin Stone Westmoreland, a.k.a. Rock Mason. She was flipping the page to begin another chapter when a deep, masculine voice said, "Hello, Charm."

Five

Charm froze. After she resumed breathing, she lifted her gaze to the man standing across the room. The man whose voice was huskier than she remembered.

And he was smiling.

Why was he smiling like he was glad to see her after the way he'd broken her heart? And why was she studying his mouth and remembering not only their first kiss but all those they'd shared after that? He had been the one to teach her about different types of kisses and the proper way to mate their tongues for each one.

Because of the bright lights in the pool room and his proximity, she saw more of him now than she had yesterday. Not just his features, but every inch of him. He wore a pair of cut-off jeans and a T-shirt. Gone was the tall lanky teenager. He seemed taller. There were a lot more muscles in his arms. His chest appeared broader, his waist tapered and his thighs taut. And with his unshaven look, Dylan Emanuel was one sexy man. No wonder women were known to go wild over him.

Her gaze shifted back to those gorgeous dark eyes and his

gaze compelled her to not look away. So she didn't. For one breathless moment she was transported back to when they'd looked at each other across the music suite. It had been as if they'd been mesmerized the day they'd met.

Things were a lot different now. At sixteen she had been young, naive and impressionable. Now she was a twenty-eight-year-old woman who had experienced heartbreak of the worst kind and all because of the man staring at her. His smile displayed beautiful white teeth and a dimpled jaw that had gotten sexier over the years.

It would be an effort, but she would smile back even if it killed her. Pasting a smile on her face that was just as broad as his, she responded in a bright and cheery voice. "Hi, Dylan. I thought that was you I saw yesterday, but I wasn't sure."

Placing her book aside, she asked, "So, what have you been doing with yourself all these years?" Of course she knew, but there was no harm in pretending she didn't. And why was she so unnerved by the way he was looking at her? The pain he'd caused should have destroyed any response to him.

Her heart beat rapidly when he moved toward her with that Dylan Emanuel strut that was just as alluring as it had always been. When he got closer, she studied his features. He was older. Mature. Even more handsome. His angular jaw had filled out, giving it a sculpted look. Dark brown eyes that used to be warm with love were as gorgeous as they'd always been but now unreadable.

The diamond stud earring in his ear gave him a bad boy appeal. His hair was longer. She recalled he'd preferred wearing it in a ponytail. Now it flowed loosely around his shoulders. A light mustache lined his upper lip and the scruff covering his chin and jaw enhanced his features, making him look manly.

The closer he got, the more difficult it was to breathe. It was only when he slid his solid frame onto the bench across from her, with his muscular thighs straddling it like it was his for the taking, that she began to breathe normally again.

"My music has kept me busy. What about you, Charm? I'm sure life has been treating you well," he said.

Sure, life treated me real well once I got over you, she wanted to say. But she fought back the urge. She also fought back the urge to ask him how he could have chosen his music over her after claiming to love her so much.

"Life has been treating me great," she said. "I finished college with honors and then got an MBA. After that I did a lot of international traveling before taking a position as a public relations coordinator for my family's business."

She had no such position within her family's business. Her brothers often teased her about just what her job duties were. They had no idea and neither did she. That was all well and good as long as she was on the Outlaw Freight Line payroll.

"Congratulations."

"Thank you and congratulations on your success as well, Dylan. Several of my sisters-in-law listen to your music." She hoped he gathered from her statement that although they did, she didn't.

"Sisters-in-law?"

"Yes. All my brothers are married now. They're even fathers, except for Maverick and Jess. Maverick has a baby on the way, though." She paused and then asked, "What about you? Married yet? Any kids?"

"Neither apply," he said.

She wondered if that meant there was no special person in his life regardless of what the tabloids printed.

"What about you?" he asked. "Marriage? Kids?"

"No to both." Charm tried not to think about the number of times they'd talked about getting married and having kids someday.

"So whose wedding were you in yesterday?" he asked.

"My friend Lacey's. She was one of my housemates from college."

He nodded. "I recall that. Although I never got the chance to meet your housemates, you mentioned them a lot."

She again fought back the urge to say what she thought: that he would have met them during her trip to New York if had he hung around instead of jetting off to England. How could he sit here and engage in polite conversation, like he didn't recall what he'd done? Obviously, success had not only gone to his head but had destroyed a portion of his memory in the process.

When he shifted in his chair, she noticed a tattoo on his upper arm—a beautiful, blazing red flame. It seemed to sparkle under the lights. He hadn't had the tattoo when they'd been together. She then recalled his grandparents' ranch had been the Red Flame Ranch. That made her ask, "Does your tattoo have anything to do with your grandparents' ranch?"

She didn't miss the look of sadness that flashed in his eyes. "Yes. I had it done in memory of them."

"In memory of them?"

"Yes. My grandparents were killed in a car accident five years ago."

Charm drew in a sharp breath. "Oh no, Dylan. I'm sorry."

She truly meant it. Although she'd never met his grandparents, she'd known how close the three of them were. He would tell her all about them and spending summers at their cattle ranch in Idaho. She'd even spoken with them on the phone one Christmas when Dylan had introduced her as "his girl." Dylan had promised to take her to meet his grandparents one day and to see the ranch. However, that day never came.

She thought of her own family and all the changes that had taken place over the years. It had expanded with a slew of Westmoreland cousins they hadn't known about until around eight years ago, her brothers' marriages and Outlaw babies being born. Hearing about the loss of his grandparents was hard. She recalled losing her maternal grandmother when she'd been twelve and how difficult it had been. Her grief had made her unmanageable, and her grandfather hadn't been any help since he was going through his own grief. When he'd died the following year, probably of heartache, her unmanageable attitude had gotten worse. That was what had driven her mother to take Charm to Bart.

A part of her wanted to give him a hug. However, another part of her, still resentful of the pain he'd caused, felt offering condolences was sufficient.

"Thank you," he finally said. "Losing them was hard on me and my parents."

Dylan had been looking down as if studying the tile on the floor when suddenly he looked up and his gaze snagged hers. At that moment she felt the sexual chemistry between them. When was the last time heat traveled up her thighs to settle between her legs while in the presence of a man? Never. That was her clue to end this little chitchat.

Charm slid off the lounger to stand, noticing how his gaze followed her movement. Even now he stared at her bikini-clad body, making the heat stronger.

"I'm sure when you came in here to swim, you expected to have the pool to yourself, so I'll let you have it," she said, easing her arms into her mesh-trimmed cover-up.

He shifted his gaze from her body to her face. "You don't have to leave on my account, Charm."

"I'm not. I was about to leave anyway," she lied. The heat and his gaze were getting to her. His very presence was getting to her. "It was good seeing you, Dylan," she said, lying again.

"How long will you be here at the resort?" he asked.

She wondered why he wanted to know but answered anyway. "The rest of the week. And you?"

"The same."

Charm nodded as she grabbed her book and martini glass off the table. "Well, enjoy the rest of your stay."

"You do the same," he said, still holding her with his mesmerizing gaze.

She turned and was walking toward the door when he called out, "Charm?"

Looking back over her shoulder, she said, "Yes?"

"Have lunch with me tomorrow."

Lunch with him? He had to be kidding. Did he think she was still that naive girl who had loved him blindly? Or worse, did he assume she would swoon like a fan at the sound of his voice? As far as Charm was concerned, Dylan Emanuel was not her friend. He was an adversary. Evidently this arrogant ass didn't care how he'd ripped her heart in two since he sat there acting like it never happened.

"Sorry, but I have a spa appointment tomorrow." Now that wasn't a lie.

"What about dinner then?"

"Dinner?"

"Yes. I'd like to invite you to join me for dinner."

She was about to tell him just what he could do with that invitation, but something stopped her. She was Bart Outlaw's daughter and one of the things she'd learned from her father was to keep her emotions in check when dealing with an adversary. She wouldn't show any sign of anger or vulnerability.

Another thing she'd learned was when the opportunity presented itself, you got even. And she intended to get even.

"Dinner will be fine, Dylan."

"Great. I'd love to hear about what else you've been up to since I last saw you. It's been around ten years, right?"

Give or take a few heartaches. "Yes." The gall of him asking such a thing with a straight face. If she'd doubted that the one and only time they'd made love hadn't meant anything to him, she knew so now.

"I'll make all the arrangements," he said. "You still enjoy Thai food?"

Charm was surprised he remembered. "Yes."

"Great. I understand there's a great Thai restaurant not far from here. What's your villa number?"

The last thing she wanted him to know was what building she was in. "We can meet in the resort's lobby. Just tell me the time."

He nodded. "Will seven o'clock work for you?"

"Seven will be fine. I'll see you tomorrow, Dylan."

She turned and left, glad he didn't see her smile. What she planned was called exacting retribution. It was a lesson he deserved to be taught, and she was just the person to teach it to him.

Dylan sat there with his gaze still focused on the door Charm had walked out minutes ago. He'd often wondered what his reaction would be if he ever came face to face with her again. Still being attracted to her hadn't been on the list.

After ten years his emotions should be under control where she was concerned, but obviously they weren't. Even with the bitterness, resentment and anger he felt, he'd still been totally aware of her. There was no point in pretending otherwise.

Up close she was even more beautiful than she had been at sixteen, seventeen and eighteen. She no longer had the features and body of a teenager but that of a woman. She had matured into a gorgeous being who had momentarily taken his breath away. And he detected a degree of sophistication that hadn't been there before.

During the two years they'd been together, she'd been trying to fit into the Outlaw family, not in their way but her own. She'd had sass and was a bit of a renegade living in a house dominated by men. He recalled she'd fought for them to accept her as she was. Eventually they had.

Several things were different about her while a number of things were the same. Instead of long straight hair, it was curly and shorter. However, it was still a brown that highlighted her almond-colored complexion. Her dark brown eyes were still stunning and sharp, as if they didn't miss much. And where had those curves come from?

And why was his heart beating so fast? That same heart she had trampled. Knowing how much he had loved her, did she honestly believe he could forget the pain he'd suffered? The betrayal?

Yet he had invited her to join him for dinner. Why?

There had to be a reason for the madness, so what was it? Why hadn't he turned and left when he'd seen her? Why had he acted amiable in light of the pain she'd caused? The last thing she deserved was his kindness, so why had he given it to her? Especially after she'd sat there and acted like the two years they'd shared had meant nothing to her. Like after all this time she didn't owe him an explanation about anything.

And what had happened to the guy she'd become involved with after him? The one who'd given her that promise ring? Since she was here alone, did that mean she wasn't involved with anyone? She could have turned down his invitation to dinner if she was in a relationship, but she hadn't. But he knew, with her, that didn't mean a damn thing. She had a history of messing with a man's heart.

"Is there anything you'd like to drink, sir?"

He glanced up at the waiter who'd entered the pool room. "Yes, a glass of scotch, please."

A short while later Dylan had done several laps around the pool and thoughts of Charm still consumed his mind. Maybe it was time to let bygones be bygones. After all, after the heartbreak had come his career had soared due to that summer he'd spent in the UK, which in a round-about-way, he owed to her.

It was time for him to move on, like Graham said, and maybe having dinner with her one last time was the way to do it. When he left Cancún, he would finally have closure.

Six

It was a beautiful evening and instead of calling for a golf cart to transport her to the lobby, Charm decided to walk. Now that the wedding was over and she had time to relax, she wanted to enjoy the beauty of the landscaped lawns and the Italian architecture of the buildings.

A day spent at the spa had been what she needed. Afterward, she had hung out inside her villa and read, trying to convince herself the thought of running into Dylan again was not the reason for her seclusion.

Charm still intended to get even. Her telephone conversation with Piper and Ola hadn't changed her mind. Both had tried talking her out of it, saying what she should be doing was finding closure. They felt carrying around so much anger and resentment after all this time wasn't healthy.

She agreed with the part about closure, and if she had detected any remorse from Dylan yesterday she would have thought of moving on. He'd had the chance to apologize and he hadn't. Instead, he'd acted as if sacrificing their love for his music hadn't been a big deal.

When she reached the lobby, she glanced at her watch and noticed she was thirty minutes ahead of their scheduled time. Being the first to arrive might give the erroneous perception that she was anxious to see him again. So, to kill time, she decided to walk around the beautiful atrium filled with flowers and greenery. That way she could see him when he arrived, but he wouldn't be able to see her.

After strolling around the atrium for a few minutes she eased down on one of the benches. Pulling out her cell phone, she checked for any text messages from her family and smiled when she saw one from her cousin Delaney. After reading it she put her phone away when she heard a woman sitting on the bench behind her say Dylan's name.

As she shamelessly eavesdropped on the conversation, it didn't take long to discover Charm wasn't the only female Dylan had wronged who was seeking retribution. And from the sound of it, this woman's plan was even more ruthless than hers. Not only was it ruthless, it was illegal.

There were two women talking and Charm sharpened her ears to hear everything they were saying...

"And you're sure the front desk said Dylan gave specific orders not to let you into the resort, Elise?" one woman asked.

"Yes. Someone must have given him a heads-up that I was coming. Probably that damn Graham. Jimmi B was too drunk to tell anybody anything. Now what am I going to do? Chrome expects me to plant those drugs in Dylan's luggage before he leaves here."

"How are you going to do that when this resort won't allow you past the lobby?"

"I have a plan. Dylan's villa is serviced by Housekeeping every day. I'll find out who does it and pay that person to let me in when Dylan's not there."

"But you don't know his schedule."

"That's what I'll need you for, Cindy. All I need is a quick moment to get in his villa and place the cocaine in the lining of his carry-on bag. You can give him a fake name, pretend to get something started with him, and keep him away from the resort for a while."

"There's a chance he might not be interested in me."

"You're beautiful. I don't know many men who would turn down a chance to spend time with you."

"Okay, Elise, my part sounds easy, and fun. Hey, isn't that him entering the lobby? Damn, he looks good. Maybe if you use your womanly wiles on him, you'll change his mind about letting you spend time with him here."

"It's worth a try, but if that doesn't work then we'll go back to our original plan. Are you in, Cindy?"

"Yes, I'm in."

Charm drew in a deep breath, not wanting to believe the conversation she had just overheard. A crime in the making. Those women were plotting to plant illegal drugs in Dylan's luggage. She could imagine the chaos at the airport when it was found. He would claim he was innocent, but the evidence would prove otherwise. He would be arrested and the newspapers would smear his name.

Shifting on the bench, Charm tilted her head to get a better view of the lobby and saw Dylan. The woman named Cindy was right. He looked good. Unlike yesterday at the pool when he'd been wearing cutoffs and T-shirt, now he was dressed in a button-up shirt and dark pleated trousers. The outfit showed just how powerfully built he was. There was nothing like a man with masculine arms, a broad chest and muscular shoulders.

He glanced at his watch and then back up and something he saw made him frown. It didn't take Charm long to see the woman named Elise come into view. She was beautiful with dark hair that hung down her back and a model's figure. She wore a short off-the-shoulder, low-cut sundress designed to capture a man's attention.

From the looks of things, it wasn't working on Dylan. He wasn't flashing that sexy dimpled smile. It was obvious from his facial expression that he was not pleased to see the woman. In fact, he appeared downright furious.

What had the woman done to make Dylan ask the hotel to keep her out? Why would she want to ruin his reputation? Although Charm didn't follow his music like her sisters-in-law did, she knew the media considered him clean-cut. That image would definitely change if drugs were found in his possession.

A part of Charm felt Dylan was probably getting what he deserved because payback was a bitch. Too many men forgot that when they went on a heartbreaking spree. However, another part of Charm felt the woman was taking things too far.

Charm watched the woman interact with Dylan. Several times, the woman touched him and he pulled back. She'd never seen Dylan so angry with anyone. Whatever he was saying must have gotten through to the woman because she angrily tossed her hair and walked away. Instead of watching her leave, Dylan turned his back to watch the entrance door. Charm decided to stay put to hear what Elise would tell Cindy.

An idea popped into her head and she pulled her cell phone from her purse. She swiped her fingertips across the screen until she came to the Record app.

"Come on, Cindy. As usual Dylan is being difficult. We'll stick to our original plan."

"How will we get into his villa without him knowing about it to plant the cocaine in his luggage?" Cindy asked.

"Like I told you, we'll find someone in Housekeeping who wants to make some money. They will let me in. Chrome will make sure I have whatever funds I need. All of this was his idea. He has a score to settle with Dylan. Come on. Let's go to that coffee shop and map out how we'll get into his villa to plant that cocaine in his luggage. Since you're allowed at the resort, we need to make sure you and Dylan meet. Then it will be up to you to occupy a lot of his time."

"Even if that means he and I sleep together?"

"Yes. I'm with Chrome now so Dylan means nothing to me anymore."

Charm clicked off the Record app and quickly placed her phone to her ear to pretend she was talking to someone when the two women rounded the row of plants that had separated them. Neither glanced her way as they headed in the direction of the coffee shop.

Standing, Charm tucked her phone back inside her purse and headed to where Dylan stood with his back to her. When she came within a few feet of Dylan he turned around with a scowl on his face. Probably thinking she was Elise returning. When he saw it was her, he smiled and Charm nearly missed a step.

She wished he wouldn't level those gorgeous dark eyes on her. A couple of the top buttons of his shirt were undone, revealing a glimpse of a hairy chest. Just when did that happen? Ten years ago, there'd been barely a bit of fuzz there.

Charm tried to ignore the rush of adrenaline trying to take over her senses. She wanted to place the blame on her erratic hormones, but she knew better. She recognized sexual chemistry for what it was. As far as she was concerned, it had no business here. Not now. Not ever. He'd had his chance with her and had blown it. Evidently her body didn't agree since it was tingling all over the place.

"I hope you haven't been waiting long," she said, coming to a stop in front of him. Why did his cologne have to smell so good? It was almost too good for her peace of mind. And why was he standing in such a sexy stance?

"No, I haven't."

Although his smile was still in place, she could tell by the look in his eyes he was troubled by something. Did he regret sending Elise away? As far as Charm was concerned, that was the best decision he could have made.

"You look nice, Charm," he said, looking at her from head to toe.

His compliment only pleased her because he was falling nicely into her plans. She had bought this dress yesterday. It wasn't as short as the one Elise had been wearing, but with the side slit it still showed a lot of leg and thigh. Dylan used to tell her that she had pretty legs and she hoped he still thought so.

"Thank you, and you look nice yourself."

"Thanks. Are you ready to go?"

"Yes, I'm ready."

He then offered her his arm. She took it and he escorted her outside to a waiting convertible sports car. Charm knew that no matter what get-even plans she had for Dylan, she would tell him about the conversation she had overheard between those two women.

Seven

Dylan opened the car door for Charm and watched her ease onto the soft leather with such sensuality his body began to throb. He immediately blamed it on the split in her dress that exposed a lot of thigh and leg. His gaze traveled over her hands that clutched her small purse and noted her fingernails were painted a pretty coral. His gaze then lowered to her feet encased in sandals and noticed her toes were polished the same color.

He recalled her saying she'd had an appointment at the spa and wondered what else she had done. He would love to have been a fly on the wall.

"Dylan?"

His gaze traveled from her feet to her face. "Yes?"

"Is anything wrong?"

He figured she was asking because he was standing there like a nitwit and hadn't closed the car door yet. Quickly recovering, he gave her a wry smile. "No, nothing is wrong. I was just thinking about something." That hadn't been a lie. He'd been thinking about something he shouldn't.

After closing the car door, he walked around to the other side. He got inside and snapped his seat belt in place as she snapped hers. He could have offered to do it for her, but the temptation was too great. He liked the way she smelled as much as he liked the way she looked.

"Nice car," she said, pushing hair away from her face as he fired up the ignition.

"Thanks. It's the one I'm using while I'm here and it's similar to the one I drive when I'm home."

"And where is home for you, Dylan?"

He wondered why she wanted to know and then figured she was asking for conversational purposes. "I have a place in New York. I guess you can say the city sort of grew on me while I was there for college."

"You live in Manhattan?"

"In Harlem. I also own a place in Memphis not far from my parents." He paused and then added. "My grandparents left me their ranch. That's where I really consider as home. What about you, Charm? Are you still living in Alaska?"

Dylan wasn't asking for conversational purposes. He really wanted to know. To be quite honest, he wanted to know as much about her as he could. Why, he wasn't sure, but he'd convinced himself it was all part of finding closure. That sounded like a good enough reason for him.

"Yes, I live primarily in Fairbanks. I bought a home there on the other side of town from the Outlaw Estates. Dad deeded the house in Anchorage, the one I lived in during college, to me as a graduation present, so I own that home as well. I lease it out to college students." She went silent a moment before saying, "My brother Cash inherited a dude ranch in Wyoming. I visit him and his family a lot. He has twin sons who were my first nephews, and his wife is expecting again."

He could tell by the tone of her voice that she enjoyed being an aunt. "What about your father?"

"What about him?" she asked. He had brought the car to a stop at a traffic light.

"Is he well? Married or still single?"

"Dad is fine. He still hasn't convinced Mom to marry him, though. However, I think he's close. He no longer works for the company. He retired. My oldest brother, Garth, now runs things."

Dylan had met all her brothers except for the oldest two, Garth and Jess. Garth had been away in the military, and Jess had been out of town on a business trip during that dinner fiasco when Bart told him and Charm to end their summer romance. Even now Dylan smiled at how Bart said it and expected to be obeyed.

The traffic light changed and he said, "I'm surprised he hasn't talked your mom into marrying him by now."

"Not for lack of trying, trust me. She says she won't marry him until he changes his ways. I have to admit he's gotten better over the years, but I doubt Dad will ever change completely. They have gotten closer, though. They do a lot together and now she spends more time in Fairbanks than she does in Seward." Seward Alaska was where Charm had been born and had lived the first thirteen years of her life with her mother and grandparents. "And Dad and I are closer now than we've ever been."

He held back asking if that was why she'd ended things between them the way she had. Had her father found out and gotten to her and threatened to withhold her credit cards? At the time there was no way Dylan could have competed with the economic security Bart Outlaw provided for her. Sadly, he'd thought that hadn't mattered to her.

"We're here," he said, pulling into the Thai restaurant. As far as he was concerned, they'd arrived just in time. He wasn't sure how much longer he could handle inhaling her scent. Heat was now rushing through his gut.

"I'm looking forward to dinner tonight, Dylan."

He glanced over at her and said, "So am I."

Charm tried to concentrate on eating the rest of her food, which she thought was delicious. But then, so was the man sitting across from her. She was being swamped by sexual desires more powerful than those she'd experienced while in her teens. Probably because back then she hadn't understood the power of sexual chemistry. Now she did.

"You've been quiet."

She glanced over at Dylan. "Sorry, I have a lot on my mind." And did she ever. Mainly because she needed to tell him about his ex-girlfriend's plans for him. She'd thought about telling him in the car ride here, but hadn't felt up to it. Besides, she had enjoyed their conversation. He'd genuinely seemed interested in being brought up to date on her family.

She noted he'd deliberately avoided any discussion of the time they'd been together. She wouldn't let him get off that easy. If he wouldn't bring up anything about that time, then she would. "Do you have the same guys in your band? The ones I met that night in New York? And is Graham still your drummer?"

She could tell by the lifting of his brow that her question surprised him. He proved that to be fact when he stopped eating and placed his fork down to stare at her. "You honestly haven't been listening to my music have you?"

He sounded somewhat astounded. Granted she'd known they'd performed on several awards shows, but she'd had no reason to watch. "No. Did you honestly expect me to?"

She saw something flash in his eyes. Was it anger? Disappointment? Pain? If so, why? "No, I guess not," he said.

He picked up his fork to continue eating. Now he was the

one who'd gotten quiet, and she hoped he was thinking just how insensitive his question had been. Especially given the fact that he was the one who'd walked away from her and never looked back.

She decided to push all of that from her mind, since thinking about it only made her more determined to extract revenge. However, first things first. "Dylan, there is something I need to tell you."

"What?"

"First, I need to ask you something."

"Ask me what?"

She pondered how she would ask her question. There was no need to ask if he knew Elise since it was obvious that he did. So instead, she asked, "Did Elise mean something to you at one time?"

She saw surprise in his eyes and then she saw the frown that settled around his mouth. "That's rich, Charm," he said derisively. "You haven't been keeping up with me or my band, yet you've been keeping up with the names of the women I had after you?"

The women he'd had after her? Did he not care how much those words hurt?

He hadn't officially broken up with her, since he'd said in his text he would be in touch. He hadn't been. A part of her had figured from the conversation she'd overheard that Elise had been his lover. But for some reason she'd needed to hear him say it, to admit there had been others after her. Although there hadn't been anyone for her after him.

"Why did you ask me about Elise, Charm?"

She frowned. "To set the record straight. Dylan. I had no reason to keep up with you or your women. The only reason I mention her is because there's something about her you should know."

He chuckled harshly. "I think I know a whole lot more about Elise Fairmont than you do."

"I doubt very seriously that you know about this."

After wiping his mouth with the napkin, he tossed it down near his plate. "Which is?"

Charm held Dylan's gaze and, conscious of the people around them, she lowered her voice. "She's devised a plan to get into your villa and plant drugs in your luggage. She is working with this woman named Cindy and is in cahoots with some person named Chrome."

Eight

"What the hell!" Dylan shouted. He hadn't realized just how loudly he'd done so until several people seated around them stopped eating to stare. The last thing he wanted was to bring attention to himself. That was the reason he had grown the beard and dismissed the bodyguards who usually followed in his wake. He had needed time for himself.

He looked across the table at Charm. The woman he would admit had haunted him for years, even during those times he'd told himself he'd gotten over her. It was said that a person never forgot their first love. Grudgingly, he would agree. However, that didn't keep his gut from twisting every time he thought about how she'd wronged him when he'd loved her so much.

"Where did you get something like that from?" he asked, lowering his voice.

She lowered hers even more, almost to a whisper. "I overheard her plan the entire thing with this Cindy woman. I captured part of the conversation on my phone."

Dylan knew there was no way she was making this up. "We're leaving to go somewhere to talk privately."

When she nodded, he glanced around and got the attention of their waiter. Dylan was glad they'd at least finished their meal. It didn't take long for the valet to bring the car around and within minutes they were on their way back to the resort. How dare Chrome, Elise or anyone assume they could do something like that and get away with it? Dylan didn't do drugs of any kind and if some were found on him, at the airport of all places, that would be news so negative it would take him forever to clear his name.

"Are you ready for us to talk, Dylan?"

Charm's question intruded into his thoughts. "No. I need to concentrate on my driving right now. The last thing I want to think about is wishing these hands on the steering wheel were wrapped around someone's neck instead."

"I understand."

He frowned, thinking there was no way she could. As if she knew what he thought, she said. "First there was my brother Jess. He ran for the US Senate a few years ago. His opponent was so sleazy he tried paying women to claim Jess sexually harassed them."

"How did he get out of it?"

"Jess's opponent evidently hadn't ever come up against the likes of Bart Outlaw, who takes playing dirty to a whole other level. Dad was ready to drop some hidden truths on the man.

So he backed off and killed the stories. In the end, Jess won. And then there was the incident that happened to my cousin who writes as Rock Mason. Someone tried—"

"Rock Mason is your cousin?" he asked, astonished. "You never told me that. If you recall, I always kept one of his books in my backpack. Reading his adventure books was my escape from my music. In fact, I recall you telling me that other than your father, brothers and mother, that you didn't have any other relatives."

She chuckled softly. "I do recall how much a fan of his you were. My family and I found out we were related to the Westmorelands around eight years ago. After you and I broke up."

He bit down to keep from saying *they* hadn't broken up. She had been the one to end things between them. There wasn't a *we* in it. Instead he asked, "The Westmorelands?"

"Yes, Rock Mason is the pen name my cousin Stone Westmoreland uses. The Outlaws discovered they were related to the Westmorelands and we have been one big family ever since."

"How did the Outlaws connect with the Westmorelands?"

"They found us, actually, after discovering they had more relatives by way of their great-grandfather, Raphel Westmoreland. They hired a private investigator and discovered my grandfather was Raphael's illegitimate son."

"I see. Sorry I interrupted what you were about to tell me, what happened with Rock Mason."

She nodded. "Like I was saying, one day he got a call from his agent that one of his books had been plagiarized. He was furious. Then the person who did it claimed it was Stone who did the plagiarizing. Luckily, Stone proved otherwise before his reputation as an author was tarnished."

"I'm glad the outcome was in his favor," Dylan said, pulling into the entrance of the resort. "We're here. I suggest we go to my villa and talk."

"The coffee shop is still open. Why can't we discuss things there?"

"I prefer not. I've found out the hard way that even saltshakers have ears."

Dylan turned to her, noticing how she was gnawing on her lower lip. He was consumed with lust as he watched her. "Surely, you're not afraid of being alone with me."

"Of course not. Why should I be afraid?"

He could call her out and say because of all the sexual chemistry he'd felt at dinner that meant they weren't as immune to each other as they were pretending to be. "No reason. If you prefer we go to the coffee shop that's fine."

"Going to your villa won't be a problem, Dylan."

"Okay then, let's do it."

Let's do it...

Why did his words conjure much more in her mind than talking? Probably because the last time she had *done it*, it had been with him. She was certain he hadn't meant the phrase as a sexual innuendo. Charm banished the thought from her mind as Dylan opened the door to his villa and moved aside for her to enter.

He had kept the lights on and the first thing she noticed was how much larger his villa was than hers. She had a suite, but Dylan's was twice the size and the furniture was more elegant looking.

"You want something to drink?"

Dylan's question made her turn to him and then she wished she hadn't. He was leaning against the closed door with his hands tucked into the pockets of his slacks. To her way of thinking, it was one hell of a sexy pose. Pure masculinity at its finest.

"Yes, I'll take a glass of wine, although I shouldn't."

"Why not?" he asked, shoving away from the door.

"Because too many glasses knock me out. Literally. I'm known to fall asleep where I am."

"You're kidding, right?" he asked over his shoulder as he headed to the wet bar.

"Nope. I'm not kidding." She glanced around. "Nice place by the way."

"Thanks. This villa and several others in this building have private owners. This particular one belongs to Stuart Parcell."

Her jaw almost dropped. "The actor?"

"Yes. He's a good friend of mine," he said, handing her a glass of wine. He'd poured two and kept one for himself.

"Thanks."

He gestured to the sofa. When she sat down, he took a chair across from her. After a sip of wine, he said, "Now we can talk privately."

"Okay."

Charm then told him about the conversation she'd overheard. She even pulled out her cell phone and played what she had recorded. Anger lit his eyes, a deep frown settled around his mouth, and his hand tightened around the wineglass.

He stood and went back to the bar. He poured himself another glass and as if he figured he would need more later, he returned with the bottle and placed it on the table.

"I've never met Elise's friend Cindy, but she mentioned her a couple of times. She's a flight attendant. And Chrome," he said, easing back down in his chair, "we started Juilliard at the same time, but he was kicked out after the first year when the school officials found drugs in his room. They became suspicious when he was coming to class high all the time."

"So what does that have to do with you?" she asked.

"Honestly, nothing. Other than we lived in the same residence hall that first year. He swears someone on his floor ratted him out."

"He thinks it was you?" she asked.

"I doubt he even knew me back then. Once I arrived on the music scene, performing similar music to his, he considered me his competition. And then when he discovered we were at Juilliard around the same time he made me the stooge." Dylan took another sip of wine. "Over the years, he and I have been up for awards under the same categories several times and—"

"Let me guess," she interrupted by saying. "You walked away the winner."

He nodded. "Each and every time."

"Sore loser," Charm said, reaching for the wine bottle to refill her glass. She knew Dylan wasn't trying to be boastful but was stating the facts. After taking another sip of wine, she leaned forward in her seat. "So what are you going to do?"

He rubbed a frustrated hand down his face. "The first thing I plan to do is contact Seth Abraham, the head of my security team. Then I need to alert my band as to what's going on." He stood, easing his cell phone out of his pocket.

"You're calling someone now? It's late. Close to eleven."

"Seth's in LA and is a man who barely sleeps. Graham and the band are vacationing in Ireland. It's before daybreak there but Graham does most of his sleeping during the day. Excuse me a moment while I make the calls, then I'll walk you back to your villa."

"That's not necessary. I know the way back," she said, standing as well.

"I'm sure you do, but like you said, it's late. Besides, Seth is a stickler for details and he'll probably want to talk to you."

"Oh." She hadn't thought of that. Easing back down on the sofa, she said, "In that case I'll wait."

Charm watched Dylan pace around the room while talking to Seth. And just like Dylan assumed, the man had questions for her. She even played him the recorded message. When she handed Dylan's phone back, their hands touched, and she felt a stirring in the pit of her stomach at the contact.

Why was seeing him pace back and forth such a turn-on? She couldn't help noticing how well his slacks molded to a pair of taut thighs whenever he moved. Seeing his body in motion almost made her short of breath. Her throat felt dry and she took another sip of her wine. Then another.

It seemed that Seth had a lot to tell Dylan. The hard edge in Dylan's voice was an indication of how angry he'd gotten. During the two years they had been together, she'd never seen him angry. Even that day over dinner when Bart had demanded they end their summer romance he had been polite, well-mannered and respectful. Even when he had no intention of following Bart's command.

When Charm's eyes became tired, she placed her empty wineglass on the table in front of her and kicked off her shoes to get comfortable. Settling back against the sofa she checked her watch. It was after midnight.

Nine

"How soon will you get here?" Dylan asked.

As far as he was concerned, Seth was the best in the business. His security firm, which was based in Los Angeles, provided protection services for a number of well-known performers and celebrities. Seth, a former CIA agent and ex-member of the president's Secret Service, had contacts all over the world and took the job of protecting his clients seriously. Not just from physical harm, but also psychological, legal, social, and economic harms as well. Elise was going to regret the day she'd concocted such a harebrained plan with Chrome.

"I'm arriving in Cancún first thing in the morning, Dylan. In the meantime, I'm contacting a friend with the FBI. Typically, the Bureau doesn't have authority to make arrests on foreign soil. However, with the consent of the host country there are exceptions, and I intend to make this one of them."

Dylan knew if anyone could, it would be Seth. "I appreciate it. I would have thought Elise had learned her lesson after that last stunt she pulled."

"I doubt she'll learn anything without prison time. You were too soft on her. We could have thrown the book at her then since I knew the prosecutor. I'm going to make sure she doesn't get away with anything this time. You owe the woman who overheard the conversation a debt of gratitude. I don't want to think about what predicament you'd be in had they pulled this off. I knew you going to Cancún not protected by my men wasn't a good idea."

Now was the time to get Seth off the phone. If he left it up to his security manager, Dylan would have a bodyguard 24/7. "I need to go, Seth."

He was just about to place a call to Graham when he glanced across the room and saw Charm had drifted off to sleep. Seth was right. He owed her a debt of gratitude for warning him about Elise's plan.

When Charm shifted positions he couldn't help noticing, yet again, just how beautiful she was. The section of her hair that had been pinned up on her head was now hanging around her shoulders in soft curls. His gaze drifted lower and took in the dress she was wearing. He had liked it the moment he'd seen her in it; it fit her body to perfection. She was obviously comfortable in a sideways position and the side slit in her dress exposed a lot of her thigh. The male in him couldn't help but appreciate it.

Dylan forced his gaze away. He needed full use of his faculties when he talked to Graham, who would ask all kinds of questions. He moved to the balcony and opened the French doors to step out. He slid into a chair and sat in a spot that provided him a full view of Charm.

He shifted his gaze to his phone to place the call. His best friend answered on the first ring. "Yes, Dyl?"

It didn't take Dylan long to tell Graham everything and then the questions came. "You ran into Charm and asked her to dinner?"

"Yes. Merely as an old friend."

"That's bullshit, Dyl, and you know it. What's the real reason you asked her out?"

He could tell Graham that it really wasn't his damn business. However, he knew Graham would not let it go. This was Dylan's best friend. The one who'd been there to get him through the rough time after his breakup with Charm.

"For closure."

Graham didn't say anything at first. Then he asked, "Is that possible? And was taking her out to dinner a smart thing to do?"

"Obviously, it was. Otherwise, she would not have overheard that conversation between Elise and Cindy. Nor would we have a taped recording of it."

"True. Do you know what I think?"

A part of Dylan was afraid to ask. "No, Graham, what do you think?"

"That there can't be closure between you and Charm."

Dylan frowned. "And why not?"

"Because your heart won't let there be."

Dylan didn't agree. "I do need closure, Graham."

Instead of addressing what Dylan said, Graham replied, "I'll let the guys know what's going on. If we need to cut our trip short and return to kick Chrome's ass then we will."

Dylan chuckled. "Whatever."

"Where is Charm now?"

Grant's question made Dylan glance through the French doors to see her. She was still sleeping. He closed his eyes and swore he could breathe her scent even out here on the balcony. He opened his eyes and when he saw her again, the lower part of his anatomy hardened with a need he hadn't felt in a long time.

"Dyl?"

He gave his attention back to the phone call. "Why do you want to know where she is?"

"Just curious, and since you didn't answer that says a lot.

So how about telling me in a few days how that closure thing is working out for you. Keep me posted as to what Seth says."

When Dylan ended the call with Graham he stood and shoved his cell phone back in his pants pocket. He then opened the French doors to go back inside. It was after midnight. What he should do was wake up Charm to walk her to her villa. But a part of him didn't want to do that.

After crossing the room, he gently swooped her up in his arms and carried her into the bedroom, even while telling himself doing so was not a good idea. She shifted and in sleep he heard her whisper his name, but she didn't wake up. After placing her on the bed, he went to the closet for a blanket to place over her. With that done, he stared at her while his mind recalled the last time she'd been in his bed ten years ago. In New York. It had been the first and last time they'd made love. She'd been a sensuous, passionate and sexy woman; he'd fallen even more in love with her that night because he'd made her his in the most primitive way.

Refusing to punish himself any further with memories, he turned off the light and left the room, closing the door behind him.

Charm opened her eyes to the sound of male voices. She glanced around and saw she was not at her villa. Pushing the blanket aside, she saw she was wearing the same clothes she'd worn to dinner with Dylan last night.

Like a flash everything came tumbling back, including the memory of all the wine she'd had. Well, she'd warned him she was prone to falling asleep when she overindulged and obviously, she had. Why hadn't he awakened her instead of letting her spend the night in his villa? She glanced at the undisturbed side of the bed that confirmed she'd slept alone. Had she expected otherwise?

Easing out of bed she tiptoed to the door and listened. Dylan was talking to his security guy, Seth Abraham. There was no way she wanted either man to see her looking so disheveled. Glancing around the room, she saw Dylan had placed her shoes and purse in the chair. Now she hoped he had an extra set of toiletries in the connecting bath.

She moved away from the door, grabbed her purse and went into his bathroom. It smelled like him. She touched a towel that hung over the shower stall. It was damp and when she put her nose to it, it smelled even more like him. That meant he'd taken a shower recently. How had she slept through that? She didn't want to think of a naked Dylan standing beneath a spray of water, but unfortunately, she *was* thinking about it.

She moved toward the vanity and saw he'd laid out a few things for her. Namely a face cloth, an unused toothbrush and toothpaste. Within minutes she had applied light makeup and combed her hair. Satisfied she looked presentable, she walked into the living room.

"Good morning."

The two men stood when she entered. After introductions were made, she wanted to make it clear to Seth, who was eying her speculatively, that things weren't as they seemed.

Turning to Dylan she said, "Sorry I fell asleep, and thanks for giving up your bed last night."

The smile that touched his lips heightened her senses.

Now Seth was watching her and Dylan curiously. He appeared to be in his late thirties and was built like he spent a lot of time at the gym. He was all muscles. Eye candy in a hard kind of way. She had a feeling he wasn't soft on anyone's eyes unless he chose to be.

"That wasn't a problem, Charm, and I hope you slept well," Dylan said, reclaiming her attention.

"Thanks, I did." She glanced at her watch. "Well, it's time for me to leave."

"No need to rush on my account," Seth said, smiling.

The man was partly right. There was a need for her to

rush away although it wouldn't be on his account. It would be because of Dylan. He was drinking a cup of coffee and eying her over the rim of it. The look he was giving her had her heart beating faster and harder than it should.

Seth's cell phone went off and she broke eye contact with Dylan when Seth said, "Sorry, I need to take this call."

She nodded. "It was nice meeting you."

Seth nodded and then walked off toward the patio, answering his phone in the process. She turned her attention back to Dylan. "I'll be going now."

"I'll walk you to your villa."

"There is no need for that, Dylan. It's daytime."

"There is a need. We're going to need your help."

She lifted a brow. "We who?"

"Me, Seth and the FBI."

Why was her heart pounding even harder? Not from what he'd said but from the way he was still looking at her. She fully understood why a lot of women thought Dylan was not only a musical genius but also a heartthrob. Standing before her in his bare feet, wearing a pair of jeans and a T-shirt, he gave all new meaning to the word *sexy*.

She tilted her head to the side and looked at him, trying to focus on what he'd said. "You, Seth and the FBI? In what capacity?"

"From what you overheard, Elise's plan is to enter this villa when I'm not here. It will make her job much easier if I'm away."

"That's part of the plan, remember? Cindy is to keep you occupied."

"That won't be happening. I don't intend to let that woman near me."

"So what do you need me to do?"

"I need to make it seem that we've met, and I'll be spending time with you and away from my villa."

She considered his words. Why did the thought of spending more time with Dylan have nerves dancing in her stomach? After all, his suggestion would fit quite nicely with her payback plan, which was to seduce him and then before things went where he thought they would, she would reject him. But still…

"Will that be necessary?"

"We think it will. The last time I was easy on Elise. But not this time. Seth has contacts with the Feds and they will be placing hidden cameras in here today. We figure she plans to make her move later today or tomorrow."

It took a moment for Charm to fully process his words. She had a suspicion they were talking about more than spending the day together. He probably wanted to make it seem as if the two of them were involved in something hot and heavy where he would have reason to spend more time at her villa than his own. Again, such a move would fit nicely with her plan, so why was she nervous about agreeing to such a thing?

"Will that plan work for you, Charm?"

She was about to tell him that yes, it would work when she recalled something he'd said. "What do you mean you were easy on Elise the last time? Has she tried doing something before?"

"Yes." He then told her about what she'd done to his car and the two-year court injunction for her to stay away from him that had ended a few months ago.

Charm shook her head. "Sounds like your ex-girlfriend has issues."

"Elise was never my girlfriend. To this day I've only had one girlfriend and that was you."

"Yeah, right," Charm said dismissively.

He frowned. "What do you mean, 'yeah, right'? It's as if you don't believe you've been my only girlfriend."

Charm really didn't want to rehash the past with him or reopen old wounds. "Nothing." Beginning to feel agitated, she said, "I want to go to my villa, to shower and grab breakfast."

"Fine, I'll go with you."

She was about to tell him once again not to bother but instead changed her mind. He'd come up with a plan to deal with Elise and she had devised one of her own to deal with him.

Ten

"Make yourself at home while I shower and change."

Dylan nodded as he watched her go into her bedroom and close the door. Trying to get his mind off how sexy she looked in that dress from last night, he thought about his conversation with Stuart that morning. He'd told his friend about the Elise situation. Stuart had given his approval to install video cameras as needed in his villa. Since Seth's company also provided security for Stuart, he trusted whatever plan Seth put into place.

Dylan was about to sit down on the sofa when a scent invaded his nostrils. Lavender. It had been Charm's favorite and evidently that hadn't changed. When he heard the sound of the shower, sensuous visions flooded his mind. The one that held his brain cells hostage was of her standing naked beneath a spray of water.

He rubbed his hand down his face. It was too early for a drink so he decided to step out on her balcony to get a much needed breath of air. Instead of facing the beach, her balcony overlooked one of the resort's beautifully shaped swimming pools. Already it was crowded. However, since her villa was five stories up, it was far away from the noise.

He thought about the conversation when Charm had referred to Elise as his ex-girlfriend. Maybe he should have let her assume that. Instead, he'd told her that she had been his only girlfriend. A part of him had inwardly dared her to say something about it. To bring up how things had ended between them. She hadn't. It was as if she wanted to quickly change the subject. And to be quite honest, so had he.

"I'm ready, Dylan."

He turned and his breath caught. Charm Outlaw messed with his testosterone each and every time. She looked amazing. Hell, she looked better than amazing—she was absolutely stunning. Light blue always looked good on her, bringing out the honey-brown color of her skin.

"Is anything wrong?" she asked, narrowing her eyes before glancing down at herself.

"What makes you think that?"

"You were staring."

Now he was smiling because she was right, he had been. "I was admiring your outfit. It looks nice on you."

She laughed. "It's just a pair of shorts and a top."

No need to tell her that the shorts showed a pair of beautiful legs and the style of the blouse with the top button undone displayed nice cleavage. "Yes, but even when we were together, I rarely saw you wear them."

Charm rolled her eyes and he thought she looked cute doing so. "I live in Alaska, Dylan. Even the summers there aren't conducive to such attire. Not like it is in the lower forty-eight." She glanced at her watch. "I'm starving. Can we go eat now?"

He chuckled, recalling how cranky she would get whenever she was hungry. "Yes, we can go eat. Over breakfast I'll share more details about Seth's plan."

* * *

"Thanks for breakfast, Dylan," Charm said, once she'd drunk a cup of coffee and eaten the most delicious pancakes she'd consumed in years.

He shook his head and his lips curved into a smile. "You are welcome. I see you were hungry."

She knew he was talking about the fact her plate was clean. But then so was his. "I see you're in a good mood, Dylan. You were fit to be tied last night when I told you of that woman's plans."

He took a sip of coffee before answering. "In a way I still am. My reputation means everything to me. And to think Elise and Chrome planned to frame me is worth getting angry about."

"And you have every right to feel that way."

He nodded. "I said I would tell you about Seth's plans."

"What are they?" Now that he had her attention she couldn't help but connect with the beauty of his dark brown eyes.

"First, I want to say I appreciate you letting me know what Elise was up to when you overheard her conversation. Considering how things ended with us ten years ago, you didn't have to."

Charm steeled herself against his words. He was finally bringing up how things had ended, and he was right. She didn't have to tell him anything because she owed him nothing. As far as she was concerned, he owed her. However, hell would freeze over before she let him know how much he'd hurt her. Besides, he would find out soon enough. But for now...

"What happened between us was ages ago, Dylan, and I prefer we not bring up the past. We were young and thought we knew everything and discovered we didn't."

She saw his jaw tighten and wondered the reason for it. There was no way she could have hit a nerve when he was the one who'd broken her heart and not the other way around.

"You're right. What we shared is in the past."

She was glad he thought so. That way he wouldn't suspect her plans. And speaking of plans… "What are Seth's plans for Elise?"

"For starters, a tail has been placed on her."

She lifted a brow. "How was she located? She's not staying here at the resort is she?"

"She's not, but Cindy Turner is. The villa is in Cindy's name. Seth found that out. Elise is staying with Cindy but is making sure she's not seen. A tail was placed on Cindy, too. Already she met with one of the resort's employees in the housekeeping department. Money was exchanged."

"Just like that?"

"Yes. Resort Security is aware of what's going on and a trap has been set. They're cooperating with Seth and the FBI. They've been given an empty villa to set up equipment for surveillance. Unknown to Elise and Cindy, Seth and an FBI agent will not only be watching their every movement but will be listening to their conversations while inside the villa as well." Dylan smiled, making it apparent that the thought of Elise and Cindy getting caught in the trap being set for them made his day. "So, Charm, what do you want to do today?"

His question made her remember the plan was for them to spend time together, away from his villa. Today and possibly tomorrow. Before she could suggest anything, his cell phone must have vibrated in his pocket because he said, "Excuse me, I need to get this. It might be Seth."

It was. Charm could tell from his expression that whatever he was being told was serious. He held her gaze when he said into the phone, "That's fine. I'm sure Charm and I can pull it off."

When he ended the call and stood to put the phone back in his pocket, she asked, "We can pull off what?"

He gave her wry grin and said, "Pretending to be lovers."

* * *

"Pretending to be lovers?"

He found the shocked look on her face endearing and couldn't help but grin. He leaned closer over the table and whispered, "Shh, remember what I told you about saltshakers having ears."

She rolled her eyes and then spoke in a lower voice. "Then we need to leave and go somewhere so you can explain yourself."

He stood and offered her his hand. The moment she took it he felt a shiver of desire rush through him and when he heard her sharp intake of breath, he knew she'd felt the same.

A part of him knew he should not have agreed to do what Seth had asked, especially without talking to her about it first. He slid on his sunglasses at the same time she put on hers. Taking her hand again they headed in the opposite direction of the beach and pool, to a place where they could talk privately. "Feel like climbing steps or would you rather take the elevator?"

She glanced up at him. "Where are we going?"

"To the roof. There's a courtyard there and the view of the resort is breathtaking. There are benches where we can sit and talk."

Charm nibbled her lips as if contemplating her choices. His gaze followed the movement and he suddenly remembered the last time he had kissed them. When she stopped the nibbling and licked her lips with the tip of her tongue, he felt his guts tighten.

Hell, what was wrong with him? This wasn't any woman. This was Charm Outlaw, the same woman he'd given his heart to at seventeen only to get it broken at twenty. Why was he wondering how her lips tasted? What he should be doing was remembering how bad she had hurt him.

"It's only five levels," she said, interrupting his thoughts. "I'm okay taking the stairs, especially after that breakfast I ate. Maybe I can work it off."

Swallowing hard, he said, "Alright then, let's go."

Still holding firm to her hand, he walked up the steps. He liked the softness of her hand in his and was glad the space was wide enough for them to walk side by side. It was as if their steps were choreographed. While there was silence between them he couldn't help but wonder why he was anticipating reaching the top and hoping they would be alone.

"We made it," she said, grinning proudly when they finally reached the top.

His gaze drifted down to her mouth. "Yes, we made it."

"The dome-shaped roof provides the perfect shade against the sun," she said, removing her sunglasses. "And the view of grounds is beautiful from up here. The ocean is such a pretty blue."

He looked out toward the sea. "Yes, it is."

Charm glanced around. "Good. Nobody else is up here, so now will you please explain why we need to pretend to be lovers?" Charm slid down onto one of the benches.

He remained standing because he couldn't handle sitting beside her. "Remember when I told you I needed to stay away from my villa by spending time with you?"

"Yes, but what does that have to do with us pretending to be lovers?"

Even from where he stood, the luscious scent of her perfume filled his nostrils. He took off his sunglasses and placed them in his shirt pocket. "The FBI placed a bug in Cindy's room. From the conversation they've heard, I'm being watched by Cindy and someone else they've paid to keep an eye on me. That means Cindy won't suspect anything if she thinks I'm away from my villa because I'm having an affair with you. She'd assume I'd spend more time at your villa instead of my own."

"Oh."

"And remember I said we would be *pretending*, Charm." She nodded. "Okay, as long as it's all pretense."

"It will be. Hopefully with us spending time together today, whoever is spying on me will think what Seth wants them to think. Of course, that means we'll need to make plans to be away from the villa tomorrow as well."

She stood up. "That's fine."

"So what had you planned to do today?" he asked as they began walking back down the steps.

"Go into town to shop."

"I thought you said you went shopping the other day."

She smiled. "I did. You know how much I like shopping. Nothing has changed." She grinned over at him. "Besides, it isn't every day that jazz guitarist Dylan Emanuel goes shopping with a woman. Or is it?"

"Trust me, it's not."

"Then I guess I should feel special."

He fought the need to say that at one time she'd been the most special person in his life. However, that was one mistake he didn't intend to repeat.

When they reached the bottom stair, she glanced over her shoulder and frowned.

"What is it?" he asked.

"That woman named Cindy is headed in this direction. Her villa must be somewhere near this area. She's carrying a tray with enough food for two. And we know why."

"You sure it's her?"

"Yes, I'm sure. She won't recognize me, but there's no way she won't recognize you even if the two of you haven't met."

He knew she had a point. "You know what this means, right?"

"No, what?"

"Operation Pretend."

Before Charm could answer, his hands went to her hips to pull her closer just seconds before he lowered his mouth to hers.

Eleven

Charm sank into Dylan's kiss. His mouth on hers felt different than before. Maybe it was the way he had tipped her head back to claim it and how easily his tongue slid between her parted lips. She definitely hadn't expected the sensations that rushed through her the moment he did so. They were pretending, for heaven's sake. Nobody bothered to tell her hormones that. The kiss was wonderful and she suddenly felt weak in the knees.

Dylan had always been a fantastic kisser, but this adult version of him was even more compelling. He was in control and masterful. She didn't want to think about how he'd gained such expertise, only that she was benefiting from it. He had her practically melting in his arms.

Just when she was about to lean into him she was wrenched back into reality when he ended the kiss. "Whoa," he said, whispering close to her mouth. "If that's pretending then I wonder..."

She licked her lips. Her entire body was on a sensual overload. How was that possible? "You wonder what?"

He met her gaze and pushed a strand of hair back from her face. "Nothing. It's not important."

Maybe to him it wasn't important, but to her it was. Yet she wouldn't tell him that. Drawing in a deep breath, she said, "Did it work?" Why were his lips still so close to hers? So close she could feel the heady heat of him on her mouth. And why on earth did she want to reach up and place her hands on his shoulders and feel the strength of all those muscles beneath her fingers?

"Did what work?"

"The kiss," she said.

"Yes, Charm, it worked."

She nodded, as if satisfied with his answer and then took a step back. "So what do you think will happen now?"

"I imagine she will report back to Elise that she saw me and I'm already involved with someone. So, I think the kiss worked well."

As far as Charm was concerned it worked more than well. The way her lips were still tingling was proof of it.

"I guess we need to leave," she suggested.

"To go shopping?"

She chuckled. "I was teasing about you going shopping with me, Dylan."

He didn't respond. Instead, he shifted his gaze to the tiled floor before lifting his head to level his eyes on her. "I'd love to spend time with you."

His words surprised her. "Why?"

"Because it reminds me when we met, in the beginning."

How could he think that? In the beginning she had been all into him and he had been all into her. He had been the one to not only fuel her desire but he had also introduced her to it. She had shared her first kiss with him. He had been the guy she'd allowed to touch her all over, even in places she'd been warned by her mother to never let a boy touch. But it had felt so right with him.

She swallowed past the knot in her throat and said, "Okay. Just as long as you know something."

"What?"

"You made a terrible mistake ten years ago where I was concerned."

She could say that again, Dylan thought, surprised she would admit such a thing. Charm had been a mistake, one he wouldn't repeat. Was that the closest to an apology he would get from her? Probably. He wouldn't hold out for anything more. At least she'd admitted that much.

"I agree, Charm, but we're older, and I'd like to think a lot wiser, than we used to be."

He touched her hand and when she didn't pull back he asked, "Is there any reason we can't put the past behind us and rebuild our friendship?"

Dylan knew he was asking a lot of himself where she was concerned. Her own words admitted she had been his mistake. So how could he even think about befriending the woman who'd broken his heart? A woman he had loved like no other? And what about his desire for closure? Graham had been right. When it came to Charm, there could never be closure for him.

But maybe they could be friends. Like he'd told her, they were older and wiser. There had to be a reason their paths had crossed here in Cancún. Normally, he didn't believe in fate but maybe there was something to it after all.

"Is that what you want, Dylan? For us to be friends after all that has happened?"

"Yes. We can't live in the past forever." Checking his watch he said, "Come on. I'll have the car brought around so we can start your shopping spree."

A few hours later Dylan was wondering where in the heck Charm got all her energy. They had gone to four shops and a restaurant for lunch and then were back to shopping again.

By the time they returned to the resort he was tired and all he'd done was sit in a corner while she'd tried on one outfit after another.

She had modeled each one and had asked for his opinion. He recalled her telling him how her brothers would take turns going shopping with her, so she was used to a male giving opinions about her clothes.

He would have to admit he'd enjoyed spending time with her today. They'd never had a chance to spend quality time together. He now understood how a long-distance romance could have taken a toll on their relationship. Dylan only wished she would have talked to him about it instead of ending things the way she had. Her not talking to him was something he didn't understand; he thought they'd had a close relationship.

"You've gotten quiet."

He was carrying bags in both hands as they walked to the car. Except for a belt he'd purchased, all the other bags were hers. She was right, he had gotten quiet, but he wouldn't tell her what he'd been thinking since he'd been the one to suggest they put the past behind them. But he would admit one thing.

"I enjoyed spending time with you today. We never did a lot of that."

She nodded. "There was no way we could since we were in colleges miles apart."

"I know." Deciding to change the subject, he said, "What are your plans for dinner?"

"I don't have any."

"Will you join me?"

She didn't say anything as she glanced at him warily. "Are you sure you want to do that? You've been with me all day."

"Like I told you, I enjoyed spending time with you. Besides, having dinner with me is the least you can do since I'm carrying all your bags to the car. And it will let whoever is watching me believe we're building a romantic relationship."

"Yes, that's true."

In truth they weren't building a romantic relationship but trying to rekindle a friendship. But what would happen after they left Cancún? Chances were, they wouldn't run into each other for another ten years or possibly never again. There was no reason he couldn't forget her.

But could he forget that kiss?

He hadn't expected it to rock his world. How dare her mouth taste so damn good? He'd been a goner the moment their tongues had tangled.

"Do you know what I'd really like to do, Dylan?"

They'd reached the car and he put the bags in the backseat. Then he opened the door for her. He heard the excitement in her voice. "No. What would you really like to do, Charm?"

"Go dancing after dinner. But if you're afraid you might be seen, I understand."

"Dancing after dinner?" At her nod, he said, "That can be arranged. I'm not afraid of being seen."

In fact, he liked being seen, especially with her. He'd noticed more than one man checking her out and then looking at him with envy in his eyes. He understood. Charm was a stunningly beautiful woman, and any man would appreciate being seen with her.

She smiled up at him as she buckled her seat belt. He hadn't been quick enough because he'd wanted to snap her harness in place. Maybe it was a good thing he hadn't, or he would have been tempted to lean in closer and kiss her again. He could imagine their tongues—

"I'll take your word for it."

Her words butted into his thoughts, and he fought to refocus. Long moments passed as he stood there, not saying anything. "You, Charm Outlaw, don't have a choice but to take my word for it." He smiled down at her before walking to the other side of the car. He wasn't used to feeling so sexually needy where a woman was concerned. The thought of it had him off-balance.

Somehow, he had to get a grip on the situation and remember that while they were together here in Cancún, the only thing he wanted from Charm was friendship. Nothing more.

Twelve

"Hey, Charm, what's going on?"

Charm smiled upon hearing Ola's ever-cheerful voice. She put the call on Speaker as she moved around the villa getting dressed for dinner and a night of dancing. "I'm good. Still enjoying Cancún."

The last time they'd talked had been a couple of days ago when she'd gone toe to toe with her and Piper about carrying out a plan of revenge. They'd thought it was a bad idea. She couldn't wait to share the most recent developments. It didn't take her long, and it would have taken her less time if Ola hadn't asked a lot of questions. She decided not to share with her friend anything about her and Dylan pretending to be lovers. Then she would have been bombarded with even more questions.

"So, let me get this straight," Ola said. "One of Dylan's old girlfriends—"

"She's not an old girlfriend," Charm said and immediately wondered why it mattered. "What I mean is that she's a former lover and not a girlfriend. At least that's what he told me."

"He actually told you that?"

"Yes." There was no need to tell Ola that according to Dylan, Charm had been his one and only girlfriend.

"I wonder why he felt the need to set the record straight on that. It's not like he owed you an explanation. Just like you don't owe him one."

"That's true. I have no idea why he told me that."

"Well, I'm just glad you changed your mind about that revenge nonsense. You did the right thing telling him what that woman was up to and—"

"Sorry to interrupt, Ola, but I haven't changed my mind about that revenge nonsense as you put it. I am determined to go through with it. Earlier today I even told him he had made a terrible mistake ten years ago where I was concerned. That would have been the perfect time for him to apologize."

"What did he say?"

"He agreed about the mistake and then said rehashing the past wouldn't get us anywhere. That we were older and wiser. He wants us to be friends."

"I agree with that as well, but obviously you don't."

"No, I don't. I was the injured party here, Ola, so I should be the one to suggest we move on and be friends. Not him. It's like he's determined to act like nothing happened."

"Then the two of you should talk about it, Charm. Find out where Dylan's mind was back then."

"I know where his mind was. It was on his music and making it big. It wasn't on me."

Ola paused and then said, "I need to ask you something, Charm. And I want you to think about the question before you answer."

"What?"

"Do you think Dylan didn't love you at all?"

For years she had asked herself that same question. She honestly believed that he had. All she had to do was remember their FaceTime talks on the phone. Then there was his visit that second summer and how she'd tempted him to go all the way, but he had refused. Instead, he'd introduced her to other pleasures in the bedroom that hadn't involved intercourse. Pleasures she hadn't shared with any other man.

"Yes, I believe he loved me. He just loved his music more."

"Do you see him falling in love with you again or you falling in love with him again?"

"No. Absolutely not. However, we are attracted to each other, which is what I need to seduce him."

"Seduce him and then walk away?"

"Yes. I want him to know how it feels to be rejected."

"Well, I still think you're making a mistake, Charm."

"I don't. For me, it's called getting even." And she intended for things to start heating up tonight.

"Dinner was wonderful, Dylan."

He doubted Charm was aware she'd been pushing his buttons all evening in the most sensuous way. It had started when he arrived at her villa to pick her up for dinner. The moment she'd opened the door, he'd known it would be hard as hell to resist temptation tonight. And Charm Outlaw was temptation of the most irresistible kind.

This particular dress was one she'd bought during their shopping trip. It was short, complimented her figure and revealed a lot of skin. He thought it was decent but only because she was with him. When she'd modeled it for him, he'd come close to telling her he didn't like it so he could be the only one to see her in it. It was only later he wondered how he could have thought such a thing. What Charm put on her body was no business of his.

"I'm glad you enjoyed it. I recall that Indian food is your favorite behind Thai."

"Yes, it is."

Now they were on their way to a nightclub Stuart had told him about. It was one frequented by celebrities who wanted privacy from the media and paparazzi. The only reason he hadn't been hassled on this trip was because everyone thought he was vacationing in Ireland with the rest of his band.

"Have you heard from Seth today?" she asked.

"Yes. We spoke briefly. Elise hasn't been seen and they're keeping an eye on Cindy. They have reason to believe they'll make a move tomorrow. When they do, the FBI will be ready."

Deciding to keep the conversation going instead of thinking about the kiss they'd shared earlier that day, he asked, "So what are your plans when you leave here?"

He glanced over at her in time to catch her smile. "I plan to visit Cash and his family in Wyoming until the middle of July."

Of her five brothers, he'd only gotten to meet three of them: Cash, Sloan and Maverick. They had been friendly enough and nothing like her father. Bart Outlaw had been downright rude and domineering. "I caught a glimpse of Maverick at one of my concerts a few years ago in Paris."

"You did?"

"Yes. He was with a very beautiful woman."

"That was probably his wife, Phire. They met in Paris where she was living at the time. Maverick never mentioned attending one of your concerts."

Because he was curious, he asked, "Did your brothers ever find out we defied your father and didn't end things that summer?"

"No. Everyone, including Dad, still believes that we did."

He nodded. That meant Charm's breakup with him had nothing to do with her family, he mentally concluded.

"Will you be joining your band in Ireland before the end of the summer, Dylan?"

"No. When I leave here I'm headed to the Red Flame Ranch to check on things."

Moments later he pulled the car up to a huge security gate

and gave the attendant a code. The man smiled politely and said, "Enjoy your night, Mr. Emanuel."

"Thank you, we will."

When they pulled away, Charm said, "A nightclub that's tucked away behind a security gate?"

He smiled over at her. "I figured we'd want to dance the night away without worrying about photos being plastered in the tabloids tomorrow. You wanted a night of dancing, and I want to make sure you get one."

They took a number of turns around a well-lit and manicured yard before the building came into view. Although they couldn't see the ocean, they heard the sound of it. When he brought the car to a stop, a valet quickly moved forward to greet them.

Dylan came around the car to stand by Charm's side, a place he intended to be for the rest of the night. While dating, she had told him how much she liked to dance. Not as much as she liked to shop, but it had been a close second. He'd always wanted to take her dancing, but they were never together long enough for him to do so. Tonight, they would be.

"Ready?" he asked, taking her hand firmly in his.

She smiled up at him and beneath the nightclub's bright lights, he could see the excitement in her eyes. For some reason, he was glad he was the one who'd put it there.

Thirteen

The one word Charm would use to describe the nightclub was *magnificent*. Not only was live music being played but there was even an orchestra. The dance floor itself was one she hadn't seen before—a triple-decker sandwiched between beautiful spiral stairs.

When they'd been shown to their table, even before they could order drinks, she had pulled Dylan onto the dance floor. They had only danced together a few times, in the privacy of her house in Anchorage that summer he'd come to visit. She had wanted to go out but couldn't risk being seen by one of her brother Maverick's friends. At the time Maverick had been the king of nightclubbing.

They were now seated at the table to drink their wine and chill before getting back on the floor. She liked how she and Dylan danced together. He'd told her once that he wasn't a good dancer but he'd done a great job with all the line dances and was even familiar with a couple she didn't know.

"I'm truly impressed with this place," she told him, glancing around. Already she'd seen a number of television and movie celebrities, as well as musicians, vocal artists and other performers. A number of them stopped to speak to Dylan and he'd introduced her as an old friend. At least he hadn't referred to her as an old girlfriend.

"This is my first time here. Several people suggested I visit here while in Cancún, but I had no plans to do so until you mentioned you wanted to go dancing."

"Well, I appreciate you bringing me here."

When the upbeat music slowed down to the hold-your-girl-tight-in-your-arms type of music, Dylan's gaze caught hers. It was a hypnotic moment. That's how it had been with them from the beginning.

"Dance with me, Charm."

His request made her breath catch. Not because it had come as a surprise but because she'd been expecting it. "Al-right."

When he held his hand out to her, she took it.

Dylan escorted her up the staircase to the second dance floor. She wondered if he'd chosen that particular dance floor because the lighting was darker than the other two. Although she wished otherwise, anticipation had her insides shivering and when he pulled her into his arms; her body automatically sank against him.

She needed to stay in control to seduce him and not be taken in by the essence of his masculinity. Keeping her head on straight and her guard up was paramount. However, she was finding both hard to do when his hand came to rest across her back.

His touch made her ease even closer to rest her head on his chest. She couldn't help closing her eyes and breathing in his scent. It had the ability to kick-start the womanly needs within her.

"Are you okay, Charm?"

She opened her eyes and tilted her head back to look at him. She'd been totally aware of him the moment she opened

BRENDA JACKSON

93

her villa door. Dressed in a pair of dark slacks and a buttoned-up blue shirt, he looked gorgeous.

"Yes, I'm okay. Why do you ask?" Because of the dark lighting, she couldn't see his eyes, but she didn't need to do so to know they could mesmerize her.

"No reason."

There had to have been a reason. Had she made a sound? Maybe even a moan?

"Are you enjoying yourself, Charm?" His voice was low and his mouth was close to her ear.

"Yes. I told you that."

"No, you told me how impressive the place was and that you appreciated me for bringing you here. It's important to me that you enjoy yourself."

She leaned back to look up at him. "Why?"

"It just is."

A part of her wanted him to explain further, but she wasn't sure she was ready for the answers. All she wanted was for him to continue to slow dance with her, hold her close, closer. She placed her head back on his chest, inhaled his scent and, for the moment, she was satisfied.

"Do you need me to carry you?" Dylan asked, opening the car door for her hours later when they'd made it back to the resort. It was past two in the morning and he'd given her just what she'd asked for. A night of dancing. On the drive back she mentioned several times that her feet hurt.

Shaking her head in a way that made all those curls on her head tumble beautifully around her face, she said, "No, I'm fine."

Yes, she certainly was, he thought, as his gaze drifted over her and that short and sexy dress she was wearing. It was cut in an angle at the shoulders that showed how beautiful and smooth they were. She'd gotten a lot of attention in that dress and those 'have sex with me' stilettos.

They had danced every single dance, only sitting out a few when they felt the need to have more wine. He loved the slow dances the best, when he could hold her in his arms while thinking of more intimate things he'd like doing with her.

Her feet were hurting, he could tell, so he swept her into his arms.

"Dylan!"

"No need for you to torture yourself by walking in those shoes, Charm. They look sexy on your feet, by the way."

"Thanks. I had to practice how to walk in them."

"Your practice paid off." He carried her to her villa, which didn't cause him any stress because he liked carrying her. "Take out your key for me."

"I'm glad most people have gone to bed. This is embarrassing," she said, reaching up and placing her key card in his shirt pocket.

"No, it's not."

Evidently, she decided not to argue because she didn't say anything. It took him a minute to realize she had drifted off to sleep. He had totally forgotten about what happened when she consumed too much wine.

He shifted her carefully in his arms while he slid the key out of his pocket to open her door. After closing it behind them, he moved straight to her bedroom to place her on the bed. Just like the last time, she said his name in her sleep. Sitting on the bed beside her, he removed her shoes and then eased her little purse from her hand to toss it in the chair.

He stood and was about to leave the room when she said, "Kiss me, Dylan."

Had she whispered the words in her sleep? No, he saw she was very much awake. Then he wondered if it was really her talking or the wine. "Why do you want me to kiss you, Charm?"

"Because I liked it when you did it before."

Although her eyes looked drowsy, she seemed very much

aware of just what she was asking for. It was something she wanted. Hell, it was something he wanted, too.

Sitting back down on the bed beside her, he drew her into his arms and placed her in his lap. He wasn't sure what got to him the most. Her scent or the look of heated desire in her eyes. It truly didn't matter because he was a goner with either.

Looking into her eyes, he traced his finger along her chin. "Are you sure you want me to kiss you? It's going to be long and deep, Charm. I'll only stop when we need to come up for air."

"Stop talking and do it, Dylan," she said in a soft voice.

He lowered his mouth to hers. The moment their lips touched, he heard her sigh of pleasure. When he eased his tongue into her mouth a sea of sensations rippled through him. Common sense told him to take it easy, not to rush, but as their tongues mated in ways they'd never done before, he couldn't help but take it to the next level. And he had a feeling she would be with him all the way.

Never had a kiss overwhelmed Charm the way this one did. She'd known it would not only rob her of her senses but also create a sexual hunger deep within her. Even now she felt all kinds of wild movements in the pit of her stomach.

She had been kissed by other men since Dylan, but never with his intensity. His mouth took hers hungrily, as if he was trying to make up for lost time. It was drawing every single thing out of her and making her want more.

She tried to convince herself she was not supposed to want more. Her plan was to make him want her, but she was not supposed to want him. At least not with this magnitude. The only good thing about it was knowing his desire for her was real and strong. But she couldn't lose control of the situation. No matter what, she couldn't let that happen.

Charm felt him beneath her backside. His erection was

poking her. The feel of it emboldened her and when he deepened the kiss, she deepened it even more.

Suddenly his cell phone rang and he broke off the kiss. He leaned in and licked her lips before placing her out of his lap and on the bed. "I need to take this call. It's Seth."

A few minutes later, Dylan said, "Elise and Cindy are in my villa. Since it's close to three in the morning I guess they figured I would be spending the night with you and decided to make their move."

"Oh," she said, easing up to sit on the side of the bed.

"There is a question I need to ask you, though. One that has me curious as well as concerned."

"And what question is that?"

He crouched down in front of her so his face was level with hers. Their mouths were within inches and she wondered if he was going to kiss her again. Instead, he said, "This thing with you falling asleep on a whim after overindulging in wine. I don't like it."

She wondered what her sleeping habits had to do with him. "First of all, I don't fall asleep on a whim after drinking too much. Just with red wine. And when I do it's only in a place where I feel comfortable and safe. I do it around my brothers, dad and other family members. However, I have enough sense not to do so around someone with an unsavory character. So if you're concerned about me drinking too much on a date and being taken advantage of, then don't be, because it won't happen."

"You fell asleep with me twice. Does that mean that after ten years, without any contact whatsoever, you feel safe with me?"

Fourteen

Instead of answering him, she switched her gaze from his to study the pattern of the bedspread. As far as Dylan was concerned, his question was simple enough and her response should be easy. So why was she hesitating? If she thought she could ignore him then she was wrong. He wasn't going anywhere until he got her response. Why it was important to him, he wasn't sure. He just knew that it was.

Then she met his gaze again as he remained crouched in front of her. He breathed in deeply as their gazes held. Did she realize how he'd felt when she'd awakened in his bed that morning? It hadn't mattered that she'd slept in it alone. Just the thought that they'd shared such close quarters after ten years had done something to his psyche. Twice he'd gone into the room to check on her and found her sleeping soundly. Each time he'd been captivated.

Then there were the memories of when he had wanted to share every part of himself, his entire life, with her. Had fate brought them back together? Or was his mind playing tricks

on him? Setting him up for even more heartbreak if he jour-
neyed down that road?

"Yes, I feel safe with you, Dylan. There was a time we
meant a lot to each other."

Had there really been such a time? If so, what had happened? He wasn't sure, but what he did know was that she
meant something to him. It was as if regardless of how things
ended between them, regardless of who shouldered the blame,
there was something that hadn't been lost. Their desire to
keep each other out of harm's way. That had been the reason
she had shared with him the conversation she'd overheard,
and that was the reason he wanted to protect her from men
who could take advantage of her whenever she drank too
much wine.

He wanted to say something. Instead, he leaned in and
placed a kiss on her lips. It was supposed to be soft, gentle
and reassuring, and it would have been if she hadn't opened
her mouth on a luscious moan. The moment he slid his tongue
between her lips his body became a frenzy of need.

The next thing he knew he was on the bed with her. It
didn't matter that they were fully clothed. What mattered
was that their need for each other was almost out of control.
His hand was on her thigh and working its way under her
dress when suddenly his phone rang again.

He broke off the kiss and stood. After pulling the phone
out his pocket, in an annoyed tone he said, "What?"

There was a pause, and then Seth said, "I just wanted you
to know Elise and Cindy are being questioned in your villa."

"I'm on my way."

He slipped the phone back into his pants pocket. "Elise
and Cindy are being questioned. I've got to go."

She eased off the bed. "I'm coming with you."

He was surprised she would want to. He was about to tell
her that it wasn't necessary. Elise and Cindy didn't need to
know who'd overheard their plan. "Are you sure you want

to get involved?" he asked, trying not to notice how she was straightening her clothes.

She went still for a moment as if thinking about what he'd asked. "I don't relish my name being plastered across the tabloids as your current lover or anything of that sort," she said. "But I'll be fine being with you when you confront Elise. However, truth be told, Dylan, I've been involved since the night I told you what those two women were up to."

Knowing she was right, he nodded, took her hand and they left her villa. It didn't take long to reach his and he opened the door without knocking. His gaze went to Seth, who was sitting in a chair with his legs stretched out in front of him like he hadn't a care in the world.

Dylan's gaze then moved to the two women sitting on the sofa with the federal agent he'd met yesterday. As soon as Elise saw Dylan, she was off the sofa and rushing toward him, nearly pushing Charm out of the way in the process. He held firm to Charm's hand, refusing to let Elise come between them, and used his other hand to stop her from getting too close.

"Dylan, sweetheart, I'm glad you're here. There's been a huge misunderstanding. These men are saying I was not supposed to be in your villa."

He frowned, wondering what Elise was up to. "You aren't supposed to be in here, Elise. I told you a couple of days ago that you weren't welcome here."

Her expression turned stony. "No, you didn't say that. In fact, you gave me permission to come here whenever I wanted and gave me a key card, too. Why are you lying in front of these people?"

Now he was aware of what Elise was trying to do. If she could convince them he'd given her permission to come to his villa and had even given her a key, then it would be her word against his. Now more than ever he was glad Charm had recorded the conversation between Elise and Cindy.

"Nice try, Elise, but it won't work. I know all about your plan to plant drugs in my luggage."

"I have no idea what you're talking about," she said, but he'd seen the surprise in her eyes.

"Stop with the lies. Your conversation was overheard and recorded. In addition, video cameras were installed in here to watch you execute those plans and hear your conversations. Those were also recorded."

Thinking about all the evidence in his possession was probably what prompted her to say, "Don't do this to me, Dylan. It was all Chrome's idea. He forced me to do it."

He hoped she could see the coldness in his gaze and know that her plea was falling on deaf ears. "Then I guess you'll need to prove that to the authorities. We don't have any proof of Chrome's involvement, but we do have proof of yours."

"Ms. Fairmont, there is the issue of the cocaine that was in your possession as well as those illegal tapes," the FBI agent said. "We watched you bring the items into this villa, and you were watched planting them in Mr. Emanuel's luggage."

Dylan frowned. "What illegal tapes?"

The agent cleared his throat before saying, "Videos of child porn."

"What!"

When the agent nodded, Dylan looked back at Elise and then back at the agent. "Please get them out of here."

"So the two women were arrested?" Ola asked.

"Yes," Charm said. "And Chrome will be questioned since Elise claimed they were working together to destroy Dylan's reputation."

"How awful."

Charm had come back inside her villa after sitting on the balcony while eating lunch and watching people enjoy themselves around the pool. Now she was talking to Piper and Ola on the phone's speaker. She had called to tell them the latest.

"I can't blame Dylan for being furious about the entire thing," Piper said.

"I can't either," Charm said. "Planting the drugs in his luggage was bad enough but she went too far with those child porn tapes. That would have caused a scandal Dylan would never have lived down, and it would have been hard to prove his innocence."

By the time the agent had taken the women away, it had been close to six in the morning. Dylan and Seth had a lot to cover so Dylan had walked her back to her villa. That had been fine since she'd needed to put as much distance between her and Dylan as possible. Those kisses they'd shared had weakened her resolve. If she had spent any more time around him, she would weaken even more.

"So what's next?" Ola asked.

Ola's question reeled her thoughts back in. "I'm not sure, but I have a feeling what happened will make the news. Elise was kicking and screaming all the way out the door, making a scene and practically waking up the entire building."

If people hadn't known Dylan Emanuel was in residence before, they knew it now. Charm heard Seth tell Dylan he needed to call a press conference to control the narrative before Chrome had a chance to claim his innocence. Dylan's PR person was flying in and there would be a joint press conference with Dylan and the FBI. She appreciated Dylan for making sure her name would not be connected, to protect her identity.

Charm's heart pounded when she heard the knock on the door. She had a feeling it was Dylan, which meant he had finished handling the business with Elise. "There's someone at the door and it's probably Dylan. We'll talk later," she said. After ending the call, she moved toward the door. It was late afternoon and she hadn't left her villa. Instead, she had ordered lunch on her balcony.

She tried pushing the thought of just how hot she'd been

last night. Almost on the verge of begging. Those kisses had made her feel explosive but he had stayed in control. And when he'd faced down Elise, he had kept Charm by his side and held her hand the entire time. It had been as if he'd needed her there with him.

Charm opened the door and took in all of Dylan. Although he was impeccably dressed, she could tell by his eyes that he was tired. He'd had a lot to deal with and hadn't gotten any sleep last night. At least she had slept for a few hours after returning to her villa.

"Would you like to come in?" she asked him.

"Yes, thanks." He crossed the threshold and she closed the door behind him. He turned and looked her up and down. "You look nice," he said, giving her a smile that made her stomach flutter.

She'd hung around her brothers long enough during their bachelor days to recognize the look in Dylan's eyes. It was one of male appreciation. That made her glance down at her outfit. It was another sundress she'd purchased yesterday. "Thanks. So do you." He wore a pair of chocolate slacks and a button-up shirt. He smelled good, too.

"Thanks. I'll be giving a press conference at one of the television stations in town in an hour." He studied her and then said, "After it's over I've decided to come back here to pack and leave."

She swallowed thickly. "You're leaving here?" Why did the thought do something to her insides? Was it because she would miss him or because his leaving ruined her plans for revenge?

"Yes. The impact of what Elise tried to do has gotten to me. I want to get as far away from here as I can. I have a feeling that after the press conference the media will start camping outside the security gates. It will become a circus."

She nodded, clearly understanding. Social media, reporters and the paparazzi could be brutal. It was on the tip of

Charm's tongue to say that at least this time he was telling her he was leaving in person instead of sending her a text while rushing off to the airport.

"Are you going to the Red Flame Ranch, or have you changed your mind about joining your band in Ireland?" she asked.

"I'm still going to the ranch."

"Well, I hope you have a safe trip there. It was nice seeing you again after all these years."

He cocked his head as if considering her words. "I wanted to spend more time with you, Charm."

"I wanted to spend more time with you, too." That was the truth, even if her intent had been to seduce and reject him.

"Then come with me."

She blinked, certain she had misunderstood him. "Excuse me?"

"I'm inviting you to my ranch. You were to go there with me one day anyway."

"Yes, but that's when we were together," she reminded him.

"Doesn't matter. I think we should continue rebuilding our friendship, Charm."

The last thing she needed was to be around Dylan any longer. But spending more time with him would help her carry out her plan, if that's what she still wanted to do. "Won't the paparazzi bother you at the ranch?" she asked.

"No. The sheriff is my foreman, Ren's, cousin. He won't let anyone get within miles of the Red Flame. I'm catching a ride back to the States on Seth's private jet. You're welcome to join me. To throw off the paparazzi we could leave for the airport in separate cars. Seth's pilot will fly us straight to the ranch. I had an airstrip installed there a couple of years ago."

"You can fly a plane?" she asked.

"No, but several of my band members can. I also recall that you do."

She'd been taking flying lessons that summer in addition to piano lessons. "Yes, I even have my own plane now."

"Good for you." He took a step closer. "So what do you say, Charm? Will you spend time with me at my ranch in Idaho?"

She nibbled her lips again. "For how long?"

He let out a smooth chuckle. "For as long as you want."

Her heart thumped erratically at the thought of spending more time with him. No matter what, she would have to remain in control. She released a deep breath, and said, "Yes, I'll go to the ranch with you."

Fifteen

The pilot's voice came through the plane's intercom. "Time to snap on those seat belts. We're coming in for the landing."

Dylan put on his while watching Charm snap on hers. He refused to glance over at Seth who'd been eyeing him with concern for the entire flight. Dylan had little to say while Charm and Seth chatted amicably the entire time.

Shifting in his seat to glance out the window, Dylan wondered if he'd made a mistake by inviting Charm. After his grandparents' deaths, the Red Flame had been his escape. He considered this his home and he returned whenever he wasn't on tour. If there was a long stretch in between his visits, Ren would call, check on him and then boldly declare it was time for him to come home for a spell.

"That was a smooth landing, Seth. I need to compliment your pilot," Charm said, her words breaking into Dylan's thoughts. He glanced over at her. She wore a pair of jeans and a T-shirt that boldly proclaimed BORN AN OUTLAW. His breath had been snatched out of his throat the moment he'd arrived at the airport and had seen her. He'd noticed other men noticing her as well. They'd probably been wondering just what kind of outlaw she was.

Seth chuckled and responded to her comment. "My pilot enjoys getting compliments."

Dylan had to agree with Charm. It had been a smooth landing. In fact, it had been a rather calm flight. "So what's next with Elise?" he asked Seth.

"Because she implicated Chrome, he's been picked up for questioning. Of course, he denied knowing anything about it. Chances are he will make an attempt to reach out to you. When he does, don't take his call."

Dylan nodded. "Anything else?"

"No. Call me if anything new develops and I will do likewise with you."

A short while later Dylan and Charm were walking down the steps of the plane. Ren had dropped off Dylan's SUV and once he'd loaded their luggage they said their goodbyes to Seth.

"It's June. Why is the temperature cool here?" Charm asked when he opened the vehicle's door for her.

"The altitude. The ranch is located in the mountains. It's not unusual to wear a jacket sometimes as late as mid-July."

"Sounds like Alaska," she said.

Out of the corner of his eye Dylan watched Charm take in all she saw. "Everything here is so green, Dylan."

He chuckled. "We try to keep it that way. There are a lot of cattle to feed."

"That's right, this is a cattle ranch. One of my Westmoreland cousins has a sheep ranch and a few others raise horses."

He nodded. "Ranching of any kind is a full-time job. My grandparents were lucky to have Ren. Now so am I," he said.

"When was the last time you were here?"

"During the holidays. Although my grandparents aren't here, spending time on the Red Flame was a tradition my parents and I didn't want to end. It was nice because I'd needed the break. Last year I was on the concert tour from hell. With over sixty cities and five countries, that can take its toll both mentally and physically. That's why we decided to take the entire summer off."

"Well, I hope you get a lot of rest while you're here, Dylan."

He honestly didn't see how that was possible with her here. She was hell of another kind, both mentally and physically as well. Every time he looked at her, especially her mouth, he recalled kissing it and how much he wanted to do so again.

Something else he wanted to do was to make love to her. Not for old times' sake but because being around Charm had renewed something within him he hadn't felt in a long time. Namely, an intense desire for a woman. Granted he'd desired women, but not to this magnitude.

The one and only time they'd made love had been about more than their bodies finally connecting. It had been a union that could never be undone. Not even by a text message proclaiming a breakup. He was finally realizing the significance of it now.

She was still his.

That explained a number of things. Like why, after being threatened with having his fingers broken if he was to contact her again, he'd contacted her anyway. And why he'd invited her to dinner when he'd seen her at the pool a few days ago.

But more importantly, why he'd invited her to his ranch.

What did all that mean? What did he even want it to mean? All he knew was that for the last ten years he had existed but not really lived. On the outside he'd been the fun-loving, happy-go-lucky Dylan Emanuel basking in his success as a musician. However, he'd known something was missing from his life. Mainly, someone. Charm. The big question was could he move beyond the hurt and pain she had caused him? Another was, did she regret breaking up with him the way she had?

He knew discussing that time in New York was something

they had to do before they could move forward, whether they wanted to or not.

"Dylan?"

He glanced over at Charm. "Yes?"

"You're quiet. You were also quiet on the plane. Do you regret inviting me here?"

Now that she'd asked...

"No, Charm, I don't regret inviting you here. In fact, the reason I've been quiet was because I was thinking about something involving you. In fact, I think I've pretty much made up my mind about it."

She shifted in her seat to face him. "And what's that?"

"I believe there is a reason our paths crossed after all this time. I've decided it doesn't matter why things ended between us, we've been given another chance and I intend to take it."

He intended to take it...

Of all the nerve, Charm thought. Did he think she had no say so in the matter? After all, he was the one who'd ended things, not her. Granted that text hadn't said he wanted to break up with her but what had he expected when he never called? Had he thought she would go through an entire summer without hearing from him?

Even if he'd assumed that, then what about when he'd returned to the States at the end of the summer? Even if she'd wanted to reach out to him, he had blocked her number. What if she'd gotten pregnant that first time they'd made love? She would not have had any way to contact him.

His callous disregard for the pain he'd caused her, and his assumption that they could just move on like nothing had happened, made her want to get even with him more than ever. No matter what he thought, Dylan didn't deserve a second chance with her.

However, she wouldn't tell him that. She would let him assume he was back in her good graces and all was well. And then when he thought he had her right where he wanted her—probably back in his bed, no doubt—she would tell him just what she thought of him.

"Charm? Will you take that second chance with me?"

She knew she had to convince him she was more than happy to go along with what he was proposing, but with stipulations. "Yes, Dylan, I'll take that second chance with you, but a lot has happened and we're not the same people. I suggest we take the time to get to know each other."

He frowned. "We already know each other."

"Obviously not as well as we thought. Otherwise, we would not have broken up," she said, trying to keep the anger out of her voice.

He studied her for a moment and then switched his gaze to stare straight ahead. "Yes, you're definitely right about that."

Charm studied his expression and wondered why she detected sarcasm in his voice. He had no reason for it when everything was his fault. Or was he annoyed by what she'd said? Had he been counting on her sharing his bed? Zero chance of that happening. She wouldn't he sharing his bed ever again.

She was about to tell him she'd changed her mind about the second chance when he said, "We're here."

Charm glanced around in total awe when she saw the beautiful ranch house. She had been so into her vexation with Dylan that she hadn't realized he had brought the vehicle to a stop. There was something about this house that not only reached out to her but beckoned her in a way she didn't understand or expect. It might sound impossible but it seemed to welcome her.

"So, what do you think?"

She would not dare tell him what she thought—that for some reason she felt this should be a home she shared with him. That this was where they could raise their babies together like they used to talk about doing. "I think it's beautiful," she said truthfully. "And it's big."

He chuckled. "Yes, it is. My grandparents figured they would have a house full of kids but Gramma's medical condition made Dad the only one. However, they decided not to let those ten bedrooms go to waste and this place became a rooming house for college students. There's a university in town that's less than ten miles from here."

"That was nice."

"Those students thought so. Especially since free meals came with the lodgings as well as tender, loving, grandmotherly care."

Charm could imagine living here and being looked after and fed by his grandmother. "They were lucky to have gotten that."

Dylan got out of the car and opened the door for her. "I'll come back to get the luggage. I want to show you around."

As they started up the steps, the door opened and an older woman who appeared to be in her late forties walked out with a huge smile on her face. "Welcome home, Dylan," she said, coming to give him a hug. She then turned to Charm and extended her hand. "Hello, and welcome to you, too. I'm Hazel, Ren's wife."

Charm returned her smile and took the woman's hand, thinking she was very attractive. "Thanks, I'm Charm."

Hazel tilted her head as her smile widened. "I like that name."

"Thanks."

Hazel then turned back to Dylan. "Ren went into town for supplies and will be back shortly. The place is ready for your visit, and I hope you'll be here for a while to get some rest."

"Yes, I will be, but I don't want to be smothered, Hazel," he said, grinning.

"I won't promise not to do that, which means you need to come home more often." She turned to Charm. "I've prepared the guest room for you as Dylan suggested. I think I gave you enough of everything, but if I didn't, Dylan knows how to reach me. I hope you enjoy your stay here. Goodbye."

"Thanks and goodbye." As Charm followed Dylan into the house, she couldn't help but think about what Hazel had said. Dylan had told her to prepare a guest room for Charm? Did that mean she'd been wrong to assume he'd intended them to share a bed? Umm, not necessarily. He might not have wanted others to know his plans.

She glanced around at how immaculate, and yet lived-in, it looked. "Your home is beautiful, Dylan."

"Thanks. It's definitely a lot larger than the ones I have in Memphis and Harlem. I like this place for the solitude as well as for the memories."

She bet he did. He would tell her all the time about the summers he'd spent here with his grandparents and how much he'd enjoyed them. He took her from room to room and she was truly impressed. A huge window in the kitchen had a view of a barn and a gated area where several heads of cattle roamed.

He then took her upstairs and she saw the bedrooms. She noted hers was right across the hall from his. His suite was massive. She'd glimpsed the room when they'd passed by it. Like the other bedrooms she'd seen, the furniture was made of oak and appeared massive and sturdy. His bed appeared to be king-size while the ones in the other bedrooms were queens. All looked comfortable and decorated with colorful comforters.

"I like Hazel," she said, as they moved up the second set of stairs to the third floor where more bedrooms and bathrooms were located.

He smiled. "Everybody loves Hazel. Especially Ren. They've been married close to forty years."

"Forty years?" Charm said, surprised. "How old is she? She doesn't look a day over fifty."

Dylan chuckled. "Hazel is sixty and you're right, she

doesn't look it. She and Ren have teenage grandchildren. Three of their grandsons help him around here when they aren't in school."

"Where do they live?" she asked.

"A few miles down the road on their own spread. Their three sons and one daughter and their families live within throwing distance. The Burgesses are a great family and very close."

"I can't wait to meet Ren."

Dylan checked his watch. "He should be back in a little while. In the meantime, I'll bring in the luggage. Make yourself at home."

They walked back down the stairs together to the main floor and she decided to check out the wraparound back porch while Dylan went out for the luggage. She saw the porch swing and immediately moved to sit in it. The beauty of the land surrounding the ranch helped her understand why Dylan wanted to come here. She closed her eyes for a second to breathe in the peacefulness.

"Charm?"

She opened her eyes and saw Dylan standing at the back door. "Yes."

"You were asleep."

"No, I was breathing in peace."

He lifted a brow. "Breathing in peace?"

"Yes, it seems so peaceful here that you can actually breathe it in."

He nodded. "For a minute there I thought you might have found my wine cellar."

She smiled. "Do you have a wine cellar?"

"Yes, and it's stocked so stay away from the red wine," he warned.

She couldn't help but grin. "I will."

Things got quiet between them and she wondered, why was he looking at her like that? It was in a way that had her heart pounding crazily in her chest. And why was she staring back? And why were those sensations flowing toward the center of her legs again?

"Charm?"

She tried answering but for some reason no sound came out. Charm swallowed deeply, and tried her voice again. "Yes?"

"Ren is back, and I wanted to know if you'd like to meet him now?"

She nodded.

"He's out in the barn. I'll take you there."

She stood and walked toward him. He looked so yummy in his jeans and shirt. And those shoulders—those powerful shoulders she had held on to when they'd kissed. The closer she got, the more she felt his magnetism, as if she was drawn to him. And heat vibrated between them with every step. The more she felt it, the more she wondered if seducing him and then rejecting him was something she could do.

Of course you can do it, she silently told herself. *Dylan Emanuel means nothing to you anymore. Besides, you can handle a little physical attraction. No biggie.*

"I'm ready," she said, coming to a stop in front of him.

"Yes, you are." He wrapped his arms around her waist. "I don't want to rush you into anything, Charm. But damn, I want to kiss you. I *need* to kiss you."

She saw heat in the depths of his dark eyes and knew she needed him to kiss her as well. "Then do it, Dylan. Kiss me."

Sixteen

The moment Dylan's mouth captured Charm's, he realized there were a number of reasons why he should not be doing this. However, what dominated his mind more than anything was the fact that she'd told him to do it, and there was no way he would not oblige her…while satisfying himself. And he intended to satisfy her as well.

He wanted and needed this kiss. Desire clawed at him and he wanted her to feel that same intense hunger.

A part of him didn't want to cross any lines either of them would regret, but a deep sexual hunger pushed him to turn up the heat even more. That same heat shot straight to his groin. And speaking of his groin… The pounding pulse in his crotch had made him rock-hard.

That's when she pressed closer, as if she'd felt it too, and wanted more of it. A primitive force he hadn't felt in years urged him to sweep her into his arms and head up the stairs to the nearest bedroom. Once there they would both appease a sexual appetite that was robbing them of their common sense. This adult Charm aroused him as no other woman could.

Their lips parted when they needed air, but soon rejoined. A rush of heated blood passed like wildfire through his veins as their tongues continued to mate. She lapped him up just as greedily as he was lapping her. Her arms tightened around his neck at the same time his tightened around her waist.

"Harrumph…"

The sound of someone clearing their throat had Charm moving away from him so fast she nearly tripped. He reached out and caught her before she could tumble back. He knew who it was and a part of him was annoyed with the interference. Pulling her back to him to act as a shield against an erection that hadn't gone down, he glanced at the older man leaning against the wall.

"What do you want, Ren?"

"I hated to interrupt but you were supposed to bring this young lady out to the barn for me to meet a half hour ago. I thought I'd come to see what was the holdup."

And, unfortunately, his foreman had seen too much. Still keeping Charm in front of him, Dylan said, "We would have eventually gotten out there."

"Not before I left. Have you forgotten I call it a day at five?"

No, he hadn't forgotten. "Charm, this is Ren Burgess." Then to Ren he said, "This is Charm Outlaw."

Recognition lit the older man's eyes and Dylan knew why. For two years he'd told everyone who'd cared to listen that he planned to marry Charm the minute the both of them graduated from college. He would move her from Alaska and she would go on the road with him while he toured, and they would make New York their home since there was so much to do there.

Ren extended his hand to Charm. "Howdy, ma'am. Welcome to the Red Flame Ranch. It's nice meeting you."

Charm gave Ren a huge smile as she accepted his hand. "Thanks, and it's nice meeting you as well."

Ren released her hand and then glanced over at Dylan. "Hazel wanted me to tell you that both of you are invited to dinner at six and she won't accept no for an answer."

Dylan rolled his eyes. Although he was fine with it, he glanced over at Charm to get her consent. "Charm? Would you like to dine with Ren and Hazel? And just so you know, all of their kids and grands will probably be there as well."

Her smile widened. "Yes, I'd love to. Now if you two gentlemen will excuse me, I need to go upstairs and unpack so I'll have something nice to wear to dinner."

Dylan lifted a brow. "What's wrong with what you have on?" He rather liked seeing her in those jeans and that BORN AN OUTLAW T-shirt.

She rolled her eyes at him. "I can't possibly go to dinner dressed like this."

"Why not?"

"I just can't, Dylan." She then glanced at Ren. "Tell Hazel we appreciate the invitation and we'll be there at six." She quickly moved past Ren to go inside the house. Dylan watched her until she was no longer in sight. That's when he glanced back at Ren who was watching him with an amused expression. "What?"

"Damn, Dylan. What were you trying to do? Kiss her mouth off?"

Charm studied her reflection in the mirror and frowned when she saw her swollen lips. There was no way Ren hadn't seen them as well. On top of that, he'd walked in on them kissing. As far as she was concerned, losing control like that was all Dylan's fault. He made her aware of herself as a woman anytime he looked at her. She had to find a way to counter her reaction to him if she wanted to be successful at carrying out her plan.

She glanced at the dress she would wear tonight. It was one Dylan hadn't seen, since she'd purchased it the first day she'd gone shopping, before she'd realized he was still at the resort. She'd known she wanted it the minute she'd seen it. It wasn't too fancy nor was it too casual. In her opinion it was just right.

While preparing for her shower she wondered what Ren was thinking. Did he assume she was one of Dylan's groupies? Dylan had just given her name without mentioning if she was a friend, lover or a mere acquaintance. Although she wished Ren had not come upon them in such a compromising way, she hated to think what he would have found had he walked in on them ten minutes later. Probably her spread out naked in that swing with Dylan on top of her. She playfully slapped both her cheeks for having such a naughty thought.

A short while later she had showered, dressed and was ready. She headed down the stairs and found Dylan with his back to her, staring out the living room window at the vast land before him. Was he thinking about that or was he thinking about the grandparents who were no longer here? She'd noted earlier there were plenty of photographs of them everywhere. Over the fireplace, on several walls. Not only of them but also of Dylan in his growing years and of his parents.

He must have sensed her presence. He turned around and the smile on his face said it all. He liked her outfit. He slowly walked over to her and brushed a kiss on her forehead and whispered, "You look beautiful."

Charm shouldn't let his words touch her the way they were doing. But she did. "Thank you, Dylan," she said, trying hard not to sound so pleased with his compliment.

"Are you ready?" he asked in a low, husky tone.

She smiled up at him. "Yes, I'm ready."

Dylan leaned back in his chair and listened to the conversation around him. The Burgess family was a lively group and Charm fit right in. He could tell Ren and Hazel's four offspring and grandkids liked her. But then Charm had that easy friendliness about her as well as a warm and bubbly personality. His grandparents had thought she was a sweet girl just from talking to her on the phone.

"I saw your press conference, Dyl. I can't believe one of your old girlfriends tried setting you up like that. Had you been caught with the amount of coke she had planted in your luggage as well as those porn videos, you would have been arrested for sure," Karl Burgess, Ren's oldest son of thirty-four, said.

Dylan figured Karl should know since he was a state prosecutor. He decided not to correct Karl about Elise being an old girlfriend of his. He had clarified it with Charm and she was the one who mattered. "I'm glad things turned out the way they did and Seth alerted the FBI. That would have definitely destroyed my reputation and music career."

"I bet that was her intent," Renata Burgess said. She was Ren and Hazel's youngest and the only one not yet married. "I just don't understand some women. Especially those who think they need to get revenge on a man because he cuts them loose. That's over the top. They should have more pride than that."

"Hazel, dinner was wonderful," Charm suddenly said.

Dylan figured he was the only one who picked up on the fact that Charm was intentionally changing the subject. Why? What part of what Renata said bothered her? Or was it that she wanted to shut down the entire subject because she didn't want anyone to figure out she'd been the person who'd overheard the conversation? Was she wary about being implicated in some way?

"Thank you, Charm. You are invited back at any time."

"Thanks."

A couple of hours later Dylan was driving back to the ranch. Charm was quiet, although she'd kept a steady stream of conversation between her and the Burgesses at dinner. He could tell they liked her. He wasn't sure why that was important to him, but it was. On the drive to dinner, Dylan had told Charm that his father and Ren had been best friends while growing up. Whereas Dyrek Emanuel had big dreams of moving away from Idaho, Ren had been satisfied with staying put and raising his family here.

"I like them."

He glanced over at Charm. The roads between the two farms were void of any streetlights, but he knew his way around without them. There was a full moon in the sky and a silver light shone through the car's window and illuminated her profile. No matter what angle, Charm's beauty was always magnified.

"And they liked you."

That seemed to make her smile and she turned around in the seat to look at him. "You think so?"

"Yes. But then I'm sure they're curious about you since I've never invited a woman to my ranch before."

"Oh." Then as if to change the subject, she said, "I like the music that's playing on the radio."

He chuckled. "It's not the radio—it's a track and one of mine."

She lifted a brow. "You listen to your own stuff?"

"Sure I do. I listen to hear if anything could have been played better."

She nodded. "So what are the plans for tomorrow?"

"I thought I'd show you around the property. You can ride a horse, right?"

She chuckled. "Yes. And because I had planned to visit my brother's ranch in Wyoming after leaving Cancún, I brought jeans and shirts with me."

"That's good. Think you can be up and ready around eight? I plan to go over the books with Ren at six."

"Yes, that won't be a problem."

Dylan pulled into the driveway of the Red Flame and for the first time appreciated it was long and winding. He wasn't ready for his time with Charm to end. When he finally reached the ranch house, he turned off the car's ignition. "We're home."

Too late, he realized what he'd said. From her expression it didn't seem as if she'd noticed the slip. This was his home and not hers. "Thanks for inviting me here, Dylan."

He nodded. "I always wanted you to see the ranch. I just regret you never got to meet Gramps and Gramma in person."

"It was nice chatting with them on the phone, though."

"Yes, and they thought the same." Not saying anything else, he got out and walked around the SUV to open the door for her. He held her hand as they walked up the steps together.

"It's a beautiful night."

His gaze was drawn to her as he opened the front door. "That's usually how it is around here. Busy days and peaceful, beautiful nights."

When they entered his home, he closed the door behind them and she said, "I'd better go now. Good night. I'll see you in the morning."

When she turned to head up the stairs, he caught hold of her hand.

"Yes, Dylan?" she asked.

"I want to kiss you good-night, Charm."

As if she needed to kiss him, too, she turned to him and his arms went to her waist to pull her closer. He leaned forward and so did she. The moment his tongue captured hers, shivers passed through him. He figured it would not have been so bad if she hadn't seemed just as greedy.

Suddenly, she broke off the kiss and took a step back. "I need to go." Then, without saying anything else, he watched her race up the stairs.

Seventeen

When was the last time a guitar was played and a song sung beneath Charm's bedroom window? Never. No one had ever serenaded her before. Yet it was happening now. Getting out of bed, she slid into her robe before walking over to the window. Pushing aside the curtain, her breath caught. Dylan had a Stetson on his head, and he was wearing a Western shirt, jeans and boots. He looked like a cowboy.

Sliding up the window, she smiled down at him. "What are you doing?"

He grinned up at her. "I'm serenading you awake. You were supposed to meet me at eight."

She turned to glance at the clock. It was after nine. Looking back out the window, she said, "I'm so sorry. I didn't set the alarm and overslept. I'll be down in a minute."

"No rush. Eat breakfast first. I left it warming for you."

That was thoughtful of him. "Thanks. And thanks for the serenade. I loved it."

Charm closed the window. Grabbing items she needed, she quickly moved toward the shower. She had intended to wake up before eight but those hot dreams of Dylan had pushed her into a deep, relaxed sleep.

It didn't take her long to shower, dress and eat the delicious breakfast Dylan had left for her. When she walked out the front door he was there, with his guitar over his shoulder. The look in his eyes let her know he liked her outfit as much as she liked his.

"So what's the plan for today?"

"First thing is milking the cows. Have you ever done that before?"

He had to be kidding. Of course she hadn't. "No, but I thought that sort of thing was done by machines," she said, following him off the porch toward the barn.

"Usually it is, but we're not a dairy. There are just a few cows, like Molly, that we prefer milking the old-fashioned way."

Dylan's legs were long and he'd adjusted his stride so she could keep up with him. She appreciated that. When they reached the barn, she was amazed how neat it was. She smiled when she saw Ren and waved. Then Dylan introduced her to some of the other guys who worked at the ranch. It didn't take long for him to show her the proper way to milk a cow. It felt funny at first but then she got the hang of it. A couple of hours later they had milked four cows.

"What's next?" she asked, proud of her accomplishments for that morning.

Dylan smiled. "I'd like to show you more of the property and then we'll have a picnic by the lake."

A picnic sounded nice and she told him so.

"Glad you like it. I told Hazel to have a picnic basket ready at noon. It's probably been prepared by now."

It had been and when they returned to the main house, just like yesterday, Hazel met them the moment they walked up the steps. Dylan quickly moved to relieve Hazel of the huge basket. "Is this lunch *and* dinner?" he asked, grinning, letting both women know how heavy the basket was.

"No, but knowing how beautiful that spot is by the lake, I figured you two would want to stay a while."

Although Charm smiled at the woman's words, the last thing she wanted was to stay a while anywhere with Dylan. But she had a mission to accomplish. To do what she needed to do meant taking advantage of every opportunity for them to spend time together.

"I think Hazel has the right idea," Dylan whispered while they walked toward his SUV. "You're going to love this spot."

Charm had a feeling she would. So far she'd liked every place Dylan had shown her on his ranch. A part of her wished things had been different and she didn't have revenge on her mind.

She stood by the vehicle and watched him put the basket in the back and when he returned to her he pulled her into his arms. A part of her wanted to resist him, but when he drew her closer, her body went willingly and eagerly. At that moment her mind and body were in turmoil.

"You okay, Charm?"

She pulled back to meet his gaze. "Yes. Why do you ask?"

He looked at her for a moment and then said, "Nothing."

There was something. Had he picked up on her confusion? That's the last thing she wanted. More than anything she needed a settled mind as to what had to be done. When she left the ranch, she wanted him to know how it felt to believe someone wanted you and to find out they really didn't.

Dylan lowered his mouth to hers and the touch of his lips sent sensations swirling in her stomach. She kissed him back until she remembered where they were. If any of his men walked out of the barn or if Hazel had glanced out the window, they would have seen them kissing. It was bad enough that Ren had been a witness to one of their heated kisses yesterday.

Breaking off the kiss, she said, "I think we need to leave and go somewhere private, don't you?"

She figured she could start working on him at lunch and then in a few days he would assume she was ripe to be bedded. That's when she would take pleasure in not only telling him what he wouldn't be getting but what he would never get from her again.

"You're right. It's getting harder and harder to resist you, Charm."

"Um, maybe you shouldn't try resisting me, Dylan." There, she'd given him ideas. Ideas that would hopefully set her plan into motion.

"This place is beautiful, Dylan. And the lake is huge."

Dylan had hoped she would like it. Of all the spots on the ranch, this particular one was his favorite. He would bring his guitar here many days and sit with his back against that huge oak tree and play to his heart's content. This place was also the inspiration for a number of his songs. After he'd met Charm, he envisioned sharing this place with her while he played his music to her. After their breakup, it had taken a long while before he could come to the lake and not think of her.

He pushed those thoughts to the back of his mind, not wanting to recall his heartbreak. What was important was that for whatever reason, fate had intervened and they were together again. He was willing to let bygones be bygones and move forward with a new beginning.

After spreading a blanket on the ground, he sat down and then pulled her down with him before grabbing for his guitar. "This song I'm about to play for you was one I wrote after losing my grandparents. It was a difficult time for me and my parents. I think we thought Gramps and Gramma would be around forever."

She reached out and placed her hand on his. "And they

will be, Dylan. In your heart. I told you what happened with
me when I lost my grandparents within a year of each other."

Yes, he remembered. She couldn't handle the loss and re-
belled.

"There's not a day that I don't think of them," he said. "I
feel their presence even more whenever I come to the ranch."

She nodded. "Were you surprised your grandparents left
the ranch to you and not to your parents?"

"No. Dad said years ago he wasn't cut out to be a rancher.
He couldn't wait to leave for college and didn't plan to return, other than to visit. I knew from the time I was in my
teens that the ranch would one day be mine. My grandparents had told me so. They knew how much I loved it here. I
couldn't wait for school to end so my parents could send me
to Idaho for the summer."

He chuckled. "I even tried talking them into letting me
live with my grandparents year-round but they refused to do
that. They didn't mind sharing me during the summer but
the rest of the year they wanted me in Memphis with them."

"That's the only time you came here? During the summers?"

"No. We always came as a family at Thanksgiving and
then again for Christmas. Holidays here at the ranch were
the best."

He didn't say anything else for a minute but noticed her
hand was still on his. It was meant to be comforting, but he
was beginning to feel more than comfort from her touch. He
met her gaze and knew she felt it, too. She did something
at that moment that he hadn't expected. She leaned toward
him, traced her fingertips along his lips and whispered, "Kiss
me, Dylan."

She didn't have to ask twice. He did more than kiss her;
he pulled her into his lap as he took possession of her mouth.
Nothing was better than this. Everything about her turned
him on. He hadn't seen her often in jeans but the pair she wore

today tightened around every curve. When she'd stepped on the porch, he'd done a double take. It had been hard keeping his concentration on milking the cows. She looked as if she belonged on his ranch.

When he noticed his ranch hands' gazes lingering on her more than he'd like, the look he'd given them let them know he would excuse their interest once. After all, they were men with a keen appreciation for beauty. But that same look also told them she was off-limits. Knowing his men, they got the message and would act accordingly.

He released her mouth. If he didn't, he would be tempted to start removing her clothes. Although she'd asked to be kissed, he didn't think she was ready to move beyond that yet. He was, but he wouldn't rush her.

"I guess we need to see what Hazel put in the basket for lunch," she said, licking her lips, which made his stomach tighten.

"Yes, I guess we'd better," he said, placing her off his lap to sit beside him before reaching for the basket.

He pulled out chicken salad sandwiches, chips, apples and a jug of iced tea and cups. Handing her one of the napkins that was also included he said, "You're going to love Hazel's chicken salad sandwiches. They are the best."

"I believe you. The dinner she prepared last night was great."

"Her dinners always are."

They ate while he told her more about the ranch and the land it sat on, including the number of generations it had been in the Emanuel family. After eating they took a walk around the grounds and then returned for him to play several songs. While in college he had often played for her over the phone when they'd been miles apart.

"I love those songs, Dylan. I always thought you were a gifted guitarist who would go places one day."

He didn't say anything as he folded the blanket for them to

leave. Evidently, it had been her plan that he go places without her. He started to bring it up but decided not to. They had shared a nice day together and he refused to allow the past to intrude.

"So what's on the schedule for tomorrow?" she asked him.

"I thought we'd ride the range and look for stray cattle."

"Are there many?"

He shook his head. "Not usually, and those I don't round up will be returned by the neighbors. However, since I'm here I'll make myself useful."

"And I will make myself useful right along with you," she said, grinning.

He chuckled. "I'd appreciate that. We could always use extra hands around here." He pushed to the back of his mind other ways she could be useful to him. All sexual and none he should be entertaining.

"Thanks for bringing me here, Dylan. I enjoyed my time with you today."

And he had enjoyed his time with her. "I figure after you rest up, we can go out to dinner later. There's a restaurant in town that's owned by a friend of mine who I want you to meet."

She nodded. "Alright. But aren't you concerned about the paparazzi?"

"No. The owner of the restaurant is the sheriff's brother. Trust me, the media knows not to mess with Sheriff Farmer."

"Ready to leave?" she asked.

"Yes." He honestly wasn't, but he knew they needed to do so. Still, he couldn't stop himself from leaning toward her and claiming her lips in another kiss.

Eighteen

After taking her shower Charm began dressing for the day. It was hard to believe she'd been here for almost a week already. She would admit she had enjoyed it. Only problem was her growing attraction to Dylan.

Dinner at his friend's restaurant had been delicious, and the dessert had been the best chocolate cake she'd ever eaten. After dinner they'd gone dancing at a nearby nightclub. She wasn't surprised that most of the people knew Dylan and when he was asked to perform, he did so to a standing ovation.

Every morning he'd awakened her with a serenade. She wished she didn't enjoy it so much. Nor did she want to enjoy their time together, although she did enjoy that, too. Over the past week they had ridden the range a number of times, milked the cows most mornings, gone back to the lake for another picnic and had dinner with the Burgess family a few times. Dylan had even displayed his cooking skills by preparing dinner one night. And just like he started her day with his songs, he ended the day the same way by playing for her before bedtime.

Today they would be visiting the local children's hospital where Dylan would entertain some of his younger fans. He'd had a special wing built that bore his grandparents' names. A part of her wished he wasn't coming off each day as a good guy because she still planned to get justice for what he'd done to her.

She picked up her phone off the bed and saw she'd missed a call from Cash. He was probably wondering where she was when she'd told him she would be heading to his ranch in Wyoming after Lacey's wedding. No one in her family knew she was in Idaho and they definitely had no idea she was here with Dylan.

She gave Cash the impression she had remained in Cancún longer than planned. He let her know that when she arrived at his dude ranch he wouldn't be there. Tomorrow he would be flying to Fairbanks for a business meeting and wouldn't be back for a few days. However, Brianna and the kids would be there and were looking forward to seeing her.

Before placing her phone back down, she swiped the screen to look at the photos she had taken of Dylan over the past few days. There was one of him standing by the corral with his guitar by his side. He'd been wearing a blue shirt and jeans. Because of the early morning chill he'd worn a leather jacket. Why did he have to appear so ruggedly handsome with that black Stetson on his head and looking like a cowboy? She had caught him in one of his pensive moments while waiting for her. He hadn't known she'd taken the photo and already it was one of her favorites.

She looked at another photo—one of them together. At Dylan's request one of his ranch hands had taken it. She and Dylan had been standing beside each other, holding hands. They held hands a lot, like when they'd been together before.

They also kissed a lot. And whenever they did, the kisses nearly got out of hand. However, Dylan managed to stop things from escalating. That made Charm wonder what was going on in that head of his. She was trying hard to seduce him, but it was as if he was working hard not to be seduced. Why?

Did he suspect what she planned? No, there was no way he could. So why was he acting like a perfect gentleman, so darn charming? Especially when she knew he wanted her. That much was evident every time he pulled her into his arms and gave her a kiss that made her weak in the knees.

She could feel his arousal, clear evidence of his desire for her. She saw the degree of desire in his eyes. Yet each time she tried taking over the kiss to sway things her way, he retained control and ended things before it got out of hand.

Not today. She was determined this would be the day she would seduce him and then walk away. Her plan was for them to strip down to nothing, and tumble on the bed. Then she would insist he put on a condom and while he did, she would get off the bed and tell him she had no intention of letting him touch her and why. He would be mad, but she didn't care. There was a strong possibility he would ask her to leave the ranch.

As she dressed, she pushed the thought from her mind that under any other circumstances she would like this Dylan. He was older, more mature and settled. He wasn't the ambitious, fame-seeking musician who had no problem tossing her aside. He had a down-to-earth personality, considering he was an international celebrity. Her name might be Charm but he was the one wallowing in charm. People couldn't help but be drawn to him. *She* was drawn to him and wished she wasn't.

She checked herself in the mirror. Satisfied with her appearance, she grabbed her purse as she gave herself a pep talk. "Tonight is the night. No matter what, you will not let that sexy smile and endearing personality get next to you. You are an Outlaw. Keep your emotions in check. Don't show any sign of anger or vulnerability. And when the opportunity presents itself, you get even."

She left the guest bedroom intending for the opportunity to present itself tonight, even if she had to take the bull by the horns.

"I didn't mean to keep you away from the ranch the entire day, Charm."

She glanced up at him and smiled. The way the corners of her lips turned up had heat coiling his gut. "I didn't mind. I rather enjoyed myself. The kids were wonderful. They love you."

"And I love them. I wish I could do more than play music to them. If I were a magician, I'd wave a magic wand and make them all well. It wouldn't bother me any if a single child never had to spend a night on my grandparents' wing of the hospital."

She didn't say anything; she had to be thinking of the children they'd met that day. Some had been in the hospital for months and some wouldn't be going home. That left a knot in his throat, which was why the wing itself just wasn't enough. He and his band often donated money to not just the children's hospital here but also to several others across the country.

He took her hand as they crossed the parking lot to the his sports car. The one that resembled the one he'd driven in Cancun. The moment their hands touched, he felt, like he always did, total awareness of her. Resisting her was hard, but he'd been doing just that. Did she have any idea why? Hopefully they were not only rebuilding their friendship but also a relationship. He was falling in love with Charm all over again. After having his heart broken by her once, he didn't relish such a thing being repeated. He wanted to be sure of her. Be sure of them. He wanted more than a toss between the sheets to satisfy their urges. He wanted to make love to her and not just have sex.

"You're quiet, Dylan."

Not for the first time, he noticed whenever she was concerned about something there was a change in her voice. It sounded throaty. There was no way he would tell her how it was becoming harder and harder to resist her as a woman. And dang it, she wasn't making things easy for him either. She was no longer the teenage Charm who didn't understand the full extent of her sensuality. She knew it, and he had a feeling she was trying to use it to get next to him. Why?

He would think, considering their history, that she would want to take things slowly just like he did. But then, she had been the one to break things off. Maybe for her that was what she'd gotten used to, what she preferred. Relationships with no meaning, with no intention to last. That might be well and dandy for her, but it wasn't for him. It was hard to consider something meaningless with the woman you'd once planned to marry, the woman you'd assumed would one day be the mother of your children. The woman you'd intended to love forever.

Knowing she was waiting for a response, he said, "I've just got a lot on my mind."

"You were thinking about the children, weren't you?"

He'd been thinking of the children alright, but not the ones at the hospital. He'd been thinking of the ones that they'd planned to have. But to satisfy her curiosity, he said, "Yes."

"I'm glad you and your band do so much for them."

He lifted a brow. He'd told her about the hospital wing and nothing else. "And how do you know what all I do for them?"

"While you were performing, I overheard one of the doctors tell a parent about all the donations you and your band give not only to them but to other children's hospitals as well. I think it's wonderful, Dylan."

"Thanks." He opened the car door for her, appreciating how nice she looked in her pants, blouse and blazer. It was the first time he'd seen her in what he considered professional attire. Like he'd done all week, he had introduced her as a close friend. However, he could imagine what everyone thought since he'd never brought a woman to this type of function at the hospital before.

After closing her car door, he walked around the other side to get in, remembering the compliment Charm had given him. A part of him wished he didn't put so much stock into what she thought of as his good deeds. What bothered him more than anything was the fact that, just like the old days, what she thought mattered to him. She'd always had a knack for boosting his ego and building his confidence.

Over the years he'd avoided women who liked showering him with praise and compliments because Charm had proved all those she'd given him hadn't truly been sincere. The one thing he couldn't tolerate was an insincere woman. That was the main reason he had quickly written off Elise. Only a fool made the same mistake twice.

"Are you hungry?" he asked her.

"No. I thought it was nice of the doctors to treat us to dinner."

He'd thought so, too. It was a nice Italian restaurant across from the hospital. He checked his watch. It was six o'clock. They'd been at the hospital since ten that morning. Charm had been a real trooper. She'd seemed to enjoy herself and did well with the kids. It was obvious they liked her. She'd told him that in addition to her brothers' kids, she had a lot of younger Westmoreland cousins she enjoyed spending time with.

"I have an idea."

Dylan snapped his seat belt in place and looked over at her. "And what's your idea, Charm?"

"I noticed a video collection of your concerts in the study.

Like I told you, I've never seen one. I'd love to watch one with you on that huge television in the family room."

He knew what collection she was talking about. Although his grandparents attended some of his concerts, he'd made sure they'd gotten a video of every single one. "If you're sure that's something you really want to do."

She smiled over at him. "It is and I'll let you select which concert that you want us to watch."

He smiled. "Okay. We'll do that."

Nineteen

Charm sank down on the bed after checking her appearance in the mirror. She hadn't told Dylan she would be changing clothes. Hopefully, he would assume she'd wanted to put on something more comfortable than the pantsuit she'd worn to the hospital. So what if it was one of those short caftans that hit midthigh? He'd seen her in a shorter skirt in Cancún, not to mention that bikini.

But she knew she was wearing this outfit for a particular purpose. She intended to seduce Dylan tonight. It was the culmination of her plans, the only reason she'd agreed to come with him to Idaho. So why was she having second thoughts? Just because today she'd seen another side of him— the grown-up Dylan who had found a cause other than his love for music. But, deep down, she hadn't expected less of the man she'd fallen in love with at sixteen.

And loved even now.

Charm went still.

There was no way she could still have feelings for him. Some women might be able to get over being dropped the way she had, but she couldn't. She recalled what Renata Burgess had said at dinner the other night. Was that why she'd begun second-guessing herself and her plan?

Other than self-satisfaction, what else would she be getting out of this? Shouldn't she be able to just move on? Obviously, he had. Is that what was bothering her? Knowing he'd lived his life for the past ten years and not given her a passing thought? He hadn't tried looking her up, rekindling a flame or even letting her know he had loved her but their love just hadn't been meant to last.

She could understand that, but what she could not accept was feeling used and betrayed. That's what she could not move beyond. At least she wasn't vindictive to the extent that Elise had been, but still… She wanted to leave her mark on him. She wanted to make him think twice before breaking another woman's heart. He'd taught her a hard lesson; now it was time she taught him one.

Standing, she drew in a deep breath and left the room. After walking down the stairs, she smelled popcorn and heard music coming from the huge family room. He was kneeling in front of the television, holding a DVD when she entered. Her footsteps must have alerted him she'd arrived. He turned to say something and stopped. His gaze roamed over her from head to toe and back up again.

She swallowed, seeing the intense look of desire in his gaze. "I thought I'd change into something comfortable."

He nodded as his gaze continued to roam over her. A part of her wondered if he had x-ray vision and could tell she wasn't wearing a bra or panties beneath her caftan. "I see," he said in a husky voice.

A part of her hoped he didn't see too much or else he would suspect what she was up to. "So which concert will we be watching?" she asked, moving to the sofa to sit down and making sure she intentionally flashed him when she did.

Was that a moan she'd heard? If so, that meant she was

getting to him. Good. When he didn't answer, she met his intense gaze and asked again. "Dylan?"

"Yes?"

"Which concert are we going to watch?"

He looked at the DVD he held in his hand and then back at her. "The last one my grandparents attended. I called them onstage to introduce them to the crowd."

"Oh." Not sure that particular one would set the mood she wanted, especially when she heard the pain in his voice. She didn't want to deal with his pain but with his passion. However, there must be a reason he'd chosen that video. "That sounds like a good one. I'd love to see it."

She gestured to the bowl sitting in the middle of the coffee table. "And thanks for making the popcorn."

He smiled over at her after inserting the DVD into the player. "Can't have concert night without popcorn."

Dylan picked up the remote that also controlled the lights in the room. They went off the exact moment the television screen revved to life. That's when he sat beside her on the sofa. It wasn't close enough for her so she scooted closer. He then placed his arm across the back of the sofa so they could cuddle while watching the concert.

Charm couldn't stop her body from responding to his nearness, especially when his arms felt warm and comforting. The only time either of them moved from that position was when he grabbed the bowl of popcorn to offer her some. After munching a while, he returned it to the table and drew her back into his arms.

Over the years she had convinced herself that not attending one of Dylan's concerts was therapeutic. It would rid him from her thoughts, mind and heart. No matter how often she'd tried to avoid hearing his music, it wasn't always possible when her sisters-in-law and many of her Westmoreland cousins were fans of his. Some had heard about her past relationship with him at sixteen, and many had not. But none of them had known that their relationship had continued for two years after Bart had forbidden it.

Watching the concert showed her that not only was he a great guitarist, but he was a gifted performer all around. He knew just how to drive the crowd wild, and those tight leather pants had several women in the audience drooling.

When she began singing along with the crowd, he smiled at her. "I thought you didn't listen to my music."

"I don't. I only know that song because Garth's wife, Regan, played it all the time."

He nodded. "Our next number is a love song. A slow number. Do you know what I want to do Charm, while we watch?"

She met his gaze. "No, what do you want to do?"

"I want to dance with you."

Dylan wasn't sure why he wanted to hold Charm in his arms during this song, but he did. And she hadn't shot down the idea.

He stood and offered her his hand and she took it. He then drew her into his arms while trying not to think about when she'd first entered the room. Turning around and seeing those gorgeous long legs and shapely thighs in that short outfit had sent his blood pressure flaring. It was an outfit meant to stroke every sensuous nerve in his body. If that hadn't done it for him, then her scent most definitely had. It had taken his total concentration to keep himself in control.

Now it seemed all that control he'd been battling to retain was being tested. Why did she have to fit so perfectly in his arms? Why was she the ideal height for his tall frame? And why, as they swayed in the middle of the room to the music, couldn't he stop his body from getting aroused?

He knew there were a zillion reasons for the latter. It had been a while since he'd slept with a woman. At least a good seven months. He joked that Graham was doing it enough for the both of them. He wasn't worried about his best friend, who took safe and responsible sex to a whole other level.

But he was worried about himself.

He tightened his arms even more around Charm. She had to feel his aroused state. In fact, if he didn't know better, he'd think she was pressing her body even closer against it.

Hard as it was, he tried not to think about how good Charm felt in his arms. He tried to remember the last time they'd danced together before he'd seen here again at the wedding. It had been that second summer in Alaska, when her room-mates were away and he'd spent a week with her in Anchorage. She'd been seventeen then and he'd turned nineteen. They hadn't gone dancing anywhere for fear of being seen by one of her brother's friends. So they had danced inside her home to the music on their phones.

Memories flowed through him of that night, and he closed his eyes on a moan. One he was certain she heard. It couldn't be helped.

At the sound, she buried her face in the hollow of his throat and licked him there. He actually felt molten blood rush through his veins. What was she doing to him? Didn't she know she was playing with a lit piece of dynamite? Did she not care?

The music stopped. "Thanks for the dance, Charm." He made a move to step back from her and discovered he couldn't. He didn't want to acknowledge the look in her eyes. Her gaze all but said *kiss me*. So he lowered his mouth to hers.

She could have politely refused the kiss by pulling back, but she didn't. The way she was kissing him back made a knot tighten in the pit of his stomach that extended all the way down to his crotch. Dylan broke off the kiss when he felt her hand travel low to his zipper. He caught her fingers in his and pressed their foreheads together as he released a deep breath. "That kind of kiss is liable to get us in trouble."

"There's nothing like a little bit of trouble. Don't you know there's such a thing as good trouble, Dylan Emanuel?"

He wasn't all too sure about that. "We need to talk, Charm."

"I don't want to talk. I want you."

He wished she hadn't admitted to that because he wanted her, too. But they needed to get a few things straight before they could move beyond a kiss. He was about to tell her that when her hand eased beneath his shirt to touch his skin. Her hands felt hot, making him sizzle from the inside out.

The next thing he knew, she was standing on tiptoe and had pressed her mouth to his, determined that they not talk but get into that good trouble she'd alluded to. He couldn't resist her. He slanted his mouth over hers, claiming it with more intensity than he'd ever done before. He kissed her hard, he kissed her deep and at that moment he was convinced he wanted to get into that good trouble she'd been talking about.

When Charm was swept up in a pair of strong arms and carried back to the sofa, she knew she had to retain control and not get caught up in the moment. However, she wanted to make sure Dylan did. All she had to do was remember the one and only time they'd shared a bed and what had happened the next day. For that reason, she shouldn't feel any guilt. If he didn't feel guilty for what he'd done to her, then she certainly wouldn't feel guilty about her plans for him tonight.

When he sat down on the sofa with her in his lap, she wriggled her bottom. There was no way he didn't know about her missing undies and bra now. Looping her arms around his neck, she kissed him and he kissed her back, pressing her body closer to his.

Charm's heart pounded as the area between her legs throbbed. Although she was trying not to get caught up in Dylan's kiss she was doing so anyway. She wriggled her backside again, glorying in the feel of his erection, and heard herself groan. She wasn't supposed to do any groaning. He was. But they were groaning together. She closed her eyes as sensations overtook her. When he broke off the kiss she opened her eyes, drew in a deep breath and then pressed her mouth against his again. Unable to get enough of him.

He gave her the kiss she wanted and his hands eased beneath her caftan. His fingertips moved up to the nipples of her breasts and she trembled in his arms. What was happening to her? Why was she losing control? Why did she want Dylan to touch all of her, not just her breasts?

If he could touch her then she could certainly touch him. She began unbuttoning his shirt. When it was completely opened, she covered his chest with her hands, feeling the warmth of his skin beneath her fingers.

He broke off the kiss. "Charm, you're driving me to the edge."

He was doing likewise to her. She hadn't expected it. His kisses were drugging. Because of her limited experience, he had always been the one in control of their kisses, even those times when she initiated them. Now, they were both using their tongues for pleasure of the hottest kind.

Dylan's hand gripped her bottom to stop her from wriggling at the same time he ended the kiss and groaned. "Charm, I'm trying to be the nice guy here."

She didn't want him to be the nice guy. She wanted to drive him mindless with lust. "I don't want you nice, Dylan. I've never seen the bad boy in you, and I want to see it."

He held her gaze. "Not sure that you want to."

"I do." There was no reason for him to know being bad wouldn't go as far as he assumed it would.

"Remember, I'm giving you what you want," he said, standing with her in his arms and heading up the stairs.

She felt her body flutter with every step he took. When he reached his bedroom and put her on the bed, he joined her there. "I don't want to be bad all by myself, Charm. Will you be bad with me?"

She could tell him she would, although she didn't plan to let things go that far. She was determined to remain in control no matter what. "Yes, I'll be bad with you, Dylan."

The smile that appeared on his face made her aware of everything about him. There was just something about a Dylan Emanuel smile and although she didn't want it to, it was getting to her. "Take off your clothes, Dylan. I want to see you naked," she said in a breathy tone. This was it. When he undressed, she would get up and walk out.

"Okay. After another kiss we'll both be bad."

He then leaned in and took her lips again.

Twenty

Dylan put everything he had, every part of him, all the sexual hunger he'd been holding back into his kiss. He wanted her to know just how much he desired her.

And how much he loved her.

Sexual energy consumed him, rocking him to the bone. From the way she trembled, he had a feeling it was rocking her as well.

Dylan broke off the kiss and licked her mouth from corner to corner. Her moans, a husky sensuous sound of want and need, stirred even more hunger to life within him.

"Dylan... I...please..."

He continued to lick her lips. And then she pulled up and took his mouth. Her hunger mixed with her aggressiveness heated his blood. It ignited an explosion of pleasure all through him. No woman had aroused him to this degree, where every ounce of testosterone in his body flared in response to what she was doing. When she finally released his mouth, he tugged her caftan over her head and gazed down at her. Her body was beautiful.

"Dylan, what are you doing to me?" she asked in a breathy voice.

"The same thing you're doing to me, Charm. I intend to drive you wild. What do you think of that?"

Before she could answer, he shifted her to lie on her back and she whispered, "Your clothes. Take your clothes off, too, Dylan."

Heeding her command, he moved away from the bed and pulled his shirt from his pants to take it off. After tossing it aside, he removed the rest of his clothes. He heard her sharp intake of breath when he stood by the bed totally naked.

Charm knew she was in trouble.

This was when she was supposed to get off the bed and tell him just what she thought of him. The only problem was that she couldn't make her legs move. Nor could she keep her gaze from roaming all over him. He no longer had the body of a teenager but that of a man. It boggled her mind that all these changes could have taken place in ten years.

She'd always thought he had a nice physique, but now it was muscular. Where had that chiseled stomach, rock-hard chest and those strapping shoulders come from? And then there was his manhood, that length that had the area between her thighs throbbing just from the sight of it. It was bigger, even more beautiful than she remembered. And from the way it seemed to be enlarging before her eyes, he was getting aroused just from her looking at him. Or was it from him looking at her naked body?

He pulled a condom from the wallet he'd placed on the nightstand earlier. She'd seen him sheath himself before and was just as fascinated now, amazed at how his oversized manhood could fit in such a tiny piece of latex.

When he was finished, she moved her gaze to his face and saw the depth of his desire for her. A frisson of need shot up her spine. And then he began moving toward her. She was suddenly filled with a need she hadn't expected. A need so intense, the ache reached every part of her body. She wanted to get a grip, but couldn't. The only thing she could do was reach out for him the moment he placed his knee on the bed.

The kiss they exchanged at that moment was one meant to be in a romance novel. Their lips and tongues were in sync, trying to feed a hunger they both felt. The more he gave of himself, the more she wanted. Whatever this was, these emotions ramming through her body were some she couldn't fight. Nor did she want to.

When he broke off the kiss, she moaned a protest, but he silenced her objection by trailing kisses down her neck while rubbing his hand gently across her chest. When his fingertips caressed her nipples she released another moan and when his tongue laved one nipple and then another, her womanly core pulsed intensely.

What was happening to her? What was he doing to her? When his hands lowered between her legs and stroked her there while his tongue continued to lick and suck her nipples, she came close to having an orgasm then and there.

When he lifted his head and their eyes met, he smiled. The look in them all but told her he was about to get bad. As naughty as he could get. He proved her right when he eased her down on her back and trailed kisses down her chest toward her stomach.

Knowing his intent, she could only moan out his name in anticipation. "Dylan…"

Any thought of resisting was not even possible as her body trembled beneath the onslaught of his tongue as it moved closer to its target. At the initial feel of his tongue inside her, she gasped in pleasure and spread her thighs to provide him better access. He became the bad boy he told her he would become when he used that tongue as a weapon of mass pleasure.

Then she couldn't hold out any longer when he lifted her hips and locked his mouth on her as his tongue suddenly became a gratification machine. Her womb contracted at the feel of what he was doing to her and how. As if a powder keg had gone off where his tongue connected with her flesh, she gripped a handful of his hair and pulled while screaming his name as an orgasm ripped through her. All logic was replaced by the explosion of pleasure that overtook her.

She hadn't yet come back off her organic high when Dylan shifted in position over her and whispered. "Now, we'll be bad together, sweetheart."

Charm's face had an orgasmic glow, and Dylan thought it was the most beautiful thing he'd ever seen. There was something about Charm that was still in his system after all this time, and tonight he intended to replace the memories of what happened following their last encounter with good memories they would build on. He wanted to move forward again with her, and he hoped she wanted to do the same with him. He had enjoyed her company this week, and knew there was no way he could let her walk out of his life again. He loved her.

Needing to kiss her with an intensity he felt in every part of his body, he lowered his mouth to hers. He liked kissing her because she never hesitated to kiss him back, letting him know she enjoyed the exchange as much as he did. Their tongues loved tangling, dueling and grappling in the most intimate way. Like they were doing now.

As if his manhood knew its way home, he eased inside her without disengaging their mouths. His body tensed when he discovered she was just as tight as she'd been the last time. He broke off the kiss and stared down at her. Before he could open his mouth to ask her anything, she arched her back and wrapped her arms around his neck to bring his mouth back down to her.

He felt himself buried deep inside her as her mouth took control of his, as if egging him on. As their mouths mated, so did their bodies as he thrust hard into her over and over again.

Fire seemed to spread between them, burning the sheets and causing his manhood to pound harder and deeper.

The sound of her screaming his name followed by her body convulsing in pleasure triggered his own climax and her inner muscles began milking him, clenching him tight while she was pulling his hair. He didn't mind the pain. He could no longer hold back a growl of deep male satisfaction and then he whispered, "I don't plan to ever let you go again, Charm."

Another orgasm ripped through them both. Dylan tightened his arms around her and hoped that tonight was the start of their new beginning.

Twenty-One

"I have to go."

Charm's words intruded into Dylan's sleepy, sexually exhausted mind. He opened one eye, smiled at her and released his hold. They'd been sleeping with their legs entwined and with his arms wrapped tightly around her waist. Figuring she had to go to the bathroom, he said, "Don't be gone too long," before closing his eyes again in blissful slumber.

Hours later, Dylan came fully awake when he heard the sound of the cows mooing and saw sunlight peeking through the curtains. It was past milking time. He figured Ren or one of the other guys had taken care of it. That was good, because he intended to take care of the woman in his bed.

He glanced over and frowned when he saw the empty spot beside him. Had Charm gotten up already? He didn't recall her getting out of bed, other than at daybreak to go to the bathroom. He blinked. He didn't recall her coming back, although he was sure she had.

Last night had been wild, exciting, and as far as he was concerned, it had been what both of them needed. Granted there had to be more than sex to their relationship but as far as he was concerned, with the explosive intimacy the two of them had shared all through the night, things were off to a great start.

Damn, he was getting hard just remembering. There were times when he rode her and then times when she'd insisted on riding him. It was as if neither could get enough of each other. It had been his intent to wake up with her in his arms and make love again before starting their day. Obviously, she'd gone to her room to shower and change. Perhaps she would surprise him with breakfast since she claimed she could cook a mean omelet.

Dylan eased to the side of the bed, drew in a deep breath and another smile touched his lips at the scent of lovemaking on his skin, in the bedcovers and in the air. Standing, he decided to shower and dress before searching for his woman. He liked the idea of finding her and hauling her back in here and engaging in morning lovemaking.

He chuckled. When had he become a greedy ass? The answer was ever since Charm had come back into his life, and he intended to keep her. Damn he loved her.

A short while later he was knocking on the guest room door. When she didn't answer, he figured she must have gone downstairs already. Maybe she was in the kitchen cooking that omelet like he'd thought.

Dylan had made it downstairs when there was a knock at his front door. Figuring it was Ren, he called out, "Come in."

He was right. It was Ren. He smiled over at the older man. "Morning, Ren."

Ren looked at him oddly and said, "You seem to be in a good mood."

Dylan was tempted to tell him just how good a mood he was in after a night like last night. Of course, he wouldn't. "Any reason I wouldn't be in a good mood?"

Ren shrugged. "Most men wouldn't if their woman had left them."

Dylan looked at the older man strangely, and then when he comprehended what Ren said, he replied, "What are you talking about? Charm's in the kitchen."

"No, she's not."

Not believing Ren, Dylan called out for her. When he didn't get a response, he went into the kitchen to see for himself. He even opened the back door and glanced around the porch and saw no sign of her anywhere.

Charm had left? Why? When? Returning to the living room, he saw Ren still standing by the door. "How did you know she'd gone?"

"I saw her leave. It was close to six this morning. I was getting the milking equipment set up. I found it odd that a car was coming up the driveway that early. When I saw Charm come out with her luggage and the young guy load it in the trunk, I figured she was leaving."

When Dylan didn't say anything, Ren added, "Maybe there's a reason she had to leave, Dyl. Have you checked your phone to see if she left any messages?"

He hadn't checked because he hadn't known she'd left. "No." After remembering his phone was upstairs on his nightstand he raced up the stairs to his room. He quickly snatched the phone up and swiped across the screen to find she had left a text message. Anxiously, he opened it.

The moment he read it, a feeling of déjà vu encompassed Dylan. It was so strong it nearly knocked him off his feet. A knot clenched in his belly as anger consumed him. The text was similar to the one she'd sent ten years ago. It said…
Last night was a mistake and I don't want to see you again.

Throwing the phone on the bed, he cursed and called himself all kinds of fool. She had played him and he'd let her. Charm Outlaw hadn't changed. A part of him had hoped they could put the past behind them and share a relationship he'd thought was meant to be. Only thing, it was quite obvious that whatever connected him to Charm wasn't meant to be.

After grabbing the phone off the bed, Dylan tried calling her to tell her just what he thought of her asinine text and discovered his number had been blocked...like before. He paced his room, refusing to let her have the last word. After this, he wanted no part of her in his life either, and he was going to tell her so. And no damn blocked number would stop him.

Dylan wasn't sure where Charm had gone. She had mentioned visiting her brother in Wyoming after leaving here. Had that been a lie? For all he knew she might have caught a plane for Alaska, or gone to visit those cousins she'd been telling him about—the Westmorelands—in either Denver, Montana, Texas or Atlanta. Wherever she was, he would find her, and he knew just the person with the capability to do so.

He stopped pacing and punched in another number. After a couple of rings, Seth picked up. "Yes, Dylan?"

"I want you to find someone."

"I hate to say we told you so, Charm, but we did tell you so," Ola said, although rather soothingly.

Charm sniffed a few times and wiped her eyes. "I know but I wasn't supposed to get caught up in the moment. I got caught up in the seconds, minutes, hours. The entire night. I acted like a horny hussy."

"Well, what did you expect when you hadn't been with a man since Dylan? Your body was probably starving for him. Of course you wouldn't have been able to pull it off. And Ola is right. We tried to warn you that your plan would backfire," Piper said. "Where are you, by the way?"

Yes, they had warned her, but she figured she knew her body better than they did and had been certain she could handle her plan to seduce Dylan. All it had taken to mess with her plans was seeing him naked and then him using that notorious Dylan Emanuel tongue on her. "I wasn't able to get a flight out to Wyoming until tonight so instead of hanging around the airport I checked into a hotel."

"You know what I think, Charm?" Ola asked.

She didn't want to ask but did so anyway. "No, what?"

"I think one of the reasons you couldn't pull it off has nothing to do with the sex."

Charm rolled her eyes. "Then what did it have to do with?"

"You love him. Whether you admit it or not, you never stopped loving him. And another thing, you were taking a plan from your father's playbook. There was no way that would work because you aren't manipulating, cunning and ruthless like Bart Outlaw. I suspect that deep down you honestly didn't want to deceive Dylan and couldn't go through with it."

"I would have gone through with it if he would have kept his lips to himself."

"Oh," Piper said, giggling. "Like you didn't kiss him back."

Charm frowned. "You're not helping matters, Piper."

"Sorry. Just interjecting a little honesty here."

Charm drew in a deep breath. "I haven't eaten anything and it's almost lunchtime. I'm hungry. I think I'll order room service."

"Okay. Call us back if you need to talk some more," Ola said.

She appreciated the offer, but knew she wouldn't. When she got to Wyoming, she would spend time with Brianna and her nephews and then she would seek privacy in one of those cabins on their property. Now she was glad Cash wouldn't be at the dude ranch when she got there. He would take one look at her and know something was wrong.

After ordering lunch, she went into the bathroom to wash her face, refusing to shed a single tear again. Her plan had backfired and she knew why. What she couldn't admit to Piper and Ola was that she *had* fallen back in love with Dylan.

If truth be told, even after he treated her like crap, she'd never truly fallen out of love with him. That was simply pathetic.

After applying a little makeup to make herself look better even if she didn't feel better, she went out on the balcony to sit and enjoy the fresh air. She'd known the mistake she was making by going all the way with Dylan, yet she'd done so anyway and, she hated to admit it, but she'd enjoyed every moment. The night had remarkable, terrific and totally fantastic. It had been everything she hadn't wanted but obviously needed.

Like she told him in that text, since she had no strength when it came to resisting him, it was best if they didn't see each other again. She'd managed to do without him for ten years and could certainly do without him for another ten. If that was true then why was she sitting there and replaying in her mind every single moment of making love to Dylan and him making love to her? Never had she experienced anything so explosive. Just like she'd told her friends, he'd turned her into a wild woman.

When she heard a knock at the door she stood. She was glad it hadn't taken the kitchen long to prepare her lunch because she was starving. Throwing caution to the wind she didn't bother looking out the peephole since this was a secured floor. She opened the door and gasped when she saw Dylan standing there.

Without waiting for her to speak, he said, "I know it was your desire never to see me again, Charm. That's fine with me, but first I need to tell you that I hope I never see you again as well."

He then walked past her to enter her hotel room.

Twenty-Two

"You can't just walk into my room."

Dylan turned to face Charm. "Trust me, I won't stay any longer than it takes for me to tell you what I think of you."

She crossed her arms over her chest and gave him a haughty look. "Really? Then I hope you know I have no problem letting you know what I think of you as well."

His brows furrowed, not believing she had the audacity to act like she was the injured victim. She had a lot of damn nerve. That made him more determined to say what he'd come to say and leave. "That text you sent this morning proves just what a spoiled, selfish and pampered woman you are, Charm. There's nothing charming about you, so you need to change your name. If nothing else, I would think after ten years you could have come up with another excuse for sleeping with me. Saying it was a mistake both times won't cut it."

She frowned. "I don't know what you mean about 'both times.' However, last night *was* a mistake since I didn't intend to make love to you. The only reason I agreed to come with you to your ranch was to seduce you and then walk away without giving you any part of me. I never intended to go all the way with you, Dylan. I had planned to reject you before things got that far."

"What!" He couldn't believe what she just said. "Are you saying the only reason you came to the ranch was to seduce me and then reject me?"

She had the audacity to smile. "Yes, that's exactly what I'd intended to do."

He had to fight to get his anger under control. "So agreeing to come to the ranch had nothing to do with you wanting to rebuild our friendship and relationship like you claimed?"

"Please. Do you honestly think I'd let you be my friend or rebuild any kind of relationship after what you did to me, Dylan?"

"After what I did to you?" he exploded. "What you mean is after what *you* did to me."

"I didn't do anything to you!" she shouted back. "You were the one who ten years ago sent me that crass text that said it was nice knowing me but opportunity knocks and you were taking off to England. And oh, you did take the time to say in that text that our one and only night together was great." She barely paused before adding. "I had given you my virginity and that's all you had to say!"

Dylan opened his mouth, then closed it when the full impact of her words sank in. "I have no idea what the hell you're talking about. I didn't send you any damn text ten years ago. You blocked me from your phone after sending me a text, very similar to the one you sent this morning, that said that night was a mistake. You hadn't meant for things to get out of hand, and the only reason you'd come to New York was to break up with me since you were no longer interested in engaging in a long-distance romance."

"What! That's a lie and you know it. I never sent any such text to you," she snapped.

"And I never sent any such text to you," he snapped back.

"Well, if you didn't who did?" she asked.

"I can ask you the same thing. Just so you know, I still have your text on my phone as a reminder of what a fool I was for loving you."

She lifted her chin. "And I still have yours on my phone for the same reason."

The room got quiet and he stared at her. Then as if of one accord she moved to get her phone out of her purse, and he pulled his out of his jeans. He was glad he'd decided to take a photo of the text. Like he'd told her, he had kept it as one of those mistakes to never make again.

When he swiped a few screens to find what he was looking for, he handed her his phone, and she handed him hers. The photo on her phone clearly showed the call had been made from his phone and what it said. She was right, considering what they'd done the night before, it had been a crass text.

He looked up when she gasped after reading the one he had accused her of sending to him. She met his gaze with shock on her face. "I swear on my grandparents' graves that I never sent this, Dylan."

Dylan stared at her with measured eyes. "And I swear on my grandparents' graves that I never sent this text to you either." He handed her phone back to her and she returned his. That's when he said, "And I guess you knew nothing about those goons posted outside your hotel the next day either?"

She frowned. "What goons?"

"When I got your text message I refused to believe you could write such a thing after the night we spent together. After all we had meant to each other. At least I refused to believe it until I caught a cab to your hotel and two men who claimed to be your bodyguards were waiting for me, as if they'd expected me to show up. They told me you meant what you said in the text and warned me that if I tried contacting you again they would break my fingers so I'd never play another instrument."

He heard her sharp intake of breath. "I knew nothing about those men, Dylan. I've never had bodyguards."

"Well, whoever hired them made them aware of what was in your text, which made things more believable to me."

She dropped down on the sofa in the room. "I knew nothing about them."

"What about the ring?"

She looked up at him. "What ring?"

Dylan didn't say anything for a minute and then after shoving his hands in his pockets, he said, "Even after getting that text and being threatened by those men, I still flew to Alaska at the end of the summer to see you when the band got back from England."

"So you did go to England?"

"Yes, but we didn't leave the day after our night together as that text claims. The band didn't get that promoter's offer to play the summer in the UK for at least three days after I supposedly sent that text to you. So it seems whoever sent those texts made sure I had a job in England that summer like the text said I would."

Who in the hell would have gone through all that trouble to break them up? Whoever was behind it had the means to orchestrate a deceitful scheme, especially with the timing of the text messages. He suddenly had a sinking feeling he knew the identity of the person, and from the look on Charm's face she did, too.

"When I returned from England I sought you out in Anchorage," he said. "You weren't home and one of your neighbors mentioned you often went to a coffee shop on Saturday mornings and told me how to get there." He paused a moment and then continued. "I was determined that you were going to break up with me to my face and not take the coward's way out by sending some damn text message. I walked in just when you were showing off a promise ring to your friends. That's when I turned and walked out."

She stared at him. "You left because you thought I had gotten the ring from another guy?"

"Didn't you?"

"Yes, but that guy was my brother Garth. The woman he loved and had planned to marry had been killed during a military maneuver. He'd intended to give her a promise ring the night she died with plans to buy her a more expensive engagement ring when they were no longer deployed. As a way to move on after her death, he gave the ring to me." She got silent for a minute and then said, "I do recall that morning I was showing it off to my friends. I had no idea you'd come to Alaska to see me."

"Well, I did."

The room was silent again.

"We were played against each other, Dylan. I believe I know who and I think you do, too. My father. He must have found out we were still seeing each other."

"It had to have been your father." Dylan rubbed his hands down his face. He then looked over at her. "You said he could be ruthless and manipulating, but I never thought he would go to those extremes to get back at us for defying him. But then look how far you intended to go to get even with me when you believed I had wronged you."

"But at least you know why," she said in her defense.

"I know why, but I don't understand why. I thought you had wronged me yet getting even with you never crossed my mind. When I ran into you in Cancún the first thought that came to my mind was closure. I needed closure with you after ten years. But the more I spent time with you, the more I discovered I didn't want closure at all."

He studied the floor as if in deep thought. Then he glanced back at her. "Even believing you had wronged me, I offered you an olive branch, Charm. I invited you to my ranch in good faith, believing we were moving forward in spite of what had happened between us. But now I know you had no plans to do that. Like your father, all you wanted to do was get back at me. To get even for what you thought I had done to you. You were acting just as ruthless and manipulative as he was. You are definitely Bart Outlaw's daughter."

"But now that we know the truth we can—"

"Do nothing. Think about it, Charm. All it took was one text to make you believe the worst of me. For me, it took more than that. I still went to your hotel although I was confronted by your father's hired men. And at the end of the summer, I flew to Alaska to see you after being warned of what would happen to my hands if I did. Because I loved you and truly believed in what we shared. But you let go so easily. You were so quick to believe the worst of me. And then years later, instead of asking me about what happened so we could talk about it, you plotted revenge."

He glanced out the window for a moment before shifting his gaze back at her. Looking at her hurt, because he knew he had fallen in love with her again. If he were to guess, he'd probably done so the moment he'd seen her in Cancún. Hell, he probably had never stopped loving her.

"This week spent with you on the ranch meant everything to me, Charm. I thought it was a new beginning in spite of everything that happened in our past. But all it had been was a pretense. It was a sham, part of your plot for my downfall. None of it, your words or actions, was sincere."

"Dylan, I'm sorry. I love you and—"

"No," he said, holding up his hand to stop her from saying anything further. "You don't know a thing about love, Charm. Not true love. Real love. Life is too short for game-playing, manipulations and scheming. I promised myself the last thing I wanted in my life was an insincere woman. Goodbye, Charm."

He moved toward the door. Before opening it, he turned back around to say, "At least now you know the truth about that summer and so do I."

He opened the door and walked out.

* * *

"How could you, Dad?" Charm shouted.

Everyone sitting at the dining table glanced up to stare at her when she entered the room. She had come straight to her father's home from the airport. It was dinnertime and seated at the table with Bart were her mother, Claudia; her brothers-Cash, Garth, Jess, Sloan, Maverick and the latter four's wives—Regan, Paige, Leslie and Phire. She had known Cash was here, but hadn't known Jess was in town. Just as well. Everyone would know in a few what she thought of her father. Not only was she hurt by what he'd done, she was downright furious.

Bart stood with deep concern etched on his face. "Charm? What's wrong? I thought you were flying to Cash's ranch in Wyoming from Cancún."

"I found out what you did to me and Dylan, Dad. I ran into him while in Cancún. Did you think I would never find out? How could you do such a thing? I trusted you."

Bart's features became stern. "And I trusted you. You and Dylan Emanuel sat here at this very table and I told you both that the two of you were too young to be in love and to end the nonsense. But the two of you didn't end things, did you? Imagine how disappointed I was when I discovered two years later that not only had you disobeyed me but you and Emanuel were sneaking around seeing each other. I found out about that week the two of you spent together that second summer in Anchorage and the real reason you went to New York when you lied to me and said you and your girlfriends were going there to a Broadway play."

Charm's glare sharpened. If her father thought saying any of that in front of her mother and brothers and sisters-in-law meant anything then he was mistaken. She walked farther into the room. "Regardless. That was no reason for you to have done what you did, and I will never forgive you for it.

And to have those men threaten Dylan…" She was fighting to retain her composure but was losing it anyway.

"Just what did you do, Bart?" That question was asked by her mother.

Charm had wondered if her mother and brothers were privy to her father's scheme. She could tell by their expressions they were wondering the same thing her mother had asked.

Instead of answering Claudia, Bart said, "You and I need to talk privately, Charm."

"No. I have nothing to say to you. In fact, I won't be talking to you ever. What you did was cruel and manipulative, but I guess I should not have expected anything less. I don't intend to set foot in this house again, and I also intend to change my last name."

"Why?" Bart all but roared. "Emanuel asked you to marry him?"

His question brought tears to her eyes because she knew not only did Dylan not love her, but he also couldn't stand the sight of her. "No. Even after finding out what you did, he still blames me because, thanks to you, I believed the worst about him. On top of that, instead of accepting the friendship he offered in Cancún, I took a rule from one of your playbooks and decided to get even."

Unable to hold back her tears any longer, they flowed from her eyes. "I wronged him and then too late we discovered that we were both innocents who were played against each other by you. But now he doesn't trust me because he thinks I'm too much like you." She swiped away her tears. "I am changing my name from Outlaw to Mama's last name of Dermotte and you can't do anything to stop me."

She turned to leave and suddenly felt dizzy. When the room began spinning, she tried reaching for one of the chairs before she lost her balance. Too late, she heard her brother Garth call out her name as she crumbled to the floor.

Twenty-Three

Charm felt the warmth of a cloth against her forehead. When she slowly opened her eyes, she stared up at her brother Garth hovering over her as she lay on the couch in her father's study. "What happened?"

"You fainted," Garth said. "Your stomach is growling like the dickens. When was the last time you ate anything?"

She saw her mother was also in the room. When she tried sitting up, Garth, who she knew received paramedic training while serving as a marine, placed a firm hand on her shoulder to keep her down.

"Yesterday," she said.

"Yesterday?" her mother asked, coming to stand behind Garth. "Why didn't you ask the flight attendant to serve you a meal on the plane from Cancún?"

"I didn't come here from Cancún, Mom. I left Mexico a week ago when Dylan invited me to his ranch in Idaho."

"Idaho?" Garth asked. "I thought he was from Memphis."

"He is. He inherited his grandparents' ranch when they were killed a few years ago." She paused and said, "When

Dylan and I figured out what Dad had done, I immediately left but didn't want to catch a commercial flight. I rented a plane and flew myself home."

"What!" Claudia exclaimed. "That had to be a five-hour flight. You flew home alone without anything in your stomach?"

Charm frowned. "I was too mad to pass out. I was determined to get here and give Dad a piece of my mind. I hate him."

"You did more than give him a piece of your mind," Garth said, shaking his head. "I don't think I've ever seen the old man so shaken. At least not since that time Cash threatened to disown him. He thinks you're actually going to change your last name."

"I am."

Garth shook his head again. "No, you're not, Charm. You've got to learn to deal with Bart like the rest of us. You're an Outlaw and will stay an Outlaw. You only get to change your name the day you get married."

She couldn't stop the tears from springing into her eyes. "I'm never going to get married. The only man I want to marry doesn't want me now because of Dad. I hate him and don't want to be his daughter anymore."

Garth moved aside when Charm began crying and Claudia pulled Charm into her arms as she continued to sob. "Don't cry, darling," her mother cooed softly in her ear.

Charm pulled back slightly and stared up at her mother. "So you didn't know what he'd done?" she asked, swiping at her tears.

Claudia shook her head. "I knew about that dinner meeting he had with you and Dylan Emanuel when you were sixteen. Although I agree that you were too young to get seriously involved with a guy, I would have handled the situation with a lot more diplomacy than Bart."

Of course she would have, Charm thought. "I know."

"However, I did know he discovered two years later the two of you were sneaking around behind his back. All he said was that he handled the issue. I never asked for details."

"He said he handled the issue? What he did was play me and Dylan against each other. For ten years I thought the worst of him and he did likewise with me," Charm said as new tears flowed from her eyes. She began sobbing almost uncontrollably in her mother's arms.

"Tell us, sweetheart," Claudia said as she gently stroked Charm's back. "Tell me and Garth what happened."

Charm nodded and after pulling herself together, she told her mother and brother everything.

"Is she okay, Garth?"

Garth heard both stress and deep concern in his father's voice. He saw it in his face as well. After what Charm had shared with him and Claudia, a part of Garth wanted to think his father deserved the worry for being so ruthless, manipulative and controlling. When Garth and his brothers were in their teens, they hadn't called him "Dictator Bart" behind his back for nothing.

But then Bart was Bart and ten years ago the old man had been at the top of his game. Since then, he had settled down somewhat. He still gave orders and expected them to be obeyed but these days he spent less time being a tyrant and more time as a man determined to win the heart of the woman he loved.

Garth had a feeling this issue with Charm and the heartache their father had caused her wouldn't go over well with Claudia, who was just as protective of their daughter as Bart was. Claudia didn't like Bart's shenanigans.

"Charm's fine. She just hadn't eaten since yesterday and—"

"Why hadn't she eaten since yesterday?" Sloan asked.

Garth rubbed a hand down his face. "Before she could eat

anything today, she found out what Dad had done and rented a plane to fly straight home."

"From Mexico?" Maverick asked as if shocked.

"No, she was at Dylan Emanuel's ranch in Idaho. But still she shouldn't have been in the air for five hours on an empty stomach."

"I agree," Cash said. "What if she'd passed out at the controls while in the air."

"Jesus," Bart said in anguish, probably at the thought of the picture Cash had just painted. Garth thought the old man looked faint and watched him drop down in a chair at the table. He then buried his face in his hands after saying, "I could have lost my daughter."

Garth hated to tell Bart but he'd probably lost her anyway now that Charm knew what he'd done. "I'm taking her home and will stop and get something for her to eat on the way."

Bart snatched his head up. "Home? This is her home."

Garth knew Charm usually spent more time here than she did at her own place, but that's where she wanted to go and where he'd promised to take her. "She wants to go to her own house, Dad."

Bart stood. "I need to talk to her and explain why I did what I did."

"You already have and just so you know, she told me and Claudia everything. I don't agree with what you did, regardless of why you felt you needed to do it. It's not just what you did, but how you did it. She's hurt, upset and heartbroken."

He paused a moment to let his words sink in before saying, "Charm figured now that she and Emanuel know the truth they could have another go of things, but he's not interested. She blames you for everything, and it will be a while before she comes around. You're going to have to give her time. And just so you know, she's serious as hell about changing her last name to Dermotte and is contemplating leaving Fairbanks and moving to her grandparents' place in Seward."

"Damn," Sloan said. He then looked over at their Dad. "Just what did you do?" he asked angrily.

When Bart didn't say anything, Garth said, "I think you should tell them everything, Dad. Then if you want your daughter back you need to fix this mess you made. She loves Dylan and a part of me believes he loves her, but since you're the one who broke them up, it's going to be up to you to get them back together. And just so you know, Claudia isn't happy with you either."

Garth then turned and walked out of the dining room.

"So there you have it," Seth was saying as he sat on the sofa across from Dylan. "Chrome thought that if Elise got caught he could throw her under the bus by denying knowing anything about her plan. Unfortunately for him, she had receipts. And she's produced them. Chrome was arrested this morning."

Dylan stretched his legs out in front of him as he rubbed a hand down his face in frustration. "Chrome didn't have to do that. There are enough jazz fans out there for the both of us. Why did he feel as if we were in competition?"

"I don't know. Only Chrome knows that. Jealousy and envy can make people do unexplainable things. Unfortunately, his actions will ruin his musical career for a while. And I wouldn't feel sorry for him if I were you. Just think of how yours would have been ruined if Elise had pulled off her plan."

Dylan took another sip of his coffee while studying Seth. "So what's your reason for coming here, Seth? You could have called with that information."

Seth stretched out his long legs as well. "True, but I needed to see you for myself. That call I got from you three days ago had me worried. I've never known you to be so desperate to find a woman. In fact, I've never known you to want to find a woman period."

Dylan stared into the dark liquid in his cup before glancing back at Seth. "I guess there's a first time for everything."

"Well, I hope things got worked out. I like Charm."

Dylan frowned. First Graham and his band members, then Seth and Ren. What was there about Charm that made people so taken with her? "Sorry to disappointment you, but things didn't get worked out. I hope I never see her again."

"What a pity."

He was about to respond when Seth's phone rang. He answered it. Dylan had a feeling the call was about him since Seth was looking at him and nodding. The only comment Seth said to the caller was, "Interesting." Of course Seth had an unreadable expression on his face.

Dylan wondered if Seth had received more information on that Elise and Chrome fiasco. They were the last people on his mind. Unfortunately for him, Charm was who he was thinking of. He couldn't even place the blame on Seth for bringing her up since he'd been thinking about her constantly for the past three days. Ever since he'd walked out on her at the hotel.

He thought about her upon waking and then at night when it was time to go to bed. No matter how tired he was, he closed his eyes with thoughts of her. He could still smell her scent in his bed as well as the guest room she'd used.

When he'd told Graham what had happened, his best friend had given him the riot act, reminding him that from the beginning Graham had suspected there was more to the breakup than what Charm had written in her text message. Now that the truth was out, Graham felt Charm was just as much a victim as Dylan. Graham didn't blame her for wanting to get even. That's how some women reacted, and Graham of all people should know since he had five sisters. He told Dylan there was a reason for the saying, Hell hath no fury like a woman scorned.

Dylan glanced over at Seth when he heard him click off

the phone. "That was one of my men I left posted at your airstrip. You're about to get a visitor," Seth said, with what seemed like amusement in his eyes.

Dylan frowned, wondering who would be coming to his ranch. "Who?"

"Bart Outlaw."

A scowl covered Dylan's face as he sat up in his seat. "He isn't welcome here."

Seth shrugged. "Too late. His jet has landed and he's on his way."

"I don't have to see him."

"No, you don't but I'd think you would want to."

Dylan's scowl deepened. "And why would I?"

Seth chuckled. "Because it's my guess that the two of you have an old score to settle."

After checking the peephole, Charm opened the door to see three of her brothers standing there. Cash, Sloan and Maverick. "I wanted to check on you before returning to Wyoming," Cash said as they entered her home.

She had told everyone she wanted to be left alone but evidently that edict had fallen on deaf ears. Jess had visited with her yesterday before flying back to Washington, and Garth, Regan and their son Garrison had stopped by every day. So had her mother.

"Shouldn't you be home with Phire?" she asked Maverick after leading them into her living room and sitting down on the sofa. Maverick's wife was due to deliver a baby any day now.

"Claudia is with her," was Maverick's response. "Besides, Phire sent me away, claiming I was driving her batty."

Charm smiled. "I can believe that."

"We're glad to see you smiling," Sloan said.

"Only because the three of you caught me at a good time," she said, knowing that was true. There was no need to tell

them she cried herself to sleep every night and still had tear-
ful moments whenever she thought about the love she'd lost.
First because of her father and then because of her own manipulative deeds.

"I talked to Bailey today and she suggested I come visit
her, Walker and the boys, on Kodiak Island, for a few days,"
Charm said. Their cousin Bailey Westmoreland had married
Garth's best friend Walker Rafferty a few years ago and, like
Cash, they had twin boys. Yesterday Bailey had shared the
news that she and Walker were expecting again.

"So are you going to Kodiak Island?" Cash asked.

"I think I will. I love it there."

"Just watch out for the bears," Maverick warned, grinning.

Kodiak Island, Alaska was reputed to have more bears
living there than people. "Whatever."

Her brothers visited with her for a couple of hours before
giving her hugs and leaving. She was glad they had the good
sense not to ask questions or mention Bart. He had called
every morning and she refused to answer. He'd even left a
voice message where he apologized, but she hadn't responded
to that either.

Her mother had asked last night what it would take for her
father to get back in her good graces, and she'd answered
that she didn't think he could. She then told her mother that
although she wouldn't be changing her name, she was seriously considering moving to Seward. Charm and her mother
both owned her grandparents' home located on the Gulf of
Alaska. She'd always loved it there, but hadn't wanted to stay
after losing her grandparents.

A part of her admired how Dylan had moved to his grandparents' ranch after losing them. One day she'd asked him
how he'd done so with so many memories. He'd said all the
memories were good ones and that's what he needed, to sur-
round himself with his grandparents' memories.

When Charm's grandparents had died, she hadn't thought

about memories, just their absence and the loneliness of them not being there. She believed that now she could move back and appreciate the memories.

Dylan...

She felt a tightness in her chest just thinking about him. How could a woman fall in love with the same man twice? Probably because she'd never fallen out of love with him the first time. That would explain why she'd been unable to get serious about any other guy during the past ten years. From the day she'd seen Dylan in Professor Jovanovich's music suite he had captured her heart. All it had taken was for her to see him again in Cancún to know he still had it.

Charm could now admit that knowing she could still love him after what she'd thought he'd done to her had been the crux of her problem, not wanting to get revenge. It all made sense to her now, although to Dylan it wouldn't matter. He saw her as an insincere person. One she knew he could never love again and that hurt more than anything.

She decided to take a shower and start packing. Sloan had offered to fly her to Kodiak Island. When she returned home, she would make plans to move to Seward. For now, she needed time with Bailey, Walker and the kids.

Twenty-Four

"Why are you here, Mr. Outlaw?" Dylan asked coldly when he opened the door. Seth had conveniently left to go into town to grab something to eat. Some bodyguard.

"May I come in so we can talk?"

It was on the tip of his tongue to say, *hell no*. But he knew he couldn't do that. As much as he detested the man, Dylan knew there were things that needed to be said.

"Come in and say what you have to say."

He stepped back and noted how different Bart Outlaw looked than when he'd seen him twelve years ago. On that day he'd walked into the dining room with an arrogant stride and a hubristic air about him. Now, although he still looked physically fit for a man in his late fifties, there was something defeated about him. Obviously, his precious daughter had returned to Alaska and given him the hell he rightly deserved. If he'd showed up here for pity then he wouldn't be getting any from Dylan. But then, he didn't think Bart Outlaw knew the definition of pity.

"So what do we need to talk about?" Dylan asked after closing the door.

"I owe both you and Charm an apology. As her father I did what I felt I had to do to protect her from you. Charm was too young to know her own heart."

"But you think you knew it?" Dylan snapped. "I fell in love with Charm from the moment I saw her, and I knew I would love her forever. Maybe with your history of divorcing five wives you couldn't see it, but I could. I come from a family with long marriages, where the men meet and fall in love early and love forever. It happened that way for my parents, grandparents and their parents before them. I loved Charm."

He saw the man's jaw tighten. "You and Charm disobeyed my order to stay apart. As her father, it was an order I had every right to make. She was only sixteen. She was not an adult and at the time, neither were you. Granted the way I played you and Charm against each other, along with the threats my men made about injuring your hand, that was wrong, I regret it and I'm here to apologize for it. I do apologize. I love my daughter and I didn't know you or your intent toward her." Then in a deep yet controlled voice, Bart asked, "Don't you understand that I had to keep Charm from you?"

Dylan frowned. "Of course you did. I was just a two-bit guitarist who would never amount to anything, right?"

Bart didn't say anything for a moment. "I regret saying that as well. I won't even lie and say I was in rare form because I wasn't. When I discovered the two of you had been sneaking around behind my back, I was furious. You'd heard what I told both you and Charm. Yet you both deliberately defied me and I knew she would not have done so without your influence. I saw you as a man I couldn't trust with my daughter. A daughter who meant everything to me. My actions were not those of a ruthless and manipulative man, but the actions of a desperate father."

Dylan shoved his hands in his pockets. "Are you finished?"

"Yes, I guess I am," Bart Outlaw answered, sounding even more subdued now. "But I just want to say—you told my daughter that she's just like me and you might be right about that, but not in the way you think. Charm and I love only once and we love hard. I fell in love with her mother twenty-nine years ago, and I still love her just as much today as I did the day we met. Charm still loves you as much as the day the two of you met when she was sixteen. That's a strong love. An everlasting love. There's not a ruthless bone in her body. She's too much like her mother in that regard, and a part of me is proud of that. And if what you said earlier is true, and you come from a family with long marriages where the men meet and fall in love early and love forever, then that means you still love Charm."

When Dylan didn't reply, Bart added, "Take it from a man who's loved and lost and is now trying to regain the love he lost. Life is too short to move backward. I no longer see you as a threat. Charm is her own woman and no longer a teen. I will abide by whatever decision she makes. Whatever decision the two of you make. I won't be interfering in your lives again."

Bart paused and then continued, "Twelve years ago I wanted you out of her life. Ten years ago I took drastic actions that I'm here to say were a mistake. I've discovered that you *are* her life and if having you back in it is what will make her happy, then more than anything I want to see her happy again. I'm asking if you still love my daughter to get her out of her misery."

Bart Outlaw then crossed the room, opened the door and left.

My actions were not those of a ruthless and manipulative man, but the actions of a desperate father...

Those words were still sifting through Dylan's mind a week later while saddling up one of the horses to take a ride to the lake. When he had reached his destination, he dismounted and tied the horse to a tree. Grabbing his guitar, he walked over to the edge of the lake and sat with his back against the huge oak tree, like always.

He began playing his guitar to soothe his mind. He had come here practically every day since Charm left, to sit, think and play. The more he'd done so the more he had begun seeing things from Bart Outlaw's perspective and that was pretty damn scary. In no way would he condone the man for his ruthlessness and manipulations since he still thought Bart had gone too far. Yet he had apologized.

The man had left not knowing if Dylan had accepted his apology or not because he hadn't said one way or the other. In all honesty on that particular day, he hadn't. But now after a heart-to-heart talk with his father, after telling him everything, he would admit—and his father had agreed—that although Bart Outlaw had taken things way too far by playing him and Charm against each other, Dylan and Charm weren't blameless either.

It had taken Dylan's tell-it-like-it-is and not-sugarcoat-anything father to make him see that Mr. Outlaw had been right to be upset when he'd found out Dylan and Charm had disobeyed him. Charm had been a minor at sixteen. She'd also been a minor at seventeen, although she'd been attending college. A nineteen-year-old Dylan and a sixteen-year-old Charm plotting a week together that second summer had been wrong. By rights, Bart Outlaw probably could have had him arrested. Such a thing would have revoked his scholarship at Juilliard. Also, as far as his father was concerned, if Charm had been as ruthless as her father, she would not have told Dylan about Elise's plans to ruin him in Cancún. She would have been glad for his downfall.

Dylan credited his father with having a lot of intelligence and wisdom, and the man had also given him something else to think about. Maybe it was meant for Dylan and Charm to be apart for a while... And although sending Dylan and his band to England had been part of Bart Outlaw's devious plan, it had been in England that summer when Dylan's career took off. So, in a way, he owed Bart Outlaw for kick-starting his musical career.

His dad also made him look at all he accomplished during the ten years he and Charm had been apart. He had given his music 100 percent of his time and he was now a successful musician who could still have the love of his life. The woman he'd known from the beginning was meant to be his soulmate. Now he could love her with or without her father's blessings.

An hour or so later, after he finished playing a few songs on his guitar, he thought about something else Bart Outlaw had said.

"If what you said earlier is true, and you come from a family with long marriages where the men meet and fall in love early and love forever, then that means you still love Charm…"

Dylan stood and slid his guitar back into the case and headed for his horse. Yes, he still loved Charm and it was time he let her know it. He had made the arrangements and Seth's private jet would be flying him to Alaska in the morning. It was time for him and Charm to do things right this time.

"You're going to have to forgive the old man at some point, Charm."

Charm glanced over at Garth who had flown his private plane to pick her up from Kodiak Island. She had enjoyed her week there. It was a trip she'd needed.

"No, I don't."

"Yes, you do. If Cash can forgive him for that stunt he pulled then you can, too."

She twisted in her seat in the cockpit. "I am not Cash. Besides, that stunt he pulled with Cash didn't have him and Brianna apart for ten years."

"Bart is in a bad way. The rift between the two of you is getting to him."

Her father still called her every day. She hadn't blocked his number but that didn't mean she had to accept his calls. "I'm not talking to him."

"You're as stubborn as he is."

She waited for him to say more and when he didn't, she tilted her head. "And?"

He glanced over at her. "And what?"

"What other characteristics of his do you think I have?" She couldn't push from her mind that Dylan thought she was ruthless and manipulative just like Bart.

"I can't think of any right off, but I'm sure there are a few. You're his daughter just like I'm his son. But we aren't his clones, Charm." Garth didn't say anything for a minute. "What Bart did was ten years ago. I think we both know that although there is still room for improvement, he has come a long way since then."

Okay, she would admit that.

"Hell, if you recall, ten years ago Dad was a damn tyrant. A dictator at his best. That's when the board gave him an ultimatum to resign or be fired."

She remembered that.

"As far as I'm concerned, he could have done something a lot worse…although what he did do was pretty damn bad."

"You can say that again. I'm still trying to figure out how he did it. How was he able to time it just right to send those text messages to my and Dylan's phones?"

"Who knows? At the time Dad had some insalubrious types on his payroll. People known to do whatever they were hired to do. But remember, that was then."

She lifted a brow. "And now?"

"And now he's an old man trying to come to terms with his true identity."

She knew what Garth meant. Finding out his true relations to the Westmorelands and accepting that truth hadn't been easy for her father.

"And he's also trying like hell to marry the woman he let get away twenty-nine years ago," Garth added. "The only woman I'm convinced he's ever loved. A woman he knows he will lose if he doesn't make things right with their daughter."

Charm shrugged. "He would never lose Mom. She loves him as much as he loves her. She just wants to make sure he's changed. Like you said, what he did to me and Dylan happened ten years ago, but I'm still angry and hurt about it."

"Have you talked to Dylan?"

"No. At the end of our last conversation he let me know he didn't want to have anything to do with me."

"People say things in anger, Charm. Things they might regret later."

"Dylan meant it, trust me. I was going to play him like Bart played us. I tried apologizing, but he wouldn't accept my apology."

"Just like you're not accepting Bart's?"

She opened her mouth to say something and then closed it. He was right. Just like she wasn't accepting Bart's.

Bart glanced up when his butler entered the study. "Yes, Seals, what is it?"

"There's someone here to see you."

Bart frowned. "Who is it?"

"A man by the name of Dylan Emanuel."

Surprise touched Bart's face and he released a grateful sigh as he stood. "Please show him in."

Twenty-Five

In the deep recesses of her sleepy mind Charm heard music. It was the same song Dylan had sung each morning when he serenaded her beneath her window. She was having a beautiful dream. She knew it because she was no longer on the Red Flame Ranch but was back in Alaska in her bed.

She shifted positions and slowly opened her eyes to see daylight filtering through the blinds. She was about to close her eyes again when she realized the music was still playing. How could that be? How could music from a dream still flow through her ears while awake?

She glanced at her bedroom window and a nervous shiver raced through her. After quickly getting out of bed she went to the window, threw back the curtains and looked down. Dylan stood beneath her window serenading her with his guitar.

Grabbing her robe off the chair, she slid it on and raced down the stairs and flew through the front door. He placed his guitar aside and opened his arms to her and she ran right into them. Before she could ask anything, he captured her lips in a Dylan Emanuel kiss.

When he finally released her mouth, she clung to him as tightly as if he were her lifeline. All she could think about was that he was here. In Alaska. "I'm sorry for what I did, Dylan."

He pulled back and looked at her, swiping a tear from her eyes with the tip of his finger. "And I'm sorry, too, for handling it the way I did. I love you so much, Charm. I always have and I always will."

When he glanced around and saw that several of her neighbors were either peeping out the window or sticking their heads out their doors, he said, "Let's go inside so as not to give your neighbors anything to talk about."

She smiled up at him. "Okay."

Placing the strap of his guitar across his shoulder he took her hand and they went inside. When the door closed behind them, he placed his guitar aside and pulled her into his arms again. He cradled her face in his hands. "I love you, Charm. We're no longer teenagers and will do things right this time." After sweeping her into his arms he carried her over to the sofa and sat down with her in his lap.

"When did you get to Alaska? How did you know where I lived?" she asked excitedly.

"I arrived in Fairbanks late yesterday afternoon and went straight to your father's house."

"And he told you where I lived? He actually gave you my address?" she asked as if surprised.

"Yes. Just so you know, Bart came to see me last week."

"He did?"

"Yes. He apologized for what he did to us."

"And you accepted his apology?"

"Not at the time. I was still filled with anger and had a lot to think about. And I admit your father gave me a lot to think about. When I thought through everything, I knew that although what Bart did was on the extreme side, you and I aren't blameless either. We outright defied him."

She lifted her chin. "He demanded that we not see each other. He was being unreasonable."

"At the time he *was* an unreasonable man, but he was still your father."

She frowned. "Are you taking his side?"

"No. I'd like to think that now as adults we can look back and see how perhaps we could have handled things differently with him."

"Trust me, there's no way we could have. He was a tyrant back then."

"Maybe. Possibly. However, that was back then. I definitely see some changes in him now. He seems to be less demanding and domineering. He still likes to get his point across on things, but at least he listens and appears respectful of others' opinions." He paused. "All I'm saying is that we had a part in what happened, too. We can't forget that. But it's all water under the bridge and we have to move beyond it."

"Not sure that I can. We lost ten years because of him, Dylan."

"Ten years we'll recapture and this time no one will come between us. But it's important to me that you forgive him and move on. You love him and he loves you."

Charm didn't say anything as she thought about what Dylan had said. If he could forgive her father and move on then why couldn't she? She'd thought what he'd done to Cash and Brianna a few years ago had been unforgivable, yet they'd forgiven him and moved on because they felt he had learned his lesson.

"I know Dad has had to deal with a lot lately. Namely, about his family history. He's seeing a therapist. However, I think the most positive influence on him is my mother. He loves her deeply."

"Yes, he told me that."

Her eyes widened. "He told you?" She knew how closed-mouthed her father was about expressing his emotions to anyone.

"Yes, when he came to see me at the ranch. I met her yesterday when I arrived at his home. She's beautiful and looks more like an older sister than your mother."

Charm smiled. "She had me at twenty-one and yes, Mom is beautiful. She understands Dad more than any of us—that's for sure. Mom loves him and has been his biggest supporter. But she won't put up with his foolishness and he knows it."

Dylan nodded. "And just so you know, we've been invited to dinner. I think we should go. I've already told your parents my intentions toward you and—"

"What are your intentions?" she interrupted to ask.

"The same as they've always been. You are the woman I want to marry and love for the rest of my life, Charm. You told me at sixteen you would marry me and now I want to ask you again. Besides, I heard that second time's the charm."

Placing her off his lap on the sofa, he eased down on his knee in front of her. "Will you marry me, Charm Outlaw? And just so you know, I got your father's blessing this time. And I got your mom's blessing, too."

"Yes! I will marry you, Dylan."

He then slid the most gorgeous diamond ring on her finger. Her breath caught looking at it. "It's beautiful, Dylan."

"Thanks. It was my grandmother's ring and I believe she would have wanted you to wear it."

Tears filled her eyes and she wrapped her arms around his neck and whispered close to his ear, "Take me upstairs and make love to me, Dylan. And just so you know, that night we made love at your ranch was the first time for me since you."

Dylan blinked. "Are you saying you haven't made love to anyone in ten years?"

She nodded. "Yes, that's what I'm saying. I guess deep within my heart I knew you were the only one for me."

He swept her into his arms and looked down at her. "And in my heart, you are the only one for me. My one and only. The woman I've always wanted to marry. Now we can concentrate on new beginnings."

She nodded and smiled brightly. "Yes, new beginnings."

He headed up the stairs, and placed Charm on the bed. Dylan stood and stated at her, thinking of how he'd known twelve years ago that he'd loved her. The path to making her his forever hadn't been easy, but they were here now and he saw happiness in their future.

"What are you thinking about?" Charm asked.

"How much I love you."

She smiled. "And I love you, too, Dylan."

He joined her on the bed. It didn't take long for him to remove her PJs, but it took her a while to work his jeans and briefs off him. Then she tugged his T-shirt over his head and tossed it aside.

Leaning back on her haunches her gaze roamed over his naked body. He could actually feel the heat from her eyes. Moments later, when her gaze met his, every part of his body was aroused. He loved how she looked and the lusciousness of her feminine scent. He loved every single thing about her.

When she licked her bottom lip with the tip of her tongue, he pulled her into his arms.

"Make love to me, Dylan," she whispered. "I need to feel you inside me now."

"Baby, there's no place else I'd rather be."

Drawing her closer, he kissed her and her tongue tangled with his fueled by the same desire raging through him. He lowered her to the mattress, unable to hold back any longer. Just like that night on his ranch, he intended to pleasure every inch of her. However, right now, he wanted to be inside of her.

Her legs parted the moment his hard erection touched her inner thigh. He groaned her name when she arched her hips and he eased between her legs. As he thrust into her, her inner muscles clamped hard around his manhood.

"Charm..." He captured her mouth in another kiss, needing her as much as he needed to breathe.

Dylan released her mouth on a tortured groan as she moved beneath him. The force of his thrusts had her calling his name over and over.

Suddenly an orgasm ripped through them both. It was powerful. It was amazing. It was filled with love. Love that had withstood the test of time. Love that was meant to last forever. He knew in his heart that it would. And from the satisfied and happy smile on her face, Charm knew the same thing.

Claudia had a huge smile on her face as she closed the door behind Dylan and Charm, who'd been the last ones to leave. Dinner had gone great and all the Outlaws living in town had come. It had been amusing to see Garth's, Sloan's and Maverick's wives fangirling over Dylan. However, her future son-in-law only had eyes for one woman. Charm.

"What's the smile for, Claudia?"

She glanced over at Bart who wore a smile that was just as big as hers. He and his daughter were back on speaking terms and all was well. Crossing the room, she walked right into Bart's open arms. "I...we...have a lot to smile about. Our daughter is getting married."

Dylan had stated over dinner that he wanted a wedding to take place before the band's tour began in October. That meant a September wedding. Because weather in Alaska that time of year could be dicey, they would get married in Westmoreland Country in Denver, Colorado. Bart had spoken with his cousin Dillon who said the family would be more than happy to accommodate everyone. A few years ago, Dillon had built a multi-purpose family center he called Westmoreland House on his three hundred acres of property. It had an auditorium large enough to accommodate five hundred guests along with numerous additional banquet and meeting rooms.

That was another thing Claudia was happy about. Mainly how Bart was finally establishing a relationship with his Westmoreland kin. She could tell Dillon had been both surprised and elated by Bart's request. Finally, after all these years, Bart saw that his fear of losing his identity as an Outlaw was no longer a threat. The Westmorelands were a family of love who stood together, supported each other and would fight to protect their own until the end. And Bart was a part of them.

"You know what I think, Claudia?"

She smiled at Bart. "No, what do you think."

"I think it would be nice if the parents of the bride got married as well…before the wedding. What about it? Will you marry me next weekend while we're in New York?"

She held his gaze and could feel his nervousness. After all, this would make the sixth time he'd asked her to marry him. It was time she gave him the answer she wanted to give. "Yes, Bart. I will marry you next weekend in New York. I feel like the mother and grandmother of your sons and grandchildren anyway, and with another baby due to be born any day now and a wedding to plan, not to mention how much I love you, I think the time for us is right. Yes, I will marry you, Bart Outlaw."

An even bigger smile spread across his face. "I love you, Claudia. I am not perfect but—"

"I don't want a perfect man, Bart. There aren't any of them anyway. I want a man who loves me and his family and I know you do. Besides, I love how you're trying to be a better person each and every day."

"It's not easy, Claudia. Some habits are hard to break, and I might slip once in a while."

"And I'll be there to make sure your slips don't become falls. I love you."

Bart threw his head back, his laughter filled with happiness before swinging her around the room a few times. After placing her feet back on the floor, he drew her closer into his arms for a long and meaningful kiss.

Bart had finally captured the heart of the woman he loved.

Epilogue

"Who gives this woman away to this man?" the minister asked.

"I do."

Charm could hear the emotion in her father's response, and it touched her deeply. She knew how much he loved her and that she would always be a "daddy's girl." When she saw the mistiness in his eyes, she hugged him. "I love you, Daddy. Thanks for loving me so much."

She then turned to face Dylan when her father placed her hand in his. Dylan said in a husky voice, "I promise to make her happy."

"See that you do," was Bart's gruff response. Charm and Dylan couldn't help but grin at Bart regaining his composure to be Bart.

A short while later the pastor said to everyone gathered, "I now pronounce you husband and wife. Dylan, you may kiss your bride."

Dylan pulled her into his arms to seal their marriage with a kiss.

* * *

Deciding to host the wedding in Denver in Westmoreland Country had been a great idea, Charm thought, as she walked around holding her husband's hand while mingling with their many wedding guests. Not only was her Westmoreland family present but her three BFFs from college and close friends had been part of the wedding party. So had all of Dylan's band members. They were also providing the entertainment along with several other nationally known bands who were friends of Dylan's. Also included on the invitee list were a number of television and movie celebrities who were also Dylan's friends.

She had flown with Dylan to meet his parents a couple of months ago, and he'd flown with her to Atlanta, Denver, Montana and Texas to meet the Westmorelands. Most of the females in the family were in awe at meeting Dylan, and her cousin Dare's teenage daughter had exclaimed, "We have another celebrity in the family."

"Happy, sweetheart?"

She glanced up at her husband and smiled. "Yes, I am happy. What about you?"

"Very happy but I'll be happier once we leave for our honeymoon."

His band members had surprised them with a two-week trip to Ireland and a stay in a castle. Since he'd missed out on their summer fun trip to Ireland they thought he deserved it and since they considered Charm his queen it was fitting they stay in a castle for their honeymoon.

"Are you being replaced already?" Dylan asked as he looked across the room.

She followed his gaze and saw the moment Sloan placed his baby daughter Cassidy, dressed in a beautiful pink lacy dress, into Bart's arms. Charm smiled and admitted it was a heartwarming sight. She could tell others who knew her gruff father thought so as well.

"I might very well be getting replaced. I don't mind. Cassidy is the one and only granddaughter for now and he looks like a natural holding her." But then he'd looked like a natural holding Maverick and Phire's newborn son a couple of months ago as well. The Outlaws were growing, and she knew her father was happy about that.

Her heart felt full of love and joy at seeing her parents together. Bart had finally put a ring on her mother's finger and everyone, especially Charm's brothers, had been happy that Claudia was now an official member of the Outlaw family. Winning her mother's love and making her his wife had been the icing on the cake for Bart. These days he seemed like a different person. *Almost.* She also liked how well her parents and Dylan's were getting along. Dylan had explained that as an entertainment attorney his father was used to dealing with people with various attitudes and personalities.

She was about to look back at Dylan when she noticed her cousin Jaxon Ravnell talking to Westmoreland family friend Nadia Novak. Nadia was the youngest sister of Pam, Dillon Westmoreland's wife. Was Charm mistaken or did she see male interest in the depths of Jaxon's eyes? Umm…

At that moment one of Dylan's band members went onstage to get everyone's attention. It was Graham Ives, Dylan's best friend and who had also been his best man.

"Well, everyone, we've had the father-daughter dance, first dance of the wedding couple, cutting of the wedding cake and all the champagne toasts. By special request of the groom, we now have the first song. It's a special one that Dylan wrote just for his wife and it's titled 'Second Time's the Charm.'"

A surprised Charm glanced up at Dylan who grinned broadly before placing a kiss on her lips. He then moved toward the stage, took the mic from Graham and said, "I am dedicating this song to my beautiful wife who I fell in love with when she was sixteen and I was seventeen."

After being handed his guitar, he began singing. The combination of words, melody and music brought tears to her eyes. Her husband was putting his heart, love and soul into every lyric. When he finished, he walked back to her with that Dylan Emanuel strut and swept her into his arms. After kissing her in front of everyone, he then headed toward the exit of the Westmoreland House.

The wedding was over and their lives together were beginning.

* * * * *

HER SECRET BILLIONAIRE

YAHRAH ST. JOHN

To my publicist, Keisha Mennefee, for encouraging
me when I'm down and out.

Prologue

One year ago

Egypt Cox stared at the clock from the plush king-size bed of Helaine Smith's mansion. It read 1:00 a.m. Usually she slept like a rock, but so much had happened over the last week, her mind was wandering.

Helaine was her best friend Wynter Barrington's aunt, and she'd always treated Egypt with kindness, respect and, dare she say, love. She'd invited Egypt to her home countless times and hadn't minded if Egypt wanted to try cooking a dish or two. When Egypt mentioned opening her own restaurant someday, Helaine championed her and told her all things were possible. Egypt came to think of the older woman as the grandmother she never had. So, it was strange to be sleeping in her home without her. Over a week ago, Helaine had passed away from a brain aneurysm.

Despite how busy she was with her food truck in Raleigh, North Carolina, Egypt knew she had to come to San Antonio and support her bestie. Wynter had rushed home from Bali, where she'd been working as a content creator, for the funeral. Neither of them knew what was in store for them after the service.

Earlier in the week, Egypt had received a call from an attorney named Sidney Carter, but between the food truck and making last-minute travel arrangements, she'd been too busy to respond. She wished she had. Then perhaps she, Wynter and the other women who made up the Six Gems, Asia Reynolds, Shay Davis, Lyric Taylor and Teagan Williams—her best friends for life—wouldn't have been blindsided at the reading of Helaine's will.

After the funeral, Mr. Carter asked each of the women to accompany him along with the Barrington family into the study at the Barrington estate. Then he proceeded to drop the bombshell that Wynter was inheriting the lion's share of Helaine's estate, and the kind older woman had left each of the remaining Six Gems two hundred thousand dollars each to pursue their dreams of opening their own businesses.

Egypt had been stunned and so appreciative, but the moment hadn't lasted. Wynter's family was furious and threatened to challenge the will. To make matters worse, the Barringtons turned against one of their own, accusing Wynter of bamboozling Helaine. It was unthinkable. Egypt was ready to go for battle for her friend, but she didn't have to. Wynter packed her bags and left the estate for Helaine's, and the other five Gems had come with her.

But that didn't mean Egypt knew exactly what to do next. Although her food truck was thriving and she'd been saving for her own restaurant in the hopes of getting a loan one day, she'd always thought that day would be far off in the future. She would've had her restaurant much sooner if her lying ex-boyfriend hadn't taken all her savings and left her with nothing. Because of Antwan, Egypt steered clear of emotional entanglements with men and kept it to the physical. It's all she had to give because she had to build her next egg from scratch. Helaine's generous endowment would go a long way with the banks in proving she had some financial backing to proceed with a big undertaking like this.

And she *would* make this dream come true, because whenever Egypt set her mind to do something, like Helaine said, there wasn't anything she couldn't accomplish.

One

Present day

Egypt stirred the Cajun aioli that would be a condiment to her crab-and-corn fritters. They were one of her specialties, because everyone in town loved the fritters filled with cheddar cheese, pickled onions and bacon. It was one of the many dishes customers had come to love since she opened Flame in her new hometown of Raleigh.

She'd moved here from San Antonio in search of a place that spoke to her Southern roots and the food she longed to cook. Her mother, Virginia, God bless her soul, had died when Egypt was six years old from breast cancer. She was from Raleigh, so Egypt felt like the city was a good place to start.

Her father, Anthony Cox, missed his baby girl and soon followed Egypt to Raleigh. He was now working for the city's planning department. It wasn't a glamorous job, but it paid the bills. It had always been Egypt and her dad. He was her hero and the man she measured every other man against.

"Chef, would you like to taste this dish?" her sous-chef, Quentin Coleman, inquired. Quentin was tall and lanky with a warm smile and a nut-brown complexion. He wore his hair faded around the crown and in short twists on top.

"Absolutely." Egypt took the proffered fork. When she placed the morsel in her mouth, the flavors burst on her tongue. It was amazing. She was glad she'd hired Quentin. He only had experience as a line cook when she interviewed him, but when Egypt asked Quentin to cook his signature dish on the fly, he hadn't hesitated. His shrimp and grits were phenomenal, and she'd offered him the job on the spot. She hadn't regretted her decision.

"Phenomenal." Egypt smiled. "Really great work, Quentin."

"You think so?" She hated that he was still unsure of himself. To be in the kitchen, you had to be arrogant about your craft, but he was young, only twenty-two. They were going to have to work on his confidence.

"Yes. Go ahead and prepare the dishes so the staff can have a taste."

Egypt left the kitchen to check on the front of the house and make sure everything was in order. The restaurant wasn't opening for another two hours, but she liked her staff to taste the meals on the dinner service.

When she stepped into the restaurant, Egypt's heart became full. Sometimes she still couldn't believe this place was hers and they'd been open two months.

She'd been lucky to find this storefront location in Glenwood South. It was an up-and-coming area exploding with young professionals and progressive restaurants. It was the right place for Flame. The restaurant wasn't large and only sat eighty at wooden tables with padded leather seats and a few booths. She loved how the overly large windows let in plenty of natural light and showed off the warm yellow and beige tones she'd chosen.

As for the floors, they were a polished concrete, stained with a swirl design. The fully-stocked bar was surrounded by dark planks of wood while the counters were a stainless steel that could withstand wear and tear. Tall bar stools abutted the bar and sat at least eight. The rest of her decor was minimal—metal art along with some eclectic pieces from her best friend Asia covered the walls. Flame was exactly how she envisioned. Her blood, sweat and tears, along with a little help from a heavenly angel, had made it all possible.

She found her hostess, Tessa Rogers, chatting it up with several of the servers. Five foot eight with silky brown hair and a slim figure in a black tank minidress, Tessa was easy on the eyes and exactly the person she needed up front. Egypt wasn't oblivious to the fact that first impressions mattered.

Tessa was friendly, gregarious and made guests feel at home, which was exactly what Egypt wanted for Flame. Most of the servers were college students. Then there were the veterans that she'd been able to entice away from the restaurant where she used to work. Her former boss, Chef Raphael, was a horrible human being who belittled the cooks in his kitchen. Egypt had been one of them. She'd hung in long enough to gain the knowledge she needed, but as soon as she could, she struck out on her own and opened her own food truck.

It had taken her longer than she'd hoped, because her ex-boyfriend took her savings and ran. Thinking about him was distasteful, so Egypt returned to the task at hand. It didn't stop her from remembering how foolish she felt for believing Antwan, hell, any man. Above all, she needed honesty in a relationship and since she didn't have time for one, she would only trust herself and the Gems because they'd never let her down. After she ensured the servers were on top of things, Egypt made her way to the kitchen. Quentin had several family-style platters from their winter menu ready for the waitstaff to sample. There were appetizers of pan-fried chicken livers with caramelized onions with a Madeira demi-glace and crispy Brussels sprouts with bacon in a sweet chili glaze. For the entrée, she'd whipped up blackened catfish with red rice, fried green tomatoes with a habanero chutney and a sautéed shrimp and scallop dish over creamy white grits in a lobster-butter sauce with fried spinach.

Soon, Egypt was sitting down with her staff and enjoying the meal. Everyone passed around the dishes and oohed and ahhed over her and Quentin's creations. It was a collaborative environment, something she'd always craved and had now achieved. Egypt glanced upward to heaven. *Thank you, Aunt Helaine.*

"Mother, Father." Garrett Forrester nodded at his parents as he walked into the living room of their palatial six-bedroom, seven-and-a-half-bath family home in Wakefield Plantation. It was a cold night in early January, and there was a large roaring fire in the two-story stone fireplace.

Garrett had endured a long day at the office of the family company, Forrester Holdings Corporation, and wanted to go home to a hot meal and a scotch. Instead, he'd been summoned to a family meeting. He wondered if it had something to do with his maternal grandfather, Cyrus Walker, who had died a couple of weeks ago and bequeathed him Walker Farms. Garrett hadn't decided what he wanted to do with it.

"Please have a seat, Thomas." His father, Hugh, motioned to the chair across from his parents, who sat on the love seat. Hugh Forrester was imposing man with his six-foot-four stature, black hair graying out at the temples and piercing dark eyes.

His father knew he preferred to be called Garrett, his grandfather Cyrus's middle name, but Hugh persisted in using his given name. Garrett wasn't in the mood for a battle, so he sat on the edge of the chair and unbuttoned his suit jacket. He'd come straight from work and after removing his overcoat was still in his usual attire of a single-breasted suit and shirt and tie, like his father. What he wouldn't give to dress like an everyday joe once in a while. "What's going on?"

"Have you decided what you're going to do with your grandfather's farm?" his father asked.

"Not yet." Some of his fondest memories were when his mother sent him to the farm to be with his grandparents for the summer. Instead of looking at boring facts and figures, Garrett had spent his time on top of a tractor or helping his grandfather pick vegetables.

Losing him hurt, but Garrett tried not to show it, because that's not what Forresters did. They had a stiff upper lip. Even so, Garrett still hadn't accepted he'd never see the old man again. Lowering his head, he closed his eyes tight. His eyes were burning with the effort to rein in his emotions. He loved Cyrus, sometimes more than his own father, because he'd been kind, patient and *loving.*

"Don't you think it's time you figure it out? We can't afford to have you distracted dealing with a ramshackle farm."

"The farm was Daddy's pride and joy, Hugh," his mother, Corrine, responded. "Daddy took excellent care of the land." His mother, with her gentle brown eyes, long bob to her shoulders and a keen eye for fashion, sat in slacks and a matching camisole and sweater set. She was the epitome of class and sophistication, but she was too soft-spoken and often allowed his father to rule their house.

"It's been hanging on for years, Corrine. It's time it was sold. Maybe someone can make good use of the land and build a hotel or something."

"No!" The word was out of Garrett's mouth before he even realized he said it. Hearing his father talk about getting rid of the farm that had been in his maternal family for years was sacrilege.

Hugh frowned. "What do you mean, no?"

"You heard me," Garrett responded. "I won't be selling."

"Garrett…" He didn't like his father's condescending tone, as if he alone knew everything. His parents had had Garrett later in life and were now in their mid-seventies, after his mother struggled with several miscarriages. Garrett had been their miracle baby and the one on whom they laid all their hopes and dreams, including running the family business. He'd done everything they'd ever asked of him, but not this. He'd put his personal life on the backburner keeping his relationships brief and as an outlet for physical release because he couldn't offer anything more. His work was his life. Garrett was even sure if he wanted to have a family some day. Maybe. It was so far off in the future, he never thought about it.

"Don't start, Father. I run a billion-dollar company—I'm more than capable of dealing with three hundred acres of land. I don't have all the answers on the farm's next steps, but when I do, you'll be the first to know."

His father was about to speak, but when he looked toward his wife, her expression brooked no further discussion, and for once he let the matter drop.

Garrett rose to his feet. "If that's all, I'm going to head home."

"Don't say I didn't warn you," his father replied as he left. "That farm will be the death of you."

Minutes later, Garrett was hopping into his Rolls-Royce Dawn and heading for the highway. The fresh air helped him clear his mind. He hadn't actually thought about what he was going to do with the farm; he just knew he couldn't sell his family legacy. He would visit Walker Farms, scope out the land and figure out his next move.

He dialed Kent Howell, the foreman of Walker Farms. "Kent, can you be sure all the farm's records for the last five years are placed in my grandfather's office?"

"Hello to you, too, Garrett. And yes, of course," Kent replied.

Garrett and Kent went way back to when they were kids working on his grandfather's farm, but it was Garrett who'd gone on to college while the other man stayed as a farmhand. "Thanks, Kent. I'll see you then." He ended the call. When he arrived, he would be able to dive in and see just how bad the farm's finances really were.

In the meantime, he was starving. He thought about his penthouse and remembered there wasn't a thing to eat at his place. He'd heard about an up-and-coming eatery in Glenwood South from his assistant, who'd raved about it recently. On a whim, Garrett decided to head there and check it out. The drive to Flame didn't take long, but it didn't stop him from thinking about how annoyed he was with his father's heavy-handed approach. Hugh thought he could bully Garrett into doing his bidding, but he was sadly mistaken. Garrett was his own man, and he would do *what* he wanted, *when* he wanted.

He arrived after 8:00 p.m. and, as he suspected, the restaurant was packed, but peering over the couple in front of him, Garrett noticed an empty seat at the bar. After the hostess seated the couple, she returned to the host stand, and for a moment the brunette just stared at him.

Garrett was used to his effect on the opposite sex. Women often threw themselves at him, giving him their number on a business card or sliding into his DMs on social media. The bold ones propositioned him outright. If time permitted, he sometimes indulged in the odd fling, but usually he was too busy building the family business.

"Can I sit at the bar?" Garrett inquired.

"*Bar?*" she asked, bewildered. She must have caught herself staring, because she snapped out of it. "Yes, yes, of course." She motioned him to an empty bar stool. "Here's a menu." She handed him a single piece of cardstock. He'd heard the menu changed weekly based on what was in season.

"Thank you."

She gave him one final smile before leaving. He wasn't alone long. The bartender, a dreadlocked young man, asked him, "What can I get you?"

Garrett's stomach rumbled. "Everything."

The bartender chuckled.

"I'll have a scotch."

"Coming right up."

While the bartender went to fetch his drink. Garrett perused the menu. The chef was offering a variety of Southern dishes that spoke to his palate, but the special sounded like a winner. He pulled out his phone from his pants pocket and reviewed his emails.

The bartender slid two fingers of scotch toward him. "Have you decided on dinner?"

"I'll have the catfish special."

"Excellent choice," the bartender responded. "Chef Egypt really knows how to throw down in the kitchen. You won't be disappointed."

"I'm sure I won't be."

"Speaking of, there she is now."

Garrett spun around on the bar stool in time to catch sight of the woman in question. And what a sight she was to behold. She was tall, maybe five feet nine or ten. She wore a black chef's coat over black slacks, but that couldn't hide her aura. There was a brightness around her—so she simply radiated.

Her clear caramel-brown skin shone even from where he sat, and her lips looked sumptuous, but it was the high-kilowatt smile on her full lips and her delectable round ass that mesmerized him. Hunger shot through Garrett with an intensity he'd never felt. He'd been working so hard for so long that he'd had no time for the call of flesh and sin. And something told him being with Chef Egypt would be all about sin.

Her peal of laughter caught his ear and ripped through the air. Garrett couldn't stop watching her. He wanted her to give him—and only him—that same effervescent smile. Garrett scrubbed his jaw. Was he really so overworked that he was lusting after a woman he knew nothing about? Hell yes! And he would meet her *tonight*.

As she chatted with another delighted patron, the hairs on the back of Egypt's neck stood up. She felt as if she were being watched. Her eyes spanned the restaurant and connected with a pair of onyx ones laser focused on her. Egypt stared right back, because she was enjoying the view. The stranger was tall, chocolate and broad-shouldered with close cropped dark curls, just how she liked her men. She also loved the sexy beard and sensuous lips. He looked like he knew exactly how to use them to give a woman the ultimate pleasure.

There was a flash in his gaze that made Egypt's skin tingle. She was suddenly aware of herself. Her breasts ached and felt heavier than usual, and that was saying a lot, since she had an ample bosom and wore a triple D cup. There was a shivery sensation between her legs, and Egypt felt her cheeks flush. Or perhaps she had spent too much time in the kitchen and was overheated?

She blinked, breaking the spell, and continued around the restaurant, checking in with guests to make sure they enjoyed their meal and were fully satisfied. Consciously or unconsciously, she stayed away from the bar. She didn't trust herself if she got too close to the magnetic stranger with the deep-set eyes. Instead, she kept to the outskirts and, when it was time, quickly made her way to the kitchen. But she still felt his eyes on her back as she entered her safe haven.

"Service going well?" Quentin asked.

She nodded. "Yes. Everyone is enjoying their food. It's a good night."

"Excellent, Chef," Quentin responded. "We have an order of your blackened catfish along with a request to meet you."

"Is that right?" She didn't need to ask who it was. She knew. It was the man at the bar. She could refuse the request and appear childish or she could be the bold boss babe she'd always been and face him head-on.

Egypt wasn't going to make it easy on him, though. She sent out the dish but made him wait twenty minutes to meet her. Once she was sure her long hair was in a sophisticated topknot and added a glide of mauve lipstick, she walked to the bar.

As if he sensed her presence, he turned around. "Chef Egypt, I presume?"

Damn! Why did his low, rich voice sound as decadent as syrup drizzled over her amaretto brioche French toast? It made Egypt's lungs draw tight in her chest and goose bumps scatter across her skin.

She offered a bright smile. "That's me. I hope you enjoyed your meal." She glanced at the now-empty plate sitting on the bar. Up close, the man looked even more attractive than he'd been from afar. He was powerfully built, and she could see the outline of his biceps in the button-down shirt he wore that easily cost more than anything in her closet. He breathed so-phistication.

"Yes, I did, and I wanted to thank the chef who prepared it. I'm Garrett, by the way." He grinned and held out his hand.

For a moment, she stared at down at his outstretched hand and even thought about refusing him, but then she took his hand, sliding her palm across his much larger one. "Pleasure to meet you, Garrett. As for the food, it was a group effort."

"Beautiful and humble. A rare combination," Garrett replied with a smile. Egypt's stomach flipped when he revealed pearly white teeth. Did he get them brightened? They were perfect!

Not to mention his eyes. They were trained on her, and Egypt found herself standing a little straighter in her Crocs. She couldn't seem to stop herself from looking away from him, either. He wasn't the usual guy she came across. She doubted a worldly gentleman like him ever ate in a place like this. She supposed that's what made him seem so out of place, but that didn't stop her heart from ratcheting up to a dizzying pace.

"I'm glad you enjoyed your entrée. May I propose dessert or coffee?"

"Only if you can share it with me," he responded boldly and looked her straight in the eye, as if daring her to turn him down.

Egypt was taken aback. Since the restaurant opened, she'd never had a patron be quite so bold. Though there had been the odd one here or there who tried to cup her behind and she promptly showed them the door, this man was different, be-cause she was attracted to him—and she suspected he knew it.

"I'm afraid not," Egypt responded. "As the chef and propri-etor of this establishment, I have a lot to do before the night is over."

"Which is precisely why you can get someone to do it for you."

Her eyes narrowed, and Egypt had to give it to him, she liked a man who knew what he wanted, but *she* wasn't on the menu. "Are you always this persistent?"

"I have found it serves me well in life."

"Well, it won't tonight, but thanks for the offer. I'll have dessert sent over. I hope you'll enjoy it."

Egypt spun on her heel and escaped to the confines of her kitchen, but all the way there, she felt Garrett's laser-beam focus on her. A shiver raced across her skin and heat flared low in her belly at the appreciative way he'd looked at her. A man like him screamed *Danger!*

Once there, Egypt leaned against the double doors and began fanning herself as she took a deep breath. The problem was, when she closed her eyes, she thought about *him* and what he would look like without any clothes on. He was all dark, sinful temptation wrapped in refined elegance, and she craved a taste.

What was wrong with her? She'd never had such a visceral reaction to a man before, not even her ex-boyfriend Antwan Dixon, who she'd thought was the love of her life. Antwan had liked being in charge and telling her what to do. He was a narcissist, which Egypt had figured out too late. She'd thought she would marry him, because in the beginning, he was everything she could wish for, but he'd been hiding behind a mask. Soon, he was criticizing Egypt about her weight and her cooking.

To make matters worse, he was a control freak. Egypt never had a voice, because he had to be the center of attention. When that hadn't been enough, he'd taken the money she'd saved for her own restaurant and left her holding the bag on a ton of debt. Egypt had never felt so used in her life. For the last seven years, she'd kept men at a distance, only bothering with them when she needed physical affection.

But *that* man out there made her *feel*. Something she'd sworn never to do again. Egypt didn't like it. It was a good thing he was probably passing through town and she'd never see him again. Otherwise, she would be in big trouble.

Nothing could have prepared Garrett for the spellbinding allure of Chef Egypt—and he didn't even know her last name. There was just something about her that…transfixed him. The way she drew his eye without having to try. Lots of women postured around him, wanting to be seen, but not Egypt. She acted as if she wasn't interested, but there was something in her gaze when he stared at her that told Garrett she was far from unaffected by him.

Much to his chagrin, she'd turned down his offer for dessert. Did she know he'd been hoping for more and making *her* his after-dinner treat? Garrett wasn't interested in anything serious. He didn't do long-term commitments. Short, expedient hookups were his MO. His relationships with women lasted as long as was mutually beneficial for both parties. Recently, he'd taken on more and more at Forrester Holdings Corporation, and any woman he dated had understood she would always come second to his work. Most did, and those that didn't received their walking papers.

It's not that Garrett didn't want to get married one day—he did—but he had too much he wanted to achieve. Although he was CEO, his father still had his hand in running the company. Garrett felt as if he was constantly proving he had the cojones to lead the billion-dollar company. It seemed like the goal line was constantly pushed farther and farther away, but there had never been anything Garrett couldn't achieve. Whether it was graduating from Harvard or being top of his class at Wharton, he was no stranger to hard work. He thrived on success.

He glanced at the double doors of the kitchen Egypt was hiding behind. She would learn that he didn't give up easily. This woman was a challenge, and he was man enough to rise to it.

Two

"You should have seen him, Wynter," Egypt said into the phone from her office in the rear of Flame. The dinner crowd had waned and Quentin had the kitchen under control, so she had time to dish with her best friend over FaceTime. "He was the definition of tall, dark and handsome. If I could have, I would have eaten him up with a spoon."

Wynter laughed on her end of the screen. "Of course you would have, but there's more than the physical, Egypt."

"Not *this* again." Egypt rolled her eyes and glanced around her sparsely decorated office. It had the essentials from IKEA— a desk, her executive chair, a couple of file cabinets, a round table surrounded by chairs, and a comfy sofa and throw blanket for when she needed a nap.

"Don't knock it, Egypt. Just because you had one bad experience with Antwan doesn't mean all men are bad."

Ever since Wynter and Riley, their best friend Shay's brother, had gotten together last year, Wynter had been spouting about how wonderful being in love was and how she wished each of the Six Gems would find their special someone.

"That's easy for you to say—you met the guy of your dreams

when you were a teenager," Egypt responded. "The rest of us have to weed through all the rotten apples to find a good one. And quite frankly, that's too much work when I can take what I want and keep it moving."

"C'mon, don't you want a husband and children one day?"

Egypt shrugged. "If it happens, it happens, but I don't have the time to go searching for it. Flame has only been open a couple of months. You know how many restaurants go belly up the first year or after? I have to keep my foot on the gas and never take my eyes off the road."

"I get it, but surely there's room in your life for more?" Wynter inquired.

"You want us all to be as happy as you and Riley are," Egypt replied. "And I appreciate that, but it may not be in the cards. But that doesn't mean I won't be cheering you and Riley on at your wedding."

Wynter smiled, and her heart-shaped face beamed on the screen. "I never knew I could be this happy, considering how we started." Last year, Wynter and Riley had reconnected at her aunt Helaine's funeral. Unbeknownst to any of the Six Gems, Wynter and Riley had a one-night stand. A couple of months later, they ran into each other again and rekindled their affair, which eventually led to them both realizing they were in love.

"I'm so ready to marry him," Wynter continued with a dreamy sigh. "And to my surprise, my family is being supportive."

"Are they?" Egypt queried. "The relationship between you and your folks is better?"

Her bestie nodded. "My mother has made a concentrated effort to repair the damage that was done after they contested the will. They are also footing the bill for the wedding. Honestly, Riley could care less. He said he would marry me even if I was wearing a potato sack, but I told him I'd be in couture."

Egypt laughed. "I'm so happy for you." And she genuinely was. Last year, she'd worried about the effect fighting the Barringtons might have on her best friend, but Wynter had been adamant her aunt's choices be honored. And because of it, Egypt had been able to open Flame. "I'll even put on a hideous bridesmaid dress for you."

Wynter scoffed. "Do you really hate the dress?"

"Of course not!" She chuckled wryly. "I'm just busting your chops. The dress is absolutely lovely, and I can't wait to stand up for you on your big day."

They ended the call with talk of seeing each other soon for Wynter's prewedding festivities. Shay and Lyric were arranging her bridal shower, while Egypt and Teagan were handling the bachelorette party. Wynter may have been the one who normally planned their annual girls' getaways, but Egypt had a few tricks up her sleeve, and they were going to have epic adventure in Vegas.

After she disconnected the call, she returned to the front of the house. She'd been under the illusion that Mr. Tall, Dark and Handsome would have gone.

She was wrong.

Only one person remained. Garrett.

"Well, well, well, you finally emerge from your cocoon," Garrett said as Egypt sashayed across the floor. He didn't even try to stop staring. Because he wanted her and was willing to wait. Earlier, he'd felt the electricity between them when she shook his hand. It felt as if he'd touched a live wire. Her handshake had been firm, but that hadn't stopped his attention from dropping to her mouth. To those deliciously full lips of hers he wanted to crush beneath his.

So here he was.

Waiting for her.

Egypt cocked her head to one side and regarded him. "I declined your invitation to dessert."

"Yes, I know. But now that the evening is over, I was hoping to entice you with a different one." When her brows rose, he clarified, "A date." Though he did want something else— *her* in his bed. "What do you say, Egypt?"

She pondered his request too long for Garrett's liking, but then she surprised him and said, "Sure, why not?"

"Don't sound so excited."

She chuckled. "I hope you're not one of those guys that think big girls are easy and lack self-confidence, because I'm not one of them. I'm discerning about who I sleep with."

"That's good to know," Garrett responded. "I wouldn't want it any other way." He liked that Egypt wasn't afraid to speak her mind. The women he dated tended to cater to his every whim rather than having their own thoughts or opinions.

"Good, because I'm picking the restaurant," Egypt stated.

He quirked brow. "Is that right?"

She folded her arms across her ample bosom. "It is indeed. Some of the restaurants out there are all fluff and no substance. If I choose, I promise your taste buds will be as tantalized as they were at Flame's."

"Promises, promises." He grinned.

"Are you always such a flirt?"

Garrett thought about her question, and the answer was no. He was usually reserved and some might stay uptight, but for some reason he felt at ease with Egypt. "Actually, I'm not. I would probably be considered boring to some."

"Then you're hanging around the wrong people," Egypt retorted. "No wonder you came driving to my neck of the woods."

"What made you pick this place, anyway?"

"Young adults and couples are moving here because it's more affordable. With their word of mouth, this 'area'—" she made quotation marks with her hands "—is becoming the new hot spot. Everyone will be looking for restaurants. That's where I come in. I bring bold flavors and a new twist to Southern cuisine."

"Yes, you do." His gaze roamed over her gorgeous face and landed on her mouth. Her full lips called, once again beckoning him to have a taste, and Garrett might have leaned over and indulged if the sous-chef hadn't come out and interrupted them.

"Chef, you coming back to finish up?" the young man asked from the double doors leading to the kitchen.

"Yes, I'm coming." Egypt turned back to him. "Listen, I have to go. We've got to get the kitchen cleaned up."

"Absolutely. I wouldn't dream of keeping you."

"But you will need my number," Egypt said. "That's if you were serious about a date."

"I was—I mean, I am."

"Good. Then hand me your phone."

Garrett unlocked the device and quickly handed it to her. He watched her nimble fingers move across the screen as she added her digits to his phone. When she was finished, she handed it back to him. "Now you can reach me. I expect a call. If you ghost me, never darken my restaurant's doorstep ever again."

He chuckled. "You don't have to worry about that—" He glanced down at the screen and read her full name. "—Egypt Cox." Tipping his head, he headed toward the door, but something stopped him and made him look backward. When he did, he found Egypt at the kitchen doors staring back at him. It made Garrett's chest tighten, because it had been a long time, if ever, since he'd felt such a strong attraction to a woman. Although he wasn't looking for anything serious, he couldn't wait for their first date.

He gave her a quick nod and headed outside. He clicked Open on the door and was walking to his Rolls-Royce at the back of the restaurant when he was distracted by a text from his father asking him to reconsider selling the farm.

Garrett was so preoccupied with his phone he didn't see the two men in dark attire approach him from either side of his car until it was too late.

"Someone was mooning over a customer," Quentin commented when Egypt returned to the kitchen to help package the remaining food to give to a homeless shelter in the neighborhood. "And I don't blame you—if I had a man like that chasing after me, I would absolutely give him the digits."

"Quentin, you're a mess."

"And you're stalling. Tell me about him. Who is he, what does he do?"

"It was all flirtatious banner, nothing more. I'll find out more once we have our first date," Egypt responded, wiping down the kitchen counters. When she was finished, she headed over to take out the trash.

"You agreed to a date?"

She nodded. "The man waited all night for me. He was clearly determined, so I figured, what could it hurt? Plus, he's easy on the eyes." As she pulled out the overflowing bag, Egypt tried to act like she didn't care, but Garrett was the first man to pique her interest in a long time. After Antwan, she'd erected walls around her heart to protect herself from ever getting hurt again. But this man was the first to make Egypt want to consider lowering them.

"If you say so, but me thinks thou doth protest too much," Quentin replied. Then he walked over and tried to take the trash bag. "I've got this."

"Hey, it's my place. I'm not above taking out the trash."

"I know, but this area can be a bit sketchy after dark," Quentin said. "But if you insist, I'm coming with you."

She did.

Egypt opened the rear door of Flame that led to the parking lot. As she did, she heard loud voices. Then she saw Garrett, the man she had been flirting with, being attacked by two men. It was too dark to see their faces, but Garrett was giving as good as he got and punched one of them in the face.

"*Stop! Stop!*" she yelled.

Garrett turned around, motioning for her to stay away, but in doing so, it allowed one of the men to get a jump on him. In slow motion, she watched as one of them swung at his head with a bat. Seconds later, Garrett crumpled to the ground. She watched as they kicked him to make sure he wasn't moving.

"Omigod!" Egypt cried, covering her mouth with her hand.

Then she snapped out of it and turned to Quentin at her side. "Call 911!"

With no thought for her safety, Egypt rushed outside and toward Garrett. One of the attackers immediately hopped into the driver's side of Garrett's car, while the other young man took the Rolex off Garrett's wrist and rummaged through his pockets, no doubt to steal his wallet and phone, and then rushed into the passenger side of Garrett's vehicle and peeled out of the parking lot.

When she reached Garrett, he was unconscious. She crouched down beside him, checking for a pulse. She'd taken a CPR class years ago. In the restaurant industry, she'd thought it was practical, considering the possibility someone might choke and need assistance.

"Garrett! Garrett!" When he didn't answer, Egypt tried to lift his head, but when she did, blood oozed on her hand. She glanced down and saw the bat they'd used to hit him. "It's going to be okay." She didn't know if she was saying it more for herself or for him. After Quentin called the police, he rushed over to help, but Egypt wouldn't let him go.

Instead, she held Garrett's head cradled in her lap with Quentin by her side until the police and ambulance arrived. She wanted to go with him, but the detective wanted a statement from her and Quentin about what occurred, so she remained at Flame.

She recounted the incident to the officer who identified himself as Detective Simpson. It seemed so unreal. One minute, she and Garrett were flirting and making plans to have their first date, and the next minute he was being carjacked in her parking lot! This was terrible. She was not only worried about Garrett and hoping he would recover, but if word got around Flame wasn't a safe place for dinner, it could ruin her.

Egypt had taken out an incredibly large loan to cover opening the restaurant, from the renovation to the equipment to stocking the shelves. The only reason the bank agreed was because she'd put the entire two hundred thousand dollars Wynter's aunt Helaine gave her into a down payment. She'd invested everything she had into this place. It had to succeed.

"Ma'am." Detective Simpson interrupted her thoughts. "How did you know the victim?"

"Garrett?" Egypt asked. "He was a customer and asked me out."

Egypt's voice trailed off, and she glanced up to see the police detective was waiting on her expectantly. "And?"

She shrugged. "He was charming and good-looking, so I said yes. I gave him my number, and we made plans to go out a date. And now this."

"When he awakes, I'm sure he'll appreciate that you and your assistant were there to help."

"I hope so."

"In the meantime, are you able to give us a description of the men?" Detective Simpson asked.

Egypt shook her head. "It was dark and I didn't see much. They were wearing hoodies, so it was hard to see their faces."

"What about cameras? Do you have any?"

Egypt nodded. That's the one thing her father had insisted on when she'd selected this location. "Yes, I do." He followed Egypt to her office in the rear of Flame. The cameras showed the two men, which was exactly what the police needed to apprehend them. Egypt downloaded the video and handed the detective the USB drive.

"We really appreciate your assistance, Ms. Cox," Detective Simpson said, "A luxury car like the one Garrett was driving will bring a lot of attention and hopefully help us nab them."

"I hope so," Egypt asked, "In the meantime, can you tell me what hospital they took Garrett to? I'd like to check on him and make sure he's okay."

"Of course. He'll be at WakeMed."

"Thank you," she murmured.

"I plan on heading there myself to see if he's conscious and can give us a statement."

It took another hour before Egypt and Quentin could leave

Flame. The police were still outside and promised to keep up a heavy presence over the next few days in case the perpetrators came back. Egypt didn't care about any of that. She wanted to get to the hospital and check on Garrett. The hit he'd taken was pretty severe. If nothing else, he would have a serious concussion.

When she arrived, she found Detective Simpson had beaten her to the hospital and was already talking with the doctors in the hospital lobby. Egypt didn't wait for them to finish—she had to know what was going on. "How is he?" Egypt asked, interrupting their conversation.

The doctor, dressed in blue scrubs, looked annoyed at the disruption. "Who are you?"

"She's the Good Samaritan who saw the incident take place and stayed with Garrett until the police and help arrived," Detective Simpson answered.

"Is he okay?" Egypt inquired. "How badly was he hurt?"

The doctor looked at the detective, who nodded. "Until all the test results come in, we are not sure of the extent of his injuries. Because he's still unconscious, we're running a head X-ray and CT scan to rule out a brain bleed."

"Omigod!" Egypt's hand flew to her mouth. "This is horrible."

"Do you have any idea who he is?" the doctor inquired. "All the detective could tell me was his first name. We would like to notify his family."

Egypt shook her head. "No, I don't. We hadn't gotten that far. He'd asked me out and I…" Her voice trailed off. Garrett had come to her establishment to get a meal. Instead, he'd been beaten and robbed. And now, they couldn't tell his family, because she didn't even know his last name. "I'm sorry."

"It's all right, Ms. Cox," Detective Simpson said. "I'll work on figuring out his identity. In the meantime, should you remember anything else, please contact me." He handed her his business card.

Egypt nodded and accepted the card. "Of course. I'd like

to stay here and see if he wakes up. Is it possible I can be put on the list for updates?" she asked, looking in the detective's direction.

The doctor shrugged.

"Since Ms. Cox is the only person who knows Garrett at this point, I see no reason why she can't be on the list, Doctor. Please contact me if he regains consciousness?"

"Absolutely."

Moments later, Egypt was alone with only her guilt to keep her company in the waiting room. She stared out of the window into the night sky. Most of Raleigh had long since retired to bed, while Egypt was dealing with this nightmare. She felt terrible that this had happened to Garrett, all because he wanted to take *her* out. Glancing around, she looked for signs for the waiting room, and that's where she parked herself until the doctor could update her on Garrett's condition.

Three

Two months later

He was in a cloak of darkness and wanted to stay there, but he heard a soft feminine voice saying his name, tugging him forward, toward her.

She squeezed his hand and her voice grew louder and more insistent, yet it felt far away. He wanted to stay in the peaceful sleep where he was, but he couldn't. *She* was pushing him out of it. Slowly, he opened his eyes—and instantly regretted it. Garrett felt dizzy, and his head felt heavy. He immediately shut them.

"Garrett, please wake up." There it was again, that soft, pillowy voice calling out to him.

He opened his eyes once again and became aware that he was lying in a bed. There was a humming noise coming from machines. A beeping sound. An antiseptic smell. Was he in the hospital?

As everything came into focus, he made out the woman at his side. She was holding his hand and smiling down at him. He didn't mind at all, because he knew her. A name popped into his head. "Egypt?" His voice sounded scratchy.

She smiled broadly back at him, and was that a tear trailing down her cheek? She spoke to someone, and that's when he realized they weren't alone in the room. Glancing around, he noticed a couple of other people. A blond man in light blue scrubs and a brunette woman in dark blue scrubs with brown eyes and a gentle demeanor.

"Garrett, I'm Dr. Burke. We're happy to see you awake" He heard the relief in the doctor's voice as he spoke. "You recognize this woman?"

He returned his attention to Egypt, who had slipped her hand out of his grasp. For some reason, he felt bereft and returned his attention to her. He couldn't tear his gaze away. Long, dark ebony hair. Round face. Deep-set chocolate-brown eyes. Wide, sensuous lips. She was wearing a pink velour track suit that was unzipped enough for him to see her full breasts wanting to break free from the camisole she wore.

"Yes. We met when I came to her restaurant the other day," he replied. "I asked her out."

He noticed the doctor frown, and Garrett felt a sense of fear for the first time. He looked at the man. "What's happened to me?" he croaked. "Why am I in the hospital?" He glanced at Egypt standing by his bed. "I can't even remember my name, my family or how I got here."

Suddenly the machines at his bedside began beeping in earnest, because his heart rate was increasing.

Dr. Burke came forward. "Please don't get agitated, Garrett. It's going to be okay."

"How can it be?" he asked, looking back and forth between the physician and Egypt. "I don't know how I got here."

"You're here because you were the victim of a carjacking two months ago."

"I've lost two months of my life!" he yelled and tried to pull himself upright on the bed. But it was impossible. It felt as if an elephant was sitting on his chest.

The doctor inclined his head to the nurse, and before Garrett knew it, she was inserting something into his IV. Fear took over him. "What is that?"

"It's a sedative to help you calm down." the nurse murmured softly. "I know now that you're waking up after all this time, everything is very disconcerting, but we are here to help."

Garrett sighed. "Fine. Then finish telling me what happened." His voice was authoritative and commanding, and the doctor responded in kind.

"The perpetrators beat you pretty badly, causing a brain injury. You've been in a coma as your body healed from the trauma. Today is a huge turning point for your recovery."

He snorted. "That's debatable."

"Why don't you rest now and we'll come back and check on you."

Garrett wanted to keep his eyes open, but the drugs were starting to take effect. Slowly, he drifted off into that peaceful world again. He hoped when he woke up, Egypt would be here again.

"Is it normal for him to not remember who he is?" Egypt inquired of the doctor after they stepped into the corridor.

"It's common with patients with a traumatic brain injury to be confused or disoriented."

That didn't really answer her question. "I don't get it. He doesn't remember his last name, but I'm familiar to him. He didn't mind me holding his hand, either."

Dr. Burke nodded. "Sometimes patients can remember short-term and not long-term memories. You were one of the last people Garrett saw before the attack, correct?"

Egypt nodded.

"That could be it. In the meantime, now that he's awake, we'll run a battery of tests to ensure there are no underlying issues causing his amnesia. You should go home and get some rest. The nurses told me you've been here keeping vigil at his bedside."

Seconds later, the doctor was striding down the hall and leaving Egypt to stare after him. She needed coffee and headed to the cafeteria. Since Garrett's carjacking, Egypt had become very familiar with the hospital's food and beverage selections, much to her consternation. They held very little flavor, and she could only guess the food was there for nutritional purposes only.

Egypt thought back to the moment when Garrett opened his eyes. The first emotion she felt was joy at finally seeing him make progress after all this time. But then she'd been hit over the head herself when he couldn't remember who he was.

Amnesia. What on earth was she supposed to do with that? Despite her busy schedule, she came to the hospital every day to check on Garrett, because they hadn't found his family. He was essentially all alone in the world. She felt bad that he had no one to depend on. The police hadn't made any headway with the case. They hadn't found his attackers, his vehicle or any clues to Garrett's identity.

It was horrible situation. Egypt felt the least she could do was visit him. Everyone thought she was crazy, but she felt like it was her duty. The incident happened in the parking lot of *her* place of business.

In the back of her mind, did she have some misconceived notion of what might happen when he awoke? Maybe she did. When she stared into his eyes after he regained consciousness, they'd been dark, almost black, like the forest at night, and it had made her heart squeeze. She could only blame her romantic notions on Wynter. Her best friend was so in love and giddy with happiness, it was infectious. Perhaps, despite what had happened with her traitorous ex, it had rubbed off on her.

When she returned a half hour later, one of the nurses called and stopped her. "Ms. Cox? Garrett is asking for you."

Egypt walked back to his hospital room but paused before going inside. She didn't know what to expect, but she wasn't going to find the answers out here. Turning the knob, she walked inside.

The bed had been placed in the upright position, but Garrett's eyes were closed. She was about to leave when he said her name. "Egypt."

Startled, she spun around and found those dark-coal eyes of his were on her once again. "I'm surprised you remembered me at all. We only met once."

His mouth curved slightly into a smile, and he motioned her forward. "You're unforgettable."

His words made her move forward, closer to him. Garrett reached out and took her hand in his. The heat of his palm rocketed through her, and Egypt looked down at their joined fingers. She had to force herself to breathe. When she lifted her gaze to meet his, her breath caught, because his dark eyes blazed with heat.

Egypt remembered how she'd felt the first time she found him watching her. How aware of herself she'd felt. Her breasts tingled, and a shivery sensation trickled down the length of her spine and lower, to the place between her legs. She felt hot. Just like she had then. She tried to remove her hand from his grasp, but Garrett held her in place. She found his strength surprising considering his stay in the hospital.

"Don't go," he rasped. "I'd like to talk to you. If I let you go, will you stay?"

She nodded, and he released his grip on her hand. Egypt wanted to touch her hand to her face to see if she was feverish, but the action might be a dead giveaway of the effect he had on her.

"Thank you."

"For what?" Egypt sat in the chair by his bed.

"For staying," Garrett responded. "The nurse told me you've been coming every day to visit."

She could strangle that nurse—she would have taken that info to her grave. "Visiting you is what any good person would do after you were injured at their place of business," she said with a smile.

His mouth quirked. "I highly doubt that. It shows me your character and that I can trust you—though…" His voice trailed off.

Crestfallen, her smile quickly faded. "Finish your sentence."

"I already knew I could trust you." Garrett's brow furrowed. "I don't know how, but my instincts have never let me down. I'm told that I have amnesia, yet I know I'm someone who is confident in my abilities to sense bullshit."

Egypt laughed. "This is the Garrett I remembered meeting. Suave. Confident. Assured."

"And that was attractive to you?"

Egypt tried not to blush, but she'd walked right into that. "Yes, it was."

"I came to your restaurant," Garrett said, more as a statement than a question. "And asked you out."

"So, you do remember something?"

"Only that you turned me down at first," Garrett responded, sitting up a bit straighter on the bed, "but I stayed until the place closed, and you agreed to go out with me."

"Your short-term memory is pretty good."

"But not my long-term," Garrett responded with a sigh. "And I don't get that. Why can't I remember my family? Was my life so terrible that I want to escape them?"

"I wish I knew," Egypt replied. "We didn't get to talk much that night."

His brows furrowed in consternation. "Yet, here you are. A woman I met only once, but who hasn't left my side. I find that curious as well as absolutely charming."

"It is my goal to charm you, Garrett." She flashed a smile. "Seriously, though, I'm here because it's the right thing to do. You were hurt at my restaurant." Egypt touched her chest. "I feel guilty."

"Why?"

"I should have done more," she insisted. "Had better cameras. Or security or something."

"It is not your fault I was carjacked."

She shrugged.

"Repeat after me. 'It's not my fault,'" he ordered.

Egypt didn't like being told what to do. Had never liked it, in school or when she'd been a sous-chef. But for some reason, she didn't mind hearing Garrett order her around. "It's not my fault," she parroted back.

He grinned, and damn if it didn't make Egypt's heart start palpitating in her chest. What was it about this man that made her giddy? Perhaps it was his wide chest and broad shoulders, which even after a month in the hospital were evident in the hospital gown he wore. He was probably naked underneath, and Egypt could only imagine how chiseled his body must be.

"Egypt." Hearing Garrett call her name made her snap out of her wayward daydreaming.

"Yes?"

"I can't remember the rest of the night," he said. "What happened *after* you agreed to go out with me?"

She rose from her chair to give herself something to do, something to focus on other than his smoking-hot physique. "We chatted a few more minutes, and then I had to close up. I put my number in your phone, and you agreed to call me for a date. I was taking out the trash when I heard a commotion in the parking lot and saw two thugs attacking you."

His expression was taut. "Go on."

"You seemed to be holding your own. When I came out, it distracted you, long enough for them to get the jump on you. One of them hit you with a bat, and then the other kept kicking you and kicking you. After that…"

Garrett patted the seat on his bed. Egypt knew it was a bad idea, but she came toward him anyway and sat down. She hung her head low, and she wasn't the least bit shocked that Garrett reached for her hand again, as if to calm her, so she went on with her story. "I didn't have my phone with me and yelled for Quentin, my sous-chef, to call the police. I saw them take your wallet and phone, hop in the car and drive off. That's when I rushed to your side. Your head was bleeding. I kept pressure on it with my chef coat until the ambulance arrived. My security cameras didn't get a good shot of your license plate so they weren't able to trace the car."

"I may not remember much, but I know this. You're one in

a million, Egypt Cox. Has anyone ever told you that?" Garrett asked hoarsely. He was still holding her hand and looking intently into her eyes. Egypt's pulse quickened.

Her reaction to Garrett was unlike anything she'd had with other men. Although she'd been in love with Antwan, she'd never felt hyper aware of him or this dizzying awareness. She was determined not to be the one to look away first, but that was hard to do with the jolt of electricity which shot back and forth between them. For some crazy reason, she wanted Garrett to kiss her. If a man didn't know how to kiss, it was usually over for her right then. It told Egypt exactly what she was working with in the bedroom department.

Garrett's other hand reached out and caught a lock of her hair. He wound it around his finger and in doing so brought Egypt closer toward him. The air was thick and full of something real and palpable. *Alive.* Egypt went very still, bracing for impact. He might have kissed her, but she would never know, because a loud cough sounded behind them.

"Excuse me." Detective Simpson was standing in the doorway. "I hope I'm not interrupting."

"Uh, no, no, you didn't!" Egypt quickly broke contact, and Garrett released her lock of hair. "Garrett, this is Detective Simpson. He can probably tell you more about that night."

When she hazarded a glance in his direction, his dark eyes were still on her. She quickly rushed out of the hospital room while she still could. Otherwise, her fantasy about kissing Garrett might indeed come true, and she was already in too deep where he was concerned. If she continued down this path, those feelings she never wanted to feel after Antwan hurt her and destroyed her trust and faith in men might not only resurface but become stronger and stronger—if they hadn't already.

Four

Garrett was angry at the interruption. He'd come very close to finally tasting Egypt. He remembered wanting to very much the first night they met. And moments ago, that lush mouth of hers had been coming toward him and those huge eyes were begging him to kiss her. He wanted to, but then the cop came in and ruined everything. He scowled at the man.

"I'm sorry to interrupt," Detective Simpson repeated, sensing Garrett's mood. "When the doctor called and said you were awake after two months in a coma, I had to come over. See if you remembered anything."

"I'm afraid not, Detective…"

"Simpson."

Garrett nodded. "When I woke up, I didn't even know who I was or how I got here."

"Has that changed?"

"No."

"But you—" The detective began to speak, but then stopped himself.

"But I know Egypt?" Garrett responded, looking at the officer. "I can't explain that. For some reason, I remember going to her restaurant and asking her out."

"And nothing else?" Detective Simpson inquired. "Because despite our best efforts, we haven't been able to find your attackers, and your car seems to have disappeared. It hasn't shown up at any known chop shops."

"What about my family?" Garrett was frustrated not only with the police, but that his own mind wasn't cooperating. Surely someone had to be looking for him?

"No one has reported you missing. We have no clue as to your real identity, Garrett. We only know your first name because of Ms. Cox. I was hoping when you woke up, you could give us information about the car and we could finally get a lead in this case."

"I'm sorry, I have nothing for you."

"If you remember anything—" The detective pulled a card out of his wallet. "Please give me a call."

The door to his room opened, and hospital staff came in. "I'm sorry, but we're going to have to borrow the patient for some tests and scans."

As quickly as he arrived, the detective was gone and Garrett was wheeled out of the room. His entire life was upended, and he had no clear direction of what was going to happen next. Intuitively, he knew that was unusual, because he always had a plan. His life was mapped out and had a purpose.

But what that was remained a mystery.

The only thing Garrett was certain of was that he wanted to see Egypt again, spend time with her. He may not remember the rest of his life, but she was the one thing that made sense. He prayed she hadn't been scared off by the intensity of his attraction toward her. *And* that she would visit him again.

"So let me get this straight," Asia Reynolds said from the other end of the line when Egypt made it home hours later after running errands. Since Flame was closed on Mondays, she had the remainder of the afternoon free. "You've been going to the hospital for months to sit by a stranger's bedside, all because he asked you out on a date? Are you really that hard up?"

Trust Asia to be blunt. Sometimes her best friend could show a lack of tact. Egypt had tried calling Wynter and Lyric to discuss the feelings Garrett evoked at the hospital, but neither of them picked up. Shay was about to start a cycling class and told Egypt she'd call her back. And Teagan was a workaholic, so Egypt didn't dare bother her. Asia had been her only option.

"Don't make it sound as if I'm some desperate seeking Susan," Egypt replied archly. "The man was attacked at my restaurant."

"In your parking lot."

"Same thing," Egypt responded. "Besides, he has no one. When he woke up today, he had no idea who he was. Can you imagine how that must feel?"

"*You* sure can," Asia replied. "Sounds to me like you have a thing for your amnesiac."

"Not a thing, but there is something about him that's intriguing."

"Do you really have the time to be chasing after some man who don't even know who he is? You're building a new restaurant. All your energies should be focused on Flame."

"Don't you think I know that?" Egypt responded tightly.

"Of course, he could be some billionaire who could make all your dreams come true," Asia responded aloud. "Or he could be a schmuck looking for a handout and you're falling prey to his charms."

Egypt remembered the night they'd met. Garrett had dressed like a man who had money, and he'd worn a Rolex, which the thieves had stolen. "Thanks for the vote of confidence, Asia."

"I'm sorry, but I haven't seen you get this soft on a man since Antwan."

"I don't want to talk about him." Egypt rolled her eyes at hearing her ex-boyfriend's name. The man who used her, stole all her money and broke her heart. She'd vowed to never believe a word that came out of another man's mouth, and she hadn't until now. Until Garrett. Was she deluding herself that the situation with Garrett was any different? Or was he just another con man like Antwan?

Asia scoffed. "Don't do that, Egypt. Every time we bring him up, you shut down. You have to let out all the anger and resentment you have bottled up inside about that man and what he did to you. Otherwise, it'll eat you up inside and you won't have anything left for when a good man comes along." She sighed. "And who knows, maybe Garrett No-Name is it and maybe he's not, but you can't close yourself off to love."

"I'm not closed off. I love the Gems."

"Uh, we love you, too, but it's not the same and you damn well know it. But listen, I'm going to get off my soapbox and stop preaching. If anyone knows how to look after herself, it's Egypt Cox. Hell, all the Gems could take pointers off a badass boss babe like you."

Egypt couldn't resist the grin creeping across her face. Asia always had a way of making her laugh. "Thanks, chick. We'll talk soon." She ended the call and stared at the phone.

Usually, she checked in with the hospital on Garrett's condition, but he was awake now. He could look after himself; he didn't need her. So, why were her fingers itching to pick up her cell?

Instead, she phoned her father and invited him to dinner. It was her one day off, and she missed hanging with him. Anthony Cox was the one man she'd always been able to count on.

Without hesitation, her finger hit the speed-dial button. Her father answered almost instantly. "Hey, baby girl. How are you?"

"I'm doing good," Egypt replied.

"Hmm…sounds like there's something more on your mind?" Her father always sensed when she wanted to talk.

"If you're free after work, I could make you dinner."

Anthony chuckled. "It's your only day off. I would think you wouldn't want to have anything to do with a kitchen."

"Cooking for my family is not a chore," Egypt responded. "Plus, I gotta eat, too."

"If you're sure?"

"Absolutely. I'll see you around seven?" She ended the call and thought about what comfort dish she would make for her father. He always loved her smothered pork chops in gravy with homemade mashed potatoes and sautéed green beans.

Cooking would keep her mind off Garrett No-Name. She had so much work to do anyway, like getting the specials ready for the next week, ordering supplies, reviewing scheduling and payroll, and making sure the HVAC was serviced. Egypt had checklists upon checklists to ensure Flame operated seamlessly.

It was hard work being owner *and* head chef. She needed to hire a manager to handle the day-to-day tasks so she could focus on the food and the branding. Unfortunately, she wasn't quite ready to hand off her baby to just anyone. It would take time to find the right person, and time was not always on her side.

She finished the menu and employee scheduling before putting work aside to make dinner. The pork chops were fried, the mashed potatoes were warming and the greens beans were finished when her father rang the doorbell.

Egypt wiped her hands on her apron and opened the door. "Daddy!"

At six foot five and over two hundred pounds, Anthony Cox was a big man, but that didn't stop him from wrapping his strong arms around her.

"Baby girl, I brought you some wine." He released her and held up a bottle of red.

"Thanks, Daddy." She accepted the bottle and brought it over to the kitchen. After uncorking it, she grabbed two wineglasses from her rack and poured them both a drink. "Cheers." They clinked glasses, and Egypt took a sip before checking on the pork chops. Her father came behind her and leaned over her shoulder.

"My favorite."

Closing the lid, Egypt regarded him. "I know. I don't get

to cook comfort food like this at the restaurant. It's always *elevated* Southern cuisine."

"But delicious," her father insisted.

"Thanks, but I have to constantly evolve," Egypt said, taking plates, cutlery and glasses from the cupboard.

"Did you think it would be easy?" he inquired, taking a seat at the small table in the nook next to her kitchen. "You're running your own business. All by yourself. It's takes grit and determination, which you have in spades, but enough about work. I'm curious about the young man you've been visiting in the hospital."

"You mean Garrett?" She set out the plates and began heaping on pork chops, mashed potatoes and green beans.

"Are there any other men who were hit over the head in your parking lot?"

Egypt couldn't resist laughing out loud. "No, Daddy. As for Garrett, he's awake now." She set his plate in front of him and then made one for herself.

"Really? And...?"

"He has amnesia," Egypt replied, sitting across from him at the table. "Doesn't remember who he is or what happened to him."

"Well, that's a doggone shame," her father replied, cutting into the juicy meat. "Were the police any help?"

She shook her head. "Nope. He has no name, no family—what is he supposed to do? Where is he supposed to live?" She scooped up some mashed potatoes and began eating.

"You're awfully concerned for a bystander," her father observed.

She put her fork down. "I can't be concerned?"

"Concerned, yes," Anthony replied, cutting another piece of the chop, "but you've visited him every day."

Glancing around for her wineglass, Egypt saw it on the counter and moved to grab it. She needed to do something to avoid being in the hot seat. She hated her father's interrogations; she could never keep anything from him. "I suppose it might be overkill, but I feel guilty for what happened and I was hoping for a better outcome when he woke up."

"What else were you *hoping* for?"

Her eyes narrowed. "Daddy!"

"Don't *Daddy* me. I call a spade a spade. And I know when my daughter is giving me a load of hogwash. You're interested in this young man." He resumed eating.

As she watched him enjoy the meal, Egypt thought about lying, but she couldn't. "I am attracted to him. I knew it the first time we met, which is why I agreed to the date, but then he was attacked. I guess now I'll always wonder what could have been."

"Do you think it's possible to create that same magic?"

Egypt thought about the moment in the hospital when Garrett circled a lock of her hair around his finger and brought her closer to him. Recalled the hot wave of desire he'd aroused in her. She was certain he'd been about to kiss her if Detective Simpson hadn't come in. "Possibly."

"Then perhaps you should take some of these leftovers over to a recovering man," her father suggested. "You always make enough to feed an army."

Egypt grinned. She didn't know how to cook in small quantities. Never had. "That's not a bad idea. I don't want any of the food to go to waste."

"Excellent. So…how are the Six Gems?"

Egypt filled her father in on the latest goings on with Wynter, Shay, Asia, Lyric and Teagan, but her mind wasn't never far away from Garrett and wondering how he was faring. Was everyone right? Did she have it bad?

Five

"We've run a battery of tests, Garrett," Dr. Burke told him midmorning the following day. "There's no obvious injury to your brain. We believe your memory loss stems from the trauma you sustained. Amnesia is sometimes your brain's way of protecting itself from upsetting events, which could explain why you remember meeting Ms. Cox but nothing else before or after."

"What am I supposed to do?" Garrett gritted out in frustration. He'd been up for hours after getting very little sleep with the nurses coming in every couple of hours to check vitals and give him medication for splitting headaches. This morning, he abandoned any idea of rest and insisted the nurses get him up so he could shower and walk.

As soon as he'd tried standing after a month in bed, his legs had given out like new fawn's. He stumbled and needed the nurse to keep him upright. Eventually, he managed the shower and to walk the hall once. He was determined to do more. He couldn't, *wouldn't* stay in bed forever. It wasn't his nature. He was used to being active—that much he knew.

"Your memory may come back in small pieces, or it could happen at one time—no one really knows."

"Meaning, it may not come back at all?"

The doctor's brow furrowed. "Yes, that's a possibility as well. In the interim, we need to keep you for a bit so we can monitor you closely."

"I need to get out of here, Doc. I'm already going stir-crazy."

"Where are you going to go?" the doctor inquired.

He hadn't exactly figured that part out yet. Then something occurred to him. "What about the hospital bill?"

"We will have to figure that out once you're well. For now, rest and I'll check on you tomorrow, Garrett." The doctor and the group of interns behind him swiftly exited, leaving him alone.

Garrett.

The name was familiar, but that was the least of his worries. He could only imagine how hefty a sum a month's stay in the hospital would cost. But why didn't that worry him? It should, because he didn't have a wallet or any money. This morning, however, he remembered another bit of his memory.

He'd been going to a farm.

Picking up the phone beside him, he dialed a number that came easily to him. A masculine voice answered on the other end. "Hello"

"Garrett?"

"You know me?"

"Of course, I do. I was expecting you a month ago, but you never showed up" Kent said from the other end of the phone. "I thought maybe you decided to shut us down after all."

"Shut you down?" Garrett asked perplexed. He had no idea what the man was talking about. "I was the victim of a car-jacking and have been laid up in the hospital in a coma for the last month. So I have no idea who you are. I just dialed the first number that I could remember."

"Holy crap!"

"Tell me about it. When I woke up, I couldn't remember who I was. All I can remember is a few details here and there. I remember…" Garrett grasped for words, and then it came to him. "Walker Farms. Was I on my way there?"

"Yes, you were," Kent replied. "And I'm sorry this happened to you. I'm Kent Howell, the foreman at your grandfather's farm. I had no idea you'd been injured or I would have come sooner."

"That's because my attackers stole my wallet along with my car. The police had no idea who I was and weren't able to contact my family. Can you?"

There was silence on the other end of the line, and Garrett felt uneasy. "Kent, are you still there?"

"Yes, of course. I'm so sorry. Where are you? I can be there in an hour."

"What about my family?"

"Let's talk about that when I get there," Kent replied, and then he ended the call.

Garrett glanced down at the receiver in his hand. He was used to being in control of every situation. Somehow, he knew that was innate to his character. He was angry that Kent had rushed off the phone. Why couldn't he tell him about his family? What in the hell was going on?

Knock. Knock.

Garrett rolled his eyes upward. "For Chrissake, can I get a moment of peace!"

Then the door opened, and he saw Egypt holding a Styrofoam box in her hand. She was wearing black slacks and her black chef's coat. Her luminous hair was in a loose updo atop her beautiful head.

"I—I'm sorry to have bothered you," Egypt stammered. "I thought you might be tired of hospital food and would like a home-cooked meal." She moved forward and put the box on the rollout table and began backing out of the room.

"Egypt, wait!" Garrett said, sitting upright. "I'm sorry. That wasn't aimed at you. I thought you were one of the nurses that keep poking and prodding me every hour on the hour. It's driving me crazy."

She cocked her head to one side. "Has anyone told you that you make a horrible patient?"

He laughed. "Has a familiar ring to it." He motioned toward the chair beside him. "Please forgive my rudeness. I would love some *real* food, especially if it was cooked with your hands."

That brought a smile to her caramel complexion, and desire squeezed Garrett like a vise. He liked this woman. A lot. He wanted to get to know her, but what did he have to offer her?

Egypt rolled the table forward toward his bed and opened the Styrofoam container. Then she pulled out a roll of linen from her purse, which he assumed held silverware, and handed it to him. "I warmed the food at the nurses' station, so be nice to them, okay? They're only doing their job."

Dutifully chastened, he took the offering. "Thank you." Once he uncovered a fork and knife, Garrett immediately started in on the mashed potatoes. He attacked the meal with gusto. He cut a tender piece of pork, and when it met his mouth, he groaned with pleasure.

When he glanced up, Egypt was watching him. "Good?"

"You have no idea," Garrett said, taking another bite. "The food they serve you in the hospital is abysmal."

"I figured as much," she stated. "I can't stay long. I have to get to Flame and get ready for the day's service."

Garrett put down his silverware. "I appreciate you thought of me at all. I know you're a busy woman, but if you can stay with me until I finish, that would be great."

"I am busy, but I can take time to help those in need."

He didn't like the sound of that. The last thing he wanted was her pity. He wasn't invalid and in need of care. He was getting stronger every day. Garrett wanted Egypt to want him as much as he wanted her. Last night, he'd dream of her lush curves against his body and he'd awoke aroused. "Is that all I am to you, a charity case?"

"Not at all," Egypt responded quickly, "and I'm sorry if it sounded like that. I… I honestly have no idea what you are to me, Garrett. I only know that I felt compelled to come and see you."

A broad smile spread across his lips. "I like your honesty."

Her pause before answering told Garrett everything he needed to know. Egypt Cox was interested in him even though he was a man without a name, without an identity. "I know I may seem like an invalid sitting in this bed, but these won't always be my circumstances. I work on a farm, and the foreman is coming today and should be able to help me figure out my past."

She leaned in as if she wasn't scared of his words. "And what happens when your circumstances change?"

"I want that date you promised me."

Egypt offered her hand. "It's a deal."

What he really wanted was to press his lips against hers and find out if she tasted as sweet as she looked. Heat shifted inside him at the thought of tasting Egypt, making his body harden with desire, but now was not the time. Instead, Garrett accepted her handshake, but in the back of his mind, he vowed that one day he would make that kiss a reality.

"So how is the patient?" Quentin asked when Egypt made it to Flame. He'd already arrived and started prepping for dinner service. The mise en place was done, the meats were butchered and portioned, and the salads were already plated.

"Quentin, oh my goodness," Egypt said as she wrapped her apron around her black chef's coat, "you've been busy."

"I finished my errands early and figured I'd get a head start on the day," Quentin told her as he worked on dessert.

"I appreciate it. I'm sorry I'm late," Egypt said. It had become a habit for her to visit Garrett on her way into Flame. Usually, she only hung around for a few minutes, but today she'd lingered longer than she intended. Her goal had been to drop the meal off and go, but Garrett had asked her to stay, and she couldn't refuse a man in a hospital bed, could she?

"No problem, but you never answered my question," Quentin responded, "about Garrett. How's he doing?"

"Better," Egypt replied, starting on the broth base for one of her soups. "He woke up, but he can't remember much."

"But he remembers you?" Quentin's mouth quirked.

She turned and glanced in his direction. "I am unforgetta-ble." She quoted Garrett's words.

"You wish," Quentin laughed and added chocolate sauce to the dessert plates. "No luck with his family?"

Egypt shook her head. "He knows he owns a farm. The fore-man is coming to the hospital. Garrett is hoping to get more information from him."

"That's great. Once he's on his feet, I'll get you back."

"I've been here," she reminded him.

"Can I be honest?"

"Please." She'd always believed in open communication with her employees, especially her sous-chef. They were a team. Egypt hadn't had that in her previous restaurant position. With Chef Rafael, it was his way or the highway. She'd chosen the latter. It's not that she couldn't take direction, but she'd always been headstrong.

Quentin put down his pastry bag. "You've been here physi-cally, but not in spirit. I feel like we've only gotten fifty per-cent of you."

"I'm sorry if I've been distracted the last couple of months." She, or rather Flame, couldn't afford her being off her game. "I promise I'm going to give the one hundred percent I expect from everyone else."

Quentin smiled, "That's all I ask, Chef."

Egypt would have to find a way to balance her work life and her personal one, because the thought of not seeing Garrett or visiting him made her feel uneasy. She didn't understand why she'd become connected to him in a short time, but she had, and that was worrisome. She didn't want to lose herself in an-other man as she had with Antwan. She'd been so committed to him; she hadn't seen his deception until it was too late and he'd betrayed her. Flame needed her focus and attention not some sexy stranger with no memory of his past.

"You're doing great, Garrett," the physical therapist stated when Garrett completed several sets of fifteen on the hand weights later that afternoon. They'd already done a series of leg exercises and stretches to help his mobility and movement.

"I can do more," Garrett stated.

"You probably can, but you've been in bed for over two months. Your muscles are weak. I don't want you overexerting yourself."

"I can do it."

The therapist smiled. "I recognize a big, strong man like you isn't used to depending on others, but that's all part of your recovery. We'll stop for now, and I'll be back tomorrow and we'll go a little further. Sound good?"

Garrett nodded. "That's fine." He was annoyed. He was ready to get out of the hospital. Kent was coming by today, and maybe he would finally get the answers he desperately needed to help him figure out who he was.

The therapist had packed up his equipment and was leaving the room when a blond man wearing a jacket, jeans, a plaid shirt and baseball cap with the Walker Farms logo walked into the room.

"Kent?" Garrett asked.

"Yes, it's me," Kent said, walking forward. "How are you, man?" He gave Garrett a one-armed hug, which he returned more out of politeness than any real memory of the man. His face was familiar, but were they friends? If so, why had Kent been so short over the phone?

"How do you think I am?" Garrett snapped when they pulled apart. "When I woke up, I had no idea who I was or what happened to me. Then I learn I've been in the hospital for over a month in a coma." He sat down on the bed while Kent sat across from him.

"I'm sorry. I had no idea."

Garrett's brow furrowed and his eyes narrowed as he looked at the man. "You've got to help me out here, Kent, because I'm confused. I was supposed to arrive months ago and didn't. That wasn't the least bit suspicious to you? And what about my family and friends? No one was looking for me?"

Kent stared down at his hands, and when he looked up, his dark brown eyes were cloudy and Garrett couldn't read him. "I'm sorry to be the one to have to tell you this, but you're an orphan, Garrett. Your grandfather Cyrus Walker has been looking after you since you were a teenager."

"An *orphan*?" The news settled on Garrett like a shroud. He didn't know what he'd been expecting, but it hadn't been that. The notion didn't sit well with him. "And my grandfather... why isn't he here?"

Kent lowered his head and this time when he glanced up, tears were in his eyes. "Cyrus passed away a couple of months ago."

"He's gone, too?" Saying the words, Garrett's throat got choked and a feeling of sadness washed over him. He might not remember his family, but in some place deep inside his psyche, Garrett knew he'd lost someone special.

"I'm afraid so," Kent replied quietly. "You weren't living here in town. You were super smart and went to Harvard and later Wharton so you could help with the farm one day. You've been up north this entire time."

"Up north where?"

"Pennsylvania."

"Then why was I in Raleigh?"

"It's the nearest airport to the farm," Kent answered. "The farm hasn't been doing well. You were going to decide whether you wanted to shut us down after Cyrus passed away. When I didn't hear from you, I assumed you'd chosen not to come and were going to sell."

"Wouldn't I have called?" Garrett inquired.

Kent shrugged. "I assumed you couldn't face me. We've never been close. At least we haven't been since you went off to college. We used to work together at the farm back in the day when we were teenagers. But once you went up north, we lost touch. Different worlds and all."

Garrett nodded as he stared at Kent. This man was literally his only lifeline to his existence outside this room. "This is a lot to absorb."

"I know," Kent replied. "It's why I wanted to tell you in person. I couldn't very well say all of this on the phone. Would have been pretty heartless."

"So, my name is Garrett Walker," Garrett stated, more for himself than for Kent. He was trying to wrap his head around it, but it didn't feel right. It felt like something was missing, but he couldn't put his finger on what it was. The doctor had told him his memory might come back in bits and pieces. Garrett sure wished it would hurry the hell up, because he was ready to get his life back. "Hopefully, the police can help me fill in the missing parts and get me an ID. In the meantime, how is the farm doing? Without my grandfather and me being MIA, a lot must have been on your shoulders."

Kent nodded. "Yes, it has, but I'm used to it. Cyrus was getting on in years and gave me more responsibility, including access to the bank accounts. I've been able to make payroll, pay the bills and such."

Garrett wasn't sure how he felt about that. You could never take your eye off the ball. Once he got out of here, he would see exactly how Kent was running things. The farm was the only thing he had left of his family. Garrett would ensure its success, if for no other reason than to honor Cyrus Walker, the man who raised him. "Thank you, Kent. I appreciate you coming. One more thing. Am I married? Or seeing anyone?" He had to know if he would compromise Egypt by getting involved.

Kent shook his head. "No, you're not married. As for seeing anyone, I don't think so. Your grandfather always said you were married to your work."

Garrett raked a hand through his hair. "That's good to know. Thanks."

"How long are you going to be in here?"

"I dunno. Maybe a week. They want to be sure there are no underlying issues before they release me. When I get out, I'll want to go directly to the farm. My grandfather had a house?"

Kent nodded. "Yes. I was able to pay the mortgage this month with some reserves, but funds are getting tight."

"I see." The farm was in trouble. Was that why Kent was afraid he'd sell? "Would you be able to get all the farm's financial records together so I can review them when I get there?" Garrett paused. An odd sense of déjà vu came over him, and he glanced in Kent's direction. The man looked as white as a ghost. "Did I ask you for the farm's records before?"

"You did. I have the last five years waiting for you."

"Great. Hopefully everything I learned at Wharton didn't disappear along with my memory."

Kent rose to his feet. "I've got to get back to the farm. Do you need anything?"

"I could use some clothes for when I get sprung, and maybe some toiletries, if you don't mind?"

"I'm on it," the other man replied, starting toward the door, but then Garrett remembered one more item.

"And a phone. It doesn't have to be fancy."

"All right. I'll take care of it. Will call you later."

Garrett watched as Kent closed the door behind him and then sank back on the bed as he tried to absorb everything the foreman had told him. There were so many things to unpack— like the fact he was an orphan. It seemed unreal that his mother and father were both gone. Garrett was having a hard time accepting it and that the grandfather who'd raised him was dead.

Garrett knew he loved Cyrus. He felt it from some place deep in his soul. It resonated with him that his grandfather had meant the world to him. They used to go fishing on the lake not far from the farm. Wow. There it was again. Bits and pieces of memory. The doctor had said they would come when he least expected them.

Garrett closed his eyes. He needed more. More of his memories. More of his family. He needed to remember the life he'd once had. A life that might include a full-figured beauty named Egypt Cox.

Six

Egypt was proud of herself. For the last week, she'd focused solely on Flame. She had the restaurant's HVAC equipment checked as part of her maintenance plan, ensured the restaurant's cleanliness, checked the food preparation and ensured proper handling, and completed her special menu for the next couple of weeks. And today, on her day off, the restaurant passed its health inspection with flying colors! All in all, Egypt felt quite accomplished, but something was off.

And she knew why.

She hadn't been to see Garrett since she dropped off lunch last week. She'd been uncharacteristically called out by her own sous-chef for being distracted. Egypt didn't get to have an off day, but that didn't mean she was made of stone. She'd gotten used to her daily visits to the hospital to see Garrett's sleeping form, but she refused to allow herself to backslide. She might be hopelessly attracted to him, but no man was worth risking Flame's reputation for spectacular cuisine and excellent service.

That hadn't stopped her from calling the nurse daily to check in. Garrett was recovering in leaps and bounds, eating up a storm and was a hit with all the female nurses. Was Egypt surprised? The man was absolutely sinful with his milk chocolate skin, dazzling white teeth and biceps that went on for days.

This morning, however, she'd been shocked when the nurse informed her Garrett was being released. The nurse couldn't give her an exact time, but she'd said it would be today. Once Garrett was gone, she would have no way of getting in touch with him. Tessa had told Egypt that Garrett called Flame a few nights ago, but she hadn't returned his call.

Why?

Because she hadn't mooned over a man since Antwan, and she wasn't about to start now. She had too much at stake. Egypt chalked up her interest in Garrett to his good looks and curiosity surrounding his real identity. It didn't matter anymore. It was best they go their separate ways. She was musing about what to do for the rest of the afternoon when Wynter rang.

"Diva, where have you been?" her friend asked.

"Hello to you, too," Egypt responded curtly.

"I left you a voice mail to call me back days ago. I wanted to know what you thought about the wedding menu. What gives?"

"I have some suggestions on how to improve the menu, and I'll email those over." Egypt pulled out one of the table chairs and sat down. "As for what gives… I've been really busy with Flame and getting things in order for a health inspection."

"You're always prepared. I'm sure you passed with flying colors."

"I haven't been lately," Egypt said, leaning back in the chair. "Quentin told me I've been distracted for the last month. When your sous-chef gives you the business and tells you to get back on track, there must be some truth to it."

"Ah, now I get it."

"Get what?"

"This is about Garrett," Wynter responded, "You think you've been spending too much time with him."

"I did. Or at least I was."

"Meaning what?" her friend prodded.

"That I haven't seen him in a week."

"Egypt!"

"Don't do that, Wynter." She was feeling guilty enough as it was. But she had to put aside the dizzying chemistry she'd felt with Garrett. She had to appear serene and undisturbed by her decision to give him the brush-off. "It might be easy for you to scoff, but I'm the sole proprietor of this establishment. It's my butt on the line if we fail, along with all the people I employ. They depend on me."

"I understand, Egypt, I do," Wynter replied. "I know the rest of the Six Gems weren't born with a silver spoon in their mouth like I was. I come from a rich family, and since Aunt Helaine left me her estate, I'm well-off. All I'm saying is you can have a life outside work. You like Garrett. What's wrong with exploring that dynamic?"

"Look what it did to me when he was unconscious and I was being a Good Samaritan. What on earth would I do with him when he's conscious?"

"Why don't you find out?" a deep voice said from behind her. Slowly she turned around and looked up into Garrett's face, his dark gaze reaching into her and holding her still. So still, the phone slipped from Egypt's fingers onto the floor.

She drank Garrett in. He was in a leather bomber jacket, dark-wash jeans, a black V-neck shirt and what appeared to be work boots. She noticed he hadn't shaved and sported a sexy five o'clock shadow, which accentuated his thick lips. Lord help her, Egypt wanted to groan out loud, but she could hear Wynter's voice.

"Hello? Hello?"

Startled out of her simmering stare, Egypt reached down and picked up the phone. "Hey, I'm here."

"Are you okay?" Wynter asked. "I heard a thud."

"That's because I dropped the phone when Garrett walked in." Heat shivered up her spine, and blood surged through her veins and made her knees feel weak.

"Garrett is there? At your restaurant? Oh my goodness!"

"In the flesh," Egypt responded. She didn't take her eyes off him, not even as he steadily approached her.

He reached for the phone. "Say goodbye."

Damn, she loved it when a man took charge. "Listen, Wynter, I'll have to call you back."

"Please do. I want all the details."

Egypt clicked to end the call, but rather than take a step back out of his dangerous orbit, she found herself moving closer to him. "You're out of the hospital." She stated the obvious.

He smiled, showing off those magnificent teeth she liked so much. "I had to get well quickly so I could come here and figure out why you haven't been by the hospital to visit me. Kent, the foreman of my grandfather's farm picked me up and is outside waiting. What happened, Egypt? I woke up and suddenly you're no longer interested?" There was a hint of bitterness in his voice.

She swallowed and looked down, but Garrett used his index finger to tip her chin up. "Well?"

Her heart skipped a beat, but she responded, "I've been busy. There's a lot to keep track of when you're the owner, manager and head chef all rolled into one."

His jaw tightened. "That's not the reason."

"What is?"

"You're scared of this," Garrett said, pointing back and forth between them, "but I'm not. I've had nothing but a week to think about what I would do to you when I got released."

Now Egypt was afraid, but not for her safety. She was afraid of the intense attraction she felt for this man, who was a stranger to her, but whom she couldn't seem to stop thinking of, *dreaming* of, even though she'd tried desperately.

She knew she was goading him when she asked, "And what might that be?" She was tired of pretending, tired of waiting for...the inevitable.

Tension was a tight coil inside Egypt's belly as she waited for Garrett's mouth to touch hers. She told herself his kiss would be like all the others, but when his mouth finally slanted across hers, it was a shock to her system. His lips claimed hers thoroughly, in a sensual exploration that intended to stir her awake, and he succeeded. A tingle shot through her, straight to her belly, and she kissed him back hungrily as she went up in a blaze of passion.

She didn't remember circling her arms tight around his neck, only that she did. Meanwhile, Garrett was sliding his fingers through her hair, angling her head so he could taste her better, and Egypt let him. A delicious madness was taking over. She wanted this more than her next breath. Garrett tasted like nothing she'd ever tasted before, and she took everything she could get. She wanted to rip his shirt from his body so she could feel *all* of him.

His chest was a wall of steel crushing her breasts. She arched closer, aching for more contact. He gave it to her by gripping her waist and bringing her flush against him. Egypt felt Garrett's arousal pressed against her lower belly, and a flood of heat rushed through her. One sinewy thigh slid between hers, and they began moving wildly together, creating friction and rippling sensation.

Egypt's sex clenched with need, and she made a low moan, which made Garrett retreat and step away from her. Both of their breathing was labored as they stared at each other. She'd suspected from the very first glance that kissing him would be this good, but the reality was much hotter. He made her body melt.

Garrett didn't know what came over him. He'd come to the restaurant to talk, to find out why Egypt had ghosted him. From all accounts he'd heard, she'd been at his bedside daily, but now that he was awake she was losing interest.

But as soon as he saw her again, the fire that raged between them came back full force and blazed right through him. All Garrett could do was let himself be consumed. He'd been lost in the moment—in pushing his tongue into her mouth, tasting her. He was desperate for her honeyed sweetness. He'd kissed her as if the entire world depended on this kiss. When she moaned and her body had grown pliant, electricity surged through him.

Garrett was certain if they had gone at it a few moments longer, he might have backed her up against the table, ripped off her jeans and plunged deep inside her. But her low moan made him realize he was losing control. They were in her place of business! Plus, he never lost control...that wasn't his usual modus operandi. He didn't know how he knew that. He just did. So he'd forced himself to pull away.

Now, he watched as Egypt touched her swollen lips with her fingertips. Was she as shocked as he was by the feverish passion that had overcome them both? "I guess we both needed that," he said softly.

She blinked and then lowered her hand. "Apparently."

"I didn't mean to come on so strong," Garrett stated thickly. "I really came because I wanted to see you again."

"You did?"

He nodded. He wasn't used to being this forthright about his feelings, but something told him Egypt appreciated his honesty. "I know we don't really know each other, but I feel there's an attraction, and I would like to explore it."

"I see." She moved away from him, and Garrett sensed it was her way of regaining her composure. He wondered what she was thinking. He wouldn't crowd her again. She needed to tell him what *she* wanted.

"I'm getting my life and identity sorted out," Garrett began. "The foreman is taking me back to the farm I now own after my grandfather passed away. Hopefully, it will help rekindle my memory. Despite the chaos my life might be, I would like to take you out on that date." When she started to speak, he interrupted her. "I know it might seem premature, but I can tell you that I'm single. I'm not married or seeing anyone."

"How can you know that for sure?"

"Kent worked closely with my grandfather and knew me. He would know if I'm married or not. As for a girlfriend, he didn't know of anyone."

Her lips pursed together. "True. But do you really want to go down this path when you're just figuring out your life?"

He walked toward her again, but not too close. "The one thing I am sure about is you, Egypt." That brought a rather large grin to her face, and it lit a fire in Garrett again. He wanted to see more of those smiles. Hell, he wanted to hear more of her moans. "Give me your phone?"

"Why?"

"Kent's bought me a new one, and I want to give you my number," Garrett responded. She handed him the device, and he punched in the digits. "Is Monday your only day off?"

"Yes. The weekends are my busiest days. I can leave Quentin on his own occasionally, with enough advance warning and prep work, but it would have to be a late dinner."

"I know you're busy at the restaurant. How about next Monday? You can drive to the farm and we can make dinner together. How does that sound?"

She nodded.

"Then it's a date." He handed her back the phone, then gave her a smile instead of the kiss he really wanted to plant on her luscious lips and forced himself to leave.

Garrett was afraid if he touched her again, he wouldn't be able to stop. He might not remember anything about his former life, but he recalled how he felt when he was with Egypt. He felt *alive*. He was fascinated by her feisty spirit and passionate nature. He couldn't wait to explore her further, but right now he had to find out who he was. Only then would he be a complete man for Egypt.

Seven

Everything looked the same, Garrett thought as they drove up to Walker Farms, but it didn't feel the same, because his grandfather Cyrus was missing. Garrett's heart sank as Kent drove past the crops toward the main house. Eventually, the truck stopped in front of a white board-and-batten house with a tin roof. There was an old barn beside it enclosed by a wire fence. Chickens were roaming around in the yard.

"We've got chickens?" Garrett inquired.

"Yeah, Cyrus loved raising them and getting fresh eggs."

Garrett exited the vehicle and climbed the wide brick steps until he came to two rocking chairs. Memories flooded his brain and Garrett's heart began palpitating in his chest. He remembered sitting in them, talking with his grandfather. A lump formed in the back of his throat. Garrett could feel himself feeling sentimental and quickly turned to Kent. "You have keys?"

"Sure thing." Kent opened the front door and handed him the key ring.

Garrett wasn't surprised to see hardwood floors, exposed beams and dark wood furniture throughout the farmhouse. When they came to the living room with its brick fireplace, he recalled sitting there with Kent. "We made s'mores here, didn't we?" Garrett asked, turning to the foreman, who had followed him inside.

Kent smiled. "Yeah, we did. We had to have been ten or eleven. I'm surprised you remember that."

Garrett nodded and went to the kitchen. He smiled when he saw the frilly curtains his grandmother had made. And the pencil marks on the wall showing his height over the years. The times he'd spent with his grandparents were good ones, but he didn't remember being here *all* the time.

"Anything else coming back?" Kent inquired.

Garrett glanced up. "I don't know. You said I lived here with my grandfather, but I don't know. It feels off."

Kent expression was tight with strain. "How so?"

Garrett shrugged. He couldn't put his finger on it, but it didn't ring true. "I'm trying to piece this all together, but its fragmented. There are chunks of my life that are a blur. I recall visiting as a child and teenager, and then poof—" he snapped his fingers "—there's nothing."

"That's odd."

"I know, right? For some reason, my mind won't go there."

"Why don't I show you up to one of the main rooms and you can get some rest?" Kent asked. "You're just out of the hospital. I stocked the fridge, and my wife, Aurora, made some sandwiches and soup. Tomorrow, I'll pick you up first thing in the morning and we can tour the farm. Sound good?"

"Sure."

Once the foreman had gone and Garrett was left alone, he walked every single bedroom, including the one his grandfather Cyrus had used, looking for something, *anything* to trigger his memory. When nothing was forthcoming, he picked one of the bedrooms and fell back on the bed, releasing a deep sigh. Not remembering his past was disconcerting, even more so because nothing here showed any indication of the man he used to be.

Surely if he'd resided at the farmhouse once upon a time, there might be some trace of him? There weren't any personal pictures or anything that made it feel as if the house had once been his home. Had Cyrus gotten rid of everything after he moved out?

Garrett's hackles were up. The doctor had said his memory loss could be temporary, and they might come back at one time. Perhaps a therapist could help him unlock the door on his mind so he could get back to his life, but how would he pay for them? He already had a hefty hospital bill to figure out.

What if his mind was retreating because he didn't like his former life? That was the scariest part of all.

"Asia, what a surprise," Egypt said when her friend arrived on her doorstep later that day. She hadn't expected the Gem. "Is everything okay?"

"All is well," Asia assured her. "I'm just passing through on my way to a jewelry show in DC and thought I'd stop in and visit for a few days. I figured you must need some company, since you've been hanging out in hospitals looking for a man."

Egypt laughed heartily. "Ouch. What's up with the shade?"

"Diva, you know you can take the heat, so let me in." The petite jewelry artist pushed her way into Egypt's apartment. At five foot two, Asia reached her chin, but she was a ball of fire. Her straight shoulder-length bob was flat-ironed as usual, and she wore stylish black spandex leggings, a long white button-down shirt and tiger-print booties.

"Egypt, your place needs a splash a color," Asia said, glancing around at the mostly blue and gray decor.

"Not all of us are artists like you."

Asia was not only skilled at making jewelry, but she was an excellent painter and could freestyle and come up with something amazing. Egypt, on the other hand, was skilled at creating masterpieces in the kitchen. "That just means I have to make you something."

"Sure you will." At times, Asia could be a bit flighty. She liked to go with the flow, whereas Egypt was a planner. When it came to cooking and baking, you needed precision. With the right technique and spices, a dish came together. "Did you come here to criticize me? Or are you here for another purpose?"

"Actually—" Asia sighed "—I was hoping you could help me with my business plan. It seems like you and Teagan already had your vision together for your businesses. Shay and Lyric are further along in opening their spots, but me..." Her voice trailed off. "I'm a hot mess, Egypt."

"Come and have a seat." Egypt motioned her friend over to the couch. "Tell me what's going on."

Asia shrugged. "I guess I assumed the money from Aunt Helaine would be enough, but I've come to realize it's a drop in the bucket if I want my own retail store."

Egypt nodded. "There's a lot of involved. It's not just the business plan. It's bank loans, leases, supplies and equipment, not to mention the accounting element and, my personal favorite, employees. Do you know how hard it is to find reliable help these days?"

Asia kicked off one boot and then the other before curling her legs underneath her. "Then how do you do it, Egypt? You made it all seem so easy. You had the restaurant up and running within six months of getting the inheritance."

Egypt leaned back on the couch. "Asia, I've wanted my own place for years. I started out as a line chef, then became a sous-chef. I watched Chef Rafael religiously, but I also talked to the restaurant manager. On my days off, I came in and shadowed him so I could learn accounting, payroll and scheduling. I think that's why Rafael got so upset. He thought I was trying to replace him, but I kept it all here." Egypt pointed to her temple. "Because I wanted to be my own boss one day and needed the tools to do it."

"I've been struggling with figuring out how to make my jewelry business viable. It's one thing to be a success at flea markets and my favorite jewelry store, but it's quite another to make a go of a retail location."

"You need to be working on your online presence, Asia, and get your own website. I've always told you that."

"I'm not good at that," Asia lamented. "I even tried dating one of those nerdy guys who love computers."

Egypt tried to smother a laugh but couldn't. Asia had no filter. "And how did that go?"

"He was really sweet guy, but he was total trash in the bedroom. He never got my engine purring, ya know?" She laughed. "But he did manage to get my website up."

"Show me."

Asia rose, walked over to her large handbag and pulled out her iPad. She swiped and typed several times before handing Egypt the tablet.

Egypt reviewed the site. "This is good, Asia. A really good start. How's it coming along?"

"It's good. Sales are strong, but it's a lot to keep up with."

Egypt rolled her eyes and glanced upward for strength. "Asia, darling, you're probably going to need to hire a web manager, preferably not one you're sleeping with. And I can help you work on your business plan, but you have to understand it won't be easy. Just because I was the first one out of the gate, don't let it fool you. Running your own business takes hard work, long hours and dedication."

"Has it really been that difficult?"

"Extraordinarily so," Egypt explained, "Much harder than I ever thought it would be. It didn't help that Garrett was carjacked in my parking lot. The press coverage of the attack hurt Flame. Revenues haven't been quite the same since. I've been trying to figure out a way to get the focus back on the food and not the area of town, but it's not easy."

"I'm sorry, Egypt, I had no idea. You've never mentioned it in the Six Gems' chats." They had a weekly FaceTime chat to catch up on what was going on in each other's lives.

"How can I?" she said. "Everyone is talking about starting their enterprises, and Wynter is planning an epic wedding. I don't want to spoil the fun about the realities of having your own business."

"Thank you for your honesty, Egypt." A smile spread across

Asia's face. "It's one of the things I've always admired about you. You give it to people straight, no chaser."

"I don't know any other way to be."

"Then you can tell me what's happening with you and Mr. No-Name."

Egypt chuckled. "His name is Garrett Walker, and he owns a farm outside Raleigh."

"Okay." Asia leaned back. "We have a last name and a job—that's a win in my book. What's next?"

"I'm going to his farm on Monday. We're going to make dinner together."

"And if it leads to more?" Asia raised an eyebrow.

Egypt thought about the mind-blowing kiss in her office earlier that day. She felt like an earthquake had erupted inside her and spread outward. "Possibly." She wasn't opposed to feeling that way again. If that kiss was any indication of how explosive being with Garrett could get, she was all for it.

Asia snapped her fingers several times. "That's my sex-positive girl. There ain't nothing wrong with a little bump and grind."

Egypt bowed her head and laughed. She'd missed the Six Gems. It was a shame they were all so far away, focusing on their own lives. She couldn't wait to see them at Wynter's bachelorette party in Vegas. Egypt and Teagan had a fun night planned. But what she was most looking forward to was her date with Garrett.

As if he'd read her mind, he called her later that night. "Garrett?" It was well after 10:00 p.m., and she was already in bed playing a game of Candy Crush on her phone. The sound of his rich, husky voice made her heart skip a beat.

"Yeah, I hope it's not too late."

Egypt pushed the pillows back so she could sit up. "No, I'm fine. I'm a night owl."

"Same here," Garrett replied, "It's strange how some things

I know with absolute clarity, but other times I struggle to remember the most basic things."

"Was it tough going to the farm?" Egypt inquired softly.

"Yes. I knew my grandfather Cyrus was gone, but it was quite another thing to be faced with the reality of walking into an empty farmhouse."

"Did it spark any memories?"

"Some. I remembered being a kid there and even as a teenager, but I don't know, Egypt. It doesn't fit that I actually lived here."

"How would you know?"

He chuckled. "Good question. I guess I…just know. For example, I may not remember our exact conversation when we met, but I knew I like you and want to see more of you."

Her heart was loud in her chest and her mouth suddenly felt dry. That was a great segue into their date. "So it seems, but are you sure you should be trying to dive headlong into…a dalliance when you have so much to remember."

"Dalliance?" He repeated the word as if he was mulling it over. "We're not going to have a dalliance, Egypt."

"Would you prefer an affair?" she asked, "Because I'm not opposed to hooking up, either. I find you attractive, you find me sexy—what's there to know?"

"I like your directness, but I think there's more between us than scratching an itch. I could be wrong—"

"But you don't think so." She finished his sentence. "Has anyone ever told you you're arrogant?"

"They have."

They were both quiet when he replied with such conviction, as if he knew it to be true.

"You soundly awfully sure of yourself."

"I am," Garrett responded. "You'll see. When all is said and done, you'll remember this conversation and that I predicted we would be more than bedmates."

After they ended the call, Egypt stared at the phone. A bolt of white heat flowed directly to her core at Garrett's heated words. She'd thought he rang her because he was interested in a booty call. Someone to warm his bed. But that wasn't it at all. Garrett wanted companionship. Someone to talk to while he figured out this crazy thing called life. Egypt's first instinct was to equate their relationship to just sex, because that's what she'd been doing with men since Antwan broke her heart. She didn't allow them to get too close. Instead, she kept her relationships physical.

Garrett didn't want that from her, though. Every time she made a move to devalue what was going on between them, he came on twice as strong. Egypt wasn't sure she could keep the walls she'd erected around her fortified if Garrett kept steadily chipping away at them.

Eight

Garrett didn't sleep well the first night at the farm. How could he? He'd gotten used to the sounds and smells of the hospital. Now he'd been thrust into a strange place, which, although familiar, didn't feel like home. Garrett struggled sleeping on the queen-size bed, which might be perfectly adequate for some, but barely fit his six-foot-three frame.

When he'd finally showered, he rambled around the farmhouse trying to find something to wear. He found some of his grandfather's clothes in one of the closets and changed into a pair of old Wranglers and a plaid shirt. Then he made his way to the kitchen and discovered he wasn't handy there, either. It took him three tries to make some halfway decent coffee. Eventually, he'd found the fixings to make some bacon and eggs, which hadn't been a total disaster. He'd learned how to cook from his grandfather. Another memory! He had just finished breakfast when Kent knocked on the door.

Garrett wouldn't say he was eager for manual labor, but it had to be better than sitting in a hospital room watching television and going to physical therapy.

"Want a tour of the farm?" Kent asked.

"Absolutely." Garrett rose to his feet. "Maybe then I can get my bearings."

"First you're going to need these." The foreman handed Garrett some plastic boots.

Kent started with the chicken coop. "First we go and check on the animals." He went inside the coop, and Garrett trailed after him. "We need to make sure they have enough food and water." He filled up the trough with the necessities, then moved over to the two cows to give them a mix of hay and oats.

Garrett assisted with opening up large bags of feed. "We have to do this every day?"

"Yep," Kent replied, not turning back to look at him. "Follow me." He took him inside the barn, which housed a couple of tractors but looked like it needed a new roof. "There are a few things I need you to do."

"And what's that?"

"Clean the tractor and grease and oil some of the machines."

"I vaguely remember doing that as a teenager."

"Good. The bucket and sponges are over there." Kent pointed to a box sitting off to the side. "Have at it. I'm going to check and see if the farm's staff have arrived so I can get them started on their duties."

"When will I get a chance to go over the books?" Garrett asked.

"Later!" Kent called over his shoulder.

Garrett wasn't above physical labor. He was fit and easily knocked out washing the vehicles. However, he was more interested in the financials and how his grandfather managed to keep this farm afloat. Kent didn't seem too keen on going over the accounting, but once Garrett's mind was set on something, there was no turning him away from it.

When Kent returned hours later, Garrett had not only washed the vehicles, he'd waxed them as well as greased the machinery.

Kent folded his arms across his chest. "I'm impressed."

"You think a white-collar guy like me is above hard work?" Garrett inquired, tossing down the cloth he'd been using to wipe down a vehicle. He'd long since removed the plaid shirt, and his white T-shirt was soaked through with sweat.

Kent nodded. "I suppose I was biased, but you've corrected me on that score."

Garrett's eyes narrowed. "Don't underestimate me, Kent. I may be having trouble up here—" he pointed to his temple. "—but I'm no slouch."

"Duly noted." Kent gave him a half smile. "Listen, Aurora made me chili. There's easily enough for two if you're interested?"

Garrett realized he would like that. Kent was his lifeline right now. "Yes, I would like that very much."

The man wasn't lying. His wife had indeed given him enough chili to feed several men. They went back to the farmhouse to eat and talked during the meal. A camaraderie was slowly beginning to form, and Garrett knew then he would have to earn Kent's trust. After their bellies were full, Garrett reminded the foreman about the books. Instantly, he noticed a change in him. His shoulders became stiff and he sat up a little straighter.

"Oh, yeah, I'd forgotten," Kent replied.

Garrett highly doubted that, but he watched the other man go to his car and bring out a laptop bag. Was there something Kent didn't want him to see? He followed Kent into the back of the farmhouse, where his grandfather had an office set up. It wasn't large and was only furnished with a large oak desk and executive chair. A ton of books on farming and mountains of ledgers were peppered throughout the room. Kent pulled out one of the ledgers and handed it to Garrett.

Garrett frowned. "What's this?"

"You wanted to see the books," Kent replied. "Well, your grandfather didn't believe in computers. Never wanted to learn them, even though I encouraged him to modernize."

"Kent, this is an antiquated way of running a business."

"I know that," he replied. "Which is why I've been moving everything over to this." He pulled a laptop out of his bag. "A year ago, you gifted it to Cyrus on Christmas, but he didn't want any part of it and gave it to me. I felt it was only right that I try and take the farm into the future. I've done my best to transfer everything over into QuickBooks. I'm no Wharton graduate, but I think it'll do."

"Thank you, and I'm sorry for thinking the worst."

"That I took an advantage of an old man?" Kent asked hotly, and Garrett sensed he'd struck a nerve. "I wouldn't do that! Cyrus was like a father to me, just like he was to you."

Garrett nodded. "I understand." He wished he could talk to his grandfather now and ask him for advice on how to pick up the pieces of his life, but he was going to have to figure it out for himself.

"I'm going to spend the rest of the afternoon going over these financials. If I was some big-time businessman in the past, it should all come back to me. It's like riding a bike, right?"

"Sure thing." Kent said and left him to his own devices.

Garrett spent hours peering through the ledgers and matching them to the laptop, and the excitement he felt at working with numbers came back. He was encouraged, because the last week, he'd felt out of sorts, as if he was a stranger in his own body, but *this* made sense to him. The first person he wanted to tell was Egypt.

Instead of calling her, because he knew she was getting ready for dinner service, Garrett texted her. Going over the farm's financials and it's fun. I'm really good with numbers.

It took a few moments, and Garrett waited anxiously for the three dots to appear. That's wonderful. I'm glad your memory is coming back.

Memory. He hadn't gotten any of those flashes the doctor had told him about. For Garrett, it was more of a feeling, an impulse that he knew what to do and when to do it. Like when he was working on the farming equipment earlier or tying the ledgers to QuickBooks. He wished his memory would come back *now*, rather than later. Garrett didn't know where the farm or Egypt fit in his life, but he would figure it out, because neither was going away anytime soon.

The rest of the week sped by for Egypt. Having Asia in town was like having a tornado in her otherwise orderly world. The woman ran about a hundred miles per minute *all* the time. Egypt wanted to tell her to slow down. Maybe then she could get figure out what she wanted to do for her store.

Instead, Egypt had to be the responsible one and work on *Asia's* business plan while she went off to a gem store in town for inspiration for her latest jewelry collection. Sometimes, Egypt wished she could be as carefree as Asia, never letting the worries of life bog her down, but then she wouldn't be her.

Not that she didn't love her fellow Gem, but when Asia departed for greener pastures in DC on Saturday, Egypt wanted to cheer. Because of Asia, Egypt hadn't had time to stress about her upcoming date with Garrett. He'd phoned her every night this week, sharing with her how each day on the farm went. Egypt lived for those calls; they were the only way to get through the long hours she put in at Flame.

There was always so much to do to keep it afloat from marketing to accounting. It was hard work, but Egypt wouldn't change a thing. She loved seeing the reactions of her customers when they tasted one of her dishes. Fortunately, she had garnered a few regulars, and was thankful for them and for the positive word of mouth, especially after the fallout from Garrett's carjacking.

She was relieved when Monday came and she could spend the day at Walker Farms. Garrett had indicated Egypt should come later that afternoon, and they would pick a few fruits and vegetables for dinner. Considering she would be out in the fields, Egypt opted to wear a comfortable outfit of a sweater over a tank top with a crisscross back and matching leggings and sneakers. She also brought a change of clothes. If they would be getting sweaty outdoors, she would need to shower before dinner.

As she drove an hour outside town, Egypt realized she'd never been to a farm before, but she'd always wanted to go to one. The drive was serene and gave her the peace that had been sorely lacking after Asia's unexpected visit. She listened to her favorite music on Spotify and soon was driving past a sign labeled Walker Farms.

She pulled her car up in front of a white farmhouse and had to admit it wasn't what she expected, but it wasn't as dilapidated as she had thought it might be, either. The fences and barn she'd passed could use a fresh coat of paint, but the farmhouse held a certain charm.

None was more appealing, however, than the chocolate gentleman rushing down the steps toward her. Garrett looked strong and powerful in his Wranglers, boots and a plaid shirt. A flood of heat rooted her where she stood as her eyes roamed his muscular body. Egypt suspected he'd never worn anything so mundane in his life. The night they'd met, Garrett had been dressed in a button-down shirt, tailored pants and a Rolex. This must be all new to him. It's why she'd brought a few pots and pans and some groceries, because she wasn't sure what Garrett might have on hand.

"Let me help you," Garrett said as she made her way to the trunk to remove all the goodies. "But first..."

She spun around. "First what?"

"First this." Garrett's gaze was incendiary as he fixed on her mouth. And then he was kissing her, and everything in Egypt's mind disintegrated under the hot, hard press of his mouth against hers. He licked into her mouth, past her teeth to join with her tongue. Egypt gripped his shoulders, and Garrett gave a low groan, crushing her hard against him and pushing her back against the car. Her breasts puckered and fire roared in her veins as they devoured each other. She needed his mouth on hers and didn't want to break away, not even to breathe.

It was Garrett who pulled his head back and looked at her through passion-glazed eyes. Egypt gave a moan of protest.

"There will be time for more kisses later," Garrett promised.

"Or all night long if you like, but if you want to see the farm, we'll have to move from this spot."

"Promises, promises," Egypt huffed and slowly stood upright. "But I suppose we should take this food inside." She clicked open the trunk and revealed an array of grocery bags as well as a box of pots and pans from her personal collection at home.

Garrett chuckled. "Did you bring your entire arsenal?" He grabbed all the bags and started toward the house.

"Something like that," she responded, picking up the box of pots to follow him inside. The house was warm and masculine, with much of the decor in beiges and dark woods. She could tell it was a bachelor's home, because it held no signs of a woman's touch.

They dumped the bags and box on the kitchen counter and began emptying them.

"You've got a lot here," Garrett said as they unpacked, "but we have some wonderful produce in the field to pick. And it looks like you came dressed for it." He eyed her up and down in her workout gear. Fire ignited in her blood from his heated gaze.

"Sounds wonderful. I can do a vegetable medley from whatever we find." Egypt spun away and stored items in the refrigerator. "You've been on the farm a week now. How has it been?" she asked, turning back around.

"Eye-opening. I had no idea what long hours farmers put in. Every night after I talk to you, I fall asleep because I'm bone tired. Then I wake up at 5:00 a.m. only to do it all over again."

"Have you been able to make heads or tails of the farm's books?" She asked, when all she wanted was more of his taste and of his touch. It was as if she'd been starving for years and this incredibly big and sexy man was exactly what she was hungry for.

Garrett nodded. "I have, and my grandfather was in debt. If I don't figure out something soon, I could lose the farm."

"Wow! Is it that dire?"

"Yeah, and I feel like I knew that, which is why I was coming here after dining at Flame."

"Did you just remember that?" she asked.

He shook his head. "The memories come in waves—mostly small, insignificant things."

"It's a start. Don't be so hard on yourself. Those thugs beat you up pretty good. They put you in a coma."

"I know, but the farm doesn't have much time." He blew out a frustrated breath. "Kent and I were able to call the bank, and they've given me a sixty-day extension, but that's not much time to turn things around."

"Do you have any ideas?"

"Well, I've been doing my research, and I think we should open the farm up to the public," Garrett told her. "Allow them to pick their own produce, like the strawberries, blueberries and some of the cucumbers, lettuce, squash, tomatoes and zucchini we grow here."

"I can't wait to see them."

After they finished putting away the groceries, Garrett took Egypt's hand and gave her a quick tour of the farmhouse. He shocked her by taking her overnight bag upstairs, but she didn't comment. Instead, she followed him outside. Egypt was amazed at the operation. There was an actual chicken coop, and she and Garrett went inside and selected at least a dozen eggs she could take back with her later. Then they were off down the road in a tractor to rows and rows of fresh vegetables.

"Garrett!" Egypt tugged his sleeve as she surveyed the produce. "This is amazing. I agree you should have a picking season for the locals."

"I know, right?" He grinned. "Speaking of buckets—" he reached over and handed her a two-gallon bucket and took one for himself "—let's get to work."

As they picked squash, tomatoes and zucchini and placed the items in their buckets for dinner, occasionally their hands or bodies would touch and it thrilled Egypt. She wanted more of it, wanted to press herself against his and feel his rock-hard body against hers. She focused her thoughts on Flame instead and it occurred to her how they could help one another. "How would you feel about partnering with Flame to provide our produce?

"You would do that?" His eyes were sharp and assessing as if he could see through her.

"Of course," Egypt stated. "Any restaurateur would kill for this kind of fresh produce."

"Then we'll make it happen," Garrett replied.

Jubilant, Egypt surged to her feet and stumbled and gripped onto his T-shirt. Garrett caught her. "You okay?" There was a fierce hungry look on his face which Egypt felt matched hers. All she could do was nod.

They stared at each other for several beats and Egypt wanted him to kiss her again, but instead he let her go and they returned to working side by side. The sexual tension between them was so tight, Egypt cut through it by asking him how the investigation was coming along. "Have you heard anything from Detective Simpson?"

"He called me a few days ago," Garrett replied, "only to tell me that nothing surfaced in Pennsylvania under my name. Isn't that odd? If I lived up there after leaving Raleigh to go to grad school at Wharton, it stands to reason I would be near there. But apparently, that's not the case. He's had to expand his search to neighboring states."

"I'm sorry there's no news." She could only imagine how frustrating it was for Garrett to not only remember nothing about his past but to be completely reliant on other people for help. Depending on others was hard for Egypt, too, especially after Antwan's betrayal. She'd loved him, and he'd abused her trust by stealing her savings. Egypt was used to being the one giving other people support, like she'd done with Garrett.

He stopped picking vegetables and stared at her. "I just want to know who I am. I know where I come from—" he glanced around the farm "—but at times…"

"At times what?"

"The past Kent told me doesn't fit, but I haven't been able to piece together anything that says otherwise."

"How are you guys getting along?" Egypt asked. "I know you mentioned there was some tension there."

"My suspicion is that Kent thinks I'm going to shut down the farm, but this is the last piece I have of my grandfather. I'm going to do everything in my power to keep it."

"That's admirable."

Once they finished with the vegetables. Egypt noticed how Garrett's hands lingered on her bottom as he helped her into the tractor with her bucket. She glanced down at him and found his gaze burning hers. He knew exactly what he'd been doing. He smiled before joining her and they moved farther down the dirt path to the strawberry fields.

"Has your friend Asia left?" Garrett inquired. "I'm sorry I wasn't able to meet her. Even though I have my grandfather's old pickup truck, options are limited without a license."

"It's okay," Egypt said. "I didn't mind getting out of the city. I needed a break from everyday life. Plus, I love my girl, but she can be a handful."

"How did you guys meet?" Garrett asked as they bent down to pick bright red strawberries.

Egypt stood upright. "We met in high school in San Antonio, along with the other Six Gems."

His brows furrowed. "Gems?"

"That's the name my friends and I gave ourselves way back when. My dad and I had moved there for his job. I didn't know anyone."

"That had to be hard," Garrett said. "New schools are never easy."

"It wasn't, but then one day I walked into the cafeteria and there were some girls sitting by themselves. One of them, Teagan had her head in a book. She wasn't paying attention to anyone. Then there was Asia, who was dressed—how shall I say this *diplomatically*?—very eclectic., Lyric was in tights and doing pirouettes around the table. Then there was Shay, who was on the track team."

"Sounds like an interesting group of friends."

Egypt chuckled. "They were and once I sat with them a friendship was born. Wynter, my best friend who's getting married, was added to the mix when her rich parents enrolled her in the public school to punish her because of her rebellious nature. All the boys wanted to date us. Asia said we were all gems and Teagan decided we should be called the Six Gems."

Garrett laughed as he rose from the crouched position he'd been in. "I love the story. And that's exactly what I'm missing. Where are my friends? Why isn't anyone looking for me? Or was I such a loner that I didn't have anyone who cared?"

Egypt walked over to him and touched his arm. "I doubt that. You're a very kind and warmhearted man, Garrett."

He leaned his forehead to hers, and Egypt's heart sped up. She longed to arch into the muscled power of his body and feel his lips on hers once more. "You're biased."

"Totally," she laughed. "Give it some time. Your memory could come back on its own."

"Not soon enough."

Egypt inclined her head in the direction of the farmhouse. "We've been out here a bit. I need to figure out this dinner situation. I hope you realize you're going to be my sous-chef in the kitchen."

"I look forward to it."

Egypt suspected she would be in big trouble if he continued looking at her with that hooded stare of his. There was no way she wasn't going to bed with him tonight. Her desire was only strengthening as she got to know him. And would that be such a bad thing? It had been too long since she'd felt this way about a guy. Would it be wrong to enjoy a night with this incredibly attractive mystery man? No strings attached.

Hell no!

Nine

Dinner consisted of the scallops and risotto Egypt had brought with her as well as a succotash of tomatoes, squash and zucchini that they'd picked in the fields earlier that day. Garrett honestly didn't care what Egypt made; he was just glad to finally have her on his turf. Before she'd arrived, he'd picked some beautiful snapdragons and placed them in a vase in the kitchen. Egypt said she was touched by his thoughtfulness. Garrett suspected he wasn't prone to acts of romance, but for this woman, he wanted to impress her.

She'd shown character in not only coming to his aid the night he was injured, but in returning day after day until he regained consciousness. That told Garrett that Egypt Cox was someone worth knowing and keeping in his life. And it wasn't like he had many people in his corner right now.

"What can I do?" he asked after she came up with the menu and pulled off her sweater to get started.

"You can chop the vegetables." Egypt pulled out a cutting board and knife set from her box. She set him up at the large butcher block countertop and went about getting the arborio rice going for the risotto.

They happily chatted, and Egypt regaled him with tales of the last week with Asia in residence. "I'm telling you, Garrett, she has no clue what she's doing. She needs someone to guide her."

"I guess that's where you come in."

"I've got my own business to look after," Egypt replied, "but I did what I could and helped finish her business plan."

"Because that's the kind of friend you are." The more they talked, the more he admired her. Clearly, Egypt did all she could for those she cared about. She listened. She was engaging, and she was sexy as hell. All day, Garrett had reminded himself to focus on picking fruits and vegetables instead of looking at Egypt's round backside when she was bent over. He wanted nothing more than to rip off all her clothes and quench his thirst.

"She doesn't make it easy," Egypt continued. "But I want to help. The money we inherited from Wynter's aunt gave us start-up down payments to start our own businesses."

"That's fantastic."

"Yeah, Aunt Helaine was like a grandmother to me," Egypt said softly. "Not having my mother growing up was tough."

Garrett paused in cutting the vegetables. "I'm sorry for bringing it up."

"It's okay—you couldn't have known."

"But I want to know," Garrett responded.

Egypt stared back at him. "Why?"

"I want to know everything about you." Garrett came toward her, and Egypt didn't move. Instead, she leaned into him, straining closer and tilting her head upward. He gave her exactly what she wanted, what they *both* wanted, and brushed his mouth across hers. It was a fleeting kiss, because the next time he kissed her, he intended it to lead to one place.

The bedroom.

Her eyes opened up when his lips barely grazed hers. "Finish your risotto," he ordered and moved away from her while he still could. "You don't want it to burn."

"Not many people get to order me around, Garrett, so consider yourself lucky."

"Oh, I intend to get very lucky tonight," he replied with a smirk and picked up his knife to resume chopping veggies.

Egypt's eyes blazed at his heated words, but she didn't respond and returned to her task.

An hour later, they were seated at his grandfather's farmhouse table in the dining room, drinking the bottle of pinot grigio Egypt had brought with her and eating one of the best meals Garrett had in his life. The scallops were seared perfectly, the risotto cheesy and creamy, and the succotash bright and delightful.

"You're a damn good chef, Egypt," Garrett said once the meal was complete and they'd taken their dishes to the kitchen. "It's one of the reasons you caught my attention."

In the dim light, he could see her swallow hard. "I'm sorry it didn't turn out as you anticipated."

"Maybe it has." He was drawn to Egypt...he had been from the start. Garrett's past might be a blank slate, but he knew with absolute certainty that he wanted her more than he'd ever wanted anyone. Something about her made him hungry to touch her, so he reached for her hand. She slipped her palm into his, and his fingers wrapped around hers, firmly and securely. He liked the feel of her and the look of her.

In that moment, Garrett recalled that he usually dated a particular type of woman—thin, poised and totally put together. Egypt was the complete opposite. Like today, for example, she'd arrived in an oversize sweater and leggings, her long black hair tousled and her beautiful features free of makeup, save some lipstick and mascara, but she looked utterly alluring.

"You think so?" Egypt asked. "How so?"

"You're here alone with me, which is exactly where I want you," Garrett replied, but then added, "Or almost the way I want you."

"Then why don't you change that?"

She was challenging him, and Garrett was more than up for

the task. He leaned over, circled his hands around her waist and hauled her into his lap. Her bottom slammed against him, but she didn't try to wiggle away. Instead, she slipped her fingers behind his head and drew his head down to her. Kissing Egypt was like coming home, and Garrett closed his eyes against the bright starburst of pleasure that shot through him.

The kiss was lush and slow, and Garrett enjoyed every minute of it. Egypt pressed against him, her softness molding to his hardness and heating him in all the right places. He deepened the kiss, and she opened up to him, giving Garrett greater access. His hands roamed over her shapely curves as his mouth plundered hers. "You've got no idea how badly I want you."

"I think I do. Because I want you just as bad," she breathed.

Suddenly, they were both kissing like hormonal teens. Garrett was unprepared for the passion Egypt unleashed, especially when she boldly slid her tongue over his. A low growl emanated from his throat. The sound of his approval ratcheted up Egypt's urgency. She rose from his lap but then returned to straddle him so his erection could be exactly at her sex. When she began moving against him, a hunger took over his whole body, and Garrett leaned her backward on the table and began to devour her whole.

Egypt could hardly believe Garrett was holding her as if she was light as a feather on the wooden farm table. He stood between her legs and pushed them wide while her fingers speared into his dark curls. Their kiss accelerated into the stratosphere, especially when Garrett moved his hips. The friction of his denim jeans against her sex made her eyes roll back, her chest heave and her heart begin to hammer loudly in her chest. But nothing was going to stop this kiss. She needed his mouth on hers, because she was hot and damp between her legs.

She couldn't wait to touch him all over and quickly began tugging at the buttons on his plaid shirt. They separated enough for her to toss the offending garment aside and bare his upper half to hers. He didn't disappoint. His body was chiseled with a slender waist and rock-hard abs. She reached up to caress his broad shoulders and tease his nipples with her tongue.

"You don't get to have all the fun," Garrett said, and before Egypt knew it, her tank top along with the sports bra underneath was lifted up and over her head until her bare D-size breasts were on full display to Garrett's admiring gaze. Then his warm mouth was covering a nipple. His hot tongue laved the pebbled peak, and Egypt gasped. Her hands moved up to his neck, and her pelvis tilted so she could get more.

"You're beautiful," he mouthed against her breast. His lips were firm and his tongue moist as he teased her while his other hand molded and kneaded the other breast. Sharp desire made Egypt hold him to her breasts as loud gasps escaped her lips. She couldn't stop him if she wanted to, because a riot of sensations was coursing through her. She and Garrett were finally going to be together. It seemed almost anticlimactic after everything they'd been through, but she was ready.

He stroked her from breast to belly, then his hand eased lower to cup her mound through the leggings she wore. Her gasp was caught in his mouth as he once again covered her lips with his. Garrett made her feel sexy and beautiful. Desired and wanted. With a deep sigh, Egypt gave herself over to the moment. When she felt Garrett's hands at her waist, she kicked off her sneakers and lifted up so he could remove her leggings and panties in one fell swoop until she was naked on the table, while he still wore his jeans and boots.

Her heart pounded, but it didn't stop her from looking at him. His eyes were dark with desire as she reached for the zip on his pants. A thrill of excitement went through Egypt as Garrett watched her tug his zipper down and ease the jeans down his slim hips. He was hard and straining against the cotton.

Egypt couldn't wait to touch him. She slipped her hands beneath the briefs and covered him with her hand. She loved the silky texture and hard, ridged length of him. Garrett groaned and grew larger as she stroked him with her hands. She wanted to put her mouth on him, but he pushed her backward onto the table. Then he removed his boots and pulled a condom from the pocket of his jeans before kicking them and his briefs aside.

"I imagined our first time in a bed, but this will work." After donning protection, Garrett was back between her thighs, exactly where she wanted him, with his hand between her legs.

Her eyes closed when his fingers slid inside her wet haven and explored, but Egypt didn't stay still. She *had* to move, because his every touch was bringing her closer to the edge. "Oh, yes…" A moan escaped her lips as excitement and desire melded into one. She could only think of Garrett and how much she wanted him with every cell of her being.

When he finally leaned over, his chest to her breasts, his breath a hot puff against her face, she shut out the world and focused only on him. On the weight of his erection as he thrust inside her slick flesh. Egypt accepted his large length and opened her eyes to find his smoldering gaze on her.

"Okay?" he asked.

"Yes. And more, please."

He laughed and then pushed in a little farther and whole lot deeper.

"Oh, God!" She clutched his shoulders, and Garrett hitched her leg up and around his waist. "That's right, give it to me, baby."

She was ready to take everything he had to give.

Garrett bent down and licked one of Egypt's juicy brown nipples in his mouth while the lower half of him made love to her. He wanted to taste *all* of her, lick her in her most intimate places and tease her until she was screaming his name. But there would be time for that later. Right now, he was seated deep inside and Egypt was circling her hips, compelling him to discover all her secret treasures.

Growling, he slipped his hand between them and found her hot and wet. She sighed with pleasure, so he did it again, fingering her while simultaneously pumping in and out. Egypt was his match and met him thrust for thrust. She didn't care that she was spread out on his table like a feast for him to enjoy.

Garrett felt like the richest man in the world right now, because he was buried inside her snug heat. Before the night was over, he would have her more than once. When she began rocking her hips harder in utter abandon, he knew she was getting closer.

He nipped at her earlobe as he fingered her nub. "That's right, Egypt. Come for me, baby."

He withdrew and thrust in again, faster and faster. Triumph filled him when her moans and gasps turned into a scream as her climax struck. Her inner muscles clenched around him, and he gripped her harder as he bucked against her. Her orgasm pushed him over the edge, and Garrett let out a ragged groan and fell forward when the undeniable force of pleasure flowed between them.

Egypt held him to her sweat-slicked breasts, and they were both silent as they took in what just happened. His heart was still thundering loudly in his chest. Had sex with any other woman rivaled this? Garrett didn't think so. His gut told him Egypt was different from any other women he'd ever been with. He also knew that this moment was a game changer.

Ten

Egypt arched her back and let the water stream down her shoulders. It was early morning and she needed to go home, but after her shower. She and Garrett had made love twice throughout the night, and she was sweaty and smelled of sex. Good sex. The best sex she'd had in her life. It didn't matter that Garrett didn't know his true identity; he knew what to do with his body, his mouth and his hands to bring her the ultimate pleasure.

She wanted a few minutes to herself, but seconds later, Garrett barged into the bathroom. He was naked and fully erect and holding a foil packet, which he placed on the sink. Egypt ate him up with her eyes as he joined her in the shower, but first she wanted something else. Dropping to her knees, she grasped his erection and took him in her mouth. Garrett groaned. When she looked up at him, he placed one hand in her wet hair to guide her exactly where he wanted her. She teased his already hard length with her hands and mouth until Garrett gasped and planted a hand on the wall to steady himself as he spilled into her mouth. She licked him up as if he were one of the decadent sauces she made in her restaurant before rising to her feet.

"You wicked woman!" Garrett murmured, leaning back against the wall, utterly drained.

"Then perhaps you should have allowed me to shower on my own." She turned away from him and began to soap her body with the body wash she'd found in the shower, but then she felt Garrett behind her. Was it possible his hard length was already thick again? Jesus, the man was insatiable!

She heard rustling behind her and a wrapper tearing, and then Garrett was sliding his hands around her round curves and lifting her bottom up to meet his. Egypt put her hands flat against the tile wall in front of her and shimmied her hips backward.

Garrett reached in front of her and began eagerly stroking her sex. Egypt leaned backward, letting the water sluice over their naked bodies as Garrett fingered her. She was already wet and ready for him, so when he drove home with one smooth, strong thrust, Egypt felt it right to her core.

"Damn!" Her breath caught. Delight rippled through her excited nerves, and she pushed backward against him. Garrett held her hips and thrust in again as they learned a new rhythm and angle. Garrett clutched her breasts, tweaking them with his fingers while his mouth sucked on the back of her neck.

"Yes, babe," she murmured when he withdrew and thrust in again, deeper and faster. "Just like that." She was incapable of thought. She wanted the incredible feeling of perfection that came from being with Garrett. It didn't take long for her inner muscles to grip him as ecstasy burst all around her.

Egypt screamed, and when she closed her eyes, she saw stars. Garrett was seconds behind her and roared out his delight. He bowed forward, bending over her, his arm around her waist. They pulsed there together in the shower, neither of them able to speak.

He'd shattered her senses, overloaded her body and jumbled her thoughts. This man had taken her to ecstasy and back again time after time, and Egypt realized she could quickly become addicted to him. But she knew it was foolish to feel so profoundly after making love. It was just sex, after all, but she felt changed somehow, and that scared her. Especially after everything she'd already been through with Antwan. She had to make a quick exit.

Slowly, they disengaged, and Garrett must have understood her need for silence because they soaped up and washed off without saying a word. Egypt dried quickly and then tied the towel around her bosom before turning around to face him. "I have to get back home."

"I understand," he said, toweling that gorgeous body of his dry. Egypt licked her lips. *Focus.*

She changed into a velour jumpsuit she'd brought and made a beeline for the kitchen for a moment to get her head together. Being with Garrett had filled an emptiness she hadn't realized was missing in her life. Her life had become about work, work. Eventually Garrett came downstairs wearing sweat pants and a T-shirt. He looked sinfully sexy and god help her Egypt wouldn't mind another go at it, but she had to get ready for work.

He followed her into the kitchen, and she let out an audible sigh at seeing the remnants of last night's meal right where they left them.

"Don't worry about it," Garrett said from behind her. "I'll clean up. You can get going."

She turned and gave him a half smile. "Thank you." After packing up what she'd brought including the fresh eggs, she looked around for her purse, but Garrett beat her to it and held it in his hands.

"I enjoyed last night, Egypt. And this morning."

She blushed and lowered her head, but he tipped her face up with his index finger. "I'd like to see you again."

"Garrett…"

He must have read doubt in her eyes, because he shook his head. "The only thing I want to hear from you is yes."

Egypt glanced into his dark eyes and found she couldn't resist him. "Yes."

"Good." Then he lowered his head and swept his warm lips over hers.

The kiss was passionate and arousing. It took effort, but Egypt pulled back. "I'll call you later."

"You'd better." Garrett winked. "I know where you work."

Egypt waved and then headed to the front door. She didn't breathe until she was alone in her car. Only then did she let out a sigh. She'd known that she and Garrett would inevitably become lovers, but she'd never anticipated it would be *that* good. Too good.

She wasn't looking for anything serious, but even though her heart was wary of getting hurt again, a man like Garrett made a secret part of Egypt hope for the happily-ever-after that Wynter and Riley had found.

Garrett felt like a rock star. Last night with Egypt had been amazing. The sounds she'd made when he'd taken her breasts in his mouths. The look in her eyes when she reached the pinnacle of pleasure and called out his name. All of it had driven him wild. He'd known she was a sexy and passionate woman, but when she knelt down in the shower and took him in her mouth, Garrett had nearly lost it. He couldn't think of anything else the rest of the day. But it also scared him. Without his memory, he didn't have much to offer her. All he could offer her with this intense heat between them until he figured out who he really was.

Kent commented he was distracted and needed to pay attention, otherwise he'd get hurt. "What's going on with you today, Garrett?"

Garrett gave him a sideways glance. "Did you forget I had a date with Egypt last night?"

"Oh!" Kent nodded his head in understanding. "And it was a good night?"

"I don't kiss and tell."

"That's all the answer I need," the other man said with a smirk. "Will you be seeing each other again?"

"I certainly hope so," Garrett replied. Egypt was exquisite. Even though he didn't know where this was heading, there was no way he wasn't hearing her hoarse cries of delight as he filled the tight, slick heat of her body. Her snug embrace was something he would crawl through broken glass for.

"She doesn't mind that you don't remember who you are?"

Garrett frowned. Why was Kent bringing that up? It's not as if it wasn't already eating at him how crazy his situation was. "If she does, she doesn't show it."

"That's good."

But that didn't mean Garrett wasn't still worried. It had been a long since time he'd heard from Detective Simpson. He was ready to get on with his life. He would call the detective after they finished picking crops for the day, which reminded him of the idea Egypt suggested and that he'd thought of himself.

"Listen, Kent. I was thinking we should open the farm to the public."

"This has always been a private farm," Kent responded brusquely.

"And it will remain that way. However, it's growing season, and wouldn't it be great if we could have the public come in and pick from the delicious variety of vegetables we grow right here on the farm? We would charge them a price per pound and start bringing in additional revenue. We would still have enough for the normal orders."

"Sounds like a lot to get started."

Garrett shrugged. "With a small investment, we could get signage, tents, additional buckets and wagons and maybe a refreshment stand? This could be a real winner."

"At the end of the day, it is your farm."

Garrett rolled his eyes. "I want you to get behind the idea, Kent, not just give me lip service. Plus, I've talked to Egypt about supplying her restaurant, Flame, with fresh produce. Who knows—she could be one of many restaurants we work with in Raleigh."

"I think both ideas are great, but I've never been good at execution."

"Then it's a good thing I am." Garrett was learning he wasn't comfortable being a follower. He was a leader, and he would steer the farm toward success or die trying.

They continued working in the fields with the rest of the crew until it was time for a break. Only then did Garrett head inside the farmhouse to call the detective, who answered on the first ring.

"Simpson here."

"Detective," Garrett began, "this is Garrett Walker. I'm the guy who was carjacked."

"Yes, I know who you are," Detective Simpson responded on the other end of the line. "What can I do for you?"

"I was hoping you could tell me if you'd finally had a hit on my identity in the Northeast. There has to be someone looking for me."

"I'm afraid not, Mr. Walker. We've contacted all the Garrett Walker in our databases and there is no match."

"That can't be." Garrett scratched his head. People didn't just disappear, not in this day and age. Was there more going on here? It was beginning to sound sinister. Was he into something illegal? He would never want to bring any harm to the farm.

"I'm afraid so. We've spent an extraordinary amount of time looking into this on your behalf and still nothing. As for your car, the thieves must have taken it to some chop shop we don't know about. And neither your cell phone or wallet has ever shown up."

"What am I supposed to do?" Garrett bit out. "I'm essentially walking around without any identification."

"Didn't the farm's foreman indicate your grandfather raised you? He might have kept copies of your birth certificate or even your Social Security card. Perhaps you can start there."

"That's a great idea," Garrett said and wished he'd thought of it himself. "But if it doesn't, what happens then?"

"Why don't we cross that bridge when we come to it?" the

detective replied. "It's always a possibility that your memory comes back on its own."

That was true, too. Every day he got stronger. Garrett was starting to feel more in control of himself and understood that he wasn't one for sitting back and letting things happen to him. He would set about finding out the truth about his existence, good, bad or indifferent. He owed it to himself, *and* to Egypt, because he would never want to bring any harm her way.

Egypt knew better than to hang her hat on a relationship based on sexual attraction alone, but Garrett had her sprung. She wanted to act as if it was just a one-night stand or friends with benefits, but deep down she knew it was more than that. For years, she'd kept her feelings locked down, and now they were trying to escape from the prison she'd barricaded them in.

Egypt went home to change into her work gear of chef's coat and black leggings, her long hair in a ponytail underneath her Flame baseball cap. Even though she'd gotten very little sleep, she had a lot of excess energy to burn off and only knew one way to do it—in the kitchen. So, she came in early to start on several bases and sauces for dinner. She wanted the flavors to have time to bloom. When Quentin arrived at noon, she'd completed all the prep work for dinner service.

"Chef, you're a beast!" Quentin said when he looked in the fridge and cooler to see everything she'd accomplished.

"Had a lot of energy," Egypt replied, stirring one of her béchamel sauces.

"Looks like the night is off to a great start," Quentin mused, putting on his white chef's coat. "I'm surprised. Didn't you have a date with Garrett? I assumed you would be booed up and I'd be in charge of the kitchen tonight."

Egypt stopped stirring to regard him. "Really? Do you think I'm that easy?" She held up her hand. "Never mind. Don't answer that. Regardless of what happens between me and Garrett, I won't ever leave you hanging. I will always give you a heads-up."

Quentin smiled as he tied his apron around his waist. "Thank you. I appreciate that."

They continued working while listening to Egypt's favorite Spotify station until the waitstaff came in. Then Egypt presented the evening's nightly special so they could all have a taste. She did her best to push down any thoughts of the man who'd made her come nearly half a dozen times last night and this morning.

All she could think about was the way he'd made her feel as if her body belonged to him. But she couldn't forget that lovemaking didn't create an emotional connection. There was still so much she didn't know about Garrett or he knew about himself. She couldn't let herself become too vulnerable or she would be opening herself to heartbreak and she couldn't bear to go through what she'd endured after Antwan. Garrett must have been thinking of her too because her phone blew up throughout the dinner rush with texts from him about the naughty things he'd like to do to her.

At one point, Egypt had to go into the walk-in to cool off, because she wasn't hot from the kitchen, but from remembering Garrett's mouth on her. Eventually, she returned to close out dinner service. It was a slow day, and they were able to leave at a decent hour. She'd just locked the front door to Flame when Quentin nudged her on the side.

"What?" She spun around and found Garrett leaning against the light post outside waiting for her. It was still cool out, so he was in the same bomber jacket and jeans he usually wore. She hadn't expected to see him again so soon, but that didn't mean an electric zing didn't go through at seeing his gorgeous face. His sensual lips made Egypt crave to touch him, to be alone with him again, to have him make her his. But she couldn't say those things. It was too early, and his murky past also posed a major complication, so she said instead, "Garrett? What are you doing here? How did you get here"

His face went grim. "That wasn't quite the welcome I was looking for. There are cabs and rideshares."

Egypt turned to Quentin, who was smiling like a Cheshire cat. Then he waved and left her alone with Garrett.

Egypt didn't rush into his arms immediately, but then he stepped forward and she met him halfway. He bent his head and kissed her. The connection between them grew and was as delicious as the night before, but maybe more so, because she knew what was in store for her. No one, Antwan included, had ever made her feel desired and beautiful like Garrett did.

A hunger took over them as they made out underneath the streetlight. Egypt was so into the kiss, she didn't hear Quentin call out from his car, "Get a room!"

"Let's go back to your place," Garrett whispered against her lips when they finally came up for air.

"To do what?" she answered cheekily. But then Garrett drew her near so she could feel the hardness between his hips. He wanted her as much as she wanted him. "I think that's a good idea."

In the darkness of Egypt's apartment, they stripped each other bare and made love slowly, leisurely, until nothing was left but mindless pleasure. Garrett held himself back, extending her sensation as if he were determined to make their time together last, but eventually he gave himself over to desire that consumed them both. And when they finally climaxed, Egypt buried her face against Garrett's warm chest.

Egypt had never felt this way. It had never crossed her mind that she could fall for a man so easily. She'd thought that sex was sex, but what was happening between her and Garrett had nothing to do with sex at all. It had to do with feelings and emotions. Those where her last thoughts as Egypt fell asleep in Garrett's arms.

Eleven

Garrett was frustrated. How could some things in his life go perfectly and the rest be a pile of crap? The last month with Egypt had been fantastic. When she wasn't at the restaurant, they were together—whether he took a ride share to her place or she drove to the farm. They'd even had dinner with Kent and his wife, Aurora. Having a love for the kitchen, the two women got on fabulously while he and Kent shared a beer.

He learned Egypt was a daddy's girl and incredibly close to the man who had single-handedly raised her after her mother's death. He also discovered she had a love of all things chocolate and had a terrible singing voice after they went to a karaoke bar late on Saturday night. Garrett, meanwhile, realized he hated baseball after Kent took him to a game, but loved basketball and wasn't a fan of beans after Egypt made a taco night with all the fixings.

They were getting to know each other, and when Garrett was with Egypt, he forgot about everything else. He thought his hunger for her might abate after the newness wore off, but it hadn't. Whenever they were together, his hands were all over silky brown skin. He liked everything about her, from the scent of her skin to her lush curves and to her sense of humor. And she was his equal in passion.

He thought about the way she'd straddled his thighs this morning and lowered herself onto his length. He'd gritted his teeth and beads of sweat had popped out on his brow when she slowly began to circle her hips. The sight of her cupping her breasts as she moved against him made Garrett hard just thinking about it. She'd writhed against him, her muscles tugging and taking him over the edge. His entire world smashed apart, and white-hot pleasure gripped him. Egypt was a potent aphrodisiac he would never tire of. However, there were times he sensed trepidation in Egypt. Was there something in her past that was making her hold back from giving herself entirely to him and he didn't mean just physically. Had someone hurt her in the past? He wanted to know everything about her and he knew that was pot calling the kettle black when he had no memory of his former life.

But on the other front, he was tired of coming up empty on his identity. He'd taken the detective's advice and gone through every box in his grandfather's office and house, but he hadn't found a single item, a birth certificate or Social Security card he could use to help him. And that was puzzling. If his grandfather had gained custody of him after his parents' deaths, wouldn't he have kept some record of it?

His memories of the farm were real. Garrett hadn't made up the moments of helping his grandfather find a stray cow that had gotten away or fixing a fence on the farm or Cyrus taking him shooting for the first time. There it was again—a fleeting memory. But they'd been coming more frequently lately.

Like the other night, when he'd remembered being in his twenties at Wharton. Garrett recalled feeling arrogant and full of himself. He didn't recognize that person, which was why he hadn't told Kent or even Egypt about those memories, because he was trying to reconcile it with the person he was today. Would either of them like the old Garrett?

Today, when he and Kent had been working on putting together the tents and tables for the upcoming public picking, it occurred to Garrett how much his father, Hugh, would hate him working outside. Hugh had always told Garrett to use his mind instead of brawn. Suddenly, an image of his mother, Corrine, with her soft brown eyes, long bob and a beautiful chestnut complexion, flashed in Garrett's mind. She was beautiful and poised and hated being reminded of her humble upbringing. But his father never let her forget it. He was determined to mold her into the perfect wife. Garrett had always hated that.

Garrett stopped what he was doing. He'd just remembered his parents' names! He left Kent in the field and rushed back to the house. Opening the laptop in his office, Garrett looked up Corrine Walker his mother's maiden name, but nothing came up. How could that be? He was certain he was on to something.

"Damn!" He hit the desk with his fist.

"Everything all right in here?" Kent asked, out of breath at the doorway of his office.

Garrett growled. "Not really. I thought I remembered a piece of my past that would be helpful, but *nothing*! I can't continue in limbo for much longer. I appreciate you getting the small bank loan in your name to start up the public picking days while I sort through this."

"Of course," Kent replied and quickly turned away from him, as if he couldn't look him in the eye. "Are you still planning on going to Egypt's later?"

"Yeah." Garrett nodded.

"Let me know if you need a ride?"

"I will." Garrett watched Kent walk away. What he really needed was the truth. For too long there had been a misty nothingness in his blurred brain, but he needed it to come back in focus, because right now, his world was very small and consisted of the farm, Kent and Egypt. Although he loved spending time with both of them, Garrett knew there was more to him than this existence—but how did he find out?

* * *

"I can't believe I'm actually reaching you," Wynter said when she and Egypt spoke later that evening at Flame.

Egypt came off the line to take Wynter's call in her office. Her best friend had called a couple of times over the last week when Egypt had been otherwise occupied. She didn't want to miss Wynter again. Plus, Quentin had everything under control in the kitchen.

"Oh, don't be that way," Egypt chided. "When you and Riley were knee-deep in the throes of your relationship, did I complain when you were busy?"

Wynter sighed. "No, you didn't, but this is my wedding and there's always decisions to be made about the food, cake, flowers, decor and more. I need my best friend around!"

"And I'm here," Egypt soothed. "Have I ever let you down?" There was silence on the other end of the phone. "Well, then, I won't now."

"Everything is happening so fast, and I guess I'm anxious," Wynter said. "I'm going to be a wife."

"To the man you've always loved," Egypt responded. "It doesn't get any better than that."

"And you, Egypt? Is there any chance you and Garrett could be more?"

"Don't go putting that out in the universe," Egypt said, putting her feet up on her desk. "It's much too soon for all that. Garrett and I are a casual fling. And even if I wanted more, that might hard to do when he has amnesia."

"All right, but I haven't seen you like this in a long time."
"Like what?"

"Happy," Wynter responded. "The last few years, your focus has been your business. First, it was the food truck, and then the restaurant. I'm glad you're finally making time for you."

"And I am. Garrett is wonderful, but after Antwan, I have to be cautious and protect my heart."

Egypt glanced up to see Garrett's six-foot-three frame standing in her doorway. She motioned him forward, and he walked toward her. She loved his swag. It was all lean and athleticism, but totally hot. Despite the uncertainty on what the future my bring, she couldn't wait to jump his bones.

Garrett clearly had other plans because he pulled off one of her Crocs and began kneading and massaging her foot. Egypt wanted to purr in delight. Standing for hours in the kitchen every day wasn't easy, but Garrett knew exactly where to press. "Um… Wynter. I… I'm going to have to call you later."

"Let me guess, Garrett is there?"

"You're correct," Egypt replied and closed her eyes when Garrett hit the right spot. She hadn't realized so many parts of her body were erogenous, but Garrett was nothing if not thorough, and he had taken it upon himself to find out every single one of them.

Wynter laughed. "Enjoy, I'll talk to you later."

Egypt tossed her phone on the desk and leaned her head back against the headrest of her executive chair and let Garrett's magic hands go to work.

"That's right, babe, let go," Garrett murmured.

She popped one eye open. "Hello."

He grinned widely. "Hello."

"You're early. Flame doesn't close for another hour."

"I know. I thought I could help out in the kitchen so you can get done sooner." When he was finished with one foot, he grasped the other one and gave it the same treatment.

"You realize you're spoiling me for any other man."

The smile on Garrett's face faded. "Good. Because I don't want you thinking about other men, just on how good I make you feel."

Egypt released a sigh when once again he hit *the* spot. "That won't be a problem, because you make me feel really good." She closed her eyes again.

That was why Egypt had her doubts. She might have to ease her foot off the pedal in the relationship because she didn't want to become too dependent on Garrett for her own emotional well-being. Garrett was missing a big chunk of her life and Egypt didn't know where she would fit it in once he did. She was trying to keep some walls up. She was afraid of losing herself like she had with Antwan. Having her own business assured that, but this time she would have to make time for herself and the Six Gems instead of being caught up in her man's world.

Wait a second.

Both her eyes popped open. Had she just thought *her man*?

She was certain he wasn't sleeping with anyone else. They had a very active sex life. He didn't have a reason to look elsewhere, and neither did she. When they were together, she felt like his. Like she was made for him.

"What's wrong?" Garrett asked.

Egypt blinked and sat up. "Uh…nothing." She pulled her feet out of his lap and put her Crocs back on. "I have to get back to work, but follow me. I'm sure I can find a use for you."

The use consisted of Garrett doing dishes and cleaning the stoves and oven. He hadn't known what to do, having obviously never done much kitchen work before, but he didn't complain and was a trouper. Consequently, they were able to clean up Flame in record time. Garrett didn't know it, but while he was working in the kitchen, Egypt had Tessa set up a table for two in the dining room.

She had prepared some of her favorite tapas—prosciutto-wrapped dates filled with goat cheese; petite rack of lamb with Dijon mustard; roasted Brussels sprouts in balsamic, brown butter and pine nuts; chicken skewers with rosemary in a lemon-tarragon sauce; and hoisin-glazed beef short ribs—for Garrett to try.

When the food and table were ready, she quickly hustled everyone out of Flame.

"Good to see you again, Garrett." Quentin shook his hand on the way out the back door. "Have fun tonight, boss."

"Thank you," she mouthed and locked the door behind him. Finally. She and Garrett were alone.

"Fun?" Garrett asked with a wicked grin. "Did you have something else in mind?"

Egypt chuckled. "Yes, I do." She grabbed his hand and led him through the double doors of the kitchen into the dining room. All the lights had been dimmed, and a candlelit table for two sat center stage. She turned to him. "What do you think?"

"No wonder you didn't want me going out front," Garrett murmured. "And to answer your question… I love it." He swept his mouth across hers. Then he led her to the table and, ever the gentleman, pulled out her chair. "This is quite a spread, Egypt. You can't honestly expect us to eat all of this."

"Whatever we don't eat, you can take home," she responded and began taking the lids off several of the platters.

"It all smells delicious. I don't know where to begin."

"Let me." She took his plate and added a little bit of everything onto it. "Try this one first." She took one of the prosciutto-wrapped dates and placed it in his mouth.

"Mmm…that's good," Garrett murmured. "What kind of cheese is that?"

"Goat cheese."

"It's very earthy." When she laughed, he corrected himself, "But I don't mind it."

"It's okay, you don't have to like everything I make. Try one of the lamb chops." She added one to her plate as well as a short rib and some Brussels sprouts.

When she glanced up, she found Garrett had finished the chop in one fell swoop and was licking his fingers. She gasped and her eyes became wide and she felt her sex clench with desire. She wanted his tongue on her. "Woman, you're killing me. This food is amazing."

Egypt grinned from ear to ear. "Thank you. It's really great to hear."

"But you know you're good."

"I wasn't always, or at least some people didn't think so," Egypt replied.

"What people?"

"My ex-boyfriend Antwan. He always criticized my cooking, like he'd gone to culinary school or something."

"How did that make you feel?" Garrett asked, reaching for another lamb chop and finishing it again in record time. Then he moved on to the chicken and Brussels sprouts.

She pressed her thumb and forefinger together. "This small. He always did that, put me down. I think it made him feel better. Like he was the big man. He was a real narcissist, but you're nothing like that."

"I would hope not." Garrett put his fork down.

"You're not," Egypt stated emphatically. "Antwan preferred it when all eyes were on him. Heaven forbid anyone look at or acknowledge me. He never let me get a word in edgewise."

"Why did you stay with him?"

Egypt shrugged. "That's a good question. I guess I was shocked that a guy like him would want a girl like me."

"What do you mean, *a girl like you*?"

"C'mon, Garrett. I'm not the average-size woman. I have a few extra pounds, and well, Antwan criticized me and told me I needed to lose weight."

Garrett reached for her hand, and she placed her small one in his palm. "Well, I'm not him. I like you just the way you are. In case you can't tell, I think your figure is hella sexy, and I can't get enough of you."

Hearing the words from Garrett's lips was like a balm to her ego. "I can't get enough of you, either."

Within seconds, they were both reaching for each other from across the table and kissing passionately. Egypt opened her mouth so she could explore Garrett's and mate her tongue with his. Desire swept through her like molten lava, and a low moan escaped her lips.

"Egypt, I want you."

She didn't have the willpower to deny him when it meant she would be denying herself, too, but they couldn't—not in her dining room.

"My office," she murmured, and to her shock, Garrett

wrapped her legs around his waist and carried her past the kitchen to her office. There was a couch she kept there for when she needed to take a quick break, but glancing down, she figured there was no way they were both going to fit.

"The floor," she urged, and Garrett tipped her backward onto the soft rug she'd thrown in front of the sofa. Then his strong arms were around her, drawing her against the solid expanse of his chest as he possessed her mouth once again. He teased her with demanding licks and flicks of his tongue. All the while his hands roamed her body, tearing open her chef's coat to reveal the lacy bra she wore underneath. Then his hands were at her waist and she was shifting her hips so he could remove her black leggings.

"I never get tired of you," Garrett rasped, and then he was drawing her panties down toward her feet.

Once again, she was in a vulnerable position, spread out naked on the rug in her office as if she were a buffet meal. And from the look in his eyes, she was. Garrett moved down her body, kissing her breasts and her belly until he came to the heart of her. He separated her, pushing her legs wide, and anointed her with his lips and tongue. Egypt's head lolled back, her eyes shutting as he moved his tongue slowly and deliberately against her nerve center. He made her writhe with pleasure, and when that wasn't enough, he added his digits. Egypt clutched his head and cried out his name when wave after wave of bone-melting pleasure took her over. "Garrett!"

She was spinning into the abyss, but before it could abate, she heard the rustling of foil and then Garrett was naked and entering her with a slow, penetrating thrust that made every hair on her head tighten. Egypt arched off the floor as she took the full weight of him. The sensation of them melding together was always amazing, and she circled her arms around his neck and kissed him. Her teeth grazed his tongue and bottom lip and he growled, tightening his hands around her hips, tilting her to him. Then he began moving in a smooth, deep rhythm that had the pressure in Egypt's body building like some tribal drumbeat.

Garrett must have felt it, too, because his movements became wilder and more urgent, and his breathing was ragged. "Don't hold back," she urged. "Give it to me."

Tension rose, so high and so tight until eventually it broke and bliss of the purest kind took over. Egypt clutched Garrett with her legs and clawing hands. She didn't know how long her cries went on, but she heard Garrett's shout as he pulsed inside her.

Egypt hugged him close, knowing in that moment that Wynter was right. This had become more—and she was falling in love with Garrett. Egypt wasn't sure her heart could withstand the fallout if they were to part ways, but she also couldn't deny that she found Garrett irresistible.

Twelve

Garrett stared off into space as he thought about last night with Egypt. She'd been unrestrained and completely without inhibitions. He'd been hungrier, harder and more demanding than ever before, and it had felt different. Not in a bad way. Egypt made him feel things, *want* things, and it felt natural. Comfortable. It made Garrett realize he was catching feelings for Egypt, but how could she want him when he didn't know who he was?

She liked the new Garrett, but who was he really? After leaving Flame, he'd asked himself that very thing. How could he be in a serious relationship with Egypt with all these unanswered questions? Yet, on the other hand, he refused to give her up. He felt like he could be whoever he was with her and she could do the same. She'd never shared anything about her past with him before until last night. It showed Garrett she was opening up and making room for him in her heart.

Now, if his mind could only see clear to helping him out and giving him all of his memory rather than these snippets, he would be a happy man. Fate, it seemed, heard Garrett's wish, because the next morning he was in the barn climbing to get a wayward chicken that had gotten stuck in some wiring when he lost his footing. The next thing Garrett knew, he was flying through the air and landing on his back with a loud thud.

Whomp!

"Garrett!" Kent rushed toward him. "Are you okay?" he asked, glancing down. "How many fingers do you see?" He held up his palm.

"Five," Garrett stated and took the hand Kent offered to help him off the floor, but when he did, he felt woozy.

"Whoa! I've got you," the foreman said, putting his shoulder underneath Garrett's arm. "You took a mighty big fall. I can help you to the house."

"Thanks, I think that would be a good idea." Garrett hadn't felt this off-balance since he'd been in the hospital.?

It took a few minutes, but eventually Kent helped Garrett up the stairs of the farmhouse. "Why don't you take it easy for the rest of the day? Me and the men can handle everything."

"The farm opens to the public in a week," Garrett said, holding the banister. "We've got to get everything ready."

"And we will," Kent replied. "Whatever it takes. You take it easy. I'll check on you in a bit."

"Thanks, Kent." He waved the man off. Once the front door had shut, Garrett glanced around the farmhouse. It looked different to him. Slowly, he walked to the living room. He hadn't changed much since he arrived here a month ago. This house, this farm was all he had left of his grandfather, and he refused to give it up, no matter how much his father wanted him to.

Where had that thought come from?

Garrett felt the back of his head, where a nice-size knot was forming. He didn't need another head injury, but that wasn't what was bothering him. It was these constant nagging feelings about his parents. As the days wore on, it was becoming increasingly apparent to him that he didn't feel like an orphan. Deep down in his gut, Garrett sensed his parents were alive and well. So, if that was true, why would Kent tell him his parents were dead?

Garrett went upstairs to his grandfather's room. He'd been hesitant before, but he had to keep looking for clues about his past. The room smelled of the old man, like pine and sandal-wood. Garrett allowed himself to reminisce for a few minutes before he tore the room apart. Eventually he found a box of old photographs in the back closet he hadn't spotted before. Slowly, he opened it and started pulling out old black-and-white photographs. There were some of his grandfather Cyrus with a young girl. It had to be his mother, Corrine. Garrett contin-ued flipping through the photographs until he came to another. This one was of his mother in her prom dress.

He kept moving through the pictures until he came across a wedding photograph. Garrett instantly knew who they were. It was of his parents and his grandfather Cyrus. He continued searching and found more pictures. Pictures of Garrett as a young boy. Pictures of him as a gangly teenager before he had an ounce of muscle.

He had parents. He had a life before the farm, but ever since he woke up, there had been nothing. But his memory was start-ing to come back, stronger and stronger each day. Garrett knew he was a businessman like his father, Hugh, who was arrogant, demanding and controlling. He'd modeled himself to be like his father so he could take over the family business one day. He didn't know what that business was, but he knew it wasn't farming or manual labor.

Once the truth came out, what would it mean for him? For the farm? For him and Egypt? The old Garrett was a leader. A businessman who made decisions that affected hundreds each day. How did he merge that Garrett with the person he had be-come today? Because he'd changed. When he woke up from the coma, Garrett had had nothing, so he'd made do with the cards he'd been dealt. He no longer cared about how many zeroes were in his bank account, but about living a life with purpose. He was living life for today and making each moment count.

He refused to go back to being a person too busy to enjoy life. Why? Because he had too much to lose now. He had a good woman with a big heart. And if he was honest with himself, he could envision having a future with Egypt. Was he alone in his feelings? Or did she feel that way, too?

"You guys really didn't have to come here," Egypt said when the other five Gems descended on Flame that Friday for what would be the restaurant's six-month anniversary.

Not only had Wynter and Shay shown up from San Antonio, but Lyric and Teagan both flew in from Memphis and Phoenix earlier today, while Asia, who'd stayed on the East Coast, had driven in late last night.

"Of course, we have to be here!" Teagan exclaimed. "Six months is a big milestone." She looked fashion-forward in a Dior pantsuit with high-heeled sandals and, her chic pixie hair-cut was as sharp as ever.

"Yeah, we couldn't let this moment pass by without acknowledging it," Lyric stated in that soft-spoken way of hers. Egypt truly hoped that one day there would be a man worthy of their former ballerina. Lyric had always had an easygoing manner, so sometimes she might get lost in the fray of the Six Gems' big personalities, but she always stood her ground.

"I appreciate it," Egypt said. "And if I had known, I would have reserved a spot for you, but as you can see—" she glanced around the packed restaurant "—it's a busy night."

"Is running your own place really that difficult?" Shay inquired. She was nearly finished with the construction of her Pilates and yoga studio and Egypt didn't want to discourage her, but she needed to know the truth.

"It can be," Egypt admitted, "because everything falls on your shoulders."

"Don't worry about us," Wynter responded. "We can wait at the bar. When a table opens up, we'll be waiting."

"But I'm wearing four-inch heels," Asia pouted. Of course, she'd come dressed as if she were going out to a nightclub in a black bustier dress that barely reached her knees and heels so tall, Egypt would topple over in them.

"I think there's one seat open," Shay said, inclining her head to the bar. "Why don't you take it, Asia?" They were all used to coddling their friend, but sometimes Egypt wanted to throttle her.

Egypt inclined her head. "I have to get back to work, but I'll be back soon."

She turned on her heel to go, just as Wynter said, "Take your time."

Egypt gave her a thumbs-up signal. Having her besties in town meant they were going to ask a lot of questions about her relationship with Garrett, and she wasn't ready to answer them. Egypt was still getting accustomed to these growing feelings she felt for her man of mystery, because she didn't have anything to compare it to other than her failed relationship with Antwan.

She didn't know what it was like to have an honest, open relationship with a man. Yet, somehow that's exactly where she found herself, and it was frightening. She was so out of her depth with Garrett, but he was a warm, kind and giving man. And proving to her more and more each day that he was someone she could rely on and trust. So why couldn't she allow herself a smidgen of hope that he could be the one?

Egypt continued working through the busy evening until the dinner rush ended, and only then did she freshen up so she could spend time with her friends. She found them seated at one of the circular booths and indulging in their meal when she approached.

"Everything has been delicious," Wynter said with a smile.

Egypt beamed with pride. "Thank you."

"C'mon in." Lyric scooted over to make room so Egypt was finally able to get off her feet.

"Flame was busy tonight. Is it always like this?" Teagan inquired.

Egypt shook her head. "Not always. Some days are better than others. The restaurant business can be fickle."

"So can real estate," Teagan replied. "Sometimes the market is hot and houses are selling within hours or days. Other times, it's a buyer's market and there's too much inventory. It's feast or famine. That's why you have to prepare yourself for those times."

Egypt nodded in agreement.

"You're making me nervous about setting up shop," Shay replied. "Fitness should be an important component of everyone's lives, but it's always the first thing to go when times get hard."

"Same goes for a dance studio," Lyric responded.

"But we're smart women," Egypt said, looking around the table. "We can weather any storm. We have to be prepared and look ahead."

"You make it sound easy," Asia responded. "From the business plan you helped me work on, it's anything but."

"Let's not be all doom and gloom," Wynter stated. "We are here to celebrate Flame." She picked up her martini glass. "Let's toast to Flame's six-month anniversary."

"Hear, hear." The other women clinked glasses. Egypt chatted with the girls until it was quitting time, and then she made plans to meet up the following day for brunch before they flew back home. She couldn't believe they'd all flown in for the occasion. She told Garrett as much on the phone later that night after she'd dragged herself home and taken a shower.

She was now in bed and wishing he were there with her.

"You're lucky to have such a wonderful group of friends who are there for you," Garrett said. "I envy you."

She hadn't realized how insensitive she was being. Of course, this was a tough subject for Garrett given his current situation. "I'm sorry. I wasn't thinking—" she began, but he cut her off.

"It's okay, Egypt," Garrett responded. "It's not your fault I can't remember who I am."

"Has there been any progress on that front?"

There was silence on the other end, and Egypt wondered

if he'd heard her or was he keeping something from her? But then Garrett replied. "Umm. . .Not really. It's very frustrating to be missing such a huge chunk of my world."

"Maybe you should go back to Dr. Burke and run some tests, make sure there's no residual effects from the carjacking?"

"That's a great idea, babe. Thank you. I don't know what I would do without you."

His words gave Egypt pause, because she didn't know what to say. Her motto since the disaster with Antwan had always been that men were interchangeable. She would get what *she* needed move on to the next one, but for the first time, she wanted to be with *one* man.

"How long are your friends staying? I would love to meet them."

"Not long. They're were here for the anniversary, and we're having brunch tomorrow before they head home." When she thought about introducing Garrett to her friends, Egypt's stomach started doing backflips. It was a big deal. It meant they were more than bed partners, but they hadn't discussed what they were to each other.

"I take it by your silence you would rather not," Garrett stated.

"It's not that."

"Then what?" The question came out sharp, and Egypt sensed she'd struck a nerve.

"Garrett, we haven't actually talked about what we're doing together or what comes next."

There was a long pause. "I thought you enjoyed our time together."

"I do. I'm saying we haven't defined what we are, what we're doing here. There's still so much unknown for you, and I don't want you to feel pushed into doing or saying something when you don't have all the facts."

"Listen, Egypt, I might have amnesia, but I also know a good thing when I see it. You're an amazing woman, and I love spending time with you. I don't want to see anyone else. I want to explore a deeper connection with you, but only if you're willing. I want you to be *my woman*—if you want to be."

Egypt damn near dropped the phone. She hadn't expected that response. But had she secretly been hoping Garrett felt this tangible thread between them like she felt? Yes. Because it was more powerful than anything she'd felt with another man, including Antwan.

She hadn't wanted to belong to anyone in so long. She'd been content with the status quo and casual relationships. Until Garrett. He wanted her to be *his woman*. She yearned for that, too, but deep down, Egypt was scared. Their relationship was so new and there were so many unknowns, but she also was afraid of letting go of the best thing that ever happened to her.

"Yes, I'll be your lady," Egypt said, "if you'll be my man."

"*Yes!*" Garrett declared. "Your words are music to my ears, Egypt. What do you say about tomorrow? Can I meet the other five Gems?"

"Yes, let's do it!" she responded.

She hoped she wouldn't regret her decision about going out on a limb with Garrett.

Thirteen

Egypt was his.

Garrett couldn't believe his luck that a woman as fine and sexy as Egypt Cox wanted to be with him, even though he didn't have much to offer her. He was a farmer with little memory of his former life, but she was still open to the possibility of what they could be. It's why he had to figure out his past. He couldn't let his lack of memory stand between them. When she asked him the other night about his memory, he hadn't exactly been forthcoming. He didn't want to share it with her until he knew more about the businessman he was before-until he knew the possible blow back. He didn't want to keep anything from Egypt, but she was trepidatious about their relationship and he didn't want her to think they weren't compatible. Because they were in, in and out of bed.

But his present beckoned. He and Kent were preparing for the grand opening of the farm to the public. Customers would be given buckets or wagons so they could pick fruits and vegetables and then be charged by the pound. With Kent's help, they'd assembled a staff to work the tents to help folks to pay and pack up their selections. Although there had been an initial outlay of costs to get the signs, supplies, tents and retail stations set up, the revenue brought in from the picking days would more than offset it. They'd advertised in the local town newspaper as well as in Raleigh.

Garrett was determined that this endeavor would succeed. It had to, because the farm needed an economic boost. Once he was sure everything was moving smoothly for the opening next weekend, he took a rideshare over to the brunch location Egypt had texted him this morning.

He was surprised to find the restaurant was packed and quite lively, but then again, that was Egypt. There wasn't anything dull or boring about the woman. She was bold and larger than life. He was looking forward to meeting the people who'd shaped her into the person she was today. Garrett had changed out of his work clothes into some black jeans and a black button-down shirt, which he'd discovered in the back of his grandfather's closet along with the photo box.

After checking in with the hostess, she led him to the terrace where Egypt and her friends were seated. "Ladies." He smiled across the table at the sea of beautiful faces, but none of them were more attractive than *his* woman. He headed straight for Egypt and planted a big kiss on her succulent lips that were tinted with red lipstick. "Hey, babe."

She grinned at him, and Garrett had to remind himself they weren't alone; otherwise, he'd be leaning in for another kiss. "Thank you for allowing me to join you," he said, sitting in the empty chair beside Egypt.

"The pleasure is all ours," a petite brunette with big brown eyes said as she smirked at him.

"Garrett, let me introduce you around the table," Egypt responded. "To my left is Asia, Teagan, Lyric and Shay, and beside you is Wynter."

Garrett turned to the caramel-skinned woman at his side who wore her hair in luxurious waves to her shoulders. "Congratulations on your upcoming marriage."

Wynter beamed back at him. "Why, thank you, Garrett. I'm very excited to jump the broom."

"We can't wait, either. It's all she and my brother talk about," the toffee-skinned woman beside her responded. She had long dark locks and looked fit and athletic.

"Tell us about yourself," another woman with a short haircut stated. If Garrett recalled correctly, her name was Teagan.

"I wish I could oblige," Garrett said, "but given that I woke up from a coma a couple of months ago without a memory, there's not much to tell."

"How are you feeling?" the woman with the chestnut hair and almond-shaped eyes asked. He suspected she was Lyric. Egypt said she was the quiet one, yet the kindest of all the Six Gems.

"Better. No residual effects, but still big pockets of memory are gone."

"That must very hard for you," Lyric empathized. "I'm sorry."

"Thank you," Garrett responded. Other than Egypt and Kent, he hadn't had many people care about his welfare other than doctors and nurses in the hospital.

"But you've been working at a farm?" Wynter asked by his side. "How's that going?"

"It was my grandfather's. And yes, I've been working hard to make it succeed. We'll be opening the farm up to the public for picking season. People will be able to come and select their own fresh fruits and vegetables. We'll even supply our products to Egypt's restaurants and hope to add more."

He slid his hand through Egypt's at the table and linked their fingers. She gave him a saucy wink, and Garrett got lost in her eyes. It wasn't until Shay spoke that he rejoined the conversation.

"That's an amazing idea," Shay replied. "Fresh fruits and veggies are what I always preach to my clients. I'm a fitness coach."

Garrett nodded. "I can tell. What's your favorite class?"

And that's how the rest of the afternoon went, with lively conversation between Garrett and the Six Gems until eventually it was time for him to leave.

"It was a pleasure meeting all of you," he said, glancing around the table. "I can't thank you enough for allowing me the chance to get to know you." He leaned down and brushed his lips across Egypt's. "I'll talk to you later, babe."

He knew the ladies wanted to gossip about him before they were due back at the airport. He hoped the other Six Gems liked him and thought he was good for Egypt, just like she was good for him.

"Well?" Egypt asked, looking around the table. She'd been quiet during most of the conversation, only chiming in here and there. She wanted Garrett to feel comfortable with these women, her *sisters*, because they were a big part of her life.

"I think he's amazing," Wynter stated without hesitation. "And absolutely perfect for you."

"Of course you would think that, because your head is in the clouds about your pending nuptials," Teagan replied. "I liked him, I really did…"

"But?" Egypt asked. She hated when Teagan got on her soapbox, but she'd agreed to bring Garrett to brunch, so she had to take it on the chin.

"Am I the only one with a little bit of reservations?" Teagan asked, folding her arms across her chest. "I think he's a great guy, Egypt, but what do you really know about him?"

Egypt's hackles went up. "I know enough. And listen, I get it, okay? Garrett doesn't have his memories and I'm concerned about that which is why I'm being cautious and taking this slowly, but I know he's a good person."

"And that's fine, but you don't know for sure there's not another woman in his life or if he's married."

"His foreman said there wasn't anyone else."

"But didn't Garrett live up north? He may not have told anyone," Teagan countered.

Her words sparked Egypt's anger. "Why are you trying to rain on my parade? Is it because you don't have a man of your own?"

"If I wanted a man, I could get one," Teagan replied tersely, "anytime, anyplace."

Egypt rolled her eyes. "And what about the rest of you? Do you share Teagan's opinion?" She looked across the table into four pairs of eyes.

"I don't." Lyric shook her head. "I think he's wonderful. So what, you don't know everything about him? You'll find it out as you get to know one another. It's not like you're marrying the guy."

"Besides, it's a short-term thing," Asia added. But her statement caused Egypt to lower her head, and her friend picked up on it. "Garrett isn't one of your casual boos?"

Egypt lifted her chin and stared directly into Asia's brown eyes. "No, he isn't. He's more, and that's scary enough without hearing all your negativity, Teagan."

"I think she just wants you to be cautious," Shay replied diplomatically. "She doesn't want you getting hurt. None of us do."

"Then trust that I know what I'm doing. It isn't easy going out on a ledge with Garrett when I don't know his past, but I'm listening to my gut. It's telling me I can trust him. He's no Antwan. He's not going to lie and deceive me."

"I tend to agree," Wynter chimed in. "Garrett gave me good vibes. Plus, I saw the way he looked at you, Egypt, and vice versa. I haven't seen you with stars in your eyes *ever*."

"Well, I stand corrected." Teagan sat up straight. "I really only want the best for you, Egypt. You're my girl. No—you're my sista, and there's nothing I wouldn't do for you."

Egypt leaned across the table and grabbed Teagan's hand. "I appreciate your concern and I'm sorry for being snippy, but I've got this."

After seeing the Gems off at the airport, she headed home for some time alone. Despite her bravado, Teagan's words gave her pause, niggling away at the questions she'd been trying to ignore. Her friend was right—Egypt didn't know much about Garrett, because he didn't remember anything about himself. Her instincts told her he was trustworthy, so she was doing her best to lean into that head space and not the other, but it wasn't easy teaching an old dog new tricks.

Teagan had planted further seeds of doubt in Egypt's mind about Garrett and whether she could trust everything he said. Time would tell if the gamble she'd made would pay off or whether she'd made the biggest mistake of her life.

Fourteen

"Today is a big day," Kent said the next Saturday when he and Garrett walked around the farm to ensure everything was in order before opening to the public later that day.

"Yes, and it will be a success." Deep down in his bones, Garrett knew this was the right direction and would help generate the revenue they needed. He still needed to pay Kent back for the loan he'd taken out. In the back of his mind, he had more ideas for expansion, such as a corn maze, food truck court area and a kids' zone. Saving his grandfather's legacy meant something to him.

"I hope so," Kent replied. "We have a lot riding on this."

"Don't I know it." Garrett said. He'd voiced those concerns to Egypt last night, but she refused to hear his negativity. Said she'd had enough of it. When he pressed her, she'd clammed up.

Garrett suspected her tight lips had something to do with the Six Gems. He'd thought the meeting with them had gone well, but Egypt had been distant the last week and they hadn't seen each other, not even on her day off. She'd claimed it was because she needed some time to herself, but Garrett suspected otherwise.

One or more of the Gems must have expressed doubt in him. He worried what a strain on their relationship would do to Egypt. Those women meant everything to Egypt and he didn't want to come between them, but they'd just met him. Surely, once they got to know Garrett, they'd realize he and Egypt were good together.

In the meantime, he would continue to prove himself. Like today, for example—Egypt was bringing her father to the farm. When she'd indicated he was a fan of sustainable living and eating well, Garrett had asked her to invite him. She'd been hesitant because their relationship was so new, but he wanted to meet the man who'd given Egypt life. He wasn't afraid of being grilled by her father. What he was afraid of was not having all the answers because of his memory loss, but that was improving daily.

Last night after his call with Egypt, Garrett had dreamed of living in a big mansion and driving the fancy sports car that had been carjacked at Flame. He remembered arguing with his father about something that was just on the edge of his memory, but he couldn't grasp it. When he woke this morning, Garrett knew his memory was returning.

Figuring out his real identity was finally within his grasp, and it was good thing because Garrett was ready to take back his life.

Egypt wasn't sure if she was doing the right thing introducing Garrett to her father. She already had her own insecurities about their relationship, given her past history, but she'd been willing to try. However, the Six Gems' visit gave her serious reservations about whether she'd foolishly led with her heart by agreeing to be Garrett's woman when she knew so little about him.

Was she making the same mistake she'd made with Antwan? Egypt refused to be lied to and deceived again. That was why she'd kept her distance from Garrett this week in the hopes of getting clarity, but in the end, her instincts told her she could believe Garrett, which was why she decided to go ahead and make the drive to the farm.

"Do you know what we're picking?" her father inquired.

"No, but I'm sure whatever they have, it will be great."

Anthony gave a sideways glance. "Is everything all right, sweetheart? You've been awfully quiet on the drive here."

She hazarded him a quick look. "I'm fine."

"Whenever a woman says she's fine," her father replied, "she means the exact opposite. Are you worried about me meeting your new beau?"

"It might be a bit early," Egypt admitted.

"Don't worry, I'll go easy on him."

Egypt shook her head. "Oh, no. You give him everything you've got. Garrett's no pushover. He'll know if you're not being one hundred percent genuine."

"I look forward to meeting him."

They chatted for another half hour before driving up the dirt road toward the farm. Egypt was thrilled to see a line of cars ahead of her as well as a nearly full parking lot. She parked where the attendant directed and turned off the engine.

They walked up the dirt path to a tent where Kent and another staff person were welcoming everyone to Walker Farms and telling them the logistics of where to pick and when to pay.

Once they had buckets in hand, Egypt and her father started toward the blueberry patch. There were rows and rows of blueberry bushes, some small, some tall. They started with the bigger ones so they'd have to bend down less. The blueberries were large, plump and deliciously sweet. They picked and ate a few while tossing others into the pail. They were getting into a steady rhythm when she heard her name.

"Egypt!"

She spun around and saw Garrett walking briskly toward them in the patch. Egypt rose and heart stuttered in her chest at how devastatingly handsome Garrett made a t-shirt and pair of jeans look. Since it was a beautiful spring day, Egypt had opted for denim capris and a baby doll top and wrapped her denim jacket around her waist.

When Garrett made it to them, rather than give her one of his usual searing kisses that left her toes tingling, he gave Egypt a quick hug and released her. Then he offered her father his hand. "Mr. Cox, it's a pleasure to meet you, sir."

Her father shook his hand vigorously. "Good to meet you as well. I've heard nothing but great things."

Garrett's dark eyes met hers and smiled. "Thank you. I think your daughter is pretty amazing."

Egypt broke into a wide open smile and her pulse leapt at his words.

Her father grinned widely and circled his arm around Egypt's waist. "I think so, too."

"When you're done picking, I'd love to give you a tour of the farm."

"I would like that," her father said.

After Garrett had gone, her father looked over at Egypt. "He's a good-looking young fella."

Egypt chuckled. "He is, but that's not the only reason I like him."

She turned to watch Garrett leave the blueberry patch. They were off to a good start. Maybe introducing the two most important men in her life wasn't a bad thing after all.

After leaving Egypt and her father, Garrett made the rounds, checking in with his staff. Everything was going exactly as he anticipated. The public seemed thrilled with the farm and the selections offered. Garrett had even convinced Aurora, Kent's wife, to sell some of her freshly squeezed lemonade and blueberry doughnuts at a stand. From the line he saw, it was a hit, and she gave him a thumbs-up sign as he passed by.

When he was certain the day was going well, he headed back to check on Egypt and Mr. Cox. Garrett knew how close Egypt was to her father, and it was important that he make a good impression on him. He returned to the blueberry patch with a golf cart and found they'd filled their buckets to the brim.

"Here, let me help you with that." Garrett took both buckets and placed them in the golf cart. When he went to help Egypt into the front, a delicious shudder heated his body, but then she shook her head. "I'll sit in the back so you and Daddy can get better acquainted."

"Of course." He felt a spark of electricity when he helped her into the cart. His eyes found hers and he knew she'd felt it too. He couldn't act on the smoldering flame he saw in her gaze, instead, he turned to give Mr. Cox a hand but found he was already seated. So Garrett returned to the driver side. "Let me show you around."

Garrett began the tour by explaining the type of farm they were on and the improvements he was making to ensure its profitability—one of which was opening the farm to the public.

"This was your grandfather's place?" Mr. Cox inquired.

"It was," Garrett replied. "He passed away and left the farm to me."

"He must have thought very highly of you to leave you his most prized possession."

Garrett nodded. "I agree, sir. Its why I'm trying to increase profits to ensure it can go on for the next generation. I feel a sense of responsibility to do right by him, because he raised me—or at least I'm told he did."

Her father glanced sideways at him. "You think otherwise?"

"Without all my memory, I'm relying on the word of others." He hadn't shared his suspicions about Kent lying to him about his parents to Egypt. He wanted to come to her when he had all the facts.

"I can't even imagine what you've gone through, but you've shown resilience to keep moving on, not knowing your past."

Garrett nodded. "Thank you."

They continued talking amiably until Garrett drove them to the produce field. "Egypt told me you're a big fan of eating green, so you'll love the cucumbers, lettuce, broccoli, carrots and asparagus we have on-site."

"I look forward to it," her father said and exited the golf cart. "You two talk. I'll find my own way."

After he'd gone, Garrett turned back to Egypt and found her grinning from ear to ear. "What?"

"He likes you," she responded, jumping down off the cart.

"You think so?" he asked, following suit.

She nodded. "I *know* so. My father respects you and appreciates your work ethic despite the circumstances."

"Good. Because I don't intend on going anywhere. Now come here, I've missed you."

Garrett pulled Egypt into his arms and grasped both sides of her face. He pressed his lips to hers, and it didn't take long for the kiss to move from soft and gentle to hot and passionate. Egypt clutched at his back as if she were desperate for purchase. He forgot they were standing in the middle of the road with people walking all around them. That's what Egypt did to him—she made her feel like he was the luckiest man on the planet.

Eventually, they broke apart so they could get air in their lungs.

"You'd better go. Otherwise, I'm going to ravish you in front of an audience."

Egypt chuckled. "All right, I'll see you soon." She headed down the row to help her father pick some veggies.

Garrett watched Egypt's lush backside as she moved away from him. He was so busy focusing on her that he didn't see a short man walk toward him until he was right in from him.

"Thomas?"

Garrett glanced down and saw the bespectacled man looking up at him as if he'd seen a ghost.

"Pardon me?"

"I can't believe it's you!" the man continued, staring at Garrett as if hadn't spoken. "Your parents will be so relieved. They thought someone kidnapped you."

Garrett shook his head. He wasn't ready for the real world to come crashing in. Not today. Not when Egypt and her father were here and he was making headway with her seeing a future with *this* Garrett. "I think you have the wrong person." He started walking away, but the man persisted and followed him.

"I'm not wrong. It *is* you."

Garrett spun around on his heel. "My parents are dead." He didn't know this man and he certainly wasn't about to get into a discussion about his past in the middle of the farm.

"They're not. Corrine and Hugh Forrester are very much alive," the man stated.

Garrett's heart began pounding rapidly in his chest, because if this man was right, his whole world was about to shift. He knew it was a possibility that some random person might know him, but he'd wanted to face it on his own terms. But those names—those were his parents' names, but when he'd searched, he hadn't been able to find anything because he had the wrong last name.

Thomas Forrester.

Was that his real name? If so, where they hell did Garrett come from? He'd given Egypt the name before he'd been knocked unconscious and beaten. Why would he lie to her? None of this made any sense, and his head was starting to hurt.

"Excuse me." He attempted to push past the man, but he adamantly stood in his way.

"I can't let you leave, Thomas. Your parents have been worried sick since you've been missing." He stated firmly, "I have to inform them."

Garrett bent down and lowered his voice. "I don't know who the hell you are, so you had better move out of my way." His stern voice must have frightened the man, because he quickly stepped aside so Garrett could march down the path.

"This isn't over!" the man yelled after him.

He was damn right, because he was about to demand answers from Kent and find out why his right-hand man had lied to him for the better part of two months. He'd allowed him to live a life that was a lie and fall in love with a beautiful woman in the process.

Garrett stopped in his tracks.

Love.

He hadn't realized that was the emotion he was feeling toward Egypt until this very moment, when his entire world was feeling flipped on its head. But he should have known, because everything between him and Egypt had felt right from the moment he opened his eyes. Something inside him had shifted, opened, making a way for her. He'd found himself in her, *with* her.

He might have told the man in the field he was lying, but deep down Garrett knew he was speaking the truth. He was indeed Thomas Forrester, but what did it mean? And how would it impact his relationship with Egypt?

Fifteen

Egypt grew still from where she stood in the fields. She saw Garrett interacting with a man she'd never met. And from the expression on his face, Garrett was agitated and angry. What could the stranger have said? Was he a disgruntled customer? She doubted it. The farm had just opened.

What could it be?

She wasn't used to seeing Garrett behave this way, and it was a red flag, because it reminded her of someone in her past. Someone who'd influenced her love life so much, she'd vowed never to repeat the same mistake.

Antwan had been hot-tempered and easily got into altercations. She remembered how jealous he would get if another man happened to speak to her. Egypt was in a field dominated by men; she was always going to be around them. Initially, she'd been too afraid as a line cook to speak about their crude jokes or offhanded remarks. However, as she'd grown in rank to sous-chef, she gained her voice and told the ole boys club where to go. That hadn't stopped Antwan from being extremely jealous and possessive, though.

She should have listened to the voice in her head when it told her to break up with Antwan, but then he'd apologize and show up with flowers and all would be well again. Until it wasn't. Until one day she came home to find he had packed up everything and taken her money along with him.

Egypt didn't know what was going with Garrett, but she would find out. No way would she return to the days of dealing with a volatile man.

Garrett found Kent at one of the retail tents helping the staff with checkouts. Since the line was short, the two staff members would be able to handle customers in his absence.

"Kent, a word," Garrett gritted out.

Kent glanced up at him and frowned. Garrett was unable to hide his displeasure. He was furious, and his expression must have shown it. "Sure thing, boss." He finished ringing up the customer and let one of the other team members take over. Kent walked over to him. "What's up?"

"Get in the golf cart." It wasn't a request. It was an order, and the foreman hopped in without saying a word.

Garrett took off down the dirt path back in the direction of the main house.

"Is everything okay?" Kent inquired, glancing in his direction.

"No." Garrett didn't speak again until they were out of the cart and inside his grandfather's home. Only then did he unleash the wrath bottled up inside him.

"Why did you lie to me, Kent? You've known I was Thomas Forrester all along."

Kent blanched, and Garrett could see the wheels turning in his mind, but he kept a death stare on him. "Well?"

Kent swallowed visibly and lowered his head. "You don't understand, Garrett."

"Enlighten me."

"When Cyrus died, your parents came to the farm, and all I heard was that this place was a dump and they were going to sell it as soon as possible. But then the will was read, and Cyrus didn't leave the farm to your mother, he left it to you."

"Go on." Garrett folded his arms across his chest.

"You had only been back to the farm a handful of times since you were a teen. I assumed you agreed with your parents and were going to close Walker Farms. This place is all I have, Garrett."

"*Garrett.* Where does that name come from?"

"It's your middle name," Kent responded. "Thomas Garrett Forrester. You never liked Thomas and preferred to be called Garrett, your grandfather's middle name, which your parents hated."

He supposed that's why he gave Egypt the name, but that was beside the point. "Let me get this straight. You were so afraid of losing your job, you not only lied to the police, but you've been lying to me for months? You let me believe I was alone in the world. That I had no one. When in fact my parents have been searching for me since the carjacking."

"They did stop by."

He frowned with cold fury. "When? I never saw them."

"When you were in the hospital. They knew you were coming to the farm. At the time, I had no idea you were in the hospital until you woke up two months after the attack. So, when your parents came, I legitimately knew nothing."

"But once I came to, you knew the truth, but you let them go on believing I was gone, lost to them."

Kent nodded. "I'm sorry, Garrett. I was scared. Walker Farms is more than a job to me. Cyrus was the father I never had, and I couldn't bear to lose this place."

"Neither could I!" Garrett responded hotly. "Why do you think I was coming here that night? Not just to see the farm, but to see how I could make it better. This is my grandfather's legacy—there's no way I would give this place up. But you didn't give me the benefit of the doubt, did you? You chose for me. You betrayed me."

"I didn't think I had a choice," Kent replied. "I felt like my back was against the wall. Your amnesia was a godsend."

Garrett snorted. "For you to rewrite history. Do you have any idea how many nights I've agonized about being an orphan? How lonely it's been living in this house with only snippets of my memory?"

Kent didn't speak. What he could say that would make it all right? He'd kept vital information from Garrett for his own selfish purposes.

"I suppose you're going to fire me now?" Kent asked.

Garrett roared, "I can't deal with you right now, Kent! Get the hell out of my house!"

The other man walked to the door and opened it but stopped short. "I know this may not mean much right now, but I'm truly sorry for lying to you, Garrett. You're right. I misjudged you. I thought you were a snob like your parents, and because of that I deceived you, and that's unforgivable. I'll understand if you want my resignation."

Garrett heard the click of the door seconds later. He felt as if all his energy had been sucked out. He sat down on the couch and pulled out his phone. The phone Kent had given him. Like an idiot, he'd believed everything his foreman said.

Opening up a browser, Garrett typed in Thomas Garrett Forrester. A ton of hits came up. The most recent ones were within the last sixty days. He tapped the first article and saw a picture of himself. He wore a suit, which was no doubt custom made, given how rich his parents were. The article mentioned their exhaustive search to find their missing son, with no success, and that he was presumed dead.

Dead.

The word was like a bullet to Garrett's chest.

All this time, his parents had been looking for him, hoping, wishing and praying he was alive, and he'd been here this entire time. And Kent had known. He could have eased their suffering, *Garrett's* suffering. Instead, he'd let this farce go on for months so he could prevent the farm from shutting down.

The joke was at Garrett's expense, because he would never have closed Walker Farms. He remembered now. That was why he and his father were arguing that day. Hugh wanted him to sell, and he'd refused. Instead, he'd decided to leave for a few days to cool off and had stopped at Flame along the way.

God, this was one giant mess.

Garrett had to tell his parents he was alive, but he didn't even know how to reach them. He supposed Kent might know or even have their address, but he was so angry with the man for his lies and deception that he would figure it out for himself. And then there was Egypt. How did he begin to explain to her that he wasn't a simple farmer, but instead the CEO of Forrester Holdings Corporation?

While he didn't want to mess up the good thing he had going with Egypt, he knew he had to tell her the truth. But he wanted to enjoy one last night as Garrett No-Name before the real world burst through the door. When the dust settled, would they still be together?

Where was Garrett?

Egypt hadn't seen him since she'd observed that tense conversation earlier. Even if he was busy, it was unlike him not to check in with her throughout the day. Egypt sent Garrett a text, letting him know she and her father were checking out. She had to get back to Raleigh. Quentin had graciously agreed to open and get started with tonight's prep until she arrived.

They had finished packing the trunk with their provisions when Garrett drove up on the golf cart. He jogged to them at her car.

"Oh, good, I didn't miss you," he said, not remotely out of breath. "Did you enjoy picking?"

"It was great. How was your day?" Egypt searched his face and could see signs of strains around his eyes, even though he was forcing a smile.

"I had some fires to put out," Garrett responded. "You know how it is on the first day."

"I remember that day well," Egypt replied, "so we won't hold you up. I've gotta drive Daddy back and head to Flame."

"Well, it was a pleasure to meet you, Mr. Cox. I'm sorry I didn't get to spend as much time with you as I would have liked."

"You're a business owner, Garrett, I understand." Her father smiled. "I hope the day was a success."

"It certainly appears that way." Garrett shook her father's hand, and then Anthony got back into her car, leaving Egypt and Garrett alone outside.

Egypt touched Garrett's chest and found his heart was pounding. "Is everything okay? You seem agitated."

"I'm sorry. It's been one helluva day." Garrett wrapped his arms around her waist and pulled her closer, into his warm embrace. "I have missed you, though."

"How much?" she asked, because she hadn't realized until now how much she depended on the close connection they shared.

He leaned down and whispered in her ear, "How about I show you later tonight?"

"What did you have in mind?"

Garrett whispered in her ear, how he would touch and taste every part of her until she shook, moaned and screamed his name.

Egypt blushed. "I…uh. I probably won't get home until eleven thirty or even midnight." She reached inside her purse. "But here's a key. Make yourself at home. I look forward to seeing you try."

"I'll be there." His hand caressed her cheek, and then he was lowering his head and fusing his mouth with hers. He slid his tongue against hers in an erotic dance that would have his taste lingering in her mouth long after she pulled away.

"I'll see you tonight." Then he waved and hopped into the golf cart and drove back down the dirt road. It took Egypt a few moments to compose herself before getting into the vehicle.

"Passion is good," her father stated, looking in her direction, "but be sure that isn't all there is."

"It's not, Daddy," Egypt assured him. Sex wasn't the only part of their relationship, but it was an integral piece, and one Egypt couldn't wait to explore later tonight. Garrett knew exactly what to do to make her body hum, and she would most certainly return the favor.

Who cared about his interaction with some stranger? She shouldn't let her fears about the past get in the way of their relationship. If something was wrong, Garrett would tell her, if not now, then later tonight. He'd always been aboveboard and honest with her, and she was counting on that to continue.

Sixteen

Garrett was grateful when Walker Farms' first official public day was over. He wouldn't have to put on a happy face any longer when he felt the exact opposite. He was enraged over the situation he found himself in. It didn't help when he went back to the main house and researched himself.

The more he read, the more he remembered that Thomas Garrett Forrester was arrogant and focused solely on making a buck...or at least that's how the press presented him. He'd earned a business degree from Harvard and gone on to Wharton, where he'd been top of his class. Immediately afterward, he joined the family firm and followed in his father's footsteps.

Although he knew he hadn't wanted to sell his grandfather's farm, Garrett wasn't altogether certain he liked the prior version of himself. Checking his social media, he didn't see much about his own personal life. It was as if he lived to work. His life today was far removed from that world. He worked hard during the day, but he made time to enjoy life, whether that was reading one of the old books he'd found in his grandfather's library, shooting pool with Kent or spending time with

Egypt—*in or out* of bed. Garrett enjoyed his life now. He didn't want it to change. At least not entirely.

It wasn't fair for his parents to think he was dead. He knew that and intended to rectify it immediately, but he also didn't want to give up the freedom and peace he'd found on the farm. The freedom to make his own choices. Garrett suspected much of his former life had been mapped out by his father. Was that why he kept remembering arguments between them? Was their relationship strained?

Garrett supposed he would have to find out, but he needed to tell Egypt first. The woman who in a couple of months had come to mean so much more to him than a Good Samaritan who visited him at the hospital. She was warm and funny and sexy as well as giving and compassionate. All qualities he never knew he wanted in a mate but somehow had found in Egypt. It was why it had been easy to fall in love with her.

The feelings had sneaked up on him. The old Garrett would have tried to suppress them, because love had never been on his agenda. He always figured he'd marry someone from his same socioeconomic class and they would produce a couple of children, but it had all been very vague and far off in the future. Not now. When he thought about his perfect woman, the woman made for him, he saw a caramel queen with lush curves and a sinful mouth that he absolutely adored. It was time he went to her and told her everything.

Garrett prayed she wouldn't see him any differently...initially he'd shown up to Flame in smart attire and a fancy car. She knew he had money, but now she knew the man underneath. He was still the same Garrett, just with a lot of zeroes in his bank account.

Egypt was dog tired. Dinner service at Flame had been bananas. She'd had back-to-back large groups, which subsequently made the night drag on, because they kept ordering dish after dish. It was great for her bottom line, but it meant she was pulling into her apartment's reserved parking space at midnight.

She turned the key in the lock, and when she opened her apartment door, all she saw was candlelight. Rose petals were sprinkled on the floor and led straight to her bedroom. Garrett appeared seconds later, holding a tumbler of dark liquid.

"I know you're not a big champagne drinker except with your girls, so I thought you might enjoy a bourbon after a long day."

Egypt sighed with pleasure as she accepted the drink. "Thank you, and you're right. Wynter and I are the only Gems who actually like bourbon." She took a generous sip.

"Long day?" Garrett asked, taking her purse and the backpack that carried all her culinary tools. He placed both items on the kitchen counter and then led Egypt over to the couch, where he sat her down and removed her Crocs.

"Yes, it was," Egypt replied. She released a low moan when, after removing the shoes, Garrett began massaging her feet. She didn't know if it was the massage, the drink or Garrett, but she felt a quickening between her legs.

"Feel good?" Garrett inquired.

"Oh, yes." Egypt laid her head back against the cushions.

"Well, there's more where that came from," Garrett said and pulled her up from the couch.

Egypt wanted to protest. "Where are we going?"

"You'll see."

Rather than lead her to the bedroom and make sweet love to her, as she was anticipating, Egypt found he'd prepared a bubble bath. Tears welled in her eyes at his thoughtfulness. "Garrett…"

Slowly, he began undressing her, freeing each button on her chef's jacket one at a time. When it was open, his eyes fixed on her ample bosom just before he slid the garment from her shoulders. Then he spun her around and unclasped her bra so that it too found its way to the floor. Egypt didn't have it in her to protest. She let Garrett push her leggings and panties down her legs in one fell swoop, and then to her surprise, he lifted her off her feet and lowered her into the warm water.

Egypt moaned again as she was instantly taken over by bubbles. "Thank you."

"Enjoy. I'll be back soon."

She rested her head back against the bath pillow he must have found in her closet. She drifted off, because when she came to, Garrett was washing her back. Egypt felt like putty in his hands. He continued his ministrations with the sponge, moving forward to massage her breasts. Despite her exhaustion, Egypt could feel dizzying pleasure build within her.

She didn't object when Garrett lowered his head and subjected her breasts to an array of licks, strokes and circles with his tongue. And when his mouth finally found hers in a long, drugging kiss, Egypt gave herself over to it. She wanted him desperately. And nearly cried with relief when his hands went lower with the sponge, past her abdomen to her sex. She parted her legs, giving him better access so he could sweep the sponge back and forth. It wasn't enough. She wanted his hands, his fingers and his mouth. She wanted him any way she could get him.

She must have spoken the words aloud, because Garrett's fingers replaced where the sponge had been. He toyed with her deliciously until she was writhing in the soapy water.

"Enough of this," Garrett muttered and unceremoniously picked her up and out of the water. He was rubbing her dry and backing her up toward her bedroom. At the same time, Egypt was pulling his wet polo shirt over his head and unzipping his jeans. She fell backward onto the bed, and after removing his jeans and securing a condom, Garrett settled between her thighs.

She wanted him inside her, but Garrett had other plans. He gripped her hips and then lowered his head to drink deep from the heat of her. The possessive warmth of his hands and mouth sent a flare of molten heat to her core, and soon she was sobbing out his name like an incantation as her entire body shuddered. "*Garrett!*"

He glided his hands up from her thighs to her hips and then to her breasts. Garrett's gaze was so intense she could hardly see his irises. Then his mouth came down on hers in another explosive kiss that sent shock waves through her body. "Please don't make me wait," she whimpered. "I want you."

"I want you, too, baby. You've bewitched me, body and soul." He splayed his hands over her buttocks, bringing her into full contact with his hardness. He teased her for mere seconds with his tip and then, with one powerful thrust, he was there. Deep at the heart of her body, and Egypt cried out. "Yes, yes!"

Garrett answered her plea, drawing her closer so he could thrust a little deeper. Egypt felt totally fulfilled—the aching and need were gone and replaced with a feeling of complete-ness. Each time they made love, it was like she was discover-ing new things about him over and over again. He was setting her up to want no one else but him, because he triggered a need in her that no other man could ever satisfy.

At first his movements were slow and measured, but as his breathing changed, so did Garrett's rhythm. A tantalizing pres-sure began to build until Egypt had no choice but to undulate her hips to meet his fast pace. It didn't take long for them to reach the crescendo, especially when he reached between them to caress her feminine nub.

Egypt shattered into a million pieces, and Garrett was with her as his body quaked and shuddered around her. Dazed, Egypt nearly said those three little words that would surely change everything. *I love you.* Somehow, she managed to keep them inside, because she wasn't sure if she was ready to say them—or if Garrett was ready to hear them.

Early the next morning, Garrett crept out of Egypt's apart-ment, because she needed her rest. She'd been exhausted last night. Yet she freely gave herself to him like she always did. Egypt held nothing back—unlike him.

Given the hour and her tiredness, Garrett hadn't had to heart to lay the truth on her doorstep. He would let her sleep—they would talk in the morning, and he would tell her everything. Or, at least, as much as he knew. He supposed last night had been a real catalyst, because when Garrett awoke the next morning at the farm, he knew who he was.

He'd gone off for a few days to check on his grandfather's farm, never to be seen again. He had to contact his parents and put their minds at ease.

He picked up the phone and called his father's cell phone. It rang a few times before Hugh picked up. "Dad?"

There was silence on the other end. "T-Thomas?" His father's voice cracked on the other end. "Is—is that really you, son?"

"Yes, it's me."

"*Omigod!* Corrine, come quick, it's Thomas," his father yelled. "My golf buddy said he thought he saw you yesterday, but I told him he was mistaken. You disappeared months ago."

Garrett heard shuffling and then his mother telling his father to put the phone on speaker. "Thomas?"

"Yes, Mother, it's me."

He heard her loud sobs through the phone. "Where have you been all these months? We've been worried sick."

"It's a long story," Garrett responded thickly. "And I want to tell you all about it. Can you come by the farm?"

"The farm?" his mother asked. "Daddy's farm? Have you been there this entire time? We came and you weren't there."

"No, not exactly," Garrett replied. "Listen, I know that you are both shocked to hear from me after all this time, and I promise I'll explain everything when you get here."

"Garrett, you have no idea how distraught we've been," his mother said. "You're our only son."

He understood because his parents had always heaped their hopes and dreams on to him. "I know, mother."

"Do you? It's unthinkable for a parent to lose their child. We always thought it would be us, that we would go first, but when. . ."

Garrett could hear his mother begin to sob again and it broke his heart.

"Son," it was his father again. "We'll be there soon and we'll want to know everything and how ended up losing you for months."

Garrett quickly ended the call before his father could hound him for more details. Their last conversation a few months ago hadn't exactly gone well. Hugh had his opinion on what to do about Walker Farms, and Garrett doubted that had changed. Then again, Garrett was more certain than ever that keeping his grandfather's legacy was paramount. Now all he had to do was wait for his parents to arrive, because all hell was about to break lose.

Seventeen

Egypt was saddened to wake up and find Garrett had sneaked out after that incredible night of lovemaking. She pushed the pillows back and leaned over to grab the note Garrett had left by her bedside. It stated she should get some rest and he would call her later. He'd been so loving and so gentle, massaging her feet and making her a bath, that Egypt realized something she'd been trying not to face.

She was in love with Garrett.

The feelings had been a slow progression, leading up to last night's culmination. She'd vowed to be cautious with her heart, but somehow Garrett had sneaked past all her defenses, and Egypt found herself a smitten kitten. She had to talk to someone about this.

Egypt called Wynter. She was thankful her travel-blogger friend was available. "Egypt, so good to hear from you, girl-friend. What's going on?"

"How did you know it was love with Riley?" Egypt asked unceremoniously.

"*Whoa!* Where did that come from?" Wynter inquired.

"Can't you just tell me?"

Wynter chuckled. "I've loved Riley since I was a teenager,

but what did it for me was after the week in Aspen. We spent a lot of time together. Told each other things I'd never confided in another man. But if I had to pinpoint an exact moment, I would say when he did something as simple as buy me a butterfly necklace because he saw me admiring it. I called you right after that."

"Oh, yeah," Egypt said. "I recall that conversation, and I believe I told you to tell him and look what happened!"

"Yes, we quarreled and broke up briefly," Wynter responded. "But it was exactly the push Riley needed to get over his fear of commitment and ending up like his divorced parents—or, worse, seeing his mother go into depression. You're not in the same situation, Egypt."

"No, but I am with a man with a lot of unknowns about his past," Egypt reminded her. "And yes, I knew that going in, and I thought I had it under control. We were kicking it, ya know? But it turned into so much more."

"I'm going to give you the same advice you gave me—be honest with Garrett like he's been with you. You might be surprised. He could feel the same way about you."

"And if he doesn't?"

"I'll jump on the next flight to Raleigh so you can cry on my shoulder. How about that?" Wynter offered.

"How did I ever end up with a sister as incredible as you?"

Wynter laughed. "You saved me from bullies when I was fourteen."

"I did do that."

"Yes, you did," her bestie replied. "Let me know how it goes."

Egypt glanced down at the clock. She had several hours before Flame opened. If she hurried, she could make it to the farm and back before the staff arrived. She knew it was crazy to rush over to Garrett's and spill her guts, but she wasn't one for beating around the bush. She'd rather snatch the Band-Aid off quick and feel the pain now rather than later. Egypt knew she might regret her hasty actions down the line, but once she was in the car, she was committed. She would find out how Garrett felt one way or the other.

* * *

Garrett heard the crackle of stones on the driveway and looked out the window of his grandfather's home to see his parents' Rolls-Royce pull up. He was prepared for his mother to be emotional after all these months, but his father was another matter. Garrett wasn't sure what he was in for, so he was pleasantly surprised when he opened the door and both parents rushed at him and pulled him into a tight hug.

The Forresters weren't known for being touchy-feely parents. So Garrett had come to learn he had to act as a grownup no matter his age.

"Omigod!" Tears were streaming down his mother's cheeks, and she cupped both sides of his face with her palms. "I can't believe it's you. It's really you." She pulled him in for yet another hug. "You have no idea how much I missed you."

"Your mother took your disappearance very hard," his father said hoarsely, tears glistening on his lashes. "Once we had exhausted the search for you with no results, she lost hope and took to her bed."

"I'm so sorry, Mom." Garrett squeezed her hand, and she held on to his. "Please come in and I'll tell you the whole story."

His father glanced around. "The house—hell, the grounds look much better than when we were here months ago. I take it you had something to do with this?"

Garrett nodded. "We can get into that later."

Once they were settled on the sofa, his father looked him square in the eye. "Tell me how we got here, son. Because it's been a terrible time. I appointed Sam Boyd interim CEO in your absence."

"You handed over Forrester Holdings to someone else?" Garrett asked. He was shocked. Hugh Forrester was all about being in control of every situation.

"You're our son," Hugh huffed. "It would have been pretty insensitive, not to mention suspect, if I didn't devote one hundred percent of my time to looking for you."

Of course, it was about appearances and not because he wanted to give over control.

"Go on with your story," his father pressed.

"On my way out of town, I stopped at a new restaurant I'd heard about in Glenwood South that's phenomenal. After dinner, when I was leaving, I was carjacked and beaten pretty badly."

His mother's hand flew to her mouth.

"I was in a coma for two months. When I woke up, I didn't remember who I was."

His father's lips took on an unpleasant twist. "Then how did you end up here?" Hugh motioned around the room.

"My short-term memory was intact, but not my long-term memory. I literally didn't remember my own name. The owner of the restaurant supplied it. And then the name Walker Farms came to me, and I called the first number I could remember—it was to the farm. The farm's foreman, Kent Howell, answered, and that's where the story branches out."

Garrett explained to his stunned parents that Kent had lied about his true identity, telling him they were dead and Cyrus had taken care of him. "I had no reason to not believe him."

"We need to sue him!" his father bellowed, jumping to his feet. "Because of that bastard we've agonized for months. We thought you were dead!" He gestured wildly. "Someone has to pay, and we need to start with Howell."

Garrett stood up. "You'll do no such thing."

"You're defending him?" His mother gasped, looking up at him. "After everything he did? After everything he took from you?"

"Kent was misguided, yes," Garrett responded, "but I got a lot in return, too. I was able to build up this farm, and..." He never got to finish his sentence and tell them about Egypt, because his father started blustering again.

"Garrett, did they give you a lobotomy when you were in that coma? You don't even sound like yourself. This man perpetrated a crime against you, against our family. He needs to pay."

"We should sue him for pain and suffering," his mother added.

"I know you've been through a lot," Garrett acknowledged,

because he was quickly losing his patience. "I know you're both upset, but this is *my* decision. It's my life. You don't get to tell me what to do."

"Someone needs to," his father stated hotly, "because you've lost your mind. So what, you've built up this piddly farm. Who cares when you have a multibillion-dollar corporation to run? It's what you were groomed to do."

"Groomed by you," Garrett reminded him, "but I'm my own man."

"I'm quickly losing my patience, Thomas."

"My name isn't Thomas. It's Garrett."

"I don't give a damn what you've been calling yourself the last few months," his father barked. "Thomas is the name we gave you at birth. It's time for you to stop playing at being a farmer and sell this dump and come home where you belong."

A loud slam sounded from behind them, and they all turned around. That's when Garrett saw Egypt staring at him with a shocked expression.

"*Egypt!*" Garrett rushed toward her, but she was already backing away and rushing out the door.

Garrett didn't think twice—he went after her. He all but jumped down the stairs and caught her in several strides at her car. "Egypt, wait!"

She shook her head. "I shouldn't have come here. I knew I shouldn't have come here. It was a mistake."

A frown flashed across his features. "What are you talking about?"

She glanced up at him. "Your memory has returned?"

He nodded.

"And those are your parents?" She pointed toward the house. "And I suppose they own this Rolls-Royce." She inclined her head toward the fancy car next to her Honda.

"Yes."

"So, you're rich?" She chuckled, but it sounded more like a cry. "I guess I should have known that after the carjacking."

"I am."

"How long?" Egypt asked, looking accusingly into his eyes.

His brow furrowed. "How long what?"

"Don't act dumb, Garrett. It doesn't become you. When did your memory come back?"

He looked down. He didn't want to answer, but he also refused to lie to Egypt, either. She deserved the truth. "It's been coming back in bits and pieces, but nothing substantial until yesterday."

Her eyes narrowed. "When that man confronted you?"

"Not exactly. He told me my real name—Thomas Garrett Forrester. Kent filled in the rest."

"Wait a minute? Who's Thomas?"

"It's my given name, but I prefer Garrett."

"But you knew the truth yesterday when I was here? And last night, when you came to my place, and you didn't tell me?" Her voice rose steadily with each sentence.

"Yes."

She shook her head. "I can't believe I thought you were different. What was I thinking?"

She turned away from him, but Garrett grasped her elbow and spun her around. "What's that supposed to mean?"

"You came over last night, and rather than tell me the truth…you slept with me. Were you using me for sex and comfort until your memory returned?"

"Of course not." Garrett was horrified she would think such a thing. "Egypt, listen, I had every intention of telling you last night, but you were so exhausted."

"That didn't stop you from having sex with me."

Garrett's jaw clenched. "Don't do that. Don't make it sound like it was all one-sided." He moved closer toward her until Egypt was plastered against her car. "You enjoyed last night as much as I did."

"That's because I didn't know who you were. That you were someone who would lie to me."

"I didn't lie!" Garrett's voice rose several octaves. "I planned on coming back to town and telling you today, but I knew I had to tell my parents first. They thought I was dead. Can't you give me some grace here, Egypt?"

She shook her head. "I can't. I can't do this!" She pushed at his chest until Garrett backed up and gave her some room. Unfortunately, it was enough for her to squeeze into her Honda and turn on the ignition.

"Egypt, please. Don't leave like this." Garrett didn't want the woman he loved thinking he'd lied to her, used her. But she wasn't listening to him now. She was backing her Honda away from him and peeling down the driveway.

"Damn!" Garrett was pissed. More with himself than Egypt, though she was being thoroughly irrational right now. But he understood it. She had a lot of baggage when it came to men. Antwan had done a number on her and caused her not to trust, and Garrett had walked right into that trap. Why hadn't he told her the truth last night? He could have avoided any doubts she might have about his honesty and trustworthiness if he'd just confided in her.

But he'd been afraid that it might change things. He'd wanted one more night where it was him and Egypt. Two people who'd found each other despite crazy circumstances. And now it could be over.

"Garrett!" He heard his father's voice behind him. "Who in the hell is that woman? Was she the reason you stayed away?"

Garrett spun on his heel and walked toward him and up the steps to look Hugh in the eye. "I told you, I had no idea who I was until yesterday."

His father pointed toward Egypt's car in the distance. "She doesn't think so."

"That's between me and Egypt."

His mother came up behind his father. "Come home, Garrett. We've missed you, and this place—" she glanced up at her father's home "—is your past."

Garrett didn't think so, but he needed to figure out a few things logistically, and going back with his parents seemed the best course of action at the present time. However, that didn't mean they'd won. It just meant he had to figure out his next move.

Eighteen

Egypt drove back to the city on autopilot. She was dazed and confused by the day's events. Garrett's memory had returned, but rather than it being a good thing, she felt like it was the worst thing that could have ever happened. Did remembering his former life change him into a different person? Into a man who lied to—or kept the truth from—her? Garrett had always been honest and straightforward. That's what she loved about him.

And there it was. She loved him. Desperately. Passionately. *Fiercely.* She'd gone to the farm to share her feelings with him and find out if he loved her, too. When she heard loud voices, she'd immediately rushed in to be sure Garrett was okay. He was fine. His rich parents had shown up to whisk him away from the farm. They'd actually called it a dump.

Her intuition was right yesterday when she suspected Garrett was keeping something from her about the heated conversation he'd had with the stranger. Rather than tell her about it, he came to her apartment and seduced her. Admittedly, she went along for the ride, because she had no willpower when it came to Garrett.

She, Egypt, who for the last seven years had been all about girl power and being sex positive, had gotten sprung on a rich man playing farmer. It made her wonder how long those tidbits of memories had been returning. Garrett hadn't shared them with her. Instead, he'd been secretive—like Antwan.

What else was he keeping from her?

Egypt wasn't sticking around to find out. She'd been there, done that, and she refused to be lied to or deceived again. She called Wynter, but her bestie didn't pick it up. Neither did Lyric or Shay. The only person available was Asia.

"Egypt, how are you, girlfriend?"

"I've been better."

"Oh, no," Asia replied, "I don't like the sound of your voice. Has something happened?"

"Garrett's memory has come back," Egypt blurted out.

"And I take it that's a bad thing?" Asia asked. "I thought that's what you wanted. What he wanted. Knowing his past would ensure you weren't walking into a mine field with other women or a potential wife, like Teagan said."

Egypt hadn't even thought about that, because she'd high-tailed it off the farm as fast as she could. "It is when Garrett knew and didn't tell me."

"Really? Why would he keep the truth from you?" Asia said, and there was a pause on the other end of the line. "Unless he has something to hide?"

"That's what I'm trying to figure out," Egypt responded. "We argued and I left. I didn't want to hear any lies or half-truths. You know what I went through with Antwan. I can't deal with another lying, deceitful man who's keeping secrets from me. Garrett's behavior is a trigger and makes me remember that horrible time with Antwan."

Asia sighed. "I'm so sorry, darling. I know how hard that was for you and how you've pushed yourself to be stronger and in charge of your dalliances since Antwan. But if I may be the voice of reason…you don't know that Garrett is like him. I got the impression he was different—trustworthy."

"Then why did he keep the truth from me?"

"I wish I had the answer to that," her friend said, "but from the way you're talking, can I assume you've fallen for Garrett No-Name?"

That made Egypt chuckle as only Asia could. "Your assumption is accurate."

"Then don't throw the baby out with the bathwater. Give Garrett the benefit of the doubt. Hear him out. You owe that to yourself before you throw away a good relationship."

Egypt was shocked Asia was being so grown-up. She'd expected her to be Team Egypt and ready to string Garrett up by his shoelaces. "I suppose you could have a point."

Asia laughed. "I know I'm not Wynter, but I can give good advice once in a while."

"Thank you, Asia. I guess I needed someone to talk me off the ledge."

"I'm glad I can be there like you've always been there for me," the other woman responded. "Let me know how it goes after your talk."

"Will do." Egypt ended the call and pulled into Flame's parking lot. Asia was right—there was still too much unsaid between her and Garrett. She supposed she did owe him the opportunity to clear things up, and hopefully things would go back to the way they were. Or was she fooling herself? Would the old Garrett want her the same way he once did?

After Egypt left, Garrett locked up the farm and came back to Raleigh with his parents. He wasn't doing it because he was kowtowing to his father—rather, he had to find out what had gone on in the last few months. On the drive back, he learned he still had his condo. Because of his mother's breakdown after his disappearance, they hadn't had the heart to sell it. Garrett was thankful he still had a home to go back to.

Unfortunately, his father was droning on and on about business, as if Garrett was interested. He could care less. Just because his memory had returned didn't mean he was jumping back into the fold. His time on the farm had changed him. He wasn't the man he was before, and he didn't think his parents got that, but they would.

"You can drop me off at the penthouse," he stated when they reached the city limits.

"Garrett, it's been months since we've seen you," his mother said, her voice soft. "Can't you at least come back to the house with us?"

"I promise I will come over later, Mother, as soon as I get settled. I need a moment, okay? My memory just returned, and I need to reacclimate and have some time to myself to absorb all of this."

"I'll make a call," his father said, "so the building knows you're on the way."

While Hugh called the property-management team, his mother responded. "Of course, it's must be a jarring change from life on the farm. Growing up, there was always some chore to be done. It was like your work was never-ending."

Garrett chuckled. "Something like that."

His father concluded the call. "You're all set. They've been informed of your arrival and will have a key ready. As far as the farm, it doesn't matter," he stated. "You'll be giving it up and coming back to Forrester Holdings."

"I didn't say that," Garrett replied.

"You don't have to. It's what has to be done. You have to take back your rightful spot as head of the company."

Garrett growled. He was in no mood to argue, not after everything that had gone down in the last twenty-four hours. He needed to talk to Egypt. "You're giving me a headache."

"Hugh, stop it!" his mother admonished, patting his thigh. "Garrett has been through a trauma."

"Jesus, I'm sorry, son," his father said, glancing back at him. "I'm going to send a doctor to check you out immediately."

"That's not necessary. I was treated at a hospital."

"Yes, it is. I don't know what care you received, but my son only gets the very best. I'll have someone over to your penthouse within the hour."

"Fine." Garrett refused to argue. When the Rolls-Royce pulled into the driveway of his plush condo building, he hopped out of the back seat. Then he went to the passenger side, where his mother rolled down the window.

"I'm so happy to have you back."

He pressed a kiss to her cheek. "I'll be by later." Then he headed inside. His appearance was a big to-do in the lobby, and the concierge practically fawned at seeing Garrett alive and well.

"It's so good to have you back, Mr. Forrester," the man said. "Here's the key to your penthouse. If you need anything, such as having your kitchen restocked or supplies, please let us know. We're here to help."

Garrett nodded. "Thank you. I appreciate that." He accepted the key and took the elevator to the top floor, where it opened onto his spacious three-bedroom penthouse. Garrett tossed the key on the console and looked around. Memories started to flood his brain about when he bought the place. How accomplished he'd felt to finally get out from underneath his parents' thumb. But as he walked around looking at the sleek penthouse with its contemporary furniture, he felt cold and empty. It wasn't like the farm, which was warm and cozy.

He walked over to the wall of windows and looked out over Raleigh. You couldn't beat the view, though. *That* was spectacular. He continued his tour and went to the master suite. His hands fingered the row of suits lining the closet. There weren't a lot of casual clothes. Just some slacks and polos and only a couple of pairs of jeans. Garrett lived in jeans now, because they were comfortable and durable. The thought of putting on a suit made him feel claustrophobic.

Garrett came out of the closet and sat on the bed. This really was another life and so removed from how he lived now. Speaking of which—he called Kent. Although he was furious with the man, he knew he would take care of Walker Farms while he figured a few things out.

"Garrett."

"I'm going to be gone for a couple of days," he responded. "I need you to hold things down on the farm."

"I'm surprised you'd want me there given…" The foreman's voice trailed off.

"I'm not ready to get into this with you, Kent. Can you do it or not?"

"Of course. I owe you and your grandfather."

"Thank you." Garrett ended the call and then made another to Egypt, but it went straight to voice mail. She must have turned off her phone. He needed to talk to her, but he had a few personal items to address first, like getting his life in order. He needed a new driver's license, some money in his pocket and a set of wheels to get around town. No more rideshares. The Rolls-Royce that was stolen was one of three cars Garrett had in the garage. He couldn't wait to get his hands on his Aston Martin.

A few hours later, after he'd showered and changed into some slacks and a polo and gotten clearance from the doctor his father sent over, Garrett made an appointment at the Division of Motor Vehicles and a meeting with his banking rep. Garrett felt like he was having an out-of-body experience. The last couple of months, he'd lived a totally different existence. Now, the big question was that he knew who he was—but what was he going to do with his life?

Nineteen

"Egypt, you won't believe who just sat down at Flame," Tessa said, jumping up and down when she rushed into the kitchen of the restaurant later that evening. "Jade Garcia."

Egypt frowned when she glanced up. "Am I supposed to know who that is?"

The hostess rolled her eyes. "Jade is, like, one of the most influential foodies in town. When she gives a rave review about a restaurant, they become hugely popular with lines out the door. She has like over a million followers on TikTok."

"Really?" Egypt didn't have time for social media because she was always in the kitchen. She continued working on the entrée she was making.

"Yes! You have to cook the meal of your life, because if Jade gives you a bad review, it could sink Flame."

"Thanks a lot, Tessa. That's no pressure or anything." Egypt wiped her hands on a towel at her waist and started thinking what she could whip up special for the TikTok influencer.

Quentin walked over to her. "It's okay, boss. We got this." He held up his hand for a high five, which Egypt returned.

Egypt wasn't going to let another person dictate her future.

She was a damn good chef, and she would do what she always did—deliver a delicious and quality meal.

Egypt looked over at Quentin and the other line chefs, who were looking at her expectantly as if waiting for their valiant leader to lead them into battle. "All right, let's do this, Team Flame!" She clapped her hands.

"Can I serve Jade?" Tessa asked and Egypt gave her nod.

The entire kitchen became energized around one purpose—to make the very best meal to serve Jade. Egypt started with a she-crab soup as the first course. Quentin helped make the accompanying fried green tomatoes with a habanero chutney. When Tessa personally came to pick up the plate in the window, Egypt's stomach clenched in knots, but she had to tell herself that Jade Garcia was no different than any other patron. However, if what her hostess said was true, Jade could sink Flame. Egypt had put everything into the restaurant, not only her heart and soul, but all her savings. Any profit she'd made from owning the food truck the last two years had gone into Flame. It had to succeed, because Egypt didn't have a plan B.

When Tessa came back and gave Egypt an enthusiastic thumbs-up, she was encouraged and set about making the entrée. It was a dish she'd whipped up hundreds of times. She just had to execute it properly.

"You've got this, Chef," Quentin said as she plated the dish, adding each component herself.

When it was complete, she told Tessa she would walk the plate out herself. Egypt wanted Jade to put a face with the name and know she was the owner and head chef of Flame. After washing her hands and checking her hair, Egypt walked out the kitchen's double doors and toward the young woman who could make or break her future.

Jade Garcia wasn't an unassuming young woman. She had pink hair in a bob and wore a glittery pink tube top and a multicolored tutu.

"Good evening. I'm Egypt Cox, owner and head chef of

Flame," she said, walking up to the table. "I hope you've enjoyed the first and second courses."

"They were divine," Jade responded enthusiastically. "I don't know what you put in that habanero chutney, but I wanted to lick the plate."

A smile spread across her lips, "I'm glad to hear it. And I hope you'll be equally pleased with the braised lamb shank with stone-ground grits, baby carrots and a mint gremolata I've prepared for you." She placed the dish in front of the other woman.

Jade picked up her plate and smelled it. "I can't wait."

"I'll leave you to it." Egypt bowed and moved on to other patrons. She checked on all the tables, making sure they were happy with their meals. The evening was going splendidly. If Jade recommended them to her followers, it could put Flame on the map. Right now, they'd been living off word of mouth and the locals, but it was still inconsistent. This was exactly what Flame needed. So why was there this gnawing sadness in the pit of her stomach? Because-she couldn't call Garrett to share this moment with him. Although they'd only known each other a short time, he'd always been rooting for her. When Egypt was certain she'd spoken to every guest, she started toward the kitchen, but Jade stopped her.

"May I call you Egypt?"

"Absolutely."

"You have a hit on your hands with this dish," Jade stated. "The lamb shank and grits are an unusual pairing, but I loved every bite of it."

Egypt beamed. "Thank you so much."

"If the first three dishes are this great, I can only imagine what dessert will taste like. Can you send it out shortly?" She picked up her fork again. "I've got to finish my entrée."

Egypt chuckled. "Coming right up."

By the end of the day, Garrett felt accomplished. He'd gone to the DMV and obtained a duplicate license, so he was finally legit. Then he'd gone shopping for new clothes, primarily a few pairs of jeans and shirts and a new Rolex and wallet to replace the items stolen all those months ago. He'd also went to the bank and ordered a new credit and debit cards, and he'd taken out cash in the meantime. Then he had a cashier's check cut to reimburse Kent for the loan he took to get the public day started at the farm. Garrett paid his debts.

Afterward, he contacted Detective Simpson and informed him of his true identity. The detective was surprised to learn of Kent's deception and advised Garrett he could have a criminal case if he wanted to pursue it, but Garrett wasn't interested in going down that road. He had bigger fish to fry.

His father fully expected him to come back to Forrester Holdings Corporation, as if he hadn't been gone the last few months, living an entirely different life. The more Garrett thought about it, the more he knew he couldn't go back to the way things were. The only reason he'd joined the family business was because it was what his Hugh had wanted.

All his life, his parents had told him how special he was after all the issues they'd had to have him. Garrett had felt as if he owed them, somehow, for his existence, so he'd always tried not to be a bother to his older parents. He wanted to please them so they would be proud of him, but they'd never once asked Garrett what *he* wanted to do with his life. They always assumed he would follow in Hugh's footsteps. And for years he had, but after the last couple of months, Garrett now realized he'd been living half a life.

In the past, all he'd ever done was work, work and work. Well, there was to more to life than being tied to his desk. His life on the farm might have been simple, but he was happy and fulfilled. Plus, he saw all kinds of ways to improve the farm's production and make it profitable. He hadn't gone to Wharton for nothing. More importantly, Garrett now knew what it was like to have a woman who cared for him and that he was capable not just of reciprocating those feelings, but of love.

His relationships with women in the past were sexual in nature and casual, because he never had the time or inclination to give them more of himself, but he had with Egypt. He'd given her everything and hadn't held back. Consequently, he fell in love with the voluptuous chef, and he couldn't wait to tell her so, but would she listen to him? Would she hear him out when she thought he'd lied to her? She thought he was like her scumbag of an ex-boyfriend who kept secrets and betrayed her. Yes, he'd made a mistake in not telling her as soon as his memories began returning, but he'd been scared. They had a good thing and he hadn't wanted to lose it. He had to convince Egypt he was the real deal, but first he had to deal with his parents.

Garrett would let them down gently, yet firmly, telling them that from this point forward, he was living his life *for him*. His parents would either get onboard or not be a part of his life. He didn't want that, because he'd known what it was like to have no one the last few months, but he also wouldn't be bullied or be his father's puppet any longer. He was his own man now.

Now that he had his license, he drove his Aston Martin to his parents' estate. Then he parked the car outside the front door and rang the doorbell. He didn't have a spare key at the penthouse. Gerard, their butler, opened the door and greeted him.

"It's a pleasure to see you again, Garrett," Gerard said. "Your parents were beside themselves when they thought they'd lost you."

Garrett could only imagine. They'd doted on him as a child, so not having him must have left a giant void. "Thanks, Gerard. Where are they?"

"Same place as usual, the drawing room."

"Thanks, I know the way," Garrett said when the butler began to lead him there.

He found them on the sofa, his father drinking his usual measure of scotch before dinner. His mother was sipping on one of her herbal teas.

"Garrett!" She jumped up when she saw him. "I'm so glad you're home." She rushed toward him, and he leaned down to embrace her. She wasn't usually given to showing PDA, but he supposed after everything they'd been through, things had changed.

"We hoped you would keep your word," his father said. "Plus, we need to continue our discussion from earlier."

"I'm a man of my word," Garrett said, walking over to the bar and pouring himself a scotch as well. He rarely drank these days except for an occasional glass of wine with Egypt, but he needed one now. "But we won't be finishing that discussion. I've already made my decision." He sipped his scotch.

"Care to inform us?" Hugh inquired.

"I'm not coming back to Forrester Holdings. I'm going to keep running Walker Farms. I have a lot of ideas to improve production and make it a profitable venture, some of which I've already started implementing."

"That's ludicrous!" His father slammed down his tumbler on the cocktail table. "You'd give up being CEO of a multibillion-dollar corporation in favor of a run-down farm?"

Garrett sighed. "I knew you'd see it that way. You don't see the potential or have the vision that I do, but Walker Farms is a gem, and I'm going to turn it into something my grandfather would be proud of, like his father before him."

"This is because of that woman, isn't it?" his father demanded, walking toward him. "I saw the way you looked at her. You have feelings for her, don't you?"

"My feelings for Egypt are irrelevant to this conversation," Garrett bit out. "I've made up my mind. I'm hoping if you can't at least support my decision, you'll accept it."

"Garrett...are you sure about this?" his mother asked.

He nodded.

She turned to her husband. "Hugh, we almost lost Garrett. Don't you remember how that felt? The hole—" she touched her chest "—that we felt here. Don't alienate him."

"I don't agree with this decision, Garrett," his father replied stiffly, "but I won't push." He turned to his wife, who looked appeased by his words.

"Thank you," Garrett replied.

He stayed for dinner with his parents, because he knew how much they'd missed him and he felt the same. He wasn't certain he believed his father, but he was going to take him at face value. And Garrett supposed he was killing time from the real task, which was to convince Egypt he wasn't a lying, deceitful scumbag like her ex Antwan. He was the man who loved her and wanted her by his side. Would she believe him?

Twenty

Egypt couldn't keep up with all the calls coming into Flame after Jade Garcia posted her rave review on TikTok. All morning long, the phone had been ringing off the hook with reservation requests. Tessa was right! Jade did have a lot of clout. Egypt had heard of the power of an influencer, but she was seeing it for herself firsthand.

She came into the restaurant early, because she was going to need to stock the shelves, fridges and freezers for the rush of activity Flame was about to receive. She left the front door unlocked, because she was sitting at the bar and waiting on a delivery, when the front door opened.

Egypt turned to see who it was, but it wasn't the delivery driver. "Hello, may I help you?" she asked. She didn't recognize the older gentleman, but he was very distinguished. He had salt-and-pepper hair, a deep brown complexion and dark eyes, and he wore a custom-fit suit that looked as if it cost a million bucks!

Was he a tourist? If so, he was far off course in this part of town.

"Are you Egypt Cox?" he inquired.

She rose from the bar stool. "Yes, I am. How can I help you?"

"I'm Hugh Forrester."

He waited and let Egypt register the name. Forrester—as in Garrett Forrester. This man was at the farm the other day when she'd arrived to tell Garrett how she felt about him. He must be Garrett's father, but that raised the question of why he'd come.

"Garrett isn't here," she informed him. Seeing Garrett's father made her heart ache because it reminded her of Garrett and how much she missed seeing him, holding him, making love with him. Her heart longed to be with the man she loved even though she wasn't sure he could be trusted.

"I'm not here for Garrett. I came to speak with you, Ms. Cox," Mr. Forrester said and moved toward her.

Egypt's brow scrunched in consternation. "Why?"

"Because you're the reason my son is willing to throw his entire life's work aside."

"Excuse me?" Egypt asked, folding her arms across her chest. "I have no idea what you're talking about, Mr. Forrester. Furthermore, you're not going to come into *my* restaurant and start making false accusations."

"Oh, trust me, I wish they were false," he responded. "But they aren't. My son has worked hard to achieve the level of success he has today. Did you know he's the CEO of Forrester Holdings Corporation, a Fortune 500 company?"

Egypt shook her head.

"Of course not, because he's been playing at being some backward farmer in the middle of nowhere. Garrett went to Harvard, Ms. Cox. Then the Wharton School. He has a top-notch mind."

"Why are you telling me all of this?"

"To get you to see that Garrett is way out of your league," Mr. Forrester responded haughtily.

Egypt was taken aback. "How dare you!" She hadn't known where he was going with the conversation, but now the gloves were coming off.

"I dare," he stated tightly, "because Garrett is *my* son, whom I have groomed to take his rightful place at the helm of our family business. And because he's been caught up with you, he's having doubts. Wants to give it all up to be with you. In what, this pathetic—" he glanced around "—restaurant, where he wasn't even safe and got carjacked, putting him in a coma for a month."

"That wasn't my fault!" Egypt cried.

"Maybe not, but you've never had the opportunities Garrett has. He has a bright future ahead of him—"

"If he stops seeing me," Egypt finished. No sense in beating around the bush. They might as well speak frankly, since it was clear Mr. Forrester thought she was scum on the bottom of his shoe and not fit to be with his son.

"In a nutshell, yes. Don't you get it? Garrett is destined for great things, not to live some ordinary life."

"*You*—" she pointed her index finger at him "—don't get to decide that. It's Garrett's life. He can decide for himself with whom he chooses to live it."

His eyes narrowed a fraction. "Oh…" He started walking around her, and it made Egypt uneasy. What did he see? She knew she was no supermodel, but Garrett liked everything he saw. "You're in love with Garrett."

Was it that obvious? Egypt spun away from Mr. Forrester and back toward the bar and began fiddling with the files on the counter. Was it tattooed on her forehead or something? Did she wear it like a badge of honor?

Mr. Forrester didn't stop his tirade. Instead, he leaned over the counter. "My son is an easy man to love—I love him with all my heart. If you do, too, which I suspect you do—" she glanced at him sideways "—you will do the right thing and let him go. Let him be the leader he was born to be."

Egypt turned to face him. "I think you should leave."

"How much?" His dark eyes rested on hers. "How much will it take for you to break up with my son and send him back to the fold? Name your price, Ms. Cox, and I will double it. From the looks of this place—" his haughty eyes looked around Flame, and she could see he found it wanting "—you could use the money."

"You're a horrible man. Does Garrett even know you're here?"

Mr. Forrester snorted. "He sent me here because he's too afraid to do what has to be done."

"Get out!" she yelled. Egypt had had enough of his condescending words. He was a snob who assumed he knew better than Garrett what was best for him. She knew Garrett wouldn't have sent his father here. When the older gentleman didn't move, she yelled a little bit louder. "Get out!"

Quentin stepped through the front door seconds later and quickly approached them. "Everything okay here, boss?" He glanced at Egypt, whose expression was mutinous.

Mr. Forrester stood taller. "Everything is fine, because I know you'll do the right thing, Ms. Cox."

Seconds later, he was gone, and it was then that Egypt crumpled onto a bar stool.

"What the hell just happened?" Quentin asked.

Tears were already streaming down Egypt's face. "That was Garrett's father."

"What was he doing here?"

Egypt laughed through her tears. "He thinks I'm not good enough for his son. He had the audacity to try and pay me off. That's when you came in."

"The bastard!" Quentin said, pulling up a stool beside her. "No wonder Garrett didn't want to remember his life. What are you going to do?"

That was a good question.

Honestly, Egypt had no idea. A part of her wanted to tell his father to kick rocks. She would be with whomever she chose, and she didn't have to give up on love. Garrett had been calling and texting her nonstop the last twenty-four hours. He'd asked to see her, and Egypt knew she couldn't avoid him forever. They had to clear the air.

The selfish part of her wanted to keep Garrett for herself, but what if his father right? Was he throwing away his life to be with her?

Garrett decided to meet Egypt at a neutral place and picked the JC Raulston Arboretum, because he remembered she had mentioned wanting to visit the gardens known for their luscious blossoms and babbling water features.

If he asked Egypt to come to the farm or he met her at her apartment after not seeing her for two days, Garrett was likely to jump her and carry her to bed until she realized he would never betray or deceive her. He'd had every intention of telling her the truth about his identity the moment it happened, but then they'd made love, and it had rocked him to his foundation.

So he'd chosen to live in the moment and planned to tell her afterward. Of course, his parents' arrival had ruined everything. But they now understood he was a new man, with a new purpose in life, to continue his grandfather's legacy—and hopefully to spend the rest of his days with the woman he loved.

Garrett had wanted to talk to Egypt last night, but she was too exhausted. Apparently, an influencer had stopped by Flame and subsequently, the restaurant had been jam-packed the last two nights. He understood how hard she worked, but he was desperate to see her and make things right.

He was thankful when she finally agreed to meet him before the dinner rush the following day. Garrett couldn't believe how nervous he was as he stood waiting for her in designer jeans and a loose white shirt. He was figuring out a more casual style of dress that worked for him without wearing plaids all the time like his grandfather Cyrus and Kent.

Speaking of which...

He had to have a talk with Kent. They'd developed a friendship over the last couple of months, which Garrett valued, but

Kent had broken that trust. It was going to take time to mend it, but any thought of Kent flew out of his head when Egypt began walking toward him.

She'd never looked lovelier, wearing wide-legged cargo pants and a beige button-down shirt that she'd tied underneath her bosom, showing off her midriff. Garrett swallowed. He had to stop himself from kissing her.

She nodded at him. There wasn't a hug, only a formal acknowledgment of his presence. "Garrett."

"Want to sit down?" He motioned to the bench behind him.

"I don't think that will be necessary," she said and remained standing.

Garrett searched her face—her eyes were cold and hard. He knew he'd hurt Egypt by not revealing that his memory had returned as soon as it came back, but surely that wasn't unforgivable? "Egypt, what's wrong?"

She shook her head. "This. *Us.*" She sucked in a deep breath, and he could see her chest was heaving. Whatever she had to say was causing her great anxiety. "This isn't going to work."

Garrett's brow furrowed. "What do you mean?"

"I'm saying it's over between us, Garrett."

"Because of one argument?" Garrett inquired. "If you'll let me explain—"

"It won't make a difference," she interrupted.

"I don't understand what's happening here."

"Don't you? You know who you are. There's no reason for you to play at being a farmer or act like you care about the full-figured chef with the heart of gold. I got you through the hard times when you had no one, but your family and the life you had before are waiting for you. You should go claim them."

She turned to spin away from him, but Garrett grabbed her arm. "Egypt, wait just a damn minute. Why are you acting like this?"

"Like what?"

"Cold and unfeeling toward me?" Garrett knew she felt differently. He remembered the way she was in his arms, before, when he didn't know who he was. He also knew he could make her feel something again if he tried.

"I'm giving you an out, Garrett. You should take it."

"What if I don't want an out!" he shouted at her. "My memory returning changes nothing. I came here today because I want to make things right between us. I'm sorry I didn't tell you. It was a mistake, a terrible mistake, but I didn't do it to hurt you."

"Stop it, Garrett! I don't want to hear this," Egypt cried. "I've made up my mind. It was never going to work between us. We come from two different worlds. You're uptown and I'm downtown. You're rich and I'm poor." When he shook his head, she kept going. "That's right—other than the restaurant, I'm flat broke. I've got nothing to offer you."

"Egypt…" He started toward her, but she backed away, refusing to allow him to even touch her. "So all of a sudden, you don't like this package?" He motioned to himself. "I was okay to be with when I was an amnesiac and had no one, but now that I have a family and I'm wealthy, we don't work? Ha!" he laughed wryly. Usually, it was the other way around. "This is absurd!"

"It's better this way, Garrett. Better for all concerned."

He didn't want to hurt her, but she was cutting him to the core, and Garrett was in fight-or-flight mode. "Tell me, Egypt, did you get a kick out of playing nurse and Good Samaritan to the amnesiac and bringing me back to life?" He said in a derisive tone, *"Poor Garrett. He has no one—"*

"It wasn't like that and you know it."

"Wasn't it?" He narrowed his eyes. "Did you have pity sex with me? Or were you just so desperate for a man after Antwan that anyone would do, even a man with no memory?"

Garrett knew the minute the words came out of his mouth that he'd gone too far. Although tears glistened in her eyes, Egypt was furious at him. "Go to hell, Garrett! You and your father!" She turned her back on him and quickly stormed away.

Garrett sat backward onto the bench, trying to absorb everything that had just happened. How had they gone from one fight when they'd never had any to a full-fledged breakup? He'd thought once he explained everything and confided his fears, Egypt would take him back with open arms. But instead, she'd kicked him to the curb.

He understood she might be confused about where she stood now that he knew he was Thomas Garrett Forrester, but she hadn't even stopped to listen to him. Allowed him to explain about Kent and his lies and deception. She'd come here with her mind made up. Why? And what the hell did she mean that he and his father could go to hell? What did Hugh have to do with any of this?

Garrett rose to his feet. He didn't know, but he was damn sure about to find out.

Twenty-One

"Egypt, are you certain about this?" Wynter asked as they sat across from one another on Egypt's sofa later that evening. Wynter hadn't lied when she'd said she would drop everything and hop on a plane to Raleigh if Egypt needed her. As soon as she heard of the events of the last couple of days, she'd done exactly that.

"Yes. It's over between me and Garrett," Egypt admitted.

"But is that what *you* want or what his father wants?" Wynter inquired. "I wish had been there when you called so we could have figured this out."

Egypt sipped on her wine. "It wouldn't have changed the outcome. It wouldn't have stopped Garrett from keeping the truth from me. More than likely his father would have still come to the restaurant."

"He intimidated you, Egypt, and you let him get away with it. I thought you were stronger than that."

"Hey—" Egypt stood up from the couch. "I *am* strong. And you're supposed to be on my side."

"I am on your side, which is why I can call you out when I see you making a horrible mistake. Asia did the same thing and I thought you heard her, but apparently not, so I'm going to beat the drum a little louder."

Egypt began pacing her hardwood floors. "I did what was best for all of us. We come from two different worlds."

"And yet somehow fate intervened and put Garrett in your path. You didn't have to stay with him in the hospital, but something kept drawing you back."

Egypt stopped at looked at Wynter. She was right. Every day she'd felt compelled to visit him. And the day he opened his eyes and squeezed her hand, Egypt had felt sparks. It was as if Garrett had marked her in some way and she hadn't been able to let go of him since—until *yesterday*.

"If you both want it, you can make this work," Wynter stated. "Hell, even when he had amnesia and with your crazy schedule, you made time for each other. You mean to tell me because he's wealthy and has some rich parents who've plotted out his future, your relationship will fail?"

"Wynter, when you put it like that, you make me feel like a fool," Egypt lamented. "I just thought if I loved him enough, I would give him his freedom."

Egypt lowered her head. "How do I keep making a mess of things? First, I'm quick to anger, believing he's like Antwan, and then I push him away."

"I'm not going to sugarcoat it," Wynter replied softly. "You have made a mess, but it can be fixed."

"What if he never wants to see me again?" Egypt asked. "I thought I was being cruel to be kind."

Wynter shook her head. "I'm sorry to tell you, Gem, but you missed the mark."

Egypt laughed and hugged Wynter tightly. It didn't matter which of the Six Gems she got—somehow they always managed to help lead each other to the right path. And her path was leading her back to Garrett. But given their last encounter, would he even hear a word she had to say? She'd botched things up terribly with her doubts, fears and insecurities. Would he give her another chance?

* * *

Garrett's head was spinning. It had only been a couple of days since Egypt broke up with him at the arboretum, and he was still shell-shocked. He'd been ready to grovel and beg her forgiveness if she would only have taken him back. Instead, she'd said no thank you. He couldn't understand it.

So, he came back to the farm, where everything made sense. Life had been good when he hadn't known he was. Sure, there had been obstacles, but he'd known his path: Stabilize the farm. Spend time with Egypt. Now? He felt adrift, and all because a voluptuous caramel beauty turned her back on him.

Knock. Knock. Knock.

Garrett glanced up and saw Kent in his doorway, shifting from foot to foot. "Don't just stand there, come in."

Kent stepped inside his office and motioned to the chair. "May I?"

"Why are you being so formal, Kent?" Garrett growled.

"Because I've been waiting for days for you to hand me my walking papers," Kent responded hotly, "but there's been nothing. I was wondering if you were going back to your family business and were going to leave us floundering."

"Damn it!" Garrett pounded his hand on the desk. "Why does everyone in my life seem to think they know me or what I'm going to do?"

Kent leaned back in fear. "Jesus, what's up with you?"

"If I wanted to shut Walker Farms down, I would have it done by now, Kent! Do you honestly think I would have gone through all the backbreaking work of fixing up the place, opening it to the public and getting the books in order if I didn't want it to succeed?"

His foreman rubbed his head. "Well, no, I guess not."

"Then give me some credit, for Chrissakes!" Garrett replied. "I meant it when I said this place is my family's legacy. Cyrus owned it and his father before him, and I'm not going to let it go without a fight."

Kent visibly sagged in his chair. "Thank you, and thank you

for the check you had delivered. You sure didn't waste any time paying me back."

"You don't have to thank me. You just have to work your butt off to ensure we achieve the big goals I have planned to make Walker Farms profitable."

"So, you're not firing me?" Kent inquired.

Garrett rolled his eyes at him.

"Okay, okay, I get it," Kent said. "I'm not fired, but what about as your friend?"

"Now, that's debatable," Garrett said with a straight face. He wasn't ready to sweep everything under the rug. Kent had put him through the wringer and more work would need to be done to repair that relationship.

Kent nodded. "Fair enough. I'll have to earn back your trust."

"Yes, you will."

"And Egypt—where is she? I haven't seen her around."

"That's because she left me," Garrett responded, his head in his hands. "She found out my memory returned earlier than I told her and after finding out I'm wealthy, she's decided we won't work."

"That's total crap!"

Garrett glanced up. "You know it and I know it, but she doesn't and I don't know what to do."

"The Garrett I've come to know and respect wouldn't take no for an answer. He would fight for her like he did for this farm."

"She doesn't want me, Kent."

The other man shook his head. "That woman loves you. Maybe she got spooked with your memory returning and thinking she wasn't good enough for you, but you have to show her that she's all the woman you'll ever need."

"That's well said, Kent. I might have to use that."

Kent smiled. "Feel free." He rose to his feet. "Thanks, Garrett. I appreciate the second chance and the faith you have in me. I won't let you down again."

Kent closed the door, leaving Garrett alone with his thoughts. He wouldn't take this breakup lying down. He had to fight for

Egypt. Show her that she meant the world to him, possibly even more than his family, because he suspected his father had been behind her turning her back on him. And it was time they had it out once and for all.

"Garrett! I knew you would change your mind," his father said when Garrett stormed into his office in downtown Raleigh later that afternoon. He'd known he would find Hugh there, because he lived to work. Once upon a time, that would have been Garrett, but not anymore.

"What did you say to Egypt?" Garrett wasted no time on pleasantries.

His father regarded him for several moments before leaning back in his leather chair. He looked like the king of the castle in his large corner office on the top floor, but to Garrett it felt cold and no longer anyplace he wanted to be.

"Are you going to answer me?" Garrett demanded.

"I said what needed to be said," his father responded. "What you couldn't say."

"Which is?"

"That she's out of your league!" he roared. "You need a woman who will complement you as CEO, not some cook who can't be bothered to stay fit."

Garrett rushed to his father's desk and leaned over him, and for once, he saw Hugh cower. "You will not speak about my woman like that."

"She must not be your woman if you're here. I was right when I told her if she loved you she'd do the right thing, and she did. She set you free, Garrett. Now you can come back to Forrester Holdings."

Garrett took away one thing from his father's tirade, which was that Egypt loved him—and that gave him all the ammunition he needed to win her back.

"I'm not returning to the fold. I told you that, not now, not ever. I have built a new life on the farm, one that doesn't include me chasing the almighty dollar. And I will do so with

Egypt by my side, so you had better get used to it. Otherwise, you won't have a place in my life anymore."

"Hugh, what have you done?" his mother cried from the door.

Garrett stood up straight and walked over to her. "It's okay, Mother. I know you had nothing to do with him talking to Egypt, that was all Father. But I have warned him—" he pointed across the room "—if he interferes in my life one more time, I'm done with him. But never with you—*never* with you."

"Oh, Garrett." Corrine wrapped her arms around his middle, and he returned her embrace. When they parted, tears were glistening in her eyes. "I love you so much. You were the blessing we never thought we'd have."

"And I love you, too, Mom, but Father, you have got to change or you'll lose me." And with those words, Garrett left his office and raced down the hall toward the future that awaited him.

Twenty-Two

"Order up," Egypt yelled at the expediter in charge of ensuring of all the tickets were handled in the order they came in. Egypt liked to garnish the plates herself. She knew she was a bit of a control freak, but she couldn't help herself.

Since Jade's rave review on TikTok, Flame's reservations had tripled. Egypt had to place a Now Hiring sign for waitstaff, a line cook and a manager to keep up with the enormous workload.

Egypt couldn't believe how far Flame had come in less than a year. She wanted to share her accomplishment and how proud she was with someone. And not just anyone. She wanted to share it with Garrett, but she'd fumbled the ball terribly. Egypt wasn't afraid of saying she was wrong, because she could. Other than not immediately telling her about the return of his memory, Garrett had never given her cause to doubt him.

It was her own insecurities that had put their relationship in jeopardy. She owed Wynter and Asia a debt in making her see how wrong she'd been in doubting him and making decisions *for* Garrett. She'd hated when it was done to her, when Antwan had stolen her choices, her future. Now, she'd turned around and done the same thing to the man she loved.

And she did love Garrett with her heart, body and soul. She was all in, and he needed to know. And she would tell him—if Flame could ease up for a moment to allow her to catch her breath. But it had been full speed ahead the last few days. She had to count her blessings that at least one thing was going right in her life.

"I need a fried green tomato all day and a lamb shank all day minus the carrots," the expediter yelled.

"Got it!" Quentin replied when Egypt failed to respond. "You okay, boss?"

She nodded. Her sous-chef had been worried about her since he caught her crying after Mr. Forrester's visit. "A bit preoccupied, but otherwise fine."

"All right." He spun around and started on the lamb dish. Ever since Jade's video, it had become the most requested plate.

Egypt and Quentin continued working side by side, but the rush didn't seem to be letting up. The more they got through the orders, the more they kept coming in.

"How many more tables?" Egypt inquired when Tessa came in an hour later.

"At least three, Chef," she stated. "And there's two more groups at the bar. Plus there's a special guest who has requested to meet you."

"Tessa, I don't have time for this."

"He's pretty insistent," the hostess stated.

Egypt pulled off her apron and went to the hand-wash sink. "Very well. Quentin, can you handle things?"

"Of course," he said with a wolfish grin.

What was *that* for? Egypt wondered, but she dismissed it as she headed into the dining room to meet the demanding patron. She pushed open the double doors and stopped midway.

Garrett stood in the middle of the dining room holding a bouquet of red roses and a sign that read Please Take Me Back. He looked good enough to eat in a black shirt with a few buttons casually undone and dark jeans. All the other guests in the dining room were looking at her expectantly.

Egypt laughed and cried all at the same time. She should be holding that sign, not him. She glanced over at Tessa, but she was backing away with a smile on her face. Slowly, Egypt made her way across the room to Garrett. All eyes were on her, as well as a few camera phones.

"Garrett, what are you doing?" Tears streamed down her cheeks.

"I'm here to win you back," he replied. "And if you say no, then I'm going to come back tomorrow and the day after that until you agree to give us a second chance."

"That's totally unnecessary."

His smile vanished, and she could see she'd hurt him. "Because you've given up on us?"

"Quite the opposite," Egypt stated, cocking her head to one side. "I'm the one who's been a fool. I owe you the apology and the grand gesture—" she motioned around the room "—for letting my fears and insecurities get in the way of us."

A broad smile spread across his gorgeous features, and Egypt wanted to jump for joy, but there was so much more she needed to say. *Without* an audience.

She leaned into him and caught a familiar whiff of his heady scent. God, how she'd missed him. "Can we go somewhere more private?" she whispered.

"Of course." Garrett turned around to the crowd. "Sorry, guys, the show is over, but dinner is still on me. Thanks for being such a great group."

Applause erupted throughout Flame. "Garrett, you don't have to do that!"

He shrugged and pushed her toward the back of the house. "It's already done."

Reluctantly, Egypt allowed him to lead the way to her office. As she did, she caught sight of Quentin and a couple of the staff peering through the peepholes of the kitchen door.

They'd all been in on it! Why was she surprised? Garrett had a way with people, including her.

When they made it to her office, Garrett tried to whisk her into his arms, and as much as she ached to feel his lips against hers, she pushed him away. She'd nearly blown a good thing with an incredible man, and she had to come clean.

"I was going to come to you," Egypt began, "but you beat me to the punch, yet again showing me how incredibly wrong I was to doubt you."

"I should have told you my memory returned."

"Yes, you should have, but I also overreacted," she confessed. "For so long, I chose sex and casual flings over any sort of relationship because I feared getting hurt again. Antwan not only broke my heart, Garrett, he made me doubt myself and my judgment. How could I have not seen the truth about what kind of man he was? It made me feel weak and small. I vowed to be stronger, fierce and independent, and never depend on another man again."

"I get that, Egypt, and I don't want to take away that feisty streak of yours. It's one of the things I love about you."

"Only one?" she asked with a smile.

"More than one, actually." He reached her, but Egypt pushed a hand against his rock-hard chest preventing him from coming further.

Her brain scrambled and heart skipped a beat because whenever Garrett was near, her body had a mind of his own, but she did manage to eke out. "That's good and although I love the bedroom eyes you're giving me, I'm not done talking yet."

"All right, woman." Garrett sat down on the edge of her desk. "I'm all ears."

"Good." She put her hands on her hips. "Because I owe you an apology. And my truth."

"Go on."

"An apology for my lack of trust and faith in you and in us. I let your father get in my head—" she pointed to her temple "—and rather than talk to you about my fears and insecurities,

I listened to him, and I tried to tell you how to live your life. I took away your choice just as he'd always done to you. And I'm sorry, because I don't want to be anything like your dad."

"No offense taken."

"And my truth is that I was attracted to you the first time we met, and I think somewhere along the way of coming to see you day after day in the hospital, you started to grow on me. I developed feelings for you while you were sleeping."

His lips twisted. "Grow on you? Like a fungus or a mushroom? Is that a good thing?"

Egypt laughed, and it was a beautiful sound to Garrett's ears, but her next words were more than Garrett could have ever asked for or dared hope.

"The truth is I've been in love with you, Garrett Forrester, from the moment, you opened your eyes and looked at me in the hospital." A tear trailed down her face, and Egypt dabbed it away with the back of her hand. "And each day since then, I've been falling deeper and deeper in love with you. With your kindness, your gentleness, your loyalty and dedication to the farm and to your grandfather's legacy, but most importantly, with how you treat me. You've opened my eyes to what it's like to be loved by a good man."

Garrett rose from the desk and walked over to Egypt and caressed her cheek with his palm. "I'm sort of speechless, because you stole my thunder." He wiped an errant tear from her cheek. "I was prepared to come in here with righteous indignation and wear you down until you agreed to be my woman again."

She grinned. "I wasn't going to take much convincing."

Garrett took one of her hands in his and brushed his lips across it. "Waking up to see you smiling down at me was a blessing." When she began to speak, he put his index finger over her lips. "I could have done without the coma, but what I'm saying, very terribly, is that these months with you have been some of the best of my life. They opened my eyes to the lonely and unhappy existence I lived before you. Being with you made me realize there was so much more to life and that I had to grasp it both hands."

He bent down and gazed deep into her eyes. "I love you, Egypt, but because I had no frame of reference, I didn't recognize the feelings. I do now, because you've shown me how to love. It's not all about receiving, but giving oneself completely and without fear. And that's what I'm here today to do, to tell you I'm all yours—if you want me?"

"Want you?" She jumped into his arms, and Garrett caught her. They fell backward onto the sofa with Egypt in his lap. "Garrett, I *love* you," she said, grasping both sides of his face. "And I will for the rest of my days."

She kissed him them, long and deep, but she wasn't in charge for long. Garrett parted her lips until she moaned and allowed him inside the delicious haven of her mouth. They kissed and greedily met each other's thrust of tongue, licking and sucking and tasting each other. Kissing Egypt wasn't just a gift, it was sheer magic and something Garrett wanted for the rest of his life.

She shifted in his lap, moving her lush derriere against his length, and Garrett halted her actions. "Not here," he rasped. "I want to make love to you properly."

"But what about the—" He cut off her words with another kiss. When they came up for air again, they were both gasping.

"I suppose Quentin can hold down the fort for a night."

Garrett grinned. "Yes, he can. I already arranged it." And then he lifted his woman in his arms and carried her from the office and out of the restaurant amid the cheers of the restaurant patrons to a limousine idling at the curb. When they arrived, the chauffeur opened the door.

"A *limo*?" Egypt asked as Garrett helped her inside the vehicle. "Isn't that a little over-the-top?"

"Nothing is too much for my queen," Garrett said after the chauffeur shut the door after him. "You do realize I'm rich, don't you?"

Egypt's brow furrowed. "I assumed the money was from your parents."

Garrett shook his head. "I'm a wealthy man in my own right, Egypt."

"Duly noted." She reached for the button to close the divider and give them privacy. Then she began unbuttoning her chef jacket.

"Baby, I thought we were going to wait..."

"I can't wait," Egypt murmured, dropping the jacket on the limo floor. Then she lifted her hips and took off her leggings and her panties right along with them until she was completely naked. Shooting him a saucy smile, she got on her knees, unzipped his jeans and freed his erection from his briefs. He was already aroused at the sight of her, because Egypt did it for him and always would.

After procuring a condom from his wallet, Egypt climbed onto his lap until she was astride him and lowered herself down on his length. Garrett lit up from the inside out. He would never get enough of her like this, naked and hot. And all *his*. A moment later, Egypt's arms slipped around his neck, and then she began riding him exactly how Garrett wanted.

And it was right there in the back of the limo that they climbed the pinnacle of ecstasy together, and, at long last, Garrett felt like he'd finally come home.

Afterward, they clung to each other, and he whispered words he'd never said to another woman. "I love you."

And Egypt said those cherished words back. "I love you, too."

Epilogue

Egypt was nervous as a limo drove her to meet Garrett at the Raleigh Rose Garden. His note had been very cryptic—it just told her to wear something fancy. She'd selected a one-shoulder, striped red dress with a side slit that reached midthigh. Pointy-toed gold stilettos and a matching clutch finished the look. She left her black hair straight and hanging down her shoulders like a curtain.

She fidgeted, wondering what Garrett was up to. He'd been her man of mystery from the start, but that had changed now that he knew who he was. Garrett had made leaps and bounds in transforming his life, starting with the farm. He'd moved permanently into his grandfather's house and had begun renovating the farm. He'd also started supplying several Raleigh restaurants with fresh produce. Walker Farms was on its way to a successful future, just as Garrett envisioned. As for his relationship with his father and Kent, both were still rocky, but Garrett hadn't given up on either of them.

Meanwhile, Flame was as robust as ever. Word of mouth hadn't slowed down since the famous TikToker's endorsement, and subsequently, Egypt had hired the manager she desperately needed, which allowed her to focus on making the best dishes. With the extra freedom, she'd been able to squeeze in a visit to calm down Wynter, the bride-to-be.

And when they weren't working, Egypt and Garrett spent all their free time together, so much so Garrett asked her to move into the farmhouse, and she wholeheartedly agreed. Their relationship was moving at warp speed, but Egypt wouldn't have it any other way. She'd found her person.

When the limo arrived, Egypt couldn't wait for the chauffeur and hopped out. She immediately started toward the garden, following a lanterned path until she found Garrett standing by a candlelit table for two. He was wearing a dark suit and a gray tie and had never looked more dashing. Garrett opened his arms, and Egypt eagerly walked toward him. Moments later, he pulled her into his embrace, and she luxuriated in him, because he smelled delicious, a heady mix of spicy cologne and gorgeous milk chocolate skin.

Garrett's head instantly lowered, and his mouth covered hers in a scorching kiss that left Egypt tingling all over. No one had ever made her feel as alive as this man.

"What's all this for?" she inquired when he lifted his head and smiled down at her.

"It's our four-month anniversary."

She grinned. "I never knew you were such a romantic."

"Then you'll be surprised by what comes next." Garrett stepped backward and then dropped to one knee.

Egypt's heart began beating frantically in her chest. *Omigod!* Was this really happening?

"I know it may seem early," Garrett replied, looking up at her, "but when you know, you know. And I've known from the moment I opened my eyes from the coma that you were meant for me. I don't want to go another day without you, Egypt Cox, knowing how much I absolutely adore you. I want to spend the rest of my life with you." He reached into his suit pocket and pulled out a velvet case and popped it open to reveal a ring featuring an oval-cut diamond encircled by round diamonds. "Will you marry me?"

Tears blinded Egypt's eyes and found their way down her cheeks. She'd never expected this, but she nodded her head all the same.

"Is that a yes?"

"Yes, yes, *yes!*" She threw her arms around Garrett's shoulders and held him close with all her strength and all the passion that always ignited when they were together. Soon, they were both on their feet, and Garrett was slipping the diamond onto her ring finger.

"Remember when I predicted we would be more than bedmates?"

Egypt couldn't help but laugh. "Yes, I do. And you were right, because you're the love of my life."

Later, after they shared a beautiful dinner under the stars in the rose garden and were on their way back in the limo, Egypt dialed the Six Gems on a FaceTime call. She couldn't wait to her tell them her big news. Once she saw their smiling faces, she held up her left hand. "I'm engaged!" she shouted into the phone.

"Omigod!" There were cheers and screams of delight from Wynter, Shay, Lyric and Teagan, but Asia remained quiet. In fact, she looked as if she'd been crying.

"Asia, sweetheart—" Egypt's heart lurched. "Is everything okay?" She glanced at Garrett, who bunched his shoulders in confusion.

Asia shook her head.

"Whatever it is, you can tell us," Egypt responded.

"I can't! It's your moment."

"Asia, we're all here for you. Just tell us," the other women chorused.

"I'm pregnant!" Asia blurted out.

Egypt was stunned by Asia's announcement and, covering the phone, turned to Garrett. "I'm going to need to fly to Denver."

"And I'll be waiting right here when you get back," Garrett replied.

"Promise?" Egypt asked.

"Always and forever." And he sealed his vow with a kiss.

* * * * *

COMING SOON!

We really hope you enjoyed reading this book. If you're looking for more romance be sure to head to the shops when new books are available on

Thursday 6th July

To see which titles are coming soon, please visit
millsandboon.co.uk/nextmonth

MILLS & BOON

LET'S TALK
Romance

For exclusive extracts, competitions
and special offers, find us online:

f MillsandBoon

🐦 @MillsandBoon

📷 @MillsandBoonUK

♪ @MillsandBoonUK

Get in touch on 01413 063 232

MILLS & BOON

THE HEART OF ROMANCE

A ROMANCE FOR EVERY READER

MODERN
Prepare to be swept off your feet by sophisticated, sexy and seductive heroes, in some of the world's most glamourous and romantic locations, where power and passion collide.

HISTORICAL
Escape with historical heroes from time gone by. Whether your passion is for wicked Regency Rakes, muscled Vikings or rugged Highlanders, awaken the romance of the past.

MEDICAL
Set your pulse racing with dedicated, delectable doctors in the high-pressure world of medicine, where emotions run high and passion, comfort and love are the best medicine.

True Love
Celebrate true love with tender stories of heartfelt romance, from the rush of falling in love to the joy a new baby can bring, and a focus on the emotional heart of a relationship.

Desire
Indulge in secrets and scandal, intense drama and sizzling hot action with heroes who have it all: wealth, status, good looks…everything but the right woman.

HEROES
The excitement of a gripping thriller, with intense romance at its heart. Resourceful, true-to-life women and strong, fearless men face danger and desire - a killer combination!

To see which titles are coming soon, please visit

millsandboon.co.uk/nextmonth

JOIN US ON SOCIAL MEDIA!

Stay up to date with our latest releases, author news and gossip, special offers and discounts, and all the behind-the-scenes action from Mills & Boon...

 @millsandboon

 @millsandboonuk

 facebook.com/millsandboon

 @millsandboonuk

It might just be true love...

MILLS & BOON

MODERN

Power and Passion

Prepare to be swept off your feet by sophisticated, sexy and seductive heroes, in some of the world's most glamourous and romantic locations, where power and passion collide.